FOUR AND TWENTY BLACKBIRDS

Battles of Christmastides

Mark A. Pierce Sr.

PITTSBURGH, PENNSYLVANIA 15238

RoseDog Books
585 Alpha Drive
Suite 103
Pittsburgh, PA 15238
Visit our website at *www.rosedogbookstore.com*

ISBN: 978-1-4809-6432-7
eISBN: 978-1-4809-6455-6

CHAPTER ONE
Heading to Paradise

A city bus gave a diesel sigh as it reached its geared maximum volume, and left sweet, oiled air—along with a momentary blast of combusted warmth, near the ground as it pulled ostentatiously away. Its exhaust trailed low along the curb of an inclined downtown Detroit street, just as a fall head wind picked up its own momentum. Of course, nearby smaller cars capitulated their right-of-way to the transit. Its departing bulk left more offense, a pale blue screen that soon turned black. Some latent diesel flatulence, a mechanical stink that fouled the air that mysteriously seeped its way through the nearby cars' air vents. Shortly, urban pedestrians passing by the bus stop subsumed the disembarked passengers like a white blood cell enveloping an infection. And amongst the mass of passersby is a frail man. Frail-beyond-elderly, a stooped and bespectacled colored man. No one seemed to notice him as he struggled against the autumn bluster and rush hour mania. They walked past him with less than deference, wearing variegated rayon and polyester shirts and pants, skirts and blouses. Their synthetic jackets, mostly made of faux leather, slid over their bodies and made unwelcome, rubbing noises. He, however, wore a time-honored classic, a brown wool suit.

It seemed everyone around him was as oblivious as they were tall, with their heels and platform shoes. They failed to not only not notice the quiet dignity of the towed, bent figure plodding upstream through their humanity, but they also failed to realize, or maybe took for granted, that he could possibly be much more complex than any of them could even imagine. Perhaps, even more than they could ever hope to be.

1

The intricacy of his personality wasn't given away in his appearance, by any means. His gait was a limping stutter, which favored the left. An exacerbation caused by a wartime service memento, lodged high and deep between nerves in his upper-right thigh. The irritant came from a round of ammunition, delivered under what would be termed in future military parlance as a "friendly fire" situation. The day's tomb dampness seemed to aggravate the flack in his leg even more than usual, though, and it made him wince. That he could still feel its effect reminded him that his mission today was as serious and necessary as any undertaken by him thirty-five years prior, when he'd first received the wound.

A slow moving, bronze Camaro with its 8-Track player cranked up, rumbled past him, the bass from its speakers at times throbbing simultaneously with the inflammation of his leg. This sage veteran, along with most everyone else, picked out the song's hackneyed chorus, "*Not goin' nowhere; somebody help me; somebody help me, yeah. I'm staying alive!*"

Street refuse, fast-food wrappers and such, swirled out towards him, and that included an inked pulping; like a bird spreading its newspaper "wings" and flying for his maimed leg. Perching around his shin, the news page glued in place, and wouldn't surrender its attachment. Though the old man tried to shake it free a few times. With unintentionally comedic earnestness. Eventually he stooped down to throw it away with his arthritic, almond-colored claw of a hand.

The old rover eyed it quickly and noted that it was from a current issue of the *Detroit Press*, dated October 11, 1978. The third page of the first section. He read that, 'the city's unemployment rate consistently hovers around eighteen percent,' and that the *Supremes* were staying disbanded. But before he could read any further, a gust, chilled with a premonition of winter, and snatched the newsprint out of his yielding hands. Only slightly surprised by the wind's ferocity, he watched the paper's wings erratically flap away from him, covering half-a-block in ten seconds. Unperturbed, he turned his form towards the continuing gusts and leaned forward with patient deliberation. As he limped his way up the metropolitan plane, he tucked his chin towards his chest as he swallowed the too-forceful air, for it was too hard to breathe through his nose, alone.

His head seemed rumpled with skin that looked similar to a brown, over-ripe apple, perhaps slightly larger than what his neck could comfortably support. His mouth, caricatured by age, formed a toothless oval on the bottom of his small face, caricatured by age. Deigned to thus look upon the ground as he walked, the elder citizen confined his gaze to only noticing his shoes.

The shoes, like their owner, were mended in unnoticeable places. The left one, showed more signs of uneven wear, and trailed behind the right leg, and its inflection. "That one," he thought to himself, "that's the shoe that will have a blowout first." He silently cursed his infirm body with a quick sucking noise behind the ridge of his false teeth. The inconvenience of old age especially agitated this still nimble-witted survivor. The wingtips he wore showed a lack of leather conditioning, causing the once expensive pair to defy polishing any longer. And that had only been in two years time. Brown, brayed, and scuffed, though ritually and vigorously brushed, he originally hadn't the heart to start wearing them, but for special occasions.

They were the last gift from his late wife, Bernice, gone now these twelve years. "She liked them shoes so much," he thought to himself. She used to beg him to buy a pair of brown shoes to match his suits. Owning but two, a brown pinstripe, and a blue gabardine, he had only black wingtips to wear with them. She knew he had better sense than to deliberately cross the conventions of fashion, and knew he shouldn't wear black shoes with a brown pant, but his stubbornness about spending money on himself would not yield. A week before her admittance to the hospital, she'd bought them for him, even though she knew he'd use them more for walking away from her, than with her.

Bernice always hated the split that her husband's diversions placed between them. He had been a faithful man, a good, supportive spouse. Even through the hard acceptance that there would be no children for them. She was also known to comment to friends of hers that after her childbearing years, he didn't seem too attentive to her emotional needs. He just wasn't amenable to doing the things with her that a man should do with the woman he claimed to love. The things people do to take their minds off their worries. One day she finally got fed up with his smoking and arguing with her and had him move a bed into his study. That's where he kept all his files and things. All his memorabilia. And as far as Bernice was concerned, if that's where he preferred spending all his time, he could roll around on those books and papers for whatever company and pleasure he needed.

Somebody had commented upon her contrary nature. Paige Garrett. Proffering his opinion about the problems between the bickering couple, both of whom he loved, he'd say, "Sack." That's what he called Frank. "Sack, that's just the way it is with you two. If you say the sky is blue, she calls it cloudy. Didn't you tell me that? Then, you say cloudy, and she turn right around and say it turned blue. Huh? You know what, though? Damn me, if I didn't hear her say the same thing about you. Now, what y'all *need* to do is start talking to—and not at, one another." Paige had advice for anyone that would listen, but poor eating habits. He died in his bed, choking on a chicken bone. But he had been right about him and Bernice, though. Sackett knew he'd let so much get away from him, from things that distracted him from her and her needs, and yet and still, she had kept on trying. But Frank was unassuming, mostly, and not too particular as to how he presented himself.

Even deathly ill, Bernice still made a fuss about him wearing the shoes she'd bought for him right before she became worse, the last visit. He tried not to show he noticed hearing her lungs rattle while she was in the bed. Even now he could still clearly see the fawning plastic tubes and wires over the hospital bed's chrome bars as he approached her room's doorway. Despite her inevitable, impending release from the bed that was to be her death prison, even though she knew she would soon be changed as summarily as the sheets beneath her, she told him he looked so good when he came in. That's one hell of a note, he thought. One helluva note. Comforting someone when you're the one in need. The inequity of her health status played a guilty tune on her husband. Upon Bernice dying, all optimism Frank Sackett had left was swallowed up in a Charybdis of continuing misfortune. Glasses could never be full again.

Yes, pessimism was now this veteran's new uniform. And the way his care was administered to him these days also didn't help to brighten his outlook any. The inattention and insensitivity he received at his veteran's facility, after becoming a widower, shaped his subconscious awareness to a point that he'd begun to second-guess his own perceptions. He wondered many times if what the doctors there had been saying about him was true.

"Frank Sackett," they said, "has a susceptibility to having narcissistic and psychosomatic tendencies." He'd overheard the practitioners talking about him between themselves, heard them saying he'd "play it for all it was worth," if given the chance. And they surmised that "it" was an appositive for any pejorative complaint. Yet, on this blustery day in Michigan, the old soldier felt every reason to be justified in worrying about his physical condition, even though he knew he couldn't keep from coming here.

He had emphysema and it was usually oppressive and chronic, a recorded, verifiable disability. But the doctors still would say things like, "Psychological indices show an aberrant psyche, one that simply craves the attention of a caregiver." He smirked when he read that in his file.

They tried telling him that he was trying to get accolades he felt due to him from his wartime service, and never received. Other doctors, the civilian ones, said his shortness of breath was just another cry for the love of a father he'd never known. And that was really too silly to get angry over.

On the last evaluation he'd had before leaving the VA it was concluded that, "If not treated and guided by therapy, this particular patient could suffer personality loss so severe, so deep and profound, that he may well never be able to discern reality from fantasy." His counter-argument was that it was proven by X-rays that emphysema was indeed taking away sixty-six percent of his lung capacity. That diverted the aspersions to his character, but suspicions were still proffered amongst the medical staff about the timing and severity of his bouts of suffocation. They always seemed to happen following one of his excursions. Not quitting smoking also helped convince the VA staff he wasn't ardently trying to help regulate his health, either.

In fact, the only mitigation that he had made was changing over to inhaling those new fangled low-tar, generic cigarettes. That only meant smoking more to get less, as far as he was concerned. The color of his gray nose hairs and praline fingernails were metamorphosing. Once stained yellow, they were now light brown. No amount of washing could get the smell of the tobacco off him.

They considered having him assigned to the psychiatric ward before he'd left, so sure some of them were of his mental delusion. "And how long before I start having all this dementia you're talking about?" he'd asked. Some of the doctors felt he was already experiencing it, but no one stated it out loud to him.

"To be truthful," his psychologist admitted, "it's not so much a matter of your mental health as it is about your meanderings around the country. The administration here frowns upon them, actually. They're close to prohibiting you from leaving at all."

Sackett didn't argue, never did because it wouldn't have mattered. To do so would be simply expending time, energy, and consternation needlessly. He knew what irked the government about his forays, and more importantly, he knew his rights. He was self-assured that they did not have the moral authority to do anything to him. But the psychologist kept on. "Four times—Mr. Sackett. Four times in two years. You go out for three weeks, sometimes more, and come back dehydrated and malnourished. You're not thinking rationally about your own health, for gosh sakes."

Sackett flared his nostrils with his sigh and stared at the practitioner unblinking, only putting forth his right hand across the desk and opening his palm, upward. "My meds, please." Without further recrimination he was given a month's supply of his medications, set up an appointment for the following month, and stopped by the bursar's office for his pension. As long as he got those two things on time, his guaranteed government prescriptions that were redeemable at any pharmacy, and his pension allotment, he could care less what the quorum of white medical personnel and psychoanalysts thought. He just couldn't be a good nigger.

What he stated as having happened rewrote history for them, and that was why they were so perplexed. Whether they acknowledged it, or not, he could tell how they really felt. What their base reaction was to any colored man, let alone one who dared to expose a lie, kept well hidden. It wasn't overt;

it was in some of the small things they'd do that let him know what the real seed of their feelings were. At first, he dismissed any notion of there being any bias because, of course, they had the best of intentions. The armed services always gave the best to those men who served, but he couldn't help being schizoid. It was the nature of life and death for black Americans. Systemic loathing created that kind of subconsciousness, after five hundred years of being referred to as the people of mud. But, waiting for the crossing light to change, Sackett thought to himself, wasn't that what God first made man from? Without warning, the light changed from the orange flashing hand to the blinking figure of the little white man—and Sackett carefully began his way across.

He pulled out the new pack of cigarettes from his coat, remembering how disgusted it had made his doctor that he would not forego having them. "If it ain't smoking, it's drinking," he muttered softly as the warning signal began to flash before he could make it a quarter of the way across. "And if they ain't worried about that, then it's eating egg yolks, or bacon. What's all this fuss over? Like the one way to die is any better than t'other." He was a few feet from the curb, now, when a car yielded for him and he waved at the driver. "We all ending up dead, no matter." He'd just as soon go to his glory by way of respiratory failure as any other, if that what was in the deal for him.

Reaching the corner on the other side of the street and looking up at the signs for direction, he knew that dying just wasn't as easy as the act of stopping breathing, and somehow separating from one's marrow. The doctors told him graphically what would occur if he kept on smoking. His lungs would collapse from the weight of the mucous and congealed blood and he would be panicked by the complete inability to breathe. Then, directly afterward he'd experience the mortifying pain of a cardiac arrest. Not a pretty death by any stretch of the imagination. "But," he said, lighting up anew, "no death ever is, really."

Turning the corner, deprived Sackett of the partial windbreak a high concrete wall provided on the former cross street. Now facing fully into the wind, he climbed a street even more pitched than the last. Walking not more than half the block, Sackett loped his way around the butt-end of an illegally parked red '67 Chevy Impala. Not only did it jut out into the street, stretching across the sidewalk, it blocked pedestrian traffic in front of the orange and white *Clark* service station. The Chevy's unconcerned driver was assuring himself a secure place in the rapidly forming gas line of cars. After ten minutes, he pulled in.

The Impala's owner, a large man, ill-dressed for the cold weather, but probably insulated by an excess hundred-fifty pounds, brought out three five-gallon buckets from the trunk. An alert attendant met him, however. "Sir, you can't pump fuel into those."

"Why the hell not?" the driver defiantly asked, "They got lids on 'em." And he tightened the grip of his distended fingers around the nozzle handle. The attendant didn't scowl, or get tensed in agitation. He just pulled on his pump key that was attached to his belt and turned the flow off to all the pumps. Groans dominoed from behind them because this surely meant an even longer delay. After two minutes of explaining commerce codes, legal transportation, and appropriate vessels of containment, the Chevy owner finally understood he would not be successful. Sackett was glad the agitator didn't press the issue; even though he made it clear he was going to get them filled, some way. Most everyone understood what that meant. There was a new market nowadays, for something unthinkable in the old man's recollection and sensibility. The manufacturing of locking gas caps was an astonishing thing to Sackett.

For years, the availability of gasoline was only one step, maybe two, from the abundance of water. But the government now pinned gas-drought consumers into desperate cages. The kind of cages where covetous stealth was the mode of society. Rationing, for some, had created a distemper of self-centered mentality. "If I had a car," Sackett thought, but he didn't finish the sentence. It didn't matter because he didn't have one. But he empathized with a car owner's position. Having to resort to protecting the storage of a simple transportation medium. The locking gas caps were the capitalist response to a new demand. People were quickly growing tired of being stranded the morning after filling their tanks the previous night.

Working his way back to the curb, and seeing the bus stop he was looking for up ahead, Sackett thought that although President Carter was a wool-dyed Democrat, he really wasn't that much better a president than Nixon had been. Sackett didn't count the Ford Administration as being a true presidency because of the way it had all come about. And Carter wasn't binding the country's wounds, either. In fact, no triage was even evident. He remembered a few years back that Nixon claimed oil imports had been pinched off by the OPEC nations during their embargo. That was the first time the country heard of an "Energy Crisis." The boldness of the lie was audacious.

The president damn well had to have known that American oil companies had fleets of tankers, full and waiting, off the coasts. Ships that was just fit to burst with oil. These companies wouldn't let the imports come in, though, until they got the price they wanted per barrel. And the whole country could line up for all they cared; the government just went along with the fraud. This all proved one thing; the standard of living for common people was sacrificial fodder to the business of politics. While they protracted their haggling over gas prices, every Joe American believed there was no oil, at all, to be had.

At the bus stop, Sackett squinted his eyes to read the approaching bus destinations and absent-mindedly hefted a dark turquoise velour case in his coat pocket. Its' small notebook size felt comfortable and warm in his hand. He put his sore backside down on the nearest paint-peeled bench and placed the case on his coat's lap to inspect it for any marks. Seeing it as pristine, he returned it to his right pocket and then reached inside his coat's lining for half of a ham and *Velvetta* cheese sandwich, still wrapped in the worn paper bag from his lunch.

He'd learned long ago to travel lightly and cheaply when he was operating "on location," as he liked to call it. Don't bother with restaurant service, was his protocol, and if you ever get a hotel room, make it one with a refrigerator. A kitchenette, even better. It had to be something like that because, as he liked to say, "A government pension don't go further than a snail on hot tar."

The sandwich spread on his meal was warm from being too close to his chest, and it made the bread a little too moist for his taste. His memory, jogged by the rumination of the mediocre sandwich along his remaining back teeth, brought his thoughts back to another such day, one where he had just as absently thought about nothing in particular while eating a similar lunchtime fare. At that time he'd been painting the exterior of a three story, white, Georgian home, in Aurora, Illinois.

It had been an atypically warm day for the three-man crew and they counted it a blessing that they'd been able to finish this late-season job before a cold weather snap would turn the paint they applied into a gummy covering. They'd worked through their normal lunch hour to ensure completion before any waning sunlight dismissed them. Lake moisture had been held in abeyance through a high-pressure trough, and the temperatures were in the upper-sixties to low seventies; a veritable heat wave that Friday, in November. Sackett had just been able to sit down on an empty, inverted five-gallon paint bucket for his late lunch. While his radio played, off around the corner from where he was breaking, he began thinking about the weekend's upcoming meeting with his wartime friends, the Blackbirds. He'd grown to look forward to the gatherings meant to make for a purposeful accounting, and not simply a reminisce about their war experience.

Knowing theirs was an undistinguished lot, they took solace in the continued longevity of each of the remaining twenty-four members. It always amazed Frank how many variations of the same story could be recounted. First, this one had the grenade; later, it would be the other one who replaced the pin. Invariably, a third interjection would disclaim foiling detonation through the entombment of the bomb. Another time it wouldn't go off because of immersion, or from an expertly placed shot. And that was only the grenade story.

Each revelation always ended up a being a piscatorial myth, and almost smelling as badly. It's like that with wars and with fishing. The respective heroes always talk about the one that got away—the exception being with this group was that there had actually been quite a bit of daring feats in their wartime exploits.

So, he'd just had time to sit down and take a bite from his too-warm sandwich, allowing it to roll quickly and clumsily around the back of his tongue before swallowing it, when he realized what was interrupting the music. The mouthful he chewed quickly became tasteless, and foreign. Like a ball of white-breaded cud. He looked at his watch and noted it was 1:35. The announcer seemed inhuman at first, his dialogue sounding more like the multiple caws of minute ravens, but the second time confirmed it—"shot, while driving less than ten miles per hour in a Dallas street—the president was taken to Parkland—now pronounced dead, at exactly..." That'd been a damn shame to hear. A damn shame. Kennedy was the only president, after Roosevelt, which he even liked. Yes, it was. A damn shame.

Then there'd been Malcolm, cursed for blaspheming the martyred leader (a chicken being left to roost for him, also) and Martin's throat being shot away. The irony of that being targeted wasn't lost on Sackett. The assassin literally destroyed the mechanisms for King's emotive oratory. And then there was another Kennedy execution. Right at the beginning of his middle age. All the martyrs of the past decade seemed to press an additional weight of guilt upon the conscience of each Blackbird. Each additional slaying was a silent shrouding of another imperfect, but noble, spokesman of humanity. Each leader, in some small way perhaps, might have tried to speak the truth for the Blackbirds, but now were quite incapable of that. And there was a whole country too afraid to pick up their torch of idealism, left lying in the streets of Dallas, Harlem, Memphis, and Los Angeles.

Teddy Kennedy knew; he forsook the cup momentarily passed his way in '68 at the Democratic Convention. The party was ready to crown him their nominee, but he recognized that it seemed Death made heroes, not heroism. And he didn't want any part of being a hero.

At a somber meeting held in late 1969, the remaining members of the Blackbirds decided that the stories—no, make that, the truths, about what actually occurred in 1945, might never be revealed. America would still believe that the country didn't have the will to interdeploy Negro and whites until the time of the conflict with Korea. The Blackbirds, sitting around two barbeque pits on that late afternoon were living proof that the lie was in fact, a lie. But would they personally do anything about it? Or would they perpetuate the unspoken shame? Would they have the fortitude to write new pages into history, pressing the point hard against the lines of unyielding white paper that recorded time? They chose, for whatever reasons, at that moment, to wait.

More time passed, and the youth of the 70's were attempting to assimilate the smoldering urban angst that was left percolating from the last decade, but they could find no focus after the fall of Saigon. The men of the Blackbirds understood the vacuum; the kids got what they'd been asking for: no more war. So, what was really left to fight over? Sackett and his colleagues saw integration come to the Armed Forces in the 50's, so what could they really complain about? The answer to that was there were people in power who would have the world believe Negro service to the country was less honorable, even though they put everything at risk as much as any white soldier. The answer was, people were saying they didn't do the unexpected, and refused to acknowledge it, all for the sake of maintaining the status quo. The answer was it wasn't enough to value yourself, that wasn't recognition.

It would have been easy for these bronze warriors to say, "No thank you. I've fought a war. Let someone with fresh legs carry this banner." But the thick keloids of their service stood out too manifest on them for there not to be any further explanation. For some inexplicable reason, almost palpable and hard to put into words, they chose to participate in a cause during a time where causes were dying at a rate similar to their champions. Indeed, even the gatherers making up the Blackbirds now had dwindled down to only ten.

They prided themselves that it was never a stranger to sift dirt upon their compatriot's sarcophagus. With not too much trouble, they all could travel and give their last respects to the fallen. Most of them lived within close geographical proximity to one another, the majority in Chicago, others in Detroit, and still more in Indiana. The remaining members stretched forth a meager network that collectively pooled their resources to try to find people to assist them. They hoped these others would lend their ears to their tale, and explain their truth. And maybe more. To do something about it. Frank was, and had been, obsessed with their agenda.

After the last twenty-five years it became a part of him, as much as he was of it. The Blackbirds had formally called upon many politicians, made up of besieged county supervisors, state legislators, congressmen and senators, who gave them homogenous rejoinders. Plausible denial, reticent disavowal, or rude disinterest seemed to be the irritated reaction caused by the ancient black veterans. Then one day, there was a forging, a liaison established, one that met the men halfway, and it was from all places, The Department of The Army.

Major Anthony Krech, an analyst from the Military Historical Records Department of the Army, sent a letter to the old man now sitting on the bench in Detroit. It had made Sackett's eyebrows tent upwards for some time upon receiving it. As he read the name at the signature block it motivated him to do even more. It got him to get on a plane to Detroit. It had him riding this half-empty bus to the west side of the city. The stationary he received had its expected formal line of dismissal, but Sackett was more intrigued by the name of the officer who'd signed it. Could it possibly be his son? Or maybe even a brother? Would he be able to, or willing to, meet with him? God forgive me, Sackett thought, but he was practically as happy as Al Jolson singing *Mammy*. And he grew in his faith as he held the letter, for to just imagine seeing Major August Krech, again was peaceful assurance.

It so happened that the major was a younger brother of the retired brigadier general who'd helped lead the Sixth Command, in Chicago during World War II. Since the general confirmed that he did personally, indeed, know the inquirer his sibling told him about, the Blackbirds were about to receive their first official audience. But the fates rebuked the meeting ever taking place. The general was killed in a car crash. Some kid ran into him after robbing a store. It happened just two days before Frank could get to Chicago. When he found out, he was shaken to the core of emotion. He wept more than he had for any Blackbird, and not even those survivors knew why. They had no idea of the tie that bound that white officer and this black noncom together, and there was only one other soldier he felt as deeply about. And he awaited Sackett in Paradise Valley.

With all the other men he served with in the war there had been an emotional detachment because during battle you couldn't begin finding yourself caring too deeply about the men you fought alongside of. It wasn't conducive to operations. But two of the original twenty-four Blackbirds could not be omitted from Sackett's fond memories: Gus Martin, and his antagonizing brother, Joe.

As opposite as they were, those two sons of Detroit were the only ones, besides Krech, who knew Sackett's secret. Frank liked Gus very much, but he had only admired Joe, and that did not actually occur until he was dead. Ironically, it was Joe who was destined to receive the only acknowledgment of what the Blackbirds really were, what they'd accomplished. That was within the folds of Sackett's overcoat. "Yes, how ironic," he thought. Joe, the man least interested in being glorified or patriotized, would end up receiving the laudatory. But that's how life operates, Sackett nodded to himself. With Krech gone, and if Gus wasn't alive, Frank didn't want to go on anymore. The missions would stop. He would stop.

The bus arriving stop-gapped the reverie of the old man, and he boarded carefully, looking down as he climbed the narrow stairs, in order to prevent a calamitous fall. Those entries and aisles were slick, especially if people tracked water and mud inside. Other passengers patiently let him ascend as he grabbed the rails and pulled himself up to the fare counter.

Sackett took out his slick, rubber change purse. It fit in his palm, a dark-green rubber oval with a slit up its middle. With a slightly ticking right hand he extracted two nickels and dropped them into the pewter slot. Then he shuffled to his immediate left and took a seat at a vacant, long, senior citizen seat near the driver. Heading out of the city with increased speed, he fought off the sleep being caused by the lulling pitch of the tires. But once he got to his transfer line he resigned himself to his fatigue. Upon entering that bus he again sat behind the driver and asked to be told when they reached the end of the line. But even though he'd soon fall asleep, he somehow sensed when that time arrived. The bus just comfortably pitched forward as it stopped and rocked Frank slightly to his left.

Exhausted, he rubbed his eyes and yawned. As he disembarked, he made a point of making a judgment about the name of the community by its appearance. Paradise Valley was no such thing, and it never had been. This newer section, built after 1965, contained ticky-tacky boxes of sameness, called tract homes. Here a blue one, there a yellow one, only colors delineating any individuality, but the heart of Paradise seemed different, slightly. The older homes showed quaint variety, not so much by their individualized styling, but by the common repairs applied to their structures.

One small cabin he passed reminded Sackett of a house he and Bernice bought once. Bought and lost in a seeming blink of an eye, a casualty of circumstances. The old man couldn't help but to stop. Even if it would delay him, some...

CHAPTER TWO
The Search in Paradise

The house Sackett stood in front of was perhaps a little bigger than the home he and Bernice had purchased, but it had the same chalk-white siding, and the same deep-green enamel on the shutters and trim. It was "such a clean look," Bernice had said to him. And so unlike the apartment they'd been renting for years. She was excited at the thought of home ownership being made available to her and Frank through the G.I. Bill. Every soldier returning from overseas received the same benefits, even though disparities existed in what their particular duty had been. Every man got a token of appreciation. Among these gifts were having the ability to procure a federal housing loan, or a small business loan, one or the other. Frank opted for the business loan, figuring the revenue from it would procure the real estate Bernice had her heart set on getting. He had no idea how long that turnover would take to come about. A lesson in life that he thought he'd learned long ago was that you try to plan for the things that might surely get in your way. And most of the time, he surmised, it was you getting in your own way.

But with no small amount of initiative, he ended up becoming the first and only Negro painting contractor in the whole county, after apprenticing with a Dutch painter for two years and getting several years' journeyman experience. Bernice hadn't seen the wisdom in taking the government money and building a business when they didn't own the roof over their heads. To make up for this non-negotiable sacrifice, he would take her for occasional Sunday drives, where they would go house hunting. Down where there were birch-lined lanes, with slab stone facades on the houses. He promised her a two-story home like that, someday. To Bernice, it seemed that every other week someday was just around the corner from their two-room apartment. After a time she stopped worrying about someday, and kept up the flat.

She waited three years for the business to take off, then five, then it was seven, but every time a sizeable profit came through she saw it getting recycled back into the business. Growing tired of the perpetuity of their lessee-status, Bernice had taken it upon her own two shoulders to get them into a home. She borrowed money from her little brother for the down payment, and purchased a loan on a little white and green cottage, buying it all by herself. She did it—is what she would tell anyone who inquired, or was within earshot of hearing. Not her man, she did it. And she let it be known that it was her house, too. Notwithstanding Frank's derelict homesteading attitude, she was the one who made sure her family was getting into their home, and it didn't matter that most American families operated in a more conventional fashion.

Frank understood all of that, and took no offense. For centuries it seemed black women had been purposely inserted into the lead roles in their families, and the men would mostly appreciate the help. After all, people of color seemed to understand more than whites that it was a partnership. Negro men would not balk at their woman holding down a job. Frank allowed Bernice's pride to flow, even though he was paying off her brother and making each and every mortgage payment without fail. For three years the Sacketts thrived in their private Americana. Then, in the fall of 1964, Frank submitted a bid on a nearby town's new government complex that was ready to have interior and exterior work done.

Painting contractors from all over the northern portion of Illinois had sealed bids on the work, which Frank figured would take half a year to complete. That was a lot of time to have set aside in your pocket because with painting, and most other building trades, when the jobs came in, it was time to feast. Contrarily, when no jobs were to be found, you did well not to starve. So, Frank wanted to make sure he had a good shot at getting considered. A kindly county engineer taught him how to read blueprints accurately, and how to decipher schematics. "Frank's Folly" was commonly snickered about when the white contractors heard about Sackett's endeavor.

The Painters' Union Hall, however, was a cave of silence when Frank went there to hire chagrined out-of-work men to work for him, once he got the nod. This job would take him through the toughest part of the year, and well past the spring. The word of Frank's good fortune got around very quickly to the other contractors, and the news was usually received with reserves of mucosal spit being hacked out. He had crossed a line that could not be forgiven for having been broken. Taking livelihood from his betters was sin.

Frank went to his savings-and-loan full of confidence when he received the bid endorsement; after all, he had a house with equity and a signed contract in his pocket. He believed that with that alone, nothing could stand in his way, and that was true, initially. His small business loan was approved practically on the spot and the loan manager set up three disbursements, one every two months. The first check came through without a hitch. Men were hired, materials procured, and the job quickly began to take shape under his generalship.

People in the community began to notice the center and many genuinely appreciated Sackett's work because, as his painters found out, unlike some other painters who owned businesses, Frank was right there slapping paint-loaded rollers on the walls, and cutting-in paint lines with the rest of his crew. The union onlookers even seemed to have forgotten about him and had gone on about their business—that is, until other residential jobs began to divert to Frank, around the same time that the fourth month's payout was due. His encroachment could have been better tolerated had it not been found out that he'd begun courting long-established customers from his competitors. In hindsight, he realized, he'd become a victim of his own hubris. But at that time, he saw no reason why he shouldn't accept the invitations from other familiar parties. The choice was entirely theirs'.

One of the biggest painting contractors in the town was in the loan office when Frank was refused to draw his second disbursement. This man worked with a large general contractor, and had been the runner-up to Frank in getting the town center contract. Between those two men, and the clout they held at the savings-and-loan, Frank found himself being boycotted. His loan was called back because it was somehow discovered that the Sacketts owed a delinquent tax bill for his shop and office. He'd missed it by one week. The tax funds had gone into procuring the bond money needed to enter his bid on the government center. Because this was a government contract, anyone doing business in the construction of the center could not be involved in any impropriety and expect financial subsidization. It was a technicality, but enforceable. Not only did Frank have to pay back all he'd used, but also he still had to find a way to finance the remainder of the job. He had to let all but one of his men go, his paperhanger. All profit margins were vacuumed into the once lucrative government center, and what was now a money pit.

At the Painters' Hall the tongues began to waggle and cluck once again, and this time nobody spat. He had to siphon off every reserve that was available to him in order to make his payroll come out, and to buy the materials he needed. But even that would not be enough. One early evening in spring,

Frank contritely took Bernice by the hand, right after he'd come home from working hard all day. She knew something major was about to be discussed because her two-pack a day smoker would be the last one she'd expect to take her by the hand and go out for a walk after working all day. His simple pretense was that the afternoon had been so uncommonly warm, the first warm spell of the year that he wanted to take a romantic stroll with his beautiful wife. By the time they made it back to their picket fence abode, though, Frank was coughing and wheezing and Bernice's face was tear-streaked. The fabric of their Americana quilt lay about them, unraveled.

Frank got their bank to finance a second mortgage, and he hoped that with that money he'd be able to forestall the onslaught of approaching creditors and disgruntled customers who'd been put off for weeks. He promised Bernice everything would be right by the end of spring. But summer began with the house going into foreclosure, and by the fall all materials in the business were sold off at an auction. The only solace Frank had was that the tobacco spitting antagonists at the union hall wouldn't have the satisfaction of witnessing his complete failure. The government center was going to be completed, in spite of their efforts.

The maimed leg had been to point that it only caused a slight discomfort, sometimes it locked his hip in place; but after the disintegration of his business, Frank's leg became an inflamed agony. He was crippled to a point where climbing and sustained standing were debilitating. Faced with that, he found he could no longer do the work anymore. It was all left up to Bernice, and she hadn't had any real job experience besides being a concierge assistant at a Detroit hotel during the war, when she met Frank. Because of their situation's hopelessness, Frank began to feel he'd truly betrayed his wife, and she repeated his failings. She couldn't help it. Totally without joy, the only thing she ever really cared taken from her, Bernice didn't have enough left in her tank to ease the two of them out of their despair. Her heart was truly broken over the loss of the home.

Life succeeded in proving it was too hard, and she was not going to argue the point. She turned the other cheek and forfeited her very will to survive, dying of a stroke the following year, her eyes cursing where her lips could not. An involuntary shudder suddenly crossed Frank's shoulders and shook him out of his mournful stupor in front of the house, his nose slightly running.

Pulling his coat collar more tightly to him, he moved on, swabbing gingerly at his nose with his blue and white rag. The house he was looking for was right ahead, a single story dwelling where a family of modest means eked out an existence. Sackett figured everyone living in Paradise had to be natural swimmers because all anyone could do here was tread water. He heard the familiar ethnic discrepancies as he walked up the warped raisers of the front porch. There were children arguing here, that much he recognized. He didn't see a doorbell, or a knocker, so it was incumbent upon him to knock as hard and long as his arthritic hands would allow him. Switching from one to the other as needed, he could also clearly hear a heated conversation between adults behind the closed door. Notwithstanding that, he had no idea why no one would answer him, for as long as he'd been knocking.

CHAPTER THREE
Trouble in Paradise

"Aw, give me a break, for chrissakes. Lorraine? Lorraine, get in here!"
A cautious, appeasing voice came from the bedroom next to the kitchen,
"Okay, all right, Jim. I'm there in a minute." She smoothed her relaxed hair
after she entered the kitchen, collecting herself while preparing the coffee.
Adding the customary cream and sugar to two white mugs. Perhaps the caf-
feinated libation would blunt the discontentment the lord of the Martin household barely held in check, at this point. He sounded pretty upset.

"Lorraine?"

"Coffee's on the way. Just a minute."

"Coffee, my butt. What's the deal with the charges this month?

"Don't yell," she mildly pleaded, "I'll be there in a second, Jim."

No answer. Outside, Sackett thought, "No answer. Must still be in the
kitchen," he concluded.

Jim Martin brushed aside the scraps of paper and palmed his temples in
his hands, which caused his thirty-year old eyes to appenge dramatically upwards. He didn't seem to look black then, more Asian. "Lorraine," he said,
shouting to make sure he'd be heard, "We got two months of charges stacked
up here and I want to know why, right now."

A firm, and firmly placed hip, peeped past the swiveling white bone-colored enameled kitchen door in response to the demand. Entering the small
den, her husband noticed how comely she was. Lorraine's complexion, like
lightly toasted white bread, was accentuated by straight, long, black hair

around her face. As she strode in with the steaming coffee, Jim could not resist admiring the flattery of his wife's tan sweater, and the pleasant ways her breast moved, or the swish her knee-length wool dress made, timed to the stride of her long legs. She set the mugs down and slid the doors closed, separating the head of the house from the superfluous activity occurring in the front room.

As if practiced for dramatic affect, Jim tapped account-payable papers on the table, his mouth slowly widening into an oval with each jab of his index finger. "I thought we were going to pay as we go," he finally got out. "You know, paying everything on time?"

"It's not that bad, Jim."

Lurching towards his spouse, she flinched, even though he had never put a hand upon her in over ten years. It was just that the barely contained anger flared and escalated so unexpectedly, like the instantaneous flash of an impotent flint lighter in the dark. It kept her anxious, off balance. To step up her anxiety even further, the muted screams of a sibling debate, coming from the living room, turned ugly, and was slowly growing louder. "Would you go see what they're up to, please?"

"What *they* were up to," Lorraine repeated silently to herself. Why did Jim state his demands for obedience like his children were always conspiring something? Sometimes even inferring she was masterminding the defiance. Straightening her sweater and opening the heavy paneled sliding doors, she exhaled a cleansing breath, controlling her unease, as well as her humiliation and left the presence of her irritated spouse to dispense some rational insight to their children. And even more to his liking, it seemed, discipline if necessary.

What had caused the consternation between fourteen-year old, Bea and her ten-year old brother, Brad, was a used *Atari* game system he'd gotten for his birthday, six weeks prior. Lorraine promised that it wouldn't turn into a problem or be a disruption to the family harmony. Either from Jim not being able to watch the evening news when he came home, or hearing children bickering between themselves. Despite its inflated price, Lorraine gave in to whining and bought it. Even though she believed it would go the way of all fads, dying a quick and unnoticed death in the hall closet. A victim of abuse or malfunction, or God forbid, maybe disuse. Then, it would really come down on her. But the dark screen and the opposing white rectangles that batted an electronic signal between them had the children bewitched. In order to possess the solitary control pad, the boisterous duo was oblivious to their mother's interruption.

"Will you all cut down that noise out there?" Jim demanded, rather than requested. His tone was louder than even he meant to use; blood-pressured agitation was probably the reason. Or maybe, he just needed to assure himself of being heard through solid doors. "Brad," he continued, "what are you playing with that mess for? Is your homework done?"

"I got it taken care of, honey," Lorraine said.

"Sure as hell don't sound like it. Don't have me come in there, you two."

There was only a veil of evaporating restraint covering that threat and the children understood the tone, and that they needed to be aware that they were toeing a line-in-the-sand. Raised and imploring eyes and eyebrows from the mother convinced them; they decided to cooperate with one another rather than risk their father's intervention. On Thanksgiving he'd gotten so mad at their mother that he'd thrown their completely baked turkey out onto the street. They didn't want that to happen with their game. Brad handed the control pad to his sister with a pout on his face and scooted himself back from the family's augmented television.

Looking up at his mother with innocence and compliance, Lorraine tapped one child and then the other on the shoulder, cautioning each with a silencing index finger to her lips. "I think your dad needs to have a little more quiet from you two, okay?" Brad nodded and gave his mother a dimpled grin, the smile only admitting to a minor affront.

Returning to the dining room for a seeming comeuppance, Lorraine fought her rising urge to contest Jim. She was not a milquetoast woman who stood silently by a domineering provider and mate. After all this was the Seventies. But she had given a verbal contract to Jim that she would follow his plan and agenda to make them rehabilitated from insolvency. When their bankruptcy would clear from their credit reports, in a few years, Jim wanted to be in a position to negotiate buying a house in a better place. The self-imposed pressure was making him unhappy and unpleasant to be around. As Lorraine closed the sliding doors, Jim could sense her unease.

He tried to temper his attitude because he knew being continually pernicious wasn't helping their fragile marriage. Retracting his anger, he made it sound more like punctuated disappointment.

"Baby, you can make or break us, here. It's sink or swim, and we can't let our arms and legs stop dead in the water. We'll drown—sure as I'm sitting here."

"I'm not all that sure what sports has to do with our finances, but—"

"They're just figures of speech."

"Are you sure your figures are right, Jim?"

"We've got late charges on all of your accounts. And I'd given you money to pay them when they were due. Late charges damage us as much as credit inquiries; I thought I made that clear to you."

"Oh, that was clear, Jim. But what you didn't make clear was how I was to buy winter coats and boots for the kids, and still pay those charge accounts."

Jim tossed aside his pencil and sighed heavily from his momentarily billowed cheeks. "Okay—I stand corrected, I guess. But I still got to figure out a way to balance things."

Lorraine placed both of her hands atop her husband's shoulders and kissed the tight curls atop of his head. "You're still the man, baby."

"For all the good that does me."

The sliding doors croaked apart partially, ending the parental conference effectively, for the moment. Bea carefully put half her body past the sliders.

"Yes, baby?" Lorraine asked.

"Someone's at the door."

"What they want, baby?" her father asked absently, absorbed in his papers again.

"Some man wants to see somebody with a name like Daddy's."

Thinking it obviously a bill collector, Jim and Lorraine looked at one another, silently asking which one of them should go to the front door. "Thank you, baby," Lorraine praised, "I'll be up there in a minute." Jim grunted his approval for her volunteering because she had, after all, been less-than-frugal.

Before opening the door, she put up one last cautionary finger to her lips for the benefit of her kids. "Don't let me have to talk to you two," she whispered. Rolling her eyes heavenward momentarily, she girded up to confront whomever stood on the other side, but when she saw the pathetic figure in her doorway, all her apprehensions turned to empathy. The old man who stood there looked lost within the folds of his too large, buck-colored Mackintosh. It seemed the next wind would spirit him away from the threshold, his fatigue was so evident.

"Hello, Ma'am. My name is Franklin Theodore Sackett," and he showed his receding salt-and-pepper hairline by doffing his hat towards her. "Perhaps you can help me—"

"Oh no," Lorraine thought, pegging the hidden agenda of the stranger—a traveling salesman, or some evangelical witness, maybe? They would show up at a time like this.

"I'm looking for a man, a few years younger than me, if you can imagine that, he began. "Would you happen to know an August, maybe, he might go by the name, ah, Gus Martin?"

Now, it was Sackett that worried he might have to catch the young lady. The sound of the name seemed to rock her back on her elevated heels, as if there had been a momentary drain of some inner-ear fluid.

"Excuse me," she said softly, recovering, "you're looking for whom?"

"Gus Martin, or if not him, maybe you know his mother, Cleo Martin?"

"How did you—," Lorraine began to expound but decided to step aside, instead. "Won't you please come in, sir?"

Sackett welcomed the warmth just inside of the door. It already made him want to get his coat off. Drawing closer to the living room he saw the augmented television but didn't quite know what to make of what he'd seen. "What will they think of next," Sackett said, as he couldn't help noticing the intense concentration of the Martin children at their *Pong* game. "Hello, children," the old man quietly greeted, only to be answered by television bleeps.

"I'm sorry," Lorraine apologized quickly, as she turned her attention from the ignored visitor to her rude children. "Hey, you two—I know y'all got better sense than to let people think your daddy and I didn't raise you any better than that. An adult was talking to you." Half-hearted grunts of acknowledgment and an insincere waving of their hands followed their mother's chastening. Lorraine threw up her hands and giggled away what little embarrassment was left. She led Mr. Sackett by his bird wing elbow. As Lorraine parted them, Sackett was impressed at her strength as she made them rumble on the coasters. Sounded like a small rocket at lift-off.

Jim didn't look up from the papers piled around him; his glasses rode the bridge of his nose, as he darted his fingers on his calculator's keypad. "Did you run off whoever it was?" he asked. No answer. He figured another percentage. An unfamiliar clearing of a throat, purely produced by a man, made Jim stop his listless scratching of pencil to pad and electronic tabulations. He looked up to see whom Lorraine had dared to bring into their home without checking with him.

"Jim, this is Frank Sackett."

"Franklin T. Sackett, young man," the mysterious codger amended.

"He's looking for your father, dear," Lorraine explained, pleading silently with her eyes to her husband not to castigate the old man.

Jim gave Frank the same befuddled look of inspection that his wife had, but Sackett could not figure out why his presence would cause such a reaction. Jim set his pencil down with a decided pause and took off his glasses. He cleaned them slowly with a paper dinner napkin. Sackett just benignly grinned at him, still waiting to be asked into the room, still feeling unwelcome. He watched Jim remotely blow the napkin lint off his bifocal lenses and set the glasses back on his face. "Twelve years," Jim began, "My whole adult life—twelve years, and I can't remember anyone outside of my family coming to ask about Gus Martin. And you probably have no idea as to why, do you?"

"Can't say as I would, being I haven't seen him since the end of the war. Son, I don't know what happened between you, but you'd be right proud if you knew how he and your uncle fought in France. They almost single handed—"

Jim held up an abeyant hand that subsequently touched his eyebrow and then lowered it, halfway covering his mouth. "There must be some kind of mistake."

"Naw, no mistaking to it a' tall. I've checked and rechecked the checking. You the one I'm looking for."

"You don't understand, Mr. Sackett."

"Franklin will do, thank you."

"Okay, Franklin." Jim did his best to hold his impatience, releasing a sigh with the appellation. "Let me put things in order for you, if you don't mind. As far as I've ever been told, my father and uncle never even made it over to Europe. In fact, my uncle died in a motor pool accident while stationed stateside. So, you must be mistaken, or have gotten a bad bit of intelligence."

"Intelligence is such a relative term, I believe," Sackett said. "What one man states for being intelligence, as I know it, could very well, under a different set of circumstances, be completely erroneous. Fabrication. Intelligence serves those that propagate it. Someone's told you that your uncle died in the United States, but I'm here to tell you he passed on in the middle of the Allied Front. I was in the Battle of the Bulge, and your uncle was there—your daddy, too."

Jim sat still and quiet for several seconds and then took off his glasses and carefully placed them down alongside of his retired pencil and paper. He glanced over to Lorraine; standing behind the old man's left shoulder. "How the hell did you find us?" he inquired.

"Up to a point, the Department of the Army gave me some information. But they wouldn't make contacts with any outside sources for me, or the families I was trying to reach. I must have gone through listings of every Martin living out here. I thought if I could contact a relative who might know something of him, his whereabouts, maybe—last known residence, I don't know, something. And finally, I come to you. Took me a while, but I knew I was on the right track. Positively confirmed it for myself, as soon as I saw you. You're his boy, all right."

"Well, the man you are looking for is not living, as you know it."

"I don't understand. Either he's living or he isn't. Is he still alive?"

Jim moved one small stack of bills on top of a larger pile next to him and scowled momentarily at both his wife and the visitor. He didn't care to revisit his family history while balancing accounts, but it was evident that there would be no relenting of the intrusion. "If you can call being hooked up to an *Erector Set* with lights and tubes, in order to breathe, being alive—then, yes, he's alive."

Sackett remembered seeing his Bernice again, at the hospital, when he heard that.

"If you can call staring without blinking, so eye drops are the only way moisture gets to your eyeballs," Jim continued with disdain, "if you call that being alive: yes, he's alive. It's a kind of living, but not what I consider being alive. Let's just say, technically, he lives."

Lorraine injected, "Mr. Sackett, you'll have to under—"

"He doesn't have to understand a damn thing, Lorraine, and don't speak for me when it concerns my father, and me," Jim flashed. "You only know what side of the story I want to let you know. It's not the whole scenario. And the only person who can shed any more light on how I got here has been institutionalized since '68."

Flesh and bones, which seemed more invigorated a short while ago, now slightly withered underneath Sackett's ill-fitted clothes. It wasn't bewilderment any longer that deflated the visitor. It was disappointment. He knew, full well, the probable condition of his one-time comrade. What's more, he knew his own rendezvous with catatonia or dementia had been said to be drawing ever closer, as well. And Sackett understood the process, the way that age made the clothes you wore grow larger on you, while the mind shrinks. "I'm sorry for your trouble," he managed to say, in a pained whisper and a resigned folding of hands. "He didn't raise you, did he? You never knew him, did you?"

"Can't even go to visit him, anymore. He's nothing to me. He just lays there like *Boris Karloff* in a mummy suit." Jim pauses after the admission and then waves his finger in the air for a moment. "You know. Come to think of it, he was never really anything more than a figurehead of what a dad is supposed to be. Somebody, you know, you could look at and account for the way you act, not just for the way your teeth grew in, or for the color of your eyes. But, actually, I misspoke a moment ago. You see, he is something to me." Jim reached into a drawer and pulled up several worn bills. He crumpled a handful of them, squeezing them into dry clumps of pulp. Like he were wringing someone's neck. "This is what he is to me. Quarterly bills from a nursing home. Money—money that I can't afford to spend. Especially on an old man who doesn't know me, or who even wants to know. He's a lump of dead weight I'd just as soon have die and cast off. So, Mr. Sackett—Franklin, you'll forgive me if your news about him and my uncle doesn't swell me up with pride."

The old man blinked once, twice. He'd never come up against any hostility from any of the families, and didn't know exactly how he should continue. His tongue went to the roof of his mouth, then pooched his lips forward while reaching for an alternative approach. "I'm sorry you feel the way you do. However, I can understand that," Sackett acknowledged. "Even if a writer finds your father of interest. But I'll not bother you any further." Sackett turned in the doorway and adjusted his coat further up on his once broad, but now narrow, shoulders when he felt the pressure of gentle hands on them. Lorraine leaned toward him in excitement at first, but then regulated her enthusiasm down to a curiosity.

"Jim, did you hear that? A book about your dad—just think." Lorraine showed the elderly visitor to a seat and offered to take his coat. Jim, for his part, didn't know how to respond.

"If he'd done something in the war to merit that attention, don't you think I'd have heard about it from somewhere by now?"

"Sometimes, it's purposely made to seem that we only know what we are told we don't know. If you'll allow me, I'll summarize the whole thing for you. It might not be as dramatic or eloquent, but it is the story, as I know it to be. Being that you never got a chance to hear much about your dad."

"Go on, Jim," Lorraine urged, feeling the old-timer must have endured more than his share of life's sundry misunderstandings, and did not want to add to them. "Let him sit down, Jim," she implored, taking Sackett's hat and coat. "Have you eaten?" she asked, "Would you join us for some pie and coffee?"

"I wouldn't want to intrude, now."

Jim gave an abrupt nod of assent and Sackett took his offered seat. He appreciated the upholstered arms and well-designed support for his lower back.

"Do you like your pie with ice cream, Mr. Sackett? Lorraine asked, happy to give the elfin visitor some type of creature comfort. Holding up his hands in grateful supplication, Sackett just grinned. "Good, I'll heat it right up, then." She left the room to the silences between the two men, knowing that only good could come from their encounter if Jim would relent in his suspicion.

For his part, Sackett just rubbed the arms of his chair, admiring the relieved texture of the fabric and other details about the seat's fashioning while Jim punched a few last tabulations. "Nice place you got," Sackett says.

"Yeah, it's all right. For the area."

"Own it, or renting?"

Jim was curious about the unabashed directness, the innocent rudeness, but let it slide. He lit himself a cigarette and gave one to Franklin. And then the words, words of unspoken decades—old truths, began to flow between the two, almost as if by a signal. "This didn't all just come about by some sort of fluke—" Sackett began. The blue smoke of their cigarettes seemed to create a signifying medium for the telling, as if their separate tendrils irresistibly moved towards each other, and washed over their faces and shoulders. This was a blues story like none other told by the people who created the genre. "This was not some isolated act," Sackett continued, growing in his passion. "Nor was it an unintentional slight of America..."

CHAPTER FOUR
1943

There was indeed no happenstance, as Mr. Sackett said to me, or a sense of there being an aberration for what happened that summer. All points being considered, from the information gathered by me through investigation, the incidents leading up to the activity on June 20, nineteen-hundred-and-forty-three could have only culminated in the social outrage that it did. I started out to write a book about that riot, but then soon found out there was an even greater story to unfold. With an MFA from Iowa University, I felt more than prepared to extricate the incidents I discovered and to turn them into my first book. I got to meet Frank Sackett, initially, through having him pointed out to me by a great uncle of mine, from some old Army pictures. He also showed me a declassified document that intrigued me to no end. And it was then and there I began to do my research for my manuscript, not knowing where its genesis would take me. Somewhere beyond the riots. These weren't the first violent demonstrations about race, and the conditions it placed upon the haves and have-nots. Nor would they probably be the last. In talking to Sackett, I could only imagine that Jim Martin, as well as I, could only remember as far back as the 1967 melee. The government had changed society a lot by the time that all came around, but it had been begrudgingly worked out. The fact of the matter was, however, that as bad as things were in '67, they were far worse in 1943. To those of you who know the particulars I'm about to explain, I apologize; for the uninitiated, the oblivious, this will make a framework for you to base your judgment upon what I wish to impart.

Try to imagine back then; emancipation was still less than a century old and a generation never got to see its promise fulfilled. But there was a lot more at stake in the hearts and minds of the 43' rioters than an eighty-year old default on a promise for forty acres and a jackass. Yet, it all essentially sprang from there. Beginning with the deceptive ploy of a rudderless liberation of slaves, aggregated with cultural non-parity and its continual hamstringing of freedmen during Reconstruction, the decided resolve of the nation against unbridled blacks manifested itself in debates within the United States Congress. They filibustered over whether to invest in educating the newly freed Negroes, or lifting trade tariffs on the South. The Dixiecrats in the legislature won that debate with the help of some northern bigots, and thereafter, seeing no welcome for them in the South, a mass of uncultured Americans of African descent moved to the North at the same time Southern Democrats parlayed into conservative Republican politics.

In the 1920's, after World War I, our military strength made America a superpower, and blacks had a significant part in that coming to pass. Many of them felt they should be able to compete with white men on the domestic playing field of economics, as well as on a battlefield. They crowded into segregated housing, trying to find any kind of work that could get them and their families out of the *Hoovervilles* that became more and more common in the country during the recession and eventual Depression.

Arrivals of "colored" migrants always caused the displacement of Poles, Slavs, Greeks, or Irish because even those ethnic minorities were not thought to be as lowly as blacks. Riots in the North over this encroachment seemed to cement the notion of what white society really felt about the Negro in America. No one realized that some kind of social mechanism was repeatedly getting broken, and no one person was willing, or able to fix it. It was like oatmeal boiling on the stove. It can seem like there's too much in the pot and it threatens to overflow, but then someone turns the heat down and everything is contained, you see that there's room enough, after all.

Such was the situation in Detroit in that summer of 1943. That summer would become, in appearance, what could easily be referred to as a boil on the complexion of World War II society. While the world raged without, on its distant borders, the stomach of America tied itself into convoluted knots of disparagements and internal dissension.

A country, like an army, propels itself forward on the substance within its stomach. Who wouldn't agree that the success of how a nation feeds its people is also a barometer of its longevity. Where this commodity comes from is the heartland, where the true pulse of America has always had its meter. Illinois, "The Land of Lincoln," is the epitome of what is known as the heartland. But the Sixth Service Command, headquartered in Chicago, had a majority of its National Guard troops stationed at Fort Custer, Michigan.

Among them was the old black troop, known affectionately during World War I as "The Regiment." It sprang from the Eighth Illinois Volunteer Infantry that had reinstated and converted to the 184th Field Artillery. Its complement of men was then moved to the base named after the martyred Indian slayer, George Custer. The absurdity of an Illinois fighting unit, black or white, stationed two states away from its headquarters was further exacerbated by the fact that the firing range for the 184th was in western Wisconsin. Fort McCoy, to be exact, which lies in the southwest lobe of Wisconsin, not far from the Mississippi. During the summer, its loping emerald hills were pocked with oak and elm groves and it looked more like the setting for a 19th century boyhood adventure than a military base for the sequestration of urban coloreds. Sackett was a first lieutenant at that training site for the better part of the year, usually pulled to Michigan's Fort Custer when they were shorthanded. He was an officer's officer.

Long of leg and trim of waist, he was a striking figure of a man in a uniform, with the exception of his teeth. They were a distraction when he smiled, and therefore he didn't do that much. There was nothing abhorrent about them. They just didn't seem to be matched well with a face that could have otherwise belonged in a Negro film, co-starring with Cab Calloway or Bobby Short, maybe. Like these stars, there were mild elements of feminine beauty in Sackett's visage, also. Men had found themselves prostrated and looking skyward for misjudging the masculinity of Sackett, however. As a civilian, even his looks brought about unwelcome overtures from questionable men, at times. In the military, marauding soldiers mistook his Greek god's countenance for a sure sign of weakness that couldn't fend for itself. They all found out that Frank Sackett was not just some pretty boy. He was a demanding perfectionist who knew not only how to elicit pain from his fists, but also by propelling vitriolic words. From someone, somewhere in his life, he'd learned the art of turning a curse into a razor. The person on the receiving end of the berating always felt as if they'd been cut physically, as well as verbally assailed. One knew right away if they were liked by him, or not, by whether he publicly judged them; anyone else needed to have a very thick skin.

Sackett told me that he seemed to remember that all the men seemed especially listless the week preceding the riot. Partly from frustration and more greatly from isolation, it seemed that since the previous winter, activation had been all they could think about. Now that wasn't going to happen. The base had learned about the possibility of being mustered for deployment through the kitchen door, so-to-speak, as did so much dissemination coming to blacks during that time. Though the overnight temperatures at the time of the news were still below zero, in the double-digits at times, many of the men were nonetheless warmed by the strong possibility of seeing action. They figured it would be a matter of weeks for a callout. But nothing happened.

Whatever the word that connotes failure is, be it sullenness, despondency, or moroseness, any adjective of nonperformance pales in comparison to the impotence those soldiers were feeling by the summer of 1943. They figured their service in World War I had allowed them to peek through the kitchen door into the dining room; service overseas in World War II should now allow them to take a seat at that table, if they were allowed to prove themselves. These soldiers, however, had no chance to prove anything. Having had their zenith of hopes taken from them, they had only to put their minds on the trivial stateside developments occurring in a three-county area, rather than military maneuvers in Europe. They would not be given a chance to prove their valor, by appearing to be more willing than whites to die for their country. They would continue to wear the stain of cowardice.

I remember how Sackett detailed the goings-on to me with some spontaneity; an extemporaneous outpouring that was surprising. He did not seem in the least the delusional veteran that VA doctors said he was. He remembered the dimensions of the 184th's headquarters. That there was a weathered RCA radio in a central place of designation between portraits of President Roosevelt and Joe Louis, hung in places of equal honor. On the next wall, he told me, to the right, there were topographical maps of Wisconsin and Illinois. Between two memorandum-filled bulletin boards there was a poster ordering every reader to buy bonds with the words "For Freedom's Sake". Sackett remembered he and Master Sergeant Davies were taking a moment's respite while digesting the surprisingly good chili they'd eaten within the past hour on that cold winter's night. Their full stomachs had made them reflective and tranquil.

"I can't get used to it, Lieu," Davis lightly commented while he momentarily groomed some chili residue from his thin mustache. "You can say what you want, but it can't be." Davies lit two non-filter cigarettes, handing one to the officer and taking the other for himself. "These *Lucky Strikes* just don't taste the same since they took the green out the wrappers. Seems they took something out the tobacco, the same time."

"It's only a different package, Sarge." Davies watched the lieutenant take a drag from the burning chalk-colored cylinder and noted that the officer didn't particularly enjoy what he'd inhaled.

"See, look at you."

"It's all in your head."

"Lieu, you all but blew that smoke out the side of your mouth, didn't you?

"You exhale the same way every time?"

"Don't ever' body?"

"A person with an untrained eye would say that, or maybe a fool."

"Fool, huh? Well, I tell you who to ask. You go and ask the colonel."

"The colonel? Now I know you is a fool." Davies chuckled after that re-mark and turned back to the requisitions he was supposed to line-item for an audit. His own cigarette dangled from the corner of his mouth and his eyes squinted as he examined papers in both hands. Smoke wafting into his eyes and face got to be too much. He put the papers down and turned again to his superior. Jabbing the air with his cigarette for emphasis.

"You know the colonel talks more about the benefits of cigarettes than most doctors, lieu," Davies said, "Did I ever tell you the story about the colonel and his bivouac cigarettes?" Sackett sat down and closed the newspaper he'd picked up.

"No—but I suppose you have to tell it me now."

"Let me prove my point, lieu."

"Go ahead, sergeant. Indulge yourself. Reclaim your intelligence."

"And I'm about to, you can believe that. Saw it myself, so you can't say this is hearsay. The colonel has this thing about tearing corners out the bottom of his packs of cigarettes, see. Says it helps him and others to know what's his, and what ain't. So, one day he's out on bivouac, and some swamp that came up from thunderstorms overrunning the groundwater waylaid the command. They end up losing they maps, compasses, and radios. I mean, man, they barely had anything, and were two days out from where they were supposed to be for maneuvers. So, they're out there in the boondocks, trying to get a fix on their position and they supplies begin running low. Things were so bad, they even had some men go up the creek and kill 'em some cottonmouths to eat. The command figured the organization stood to fall apart if they weren't found in a matter of hours."

"Wait a minute," interrupted Sackett, remembering something, "was this in '41, down south, somewhere? I think I heard about something happening in Arkansas like that—"

"Yessir, you got it right. It was down in Gurdon, Arkansas. Anyway, like I said, the supplies are running low. The command staff only has a pack of Lucky Strikes left between 'em, and they belonged to Colonel Peets. Everybody was smoking Bugler mixed with some dried up tick grass. Well, they go to bed on the third night, and the colonel, he resting real well knowing he still had them Luckies under his cheek. But come morning, them smoke's gone! He couldn't find 'em and began turning that camp down one side and up t'other. Practically had the men stripped out over them Luckies. When he looks like he's 'bout ready to do that very thing. My company comes in and finds 'em."

"What condition were they in?"

"They was all right, for the most part. But the colonel, he was powerful mad. I'll tell you one thing, f'shoah. Colonel was about to tear him some new assholes when we come through there."

"Out of control?"

"Naw, sir. Matter of fact, as decent as a deacon. On the surface. He went about carrying out his bizness, just like regs say to do. He got the men they rations and such—Evah thing's hunky-dory. Then after a while, and evah body's fed, they give all the men smokes—Luckies, in white packs, just like we have now. Colonel didn't want none. Said he'd rather have the Bugler. Well, sir, this huge, corn-fed nigra from Texarkana goes and pulls a pack of green Luckies out his boots. Peets got a gander of the bottom of that pack, and it was like he spotted a sniper, the way he didn't let on."

"Did he put him on report?"

"Y'might say he did."

"Well, he either did, or he didn't."

"What he did was hit that big-ass country nigger so hard in the mouth, it made piss run down my own damn leg. Poor fool didn't even have time enough to spit it out."

"Was it lit?"

"Does Dorothy Dandridge kiss gendarmes? Sure, it was lit. Barely taken two tokes from it. A corporal and me had to put hands on the colonel to keep him from tearing that boy's head off. The only thing Peets kept saying was they was no such thing as a horse of a different color when it came to his cigarettes. And to this day he don't smoke nuthin' but Bugler. He rolls his own."

"If that ain't the most dad-blamest crock of—"

"Ain't a crock, Lieu—Colonel gave me one of the smokes from the rations and one of his own. I'll be dad-blamed if there wasn't a lot to what he said. They taste different, all right." Then Davies added this, more as theory than an afterthought, "Probably them gals they got pickin' it, nowadays. Ain't got sense to know when the leaf ready, or not. Betcha that's it, right there." Then he extinguished his smoldering stick of tobacco in the nearby butt can. After pausing long enough to represent the end of one conversation and the beginning of another, he asked, "Colonel's causin' some kinda ruckus down in Chicago, you think?"

Sackett narrowed his eyes, realizing the surprisingly cunning subterfuge of the master sergeant. The clearly less articulate man was trying to soften the officer's defenses through an anecdote, a casual remembrance, followed by a seemingly off-handed inquiry. It didn't work, but Sackett appreciated the sergeant's moxie. Only the closemouthed grin faded, however, not the lieutenant's goodwill towards the noncom.

"What did you say, Davies?"

"The colonel, sir. Ain't he got bizness down in Illinois? Ain't headquarters called for him?"

"What do you know about him going to Chicago?"

"Actually nothing, Lieutenant. That's why I'm asking you. Seems to me I shouldn't be the one left out the loop. I mean, what do I do if the inspector general wants to talk with him? What am I s'pose to say?"

"Nobody in command asked you to say a thing, sergeant," Sackett reproached, no longer in a playful mood. "This office is no place for your personal fishing expeditions, do you understand me?"

"Why, sure, Lieu—but—"

"But not a damn thing, do you get my meaning? The colonel's business is restricted as far as you're concerned. Even if I knew—which I don't, I couldn't very well tell you about it. Your rank doesn't give you that kind of privilege. What's the matter with you?"

Suddenly, the sounds of the loose floorboards being traversed in the hallway outside of the office were unusually louder and it brought all conversation to a halt. Only one person made those planks protest as loudly. Sackett and Davies turned in unison, knowing who that was. He tried opening the door quietly, but the left corner needed planing and the silhouette of the large man could be seen shifting his frame and bulk from side to side as he attempted to push it open without breaking its vibrating pane of glass. His patience was dwindling, however, and the soldiers in the office heard him cursing under his breath. The barrier finally gave up its resistance and Colonel Peets familiarly ducked his head to enter. He filled the entryway, blotting out the door behind him, like a Kodiak bear standing on its hind legs. The lieutenant and sergeant saluted and stood motionless. Almost no sign of even breathing.

Peets closed the door with such force that it was a wonder why he'd even taken such care when opening it. The glass buzzed. Turning, he glowered at his office staff with a countenance that was bloated from being out in the cold. "What the hell are you two looking at," he scolded, hefting a wrapped three-foot square flat.

"Pleasant good evening to you, Sir!" Sergeant Davies piped, bracing himself for the possibility of some bivouac justice being delivered to both he and the lieutenant, momentarily, judging by the look the commander gave them. Peets didn't bother returning the salute, either. He just propped the package against a dully-painted wall and gave the officer and noncom a further disdainful, caustic, staring down. It seemed he was like a percolator getting ready to broil over.

"That door was to have been fixed while I was gone these two days, wasn't it? Can either of you two sorry excuses for regular army tell me why it isn't?"

"My apologies, Sir!" Davies barked back, "I'll get on it, presently, Sir!" Glancing nervously out of the right corner of his eye at Sackett, still at attention, Davies was growing increasingly uncomfortable, physically. His right arm began aching at its frozen elevation and the discomfort echoed into the small of his back. Yet, he dared not relax.

Peets drew close to both soldiers and paced back and forth in front of each man, then finally let his men off his intended hook, returning their military accolades. Following his salute with a snapping flourish, the colonel quickly removed his gloves and took off his hat. Davies immediately came to his side to receive the wool overcoat and hat, placing both on a pole that was near where the colonel had set the large flat. The sergeant assiduously reached for the parcel, to put it in Peet's office, but was rebuked. "You can leave that alone, Sergeant."

"I was just going to place it—"

"Leave it, do you hear?"

Sackett tried to ease the tension in the room by drawing his superior out of his funk with some conversation. "What's in there, Colonel? Don't tell me it's more maps."

"Lieutenant, get me battery rosters," the colonel growled, ignoring the small talk, "and I want to indicate the top infantry troops."

"Infantry, Sir?" Davies inquired with surprise.

"Sir," Sackett interjected, "aren't we strictly a field artillery battalion?"

"Battery Rosters, Lieutenant! Infantry designations, do you hear?"

"Begging the colonel's pardon," Sackett apologized, "it's just highly unusual—"

"Sackett," Peets hissed, clinching his fists and opening them, willing complacency, "you're my personal adjutant, are you not? And as my auxiliary, you need to begin to answer questions I put to you—not you asking me about piss ant observations and sundry speculation." The lieutenant was visibly taken aback with the chastisement. Never had he been upbraided in such fashion, and in front of a noncommissioned officer, at that.

Davies, felt the growing awkwardness between the two officers, desired to quell the distemper but was at a loss as to how to go about doing that. To demonstrate that the emphasis had been felt, Davies loudly clicked his heels sharply, like wood slats forcefully being cracked together. The sound reverberated, bouncing off the tactical maps, to the posters, and past Joe Louis's portrait. "They'll be in your hands within the hour, Sir!"

"Is that all, Sir?" Sackett asked. The colonel picked up the package and turned towards his office, harrumphing a little, giving way to a slight sigh. A scowl of dissatisfaction still shaded his face.

"Just get me those rosters," he restated, and closed the door to his office quietly after stepping inside, to the surprise and relief of Sackett and Davies. Neither of the men wanted to move immediately, lest any disturbance could cause that discontented soldier to set upon them again. Slowly they pivoted their heads towards one another and each quietly acknowledged the perplexity on the other's face. They hadn't a clue as to why Colonel Peets had been agitated because he really hadn't made all that much fuss about the door before.

"You'll have to excuse me, Lieu," Davies said softly, "but I'm gonna go and change my pants right about now. Can I get you a pair?" Sackett didn't laugh at the joke, but not because the attempt at levity couldn't penetrate his demeanor. He had never seen the commander in such a peevish attitude, and he didn't dare let loose a snicker, so close were they to the office.

"What's with him?" Sackett whispered.

"I'm a noncom, Lieu," Davies said tiptoeing away from the door. "It ain't for me to know."

While he and Davies went about preparing the requested list they could only hear some momentary hammering coming from behind the closed door. Thirty minutes passed before the adjutant officer worked up the nerve to appease the colonel with the initial findings. Sackett knocked lightly on the colonel's door and was bid to enter with Peet's resonant, yet disconnected voice. Transferring several manila folders to his left hand, the lieutenant then opened the door with his right. He tensed as he entered, not taking his eyes off the floor. Expecting a fusillade of berating as he turned to close the door after him, Sackett was relieved that there were no harsh words or objects thrown his way, following his entrance.

The colonel stood looking impassively out of his office window, near the opened venetian blinds behind his desk. The caramel-colored palm of Colonel Peets' right hand, folded over the left, rested at the small of his back, again opening and closing both of them while he watched something going on outside. Peets' uniform coat lay draped informally over the back of his desk chair and the paper-wrapped flat leaned against the darkly stained furniture, conspicuously. The colonel knew that Sackett was in the office, looking at him and the package, but he didn't want to talk to the junior officer just yet. He just continued to stare out the window at the parade field directly behind his headquarter window, watching the determined activity of a laboring grounds crew.

Turning from the window, the colonel closed his walnut-hued eyes and began rubbing his temples, first in clockwise, then counter-clockwise rotations, using the index and forefinger from each hand. Through a slightly opened mouth, he yawned softly and then exhaled in slow, metered breaths. Sackett recognized this calming technique of the colonel's, and cleared his throat.

"I've—I've, ah, got three rosters together for you, Sir. We'll have the rest in fifteen minutes, or so."

CHAPTER FIVE
The Question

P eets opened his eyes wide, shaken from his reverie, and motioned for Sackett to place the folders on the desk. Then turning to the window again, monotoned. "They'll never get through that. Not this time of year. I wonder who put them on such duty."

"Sir?"

"Those seven men outside. They're out there trying to lay sod, but it's too early. Ground's still frozen. Not the topsoil, but what's below it is. You can believe that. "

"Guess they figure it's about time for things to be warming up enough for it to take, Sir. But you're right about one thing. It's damn cold out, yet. That's a fact."

"Yeah," Peets responded, "seems to be winter eight months out of the year up here, doesn't it?"

"That it do, Sir. That it do."

"It's like some parts of the country don't abide by nature's laws, huh, Frank?"

"Yes, Sir. This is one crazy state. They must get cabin fever from being cooped up for so long. And I still can't help but get uneasy when I see them around with those shot deer tied onto the hoods of their cars. Tongue all lolling around. Practically to the bumper"

"Doesn't take much to figure out why that bothers you, Frank. It's too close to the way our people have been treated. That's why. It's just a little too close."

"Well, now that you mention it—I'm beginning to see your point. Never thought about that."

"It's a thing called thinking outside of the box, I'm told. Associating new ways of thinking about old concepts. Rethinking what is, and what isn't. Have you ever done much of that, Frank? Thinking outside of the box?"

"You might be surprised how much I have, Colonel. Yes, I'm definitely an out-of-the-box thinker."

"That's good, excellent in fact. Sit down please, Frank."

As the lieutenant seated himself in the chair facing the colonel's desk he couldn't help but notice, watching the commander turning to face him, that the buttoned collar of the officer's uniform appeared so constrictive. The colonel didn't appear uncomfortable, but it looked like he ought to have been. The back of his neck brimmed over the collar of his shirt and almost obliterated its neckline. His jowls were also full, Sackett noticed, and Colonel Peets reached for an amber prescription bottle on his desk as he sat. He quickly opened it and tapped out two small white pills into his mitt of a hand. Then he poured himself a full glass of water from the pitcher on his desk.

"Sir, do you want me to call the doc? Have him check your pressure?" Peets couldn't answer directly as he was quaffing the water down like a man newly arrived from a desert. Finally swallowing his medication and shaking his head, Peets finally could answer.

"Naw, I'm all right." There was some excess water at the corner of his mouth that he wiped away with the back of his hand and then, and then, just like Sgt. Davies, pointed a waggling finger skyward for momentary emphasis, continued. "I want to show you something, Frank." Peets brought the flat from its temporary placement and set it on his desktop, beginning to unwrap it. "Give me a hand with this, Sackett," he requested, rather than ordered. "My arthritis is acting up."

Sackett reached over and helped to break the twine and discard butcher paper, discovering a painted wooden square had been covered. Several coats of varnish sealed a military coat-of-arms. Both men picked it up and Peets nodded over to the wall where he'd placed two nails. They hung the plaque and stepped back to see if any adjustment needed to be made, Peets clearly admiring the artwork.

"What do you think?" Peets asked.

Withholding comment, Sackett assessed the insignia discompassionately, seeing that it had a tri-pointed shield in its center, placed upon a blue field. Nothing significant. The shield itself was comprised of an inverted white triangle, divided into three parts. One section contained a blue circle with a World War I French Army helmet; something akin to the hat made famous by Sherlock Holmes. Directly above that shield he noted there was a log blockhouse, with a scrolling banner below that declaring, "One Country, One Flag." The other two sections had similarly innocuous symbols: three yellow fleurs-de-lis in one, and a Roman sword partially obscuring a cactus in the other. "Two days in Chicago for this?" Sackett asked.

"Consolation prize, Frank. They didn't want me to leave empty-handed."

"But what about all the rumors? Hell, even white officers were talking about you."

"Premature—unfortunately. All of it, rumors I let get fanned into delusion. And that's my fault. Hell, I wanted it to be true more than anybody, believe me. To be the first at anything is every man's conquest. But to be the first colored general in this army—well, it had me thinking things. Things like making history. History, you know—that thing bigger than any man. That really had me going. Really had me believing I was John Henry and Emperor Jones, all rolled into one. I was gonna be The H-N-I-C."

"The what?"

"Head nigger in charge, Frank." Peets batted his eyes at the younger officer and heavily sighed through his nose with mild exasperation. "Don't look so taken aback. You've heard that phrase before, I'm sure."

"But not coming from you."

"You forget—command took my pedestal away. And now I got to crap in a helmet just like anybody else." Peets pointed back to the battle insignia. "But they let me take this memento with me. Our history, Frank. That log fort, on the top, that's the old Fort Dearborn. It represents all the Illinois troops. The blue field there, in the shield, that's symbolizes infantry."

"You fought infantry in the first World War, didn't you?"

"That I did," Peets replied, lightly running his fingertips over the varnish.

"Couldn't any of us get into a combat unit, back then."

"I was one of only twenty percent of colored soldiers to fight infantry."

"And a machine gun battalion, at that, so you really had to have seen some action."

Peets sucked his tongue behind his teeth and went on with his illustrative discourse, foregoing memories of distinguished service. "You see that sword there, partially hidden by the triangle?"

"Yes, Sir."

"That represents our unit's service in the Spanish-American War, the last conflict this country had before World War I. That cactus signifies our placement on the Mexican border in that war. To show our World War I service you have to look at the semi-de-lis, the triangle. It stands for France, hence the helmet."

"Sir, why does the triangle with the squares in it partially cover the sword and cactus?"

"That shows significance of duty. The Eighth Regiment had a greater service in its World War I callout, than it did in either Cuba or Mexico"

"Okay, but why are there squares in the triangle?'

"They symbolize the Hindenburg Line. The one there, at the point of the triangle, it represents that the Eighth Regiment pierced the line. And the three fleurs-de-lis around the helmet, there, that says that the Regiment was in Meuse, France when we did it. Those are the French coat-of-arms."

"One country, one flag," Sackett read.

Peets sighed. "One country, one flag—indivisible. With liberty and justice for all. Maybe we should change that pledge. I mean, what's a man got to do to get a little justice? I took a National Guard regiment and turned it into an artillery division within ten months. It would have taken anyone else two years to do that. Man, I wanted that promotion so badly, to become the first colored general—"

"Begging pardon, Sir—General Davis?"

"Benjamin Davis is an acting-general, Lieutenant," Peets corrected. "If you notice there's a little 'a' behind his name. He ain't official. It's an acting commission. And that's why I took this from Division Headquarters, for me and Ben and all the rest of us sorry suckers who believe in history. I took that chunk of plywood because it didn't have a place of honor down there, anymore. Not in my eyes. 'One Country, One Flag,' my ass. Should be 'All for one and one for all,' as far as I'm concerned."

"The three musketeers?"

"You know who it was that wrote that?"

"Alexander Dumas, wasn't it?"

"Yes. And did you know he was a colored man?"

"Are you sure? And he wrote like that?" Sackett watched Peets shake his head affirmatively several times. He didn't know if his superior was spewing leftover Marcus Garvey ideology, or simply giving his own surmises about the literature. It certainly wasn't anything Sackett remembered learning about in schools, and he thought himself fairly well read. But, of course, he wasn't about to argue the point with Peets; a man who was now talking to him more like an elder than a commanding officer.

"So, what really did happen down in Chicago, Sir? What made you think you were going to be promoted?"

"When I got that priority dispatch, Sackett. That's when. A dispatch signed by General Aurand, himself. They'd put me up here to get this unit in place, and I did it in record time. And they knew I didn't want to leave Chicago. Hell, I just knew—just knew I was about to get my just reward." The colonel chuckled, "Aw, man. Visions of sugarplums. Visions of sugarplums just jitterbuggin' in my head. That is, they did until—" Peets stopped to take another sip of water.

"Until they what, Sir?"

"Sat me down in a big ol' chair and told me Christmas was five months ago." Peets carefully sat himself down in his desk chair with a grimace, and the relenting chair responded to the action with its own protest of a drawn out creak, as it tilted back on its fulcrum when his weight shifted in its lap. "They actually didn't even bring the subject of promotion up," Peets continued. "It wasn't even on the agenda. I figured it was the same old thing. My service was not distinguished enough. My experience, not broad enough. But then General Aurand told me something that almost made up for the slight. Told me something to make me believe there's a chance for greatness even in this war, Frank. You see, in every war since Reconstruction ended, the American Negro has been given an opportunity to distinguish himself in federal service. Aurand told me that kind of opportunity was on the horizon for us."

"Permission to speak freely." The colonel nodded his head in silent assent. "A Jim Crow army cannot fight to free a world where they aren't free, themselves. You and I both know why they keep us loading and unloading everything they own—or dishing up some white soldier's mess. And I'll state it clear. They don't want us getting used to the idea of firing bullets into white men." Sackett became sorry he'd said it before he'd even finished.

"Maybe. Maybe you're not too far off the mark. But I'll say it again. There's a chance for greatness in this war. For us. You and me. And you better believe they'll try to trip us up in it, shackle us to their outdated notions, but I'm holding Aurand to what he told me. That's why I'm not upset with what you said. We can make a stand about who we are as men, in front of the whole goddam world." A knock on the office door suspended conversation. "Enter."

Sergeant Davies came in with the rest of the files and immediately saluted the officers and not waiting for a return, crossed to the desk and placed his documents alongside Sackett's, on the colonel's blotter. "Here are the remaining rosters, Sir." The colonel became absorbed in the documents immediately, cross-referencing one sheet with another. Noticing the preoccupation, Sgt. Davies gave Sackett an inquiring glance, raising his eyebrows and bulging his eyes at him, tightening his jaw.

"That will be all, Sergeant. Thank you," said Peets, without looking up.

The sergeant flinched like a cat splashed with a bucket of water, fearing his curiosity had been uncovered, but there was no reprimand following the dismissal. Davies walked out of the office taking backward steps and closed the door again. After about a minute had passed and Sackett heard only the further shuffling of paper, Frank spoke up to remind the commander he was in the room.

"Huh? Oh, yeah, Sackett. Where was I?"

"The Great American Military Benevolence Society—"

Peets laughed hard at that, though Sackett couldn't quite figure out why. "Sir? What—what's so funny?"

"Don't you get it?" Peets continued chuckling, "The Great American Military Benevolence Society. The acronym for that is G-A-M-B-S, gambs. You get it? Gambs! Whoa, you're pretty good, kid. Pretty good. I'ma remember that one. Great American Military Benevolence—" A coughing spasm.

"Sir, are you all right?"

"Yeah—fine. Fine. Let me get my breath, a minute." Peets coughed into a white handkerchief and dabbed at the wetness in the corners of his eyes. "What General Aurand told me, in Chicago, was that we should expect an allied invasion in Europe, within two years."

"How are they going to do that, Sir? You've basically got two fronts, now. And that's not saying there couldn't be an Italian resurgence. We can't march into Poland with the Japs tearing us a new asshole in the Yellow Sea, not with that likelihood. Not enough—"

"Men, Frank?" Peets lifted up the files in his lap. "Men like these, here?"

"Now I know you need to see a doctor. As a matter of fact, the whole world's definitely gone completely on end, if you believe that." There wasn't a hint of a smile on Frank Sackett's face when he said that.

"Frank, you and I both know that invasion is inevitable; it's tactical convention, but there are pragmatics at play here that even the government can't overlook any further. They very well might have to invade Japan and Germany simultaneously; they might not have the luxury of shutting down one front and then the other. Think about it, Lieutenant. It's simply a matter of logistics, isn't it? Unilateral or bilateral invasion will bring enormous casualties, and when they grow massive enough the expeditionary forces will have to turn to the only reserve troops they have—us."

"Well, sure, I agree with you that colored regiments have moved in to replace—"

"Not replace, Frank—augment. They want to deploy colored men in white units while the battle's hot. Not mopping clean-up. Not anymore."

"And they'll have practically assured Hitler a victory, if they do."

"Are you going to stand there and tell me the initiative the War Department is taking isn't something were up for? Are you, yourself, afraid to go through that opened door?"

"If they mix our troops we'll be too busy fighting each other, instead of the Germans, I can guarantee that. The enemy will mow down what's left."

"That's how you honestly feel?"

"You gave me permission to say what was on my mind, Sir."

"Frank—haven't you been listening to what I've said? If you get a chance to do something that will move you up quickly, you do it. That's why I came up here. Do you have any idea how long it took me to get from where you're at, to become a captain? Five years. Sixteen years to go from captain to major. That's practically a career's span. And that was the ceiling for me. I couldn't have bought a promotion until this war started. As soon as Hitler refused to leave Poland I became a junior colonel. Four months afterwards I made full-bird."

"And begging pardon, Sir. The fact is you're still a colonel now. If what you're telling me is that that is how things do indeed work, then you should have come back here a brig general."

"But it's not about me, Frank. Don't you see? Yeah, it would have been nice, to say the least. I meant what I said earlier, believe me. But the fact of the matter is, I'm tired. It's you I'm trying to line up, now. By the time this war is over you might not have the opportunity to wait around sixteen years for your next set of bars. Talk is the Nazis have a super bomb they're developing. Hell, we might all be dead within two years. I dunno, but, the reason I asked for these rosters is because every colored division in the country is transferring their best foot soldiers to a classified camp."

"Where at?"

"Fort Benning, this summer."

"Georgia!"

"Well, I guess you won't be needing a map to try and find it, will you?"

"Colonel, I can't sign on to that. I'm not from the South—don't have any reason to want to be in the South. I can't—"

"Frank—Frank, don't whine. It's not dignified."

"Well, Sir, dignity is a very rare commodity for any black in Georgia. Let alone a soldier. Dignity rhymes with uppity down there, and you know what that'll get you."

"Put yourself out there, Sackett. Don't you see that's what's needed to build, to breed the character of all the men who've been turned out for this call? Regardless of how white troops feel about you, a sterling demeanor will outshine any dispersion put to you."

"I'm not one to grin and bear it, Sir."

"It's not about what you can bear, Frank. This will be about what you can exemplify to our men under circumspect situations."

"I'm sorry, Sir. But besides the solitary honor of your faith in me, I'm at no good understanding as to why I still wouldn't let the assignment pass me by."

"All right. Here it is, then. Plain and simple. The War Department is deploying men who have sucked the mud off the roads of battle consistently for two hundred years. Now they're telling us we're needed, that we're going to be counted--well, they also told my grandfather he was going to receive forty acres and a jackass. So, you can see why I don't want to let Uncle Sam completely think he's got all us niggers in his back pocket. I have to have you be my ears, my eyes, at Fort Benning. I don't want to analyze the training by reading unclassified reports or by making follow-up phone calls that will never get answered. No. I want you to tell me the real skinny. I want you to assure me that Negro soldiers, *my* soldiers that *I'm* sending there, are being treated with the dignity they deserve."

"But, Sir. Think about it, I'm just a lieutenant. Aren't there more experienced—"

"They can't do what you'll have to do."

"What?"

"They're too old."

"Too old for what"

"To pose as a non-com."

The air in the room became quiet for a protracted pause. "That's a court martial."

"Frank, those are the only people they're considering. The Army knows they couldn't have any colored field officers. What would happen the moment a Negro officer told a white non-com what to do, huh? There'd be bloody hell. And that's why only NCOs are being drafted for this."

"But if I'm caught, according to regulations, I'll lose my commission, Colonel."

"Yeah, well, let me clue you in on something. Not everything they're planning on doing down there is going to be according to regulations, either. In fact, you can believe the Inspector General's office is planning on doing the same thing I'm suggesting."

"But I'm still the one being asked to take all the risk, Colonel. If I'm found out, will you come to my aid? Where's the payoff in the charade?"

Sackett became more worried the longer it took the colonel to respond. He was no stranger to subterfuge when it was needed, but this could quickly turn into a double jeopardy situation; in ways that were only known to him. He needed more than a little assurance from Peets that he wouldn't be left out to tether on a rope all by himself.

"The truth of the matter, Frank, is this," Peets finally said, "I can't say there is some great stipend that will befall you. Because there's not any compensation that could be made manifest that would come close to compare to what colored soldiers have endured, and what you would assure to end. Sometimes, the journey is the only reward. And perhaps you're lucky enough along the way to find some terms of engagement in the struggle that will satisfy your needs. Hell, I'd go myself if I weren't too damn old. I envy you, the opportunity, and I could only think of you who could be the one to replace me. You are the one who has the demeanor—you, are the one who has the focus I have. But, for what it's worth, let's make it interesting."

"How could it be any more interesting?"

"For the sake of argument, and your peace of mind, let's say you get an incentive to set you on your way."

"I'm listening."

"If you accept this assignment—" Peets went to his desk and pulled out a bottle of cognac and some bucket glasses. Frank dreading that the colonel would attempt to bribe him with the mere offer of a drink.

"If you accept, I'll give you a promotion as of tomorrow. Captain Franklin Sackett. Then, if the going gets too rough, you pull that trump card, and you have me contacted. I'll say you were acting under my orders. What do you say?"

Sackett was in a focused tunnel of self-determination, hearing the whistle of Peets' train of authority coming from behind, inevitably overrunning his will. "Well, I do want to promote."

"Yes."

"And it does sound intriguing."

"Ah, huh."

"And it could be worse."

"How's that, Lieutenant?"

"It could be Georgia, in Russia, instead of Ft. Benning, Georgia. Pour them up, Colonel. Make mine a double."

Peets chuckled at the brave face Sackett was attempting. "But don't turn that card over quickly, mind you. Because then the heat will come back to me, and I'd rather it didn't. But, nonetheless, I'll go your bail." He gave them each a glass half-filled with the honey-colored alcohol, and Peets lifted his glass in front of him, in the manner of a toast, towards the junior officer. "To the Great American Military Benevolence Society." Peets began laughing again over the reiteration, but couldn't help but notice the sad eyes above the close-mouthed grin of Lieutenant Sackett. He felt badly for him.

"Remember, Frank. Sometimes there's no method to the madness, but only madness. The thing we have going for us with this is that we'll be a factor in the methods used. It gives us a little control over what madness prevails."

Sackett nodded. The seed had now been put to soil. Planted at a time when Peets thought nothing could grow. It was not a treacherous seed, meant to prosper a choking weed of sedition. This seed, germinated by hope, had all the moral conviction that fertilized the nation's original independence fight, yet it had not the care of a good farmer to nurture it. The growing seed is vulnerable, and the colonel's plant could easily have its limbs torn by grazing winds of obstacles, seen and unforeseen. But someone needed to clear weeds from the plant's base and brace it to become as strong as it needed. A lack of such diligence invited parasites, and the plant would inevitably sicken, surrendering to the chaos within and around it. Only to be replaced by encroaching, heartier weeds.

Frank gave a slight nod and smile, "I guess it can't be said that we all don't go just a little mad every now and then."

"Some more than others and at some times, more readily than others. But remember, it's all according to one's point of view."

"Like grounds men putting down sod in the snow."

"Yeah," Peets chuckled, "just like crazy ass gardeners, like that."

CHAPTER SIX
Gardening on Granite

Mayor Jeffries, by all of his accounts, presided over Detroit's one hundred-forty square miles with a non-partisan hand. He felt he did right by the escalating colored population he had over in the Paradise Valley area of the city. Their two decade long influx was amalgamating within Detroit's culture without the usual visible signs of ethnic strain. That was due to one thing, predominately. They were kept busy with work. Military manufacturing, especially for the Navy, was a round-the-clock operation in Detroit. The Negroes, along with the working white women, shored up the depleted work force of white males admirably. As long as there were no scapegoats, nobody to point fingers at for the loss of a job, there'd be peace. The war meant work for all.

Jeffries considered himself a "good gardener" and a reliable steward of his constituencies' growth. The agrarian allegory, however, pragmatically speaking, was somewhat of an oxymoron. You see, a gardener wouldn't try growing seed where there's salt. And Detroit, literally, had a bedrock of salt for its foundation. Left over from the Ice Age, before the granite plates of its shelving arose and closed off the northern continent to the ocean, the area had been a seabed. The salt, the last vestiges of prehistoric legacy, were underneath the city. Two square miles of it. It was mined for commodity, and the salt manufacturers had carved out white corridors and rooms. Still, Mayor Jeffries didn't see the connection between salt and gardens. Oblivious to it.

The mayor was contented because as far as he knew, there wasn't a "colored problem" in Paradise Valley. Public Safety Commissioner Witherspoon, and his officers in the police department, usually gave the Negroes every chance to settle their own differences. Of course, if they couldn't, there was no hesitation in applying the full force of official authority. And Mayor Jeffries didn't insist that things were perfect. Yes, there were problems with housing there, but the mayor added, after conceding that fact, "Where wasn't it?" In fact, the mayor saw a bright future for the colored people of his town, once the war was over, if they could keep peaceable.

West of Paradise Valley, connected to the shore of Lake St. Clair by a large bridge, was a municipal park called Belle Island, or Belle Isle, if you listened to residents who were as persnickety about its names as some San Franciscans were about hearing their city referred to as Frisco. Streetcar traffic and taxicabs are a common denominator to the ratio of visitors there on any given day. Working class Detroit came there to forget about Hitler's atrocities and tried to gather their second wind before returning to the grind of production quotas and overbearing shop foremen, who took up all of their waking hours.

On the weekend, most of the baseball fields were in use and picnickers found themselves approached by cart vendors throughout the leisure day, selling roasted peanuts. Some carried cotton candy, or snow cones. The snow cones were so big there; that by the time you leveled them off, you had a white paper funnel brimming with cold syrup.

Other park patrons would go on excursions aboard the ferry. There were actually two running between the mainland and the island, but people, especially visitors foreign to the granite, country rock isle, could be mistaken that there was only one. If they were on the Michigan pier, or the Canadian dock, it seemed that way. But unknown to the landlubbers, while one was docking on the destination shore, the other ferry motored out from its mooring. People watching and waiting for the next boarding would notice that the departing boat eventually looked like an insignificant white dot, many times mistaken for a whitecap upon the fresh water horizon. Twenty-five minutes or so into the trip, these two ships would juncture in crossing. And as they passed one another, the passengers occasionally would wave salutations to the other craft. These always-silent greetings, a universal acknowledgment that finite humanity was in the boundaries of what seemed a watery infinity, had its aesthetic lost, though, to persons of color. They were confined to travel by the bridge. There were no facilities for these free Negroes on the boats, even though, strangely enough, water is believed to be representative of freedom.

According to some scholars of 19th century literature, it's believed that on water is where the mind can ponder about things greater than itself, greater than the body in which it is contained. Bereft of land and its innate, terrained assuredness, mankind is humbled there. It is where there's landfall that always seems to bring about conflict with people, and these binaries seemed to ring true because Belle Isle is where all the trouble began. Even though the waters surrounding the island were calm and translucently pristine that day, the people on the rock were not affected that way.

If you happened to hear about the origin of the great consternation from people on Detroit's Eastside, where Paradise Valley existed (the Forrest Club, in particular), it came about from an unprovoked attack on a Negro mother and her infant by some irate whites. If you were a white defense worker, getting on the road after the graveyard shift ended downtown, the talk was a colored kid bludgeoned some guy to death. Later on, the federal government had its own interpretations of what happened, and why. So did the Army, and so did the government of Detroit. None of these bodies, however, after all their lengthy studies and testimonials could define what the malfunctioning social mechanism was that ended up resulting in the deaths of over forty people, and millions of dollars in conflagrated damage. Off the record, some Rust Belt evangelists truly felt its roots were formed in the nexus of Original Sin, and the division within the human spirit. They were not in the least surprised that things turned out as they did with coloreds. Darkness attracting dark ideas, and even darker behavior, perhaps.

On Sunday, June 20, 1943, it was another successive day of plus ninety-degree weather that drove a diverse colony of Detroit's citizenry to the lull of intermittent onshore breezes that wafted in from off the Great Lakes. All that day, foot and vehicle were constantly traversing the bridge. But it never fails that when environments become uncomfortable, practically unbearable, everyone seeks refuge at the same time. And came they did. The city poured forth people seeking freedom near the water, all driven by one single, evanescent idea. Freedom from the conventional oven of air, doming over them. Come one, come all. Surely, there is room for any that desire to refresh themselves by the cool water's edge. By mid-day, though, even the water-cooled air circulated by heat thermals made it too humid for the more than three thousand park patrons who were there.

Many of them chose to retreat under elm or sycamore tree awnings, choosing to take the time for having something light to eat. While doing so, however, looking at the street-level, the lower bodies of the far-off walking citizens appeared to warp in their heated reflection from off the pavement. Those shaded watchers could see the chimera figures approaching their way, and they curled their barefoot toes into the cool, black earth, thankful to not have to be trekking on the park's concrete frying pan of an avenue. Singularly distinct among the patrons moving about in the smoldering chimera wall were a mother and her little girl. The child held an *Eskimo Pie* ice cream while the parent tugged at her.

The blonde girl's mother was from Saginaw, staying with her sister and brother-in-law for six long weeks after having watched her husband ship out. "Mrs. Saginaw", as we'll call her, had been spoiled since childhood and never had to contend with providing for herself. Her husband managed a lumberyard and made more than enough for her to stay at home and handle her part of the deal, and produce children. Up until the war started. Now without her husband's salary, Mrs. Saginaw had to seek out her family to give her a hand. Her sibling gladly obliged, at first, but her own husband was growing tired of the sister-in-law and the irritating, precocious niece. In some ways, God forgive them, the couple feared the child's father dying more than the mother did.

A combination of exasperation, high temperatures, and a dress too warm for the day, along with her uncooperative child, caused uncharacteristic red blotches to form on the faux debutante's usually creamy neck. Her face appeared even more as a mask due to no make-up being applied below her chin. Things were getting out of control, all the way around for her. And she had had enough. "Come on, now," she complained. "Will you come on? I don't plan on taking all day. Do you hear what I'm saying?"

Mrs. Saginaw's progeny, the Pollyanna-of-the-pinafore, struggled to keep up but it was all she could do to focus on the eating of her ice cream confection. When she could not do either walking or eating very well they ended up stopping, and she had to endure her mother's white-gloved, spittle and handkerchief pawing to clean her face. "But I wanted to ride the boats!" the seven-year old protested.

"Yeah? Well, you got me wanting to whip your fanny. Now, come on, girl. I need to pee."

"Momma, wait a minute!"

"It's too damn hot for this child. Come on!"

With that final demand came a tug on the daughter's right arm. It was forceful enough to preempt her from taking another bite of the Eskimo Pie and the right wrist wobbled. The laws of inertia, the mass of the ice cream, and gravity all did the rest. The barely eaten Eskimo Pie ended up on the pavement, its wood shim handle angling towards the sky. "Oh, look what you made me do!" the girl screeched with adult indignation as she saw the treat turn into a spreading brown puddle of melted sweetness.

"Shush, now. I'll buy you another one, okay? But there better be a restroom on the way, Missy. Or you'll have more than that ice cream to cry over." The frazzled woman and her pouting offspring immediately set out for the nearest vendor.

Two sailors, wearing immaculate summer white uniforms, almost stopped directly on top of the threatening chocolate pool that everyone else had been avoiding. "Damn, but it sure is hot, today," said the taller, thin one as they came to the spot where the mother and daughter had just left. His friend, a sweaty and barrel-chested, portly individual, didn't provide immediate comment. His actions bespoke all his sentiments. He finished drawing a long swig off the sarsaparilla bottle he clutched in his doughy looking hand and mopped at his neck with a fully unfurled handkerchief. Getting no feedback, the taller sailor made another assertion. "Well, at least its far better to be here sweating, ain't it?"

"Compared to where?"

"I dunno. Anywhere there are guns firing at us—South Pacific, fer instance."

"Really makes no never mind to me," drawled the less-statured sailor. His southern accent elongated certain vowels and aborted others. He looked around and seemed disgusted, though not with himself and what he was thinking. "In fact—I'd just as soon transfer out to some action, if I'd have my druthers."

"You're nuts."

"Oh, I'm the looney one. Come on over, here." The Dixiecrat plodded over to a newly vacated, shaded bench. Though his steps towards the park fixture were deliberate, there was, oddly, an awkward sort of grace to his movement. When he and his cohort sat down, the chilled sweat from the bottle he held commingled freely with the salty moistness of his hand. As they sat they both grunted out a sigh that came from having too-full stomachs. After a moment, the tall sailor tilted his head towards his shipmate and raised an eyebrow.

"You're not serious, are you? You really want to go? Look, we have it made here. For one, we aren't catching yellow fever, or shrapnel. And I, for one, intend to keep it that way as long as I possibly can."

"Don't you see the grand scheme of things that are happening here and abroad? We have a higher responsibility," the overweight salt almost chanted, raising his double chin for emphasis, followed by another swiping of his rag on his forehead. "There is an order in this world set about by the dictates of nature that places the burden of responsibility on the race of white men—"

"Quiet—people are staring. Why don't you can all that stuff. It's not winning you over any friends."

"I could give a spit, sir. Now, you looka here. Whether it's in America, or in the Pacific. Be it japs, or be it jigs, colored is colored. We got to fight with one or the other because they breed fast as cats and outnumber the white men three times over. If not for our cunning, the entire world would be overrun with 'em."

"Yeah, pal. Well, around here, you need to keep that under your cap."

"Why? Because half the niggers in Detroit decided it was time for a barbecue, today?"

The bigot shot out his sarsaparilla occupied hand and waved it over an expanse in front of him. The pacifistic sailor followed the sweep of his self-righteous friend's arm and concurred. In every direction he looked Negroes were in the majority, some looking their way, and he also silently admitted that that realization came along with some general uneasiness. In the past two weeks skirmishes over housing and employment had polarized a good deal of Detroit, and the military had been cautioned not to become involved. "I don't want to be around any upstarts," the tall sailor said, shaking off the last of his anxiety. "That goes for whites or blacks."

"Who's starting anything? I'm just stating facts, is all."

"Well, it ain't helping nothing. So, let it go. Come on, I wanna real beer." On a nearby bluff, in the direction the sailor had pointed, a group of five teenage Negro boys lounged underneath a tree with cascading foliage, and watched. Well-used bats and mitts lay around them.

The two sailors rose from their seatee and resumed their walk, and when they stepped out into the direct sunlight again, the boys from the bluff saw the reflection of the light that made their uniforms practically turn into halos.

"Man, I sure like the way them uniforms looks. I think out of all the military, the Navy has the nicest uniforms."

"Forget them peckerwoods, brother," said Bay-Bay, the oldest, at nineteen.

Diatomaceous, sixteen and second oldest, got back on track to his original conversation, and jumped up with his Louisville Slugger and took a batter's stance. He cocked the bat, splaying his elbows out. "The trouble with you, Bay-Bay," he said, "is you ain't puttin' no ass into your swing. Now, lookey here—" Diatomaceous stroked a forceful arc, causing a subsonic whoosh of air. Bay-Bay watched the demonstration for his benefit with nonplussed concern.

He wore a sleeveless tee-shirt, that hardly contained his boulder sized pectorals and sinewy torso. His unblemished skin was the color of creamed coffee, and his relaxed hair was blue-black and worn close to the skull. The legs in his khaki pants uncrossed themselves and drew up towards his indented chest. He wrapped his arms around his knees and withdrew the wooden matchstick from his uncharacteristically thin lips. He gave Diatomaceous that look—the one that earned him the title of being called the colored Valentino, the one that made opponents second-guess their aggression, the one that persuaded girls and some married women to succumb to his advances. "Oh, please, niggah," Bay-Bay snickered.

"Well, who's hitting all the homeruns?"

"She-it," was the only thing Bay-Bay could hiss back because for as small as Diatomaceous was, it could not be denied that he had a system down for consistently applying the meat of a bat to a leather ball.

"I'm telling you. You got to hit from the bottom of your feet. You're doing it all from up here, in the shoulders."

"Go on, man," Bay-Bay rebuked.

"I'm serious," Diatomaceous insisted. "It's just like throwing a punch when you're boxing." Seeing a chance to regain his eminence through the simile, Bay-Bay went for the opening.

"Oh, yeah, Dime—like you did when you punched out all those white boys that came and ran your ass off the field the other day." The shrieks of laughter and abuses came rapid fire at Diatomaceous, now. All the boys were involved in a critique that, to an outsider, sounded like one strident, pubescent babble, one voice trying to overcome another through sheer volume. A passerby wouldn't know if they were roughhousing, or choosing sides to kill one another. Everyone but Diatomaceous began to yuck it up over the memory Bay-Bay pointedly brought to mind. Diatomaceous had tried to cajole white interlopers to let him reserve the ball field, but he was summarily cuffed and ran off. Screaming for his momma.

"I ain't scared of no white boys," Diatomaceous squeaked, in protest, his voice losing its modulation when he said 'white'. It was all from his hormones involuntarily over-compensating for his humiliation, but the crack in the pitch of his voice made his peers shriek with laughter, all the more. Bay-Bay was on his maligner like a terrier on a kitten. Now that the embarrassment was re-versed, he wasn't about to let Diatomaceous off so easily.

"As a matter of fact," Bay-Bay added, "he was too busy running to be doing much swinging by the time he got to me, as I recall." Diatomaceous's prowess on the ball diamond was now reduced to a flaccid egotism; his interjections and explanations continued to be drowned out by louder guffaws. Feeling his man-liness being directly ridiculed, Diatomaceous responded with renewed bravado. He would do something to make his stock climb back up in value.

"I'll show you who's afraid," he said. Going north, he set off with his bat. The others stood around shrugging to one another as they tried ascertaining what it was exactly their friend was up to. Without hesitation, and determined kinetic purpose, Diatomaceous was making a beeline towards a white, mid-dle-aged man, asleep under a neighboring tree about thirty yards away. As he approached the slumbering man, Diatomaceous turned towards his comrades, making sure he had all their attention. He lifted the bat he carried off of his bony shoulder and looked down at his target. "Hey. Hey, cracker."

The white man continued his oblivious and deliberate nap, adopting a semi-fetal position on the ground. Diatomaceous tapped the baseball bat against the gray soles of the man's shoes. The man awakened disorientated, at first, but then shockingly alert, seeing a perturbed and menacing colored boy standing over him with a bat. "Get on up outta, here," Diatomaceous ordered. The perplexed dreamer, trying to assess what was happening, looked over to his right and saw the wide-shouldered Bay-Bay and three other black toughs. "I said git, cracker!" And as Diatomaceous screamed this he raised the bat up over his head, as if he were going to career it down upon the man's pink head. The awakened realized he was in imminent danger and rolled to his side, bringing his hands up to the sides of his face with a shriek.

"Don't hit me. Don't hit me. I'm gone—see?" And the terrorist victim got up to his feet quickly and ran, as best he could with his potbelly and bowed legs, down the sloping grade of the knoll. He repeatedly cast glances over his right shoulder and then alternately, his left as he made his gape-mouthed escape. Diatomaceous felt triumphant. Triumphant in a way that no athletic event had ever made him feel. For the next five hours, or so, whatever was left of the day, he could gloat about the momentary dominance he'd had over a member of the establishment. How his peers saw that dominance displayed for their benefit. They joined him with slaps of congratulations and plaudits, characterizations of being "one crazy niggah." The talk about the scene was remembered throughout the day and into the evening. Into the magic hour.

Everyone seemed to be waiting for the evening to consider leaving and the cooling of temperatures promised with the tide. The twilight and the dwindling hours usually conspired to cull a perpetual wind from the lake but only a mild zephyr came. The sun, a deep tangerine in the sky that came level to the car tops near the bridge did not relent. The invisible air current was warmer than the still dusk's temperature that it streamed through. There was little to no relief as families, couples, and solitary visitors began to migrate towards the Belle Island Bridge exit, hoping to escape being sequestered in the pilgrimage of traffic that would occur.

The movement of the crowd was impeded by such things as the number of items being hauled out, the sizes of groups struggling not to lose sight of one another, and the insipid wanderlust of patrons whom habitually stopped in the middle of such masses, and for no apparent rationale, began their own discourse with whomever they're with. A large lobster-colored woman, wearing a recent mail-ordered print dress, led her equally obese and Bermuda-shorted husband around such a small clot of immobile humanity. She plodded forward, carrying more than half of the belongings she and her husband had brought, and cast a long, purposefully pointed glare of disgust at the human obstacles in their way. Further irritating her was that her spouse couldn't seem to keep up with her marching pace.

Several hundred yards back from the lobster woman, Mrs. Saginaw and Pollyanna were still testing each other's assertiveness, only reversing polarity. Now, it was the banana-curled tyrant who tried to drag her sluggish mother back into the recesses of the park. "No. We got to catch our street car," the mother insisted. It was evident to the woman that her daughter was overly tired, so tired that the poor dear didn't realize how much she needed to rest. The child bleated out loud, despairing pleas, her tear-induced crankiness continually interrupted by runny-nosed snorts. Her cheeks were flushed and had salt from tears and sweat on them.

"But—it's not—hot, anymore," five hiccoughing sobs, "Mommy, it's not!" And the daughter timed her imploring with tuggings at her mother's dress and limbs, seemingly with no effect. Their departure was not to be delayed by emotional outbursts.

"That's enough, young lady! I've let you play all day. Now, quit making all this fuss and let's get moving."

Nearby, a group of Negro mothers smiled knowingly to each other amongst themselves as they overheard the parental exchange. To them, the over-dressed white woman and her once pristine, but now disheveled and tantrum-throwing daughter were disciplinary enigmas. The Negroes wouldn't have gone half as far with the demonstrations of that child. They couldn't help but smiling at the tug-of-war developing between the two. Then the unexpected happened.

Pollyanna suddenly stopped pulling, and relaxed. Ceasing her exertions practically caused her mother to fall atop of her. Now free, the child snatched her hands to her sides and refused to give them back to her parent. The child knew she wouldn't be able to physically pull her mother back into the park, but she also seemed to realize that she wouldn't have to. Mrs. Saginaw would have to carry her out, and that was only if she could catch her. "I'm going to stay, anyway, and you can't stop me!"

"You come here, right now!" The mother yelled as her child ran away, the rebellion stunning her and leaving her motionless. Stopping her mother in her tracks, as it was, the youthful escapee gained a sizeable lead in distance. The race was one of sheer audacity and surprise and quite comical to the Negro mothers. Mrs. Saginaw was not going to catch that girl, running in her pumps and a hip-hugging skirt. "If you don't get back here," Pollyanna's mother screamed after her, "I'll tan you, good!"

About fifty yards or so away, directly in line of the oncoming chase and pursuit, three Negro girls, all around secondary school age, were engrossed in a game of keep away with a soccer ball. Long, ochre and mahogany legs, and accompanying arms, playfully batted the ball through the air with athletic purpose and beauty, running to get possession. They didn't see what was headed straight for them. And that was verified by at least one eyewitness. Because you have to remember that there were police investigations about everything that could have been a precursor to the riot.

Therefore, we must take the viewpoint of the casual observer for a moment, which is the legal criterion of a witness. The casual observer on the scene would have observed that a bigger human object was heading in the direction of a smaller human object, and both were traveling towards one another at about the same rate of speed. Now, laws of physics dictate that the smaller object, Pollyanna, should be violently deposited on her backside upon running into the larger object. And the laws of physical nature held sway, Pollyanna hit the asphalt hard, while the Negro girl as well was bowled over. The former ballplayers surrounded their friend immediately, trying to help the older girl regain her breath while simultaneously brushing off the devastated Pollyanna, who rolled on the ground in pain.

From a distance, seeing the preclusion and inevitable conclusion of the accident, Mrs. Saginaw could only manage to gag out a warning. Her voice was strangled by invisible fingers of anxiety and alarm, and suffocated by her exertion in running to her fallen child. She expected, by the banshee moan of pain that her daughter sirened forth, that the older girls were about to pummel her. By the time she reached her daughter, the mostly Negro crowd couldn't help but take notice of what was going on. "Get away from her," Mrs. Saginaw screamed finally. "You heifers! Get away from her!"

The dusky children and onlookers didn't know what to make of all the fuss. The little white girl only appeared to have been moderately injured, some abrasions of varying severity on her right hand and hip, and the right knee was skinned pretty badly, weeping a clear sap. She also had a bloody nose and a contusion under her left eye innocently inflicted. Yes, she was banged up, but nothing to be confused with being mortally wounded. Not as injured as all the screaming she did would have you to believe.

One of the older girls, one who was maybe sixteen or seventeen years old, tried to help the smaller child get up and offered her some comfort. But for all of the compassion she gave, she was shoved aside by the irate and protective mother. "I said move, you clumsy nigger bitch!"

"What did you just say?" the girl incredulously asked, aghast at the slur having been spoken aloud. Everything at that instant seemed to start happening in slow motion, like the slap from the verbal bullet shattered the dusk's reality and placed a vacuum over the crowd. But lasting for only the moment it took to ponder the weight behind the epithet. For when reality became manifest again, and emotions became fired, the concern and incidental interest of the Negroes gathered turned into anger.

Mrs. Saginaw knew in her heart how she felt at the moment. She knew she meant for the words to hurt "them nigras" because she physically couldn't. She wanted some immediate compensation for the injuries to her daughter and the only payment that she could exact was the satisfaction of a verbal whipping. This was as it should be, she thought, they got to know their place. But no matter how righteous her indignation, or how virulent her outrage; she couldn't let her fearlessness become a vehicle for foolheartedness. She was clearly outnumbered by the others, and therefore didn't respond to the girl asking her a second time what she had said. Mrs. Saginaw didn't feel her worthy of a reply. She simply stared the colored child in the eye with a fixed and leveled contempt on her face and picked up Pollyanna. "Come on, honey," she said quietly, "let's go home, now."

"These white people sure is crazy," one of the girls was overheard to say.

Clutching her child up into her arms, the mother backed away from the scene of conflict, warily eyeing any potential or imagined attackers. She patted her whimpering girl's back with her still gloved hand, growing all the more thankful when she saw a group of whites approaching quickly. The screams apparently had attracted them and Mrs. Saginaw's vivid distress seemed to feed into their own apprehensions about the scene they came upon. Some murmuring and hard stares among the witnesses, both colored and white, escalated the always-subsumed distrust between the two groups. The mother and child left under an escort of Saxons. The maligned minority viewers watching them go, placing their hands on askance hips or scratching their ears and heads from being pestered by insistent mosquitoes, held their ground and did nothing to re-engage.

This incident with Mrs. Saginaw, whose only claim to fame had been a former beauty contest placement, and the assault by Diatomaceous, could have by themselves formed any number of social configurations and radical motivations capable of erupting in an uprising. Any of the details in the two scenarios could have turned into an emotional trigger, and a riot only needs one trigger to fan a fire of ill repent. This uproar had three. The third happening, in timing almost with the second, where coincidentally Diatomaceous and Bay-Bay happened to be in the vicinity of, occurred while Pollyanna and Mrs. Saginaw were running their meandering course over the hills and dells of Belle Island.

The parties in this memorable occasion were Charles Gelving, a man approaching the latter years of his middle age, and Delores Crawford, who was on the younger side of thirty-five, though you'd never hear it from her lips. Charles, shorter than his date, was of medium height and about fifteen percent over his fighting weight from years earlier. You could barely distinguish, however, where a quarter of a century hadn't entirely obliterated his fundamental musculature. The squat frame still appeared to possess latent power. They both worked at the machine yard because, well, for Charles it was all he'd ever done for twenty-five years. But Delores, however, was a new hire, looking to make ends meet until her husband came back. And Charles was a widower.

Clumsy flirtations and gentle nudging from Charles came after an incident on the loading docks, where he'd taken the blame for her on a safety violation. The first time in fifteen years, the super noted. He'd only been given a good ribbing over the missing chocks, but the girl would have been let go if he hadn't stepped in. That would have meant her losing her apartment, and maybe even going hungry. Charles wasn't about to let that occur. Delores had tried to thank him at the end of their shift, while they were punching out, but Charles played it all off to momentary insanity. Outside, on the way to the parking lot she kissed his cheek. His grin was hidden as he quickly walked away without so much as a word. But from there on, they'd pass small talk, or kidded one another about how the other person worked, but it was all-playful. People were beginning to talk, though.

Considering his monkish existence, however, Delores soon realized that any ideas about her and him becoming an item were overblown, and as unfixable as the bump on her nose. She needed male company, but could not afford having some young provocateur vying for her affections, failing to understand he would only be an interim interloper. With Charles, she felt the "safe" relationship she'd been looking forward to developing. Like most men, he talked a lot about what he would do to her if given a chance, but she knew he would never attempt any of it. Charles kept his distance from appearing in any way lecherous, but Delores was getting to a point that she desired him maybe placing a squeezing, meaty hand on her still, as yet, firm flanks. That wouldn't have sickened her, in the least. Others were interested, that was for sure. She saw the looks they'd give her, when she'd walk over to the candy machine or to go to the restroom. But she simply couldn't trust the younger guys. They had a grapevine that tended getting too overheated and it wouldn't do for family finding out she'd been wayward. She thought Charles was interested, but just couldn't get a read on him.

However, had she known the desirously sensuous shadow dances her image played out in his mind, before the cold cave of his libido, she'd be proud. The feelings he had for her were very real. Too real. And his upbringing wouldn't allow that reality to manifest. Not that kind of reality, one to turn their relationship into some promiscuous façade. A man's forgotten indulgences. A denial of small urgings that twinged inside his manhood more than he'd care to admit. He felt it would not only cheapen her, but the memory of his wife, for if that kind of companionship was meant for him again, surely it wouldn't be from a woman too eager to please. But, still, he found himself particularly captivated by Delores' full curves and tight, thick muscles. Her light green eyes reminded Charles of what he had poetically heard referred to as jade pools. One of her best features, she'd said. Making up for the dark amber hair and the slightly bulbous nose that she hated. It didn't matter a whit to Charles, though. Any of it. In his lonely eyes, he thought her a goddess.

Gelving crossed his arm over towards Delores while they walked and offered her some peanuts he carried in a bag. That was the way her "Chuck," as she preferred to call him, would run a diversion from probing questions. He pulled out some peanuts. It was a defense that a school kid could see through, so it didn't deter Delores. "So, you got word from the State Department recently?"

"Hmm?"

"Last week. You mentioned some news," she persisted and took a few peanuts.

"Oh—ah, yeah. Well, y'know it's only preliminary stuff."

"What did they tell you, Chuck? It's not bad, is it?"

"No—nothing worse. They, ah, just confirmed that he's been a P.O.W. since March. That's all they were doing."

"Do they know where?"

"Somewhere in the Pacific, I guess. I don't know."

"So, he was stationed at sea, last?"

Charles stopped in his tracks. "Uh, yeah—hey, Delores."

"What is it Chuckie-Wuckie?" There was no one else around. They solely occupied this particular place and Charles saw how the rose sunset made her amber hair look like a deep fire. He shoved his free hand forcefully into his pant pocket.

"Look," he began, "I don't mean to have you listen to all my stuff, y'know. It kinda makes me a little fidgety."

"Chuckie, you ol' stick in the mud, that's your son! You're talking about your son. That's important to you, and it should be. You don't ever have to apologize for telling me about him. Just because you're with me shouldn't mean you have to hold back about anything that is going on with you. That's not only silly, but it's unreasonable, if you want to know. A man has feelings, too."

Charles was touched, but not so much that he would be reduced to tears. He was of the Gary Cooper mold, and tears would be out of character for him. Delores cracked the peanut shell in her hand as they resumed walking. She'd never had that kind of hand strength before coming to work at the plant, and she hoped it wasn't her short nails and rough hands that were keeping Charlie at bay. How much more unfeminine could she expect to become?

"You know, you're a very special woman, Delores."

"Oh, you noticed, did you? Even in overalls?" She began to softly wring her hands.

"I don't mean, in that kinda way—although you are a looker. What I'm saying is, the help you've been to me since my Ann's passing, and now with Tim's situation, overseas. Well, you've been really kind to me. That's something I won't forget, I'll tell you that."

"Tell me that other thing, again, Chuck."

"What other thing?"

"You said I was a looker. With this frizzy red hair and big honking nose. You said I was a looker. What are you crazy?"

"Oh, come on, Dee. Most guys would have to be half-blind not to notice you. Don't play coy with me."

"Unfortunately for me, most guys aren't the guy I'm married to, Chuck.

"My gosh, I didn't even stop to think. Here I am talking about how my son is and you got your husband fighting in the teeth of the front. Am I insensitive, or what? Can you forgive me?"

"What's to forgive?"

"Isn't all this just happening because your husband is over seas? I'm sure it must have been entirely different."

"That sonuvabitch never paid me a minute's worth of attention all before the time he enlisted. And now just because he decided to join the Army, I'm supposed to turn around and put myself on a shelf?"

"Come on, Delores. Give him a break, why dontcha? He's fighting the good fight over there."

"That may be, Chuck. But he didn't have to go. He was over the age limit to enlist, so I guess he just must have been tired of me. Tired of me not willing to endure the things he wanted me to do, so he could feel younger. When I didn't fill that bill, he up and left me for his fool's adventure in the military."

"You still love him, don't you?"

"There are all sorts of different levels of love, Chuck."

Meanwhile, further up the same pavement, Diatomaceous and Bay-Bay and the other ballplayers were mired down in nonsensical conversation as they walked towards the park's exit. A street lamp switched on as they passed it, leaving an isolated circle of light on the walkway. As Bay-Bay turned to Diatomaceous and gave him back his bat, something made the eldest youth stop in his tracks. "What's the matter with you?" Diatomaceous asked.

"I'm hungry," came Bay's Bay's reply, the announcement bringing up whoops.

"Uh-oh, y'all. Better watch out, now. If we don't feed him something soon, he'll be gnawing on one of our feet like it's a pig knuckle," Diatomaceous joked.

Bay-Bay ignored the smaller boy's taunt because he lost all sense of provocation when his stomach growled. Instead of wasting time and breath by coming up with a retort, he instead re-emphasized his uncomfortable emptiness, "I ain't playin', man. I'm really hungry."

"Well, don't be looking over at me," one of the other boys added, "I ain't got the money back from last time. Bay-Bay always be asking dudes for money."

"I ain't got no money," Diatomaceous said.

"Now, Chuck. Stand still, you. Let me put this in your hair." The boys, thinking they'd all been left alone, now looked in back of them and saw a white woman with some Brown-Eyed Susan's in her hair. She was attempting to place a daisy behind some old white guy's ear. The guy looked like an old boxer, or a football player, maybe. Diatomaceous whistled through the gap in his front teeth, and smiled. Drawing close to a tree, he held the bat to his chest, like some misguided altar boy who was carrying an oversized and extinguished candle.

"There's your meal ticket, Bay-Bay. Betcha they got some money." Diatomaceous ran off, swinging wide of the path as he backtracked, so he could flank his prey. He did this before Bay-Bay's whispered warnings could be finished, or heeded. And when the gang realized that Diatomaceous was serious, they ran away from the immediate area, for their own sakes. Diatomaceous had become reckless in trying to rehabilitate his reputation, and the others wanted no part. Regretted having teased him, even.

Standing behind a tree, a trickle of sweat rolled down Diatomaceous's temple as he turned his head towards the right. Waves of heat rolling outward from the furnace within him escaped through the neckband of his tee-shirt, baking his ear lobes. The couple was almost there, the woman laughing loudly. Completely oblivious.

Delores laughed in a way that could make a man blush from her saucy pitch lilting out. It carried a tinge of sexual innuendo. In a crowd of people, one would be captivated when they heard it and then want to see where, and from whom, that carefree music came from. It was her laugh, in fact, that distracted Charles from catching the movement on his left, just out of his line of sight.

"Give me some money," Diatomaceous demanded, "right now!"

Delores' laugh aborted, cut off by the immediate threat posed by a face-off with a bat wielding, colored juvenile blocking their path. Diatomaceous felt the rapid-fire stings of about seven mosquitoes on his back as he impatiently waited.

"I ain't playin' with you. Now, give me money."

"You go right to hell," Charles said, taking Delores by the hand and beginning to walk around Diatomaceous. Diatomaceous, however, took one step to his left and called Gelving's bluff, sinking about six inches of the bat's shaft into Chuck's mid-section. Gelving's knees immediately buckled, almost collapsing completely from under him. His fingers splayed open at his stooped over sides. Incapacitated. Delores then let out a scream that was even more voluminous than her laugh.

Some park workers had heard the peal of her cries and the tirade of pleas following the initial attack. They gathered other whites and began to search, deeper into the park, but of course, by the time they arrived Diatomaceous was nowhere to be found. Charles hadn't regained the use of his voice, but the hysterical Delores managed to convey what needed to be understood by the rescuers. The group set off as one in the direction she pointed, and they were agitated like villagers in pursuit of a werewolf.

Diatomaceous made good his solo-flight of escape, however, having such a lead on his would-be capturers that he had to stifle an overwhelming urge to stop his running and succumb to a strong desire to laugh out loud. What had been particularly amusing to Diatomaceous was the noise the big old white guy made when he got hit with the bat. Diatomaceous was heard to say later that it was the noise a "sissy" would make if you squeezed his arm too tight. It certainly wasn't what he expected to hear from a guy that appeared farm-fed tough.

Finally stopping at a tree, catching his breath, Diatomaceous realized that he had gotten himself into what he called a "tight," that is, needed to relieve his bladder. He unfastened his pants quickly and his urine ran strong, almost loud enough to be reprimanded with a call for silence. But, sure enough, there had been no time for that because before he could refasten his fly, Diatomaceous saw the white mob approaching. They broke into a run when Diatomaceous took flight anew, but there wasn't a man amongst the pursuers who had the youth or stamina of Diatomaceous Thurgood Dolomite.

The former high school track star quickly put a distance between him and the mob, once again. It allowed him a minute or so to catch his breath after sprinting. Still carrying the bat, he dropped it now and bent forward, resting his hands on his knees. Looking up, he noticed a disbanding group of Negroes at a family reunion within jogging range. Diatomaceous ran at full pace towards them for purpose of dramatics.

With some amount of theatrical flair, Diatomaceous practically fell into the arms of an older, startled black man, who at same moment saw the posse of agitated whites heading for them. "What they want with you?" the man asked.

"Whatever it is," said a fellow who looked like a brother to Diatomaceous' benefactor, "it don't seem to speak to any good."

The whites, eighteen in number, massed together in front of the reunion contingent of around fifty. "Give us up that boy, now. You hear?" one of the park staff demanded.

"Wait one minute, now," Diatomaceous's defender objected, "I don't see anything here saying that any one of you is a constable, carrying out his legal duties. We are not turning over this child to a crowd with no legal authority."

"He's an attempted robbery suspect, that's what he is."

"Did you all witness this?" Diatomaceous's advocate asked.

"His victim told us directly."

"That's hearsay, anything coulda happened," a family member mitigated. "All y'all got is some allegations."

"He had a bat," a white said.

"He ain't come here with no bat," a black answered.

"Well, if you all don't want to be arrested yourself, for harboring a criminal," the park employee threatened, "I suggest you hand him on over."

"Look here, white man," the brother of Diatomaceous's defender declared, "We here can come and go, as we please. And we do not intend to let you have this boy."

"Come on," said an impatient white, "let's just go and take the black—" and he shoved the brother.

This caused for several other pushing jousts and lying on of hands to get at Diatomaceous, and then blows began to be thrown with bad intent. The hammering of bone and flesh began, and the agonies cried out, rising into the air of the humid Michigan night. The final trigger for the riot had been pulled and the shot that rang out would be heard across the country.

CHAPTER SEVEN
Emergency Plan White

Colonel August M. Krech basically consigned himself to bachelorhood as soon as he'd been placed at the Sixth Command of the United States Army. He hadn't even reached the age of forty and he'd determined that was the way it was going to be for him. Now, five years later, it seemed to be holding true. There wasn't a woman he'd met that could have swayed him to recant his sentiments on marriage. Living on Chicago's North Side, there wasn't a lack of comely female acquaintances, but Krech's address book nonetheless lacked any notation about them. It was an entrenching motif. The stars that could seduce August Krech were not the ones seen in the eyes of a willing date. The stars of commission, and his covetous desire for them, were the real enchantresses of the colonel's preoccupations. So, even though prospective females came within his day-to-day interactions, some sent by his mother's encouragement, Krech did not make any accelerated overtures to any of them. He was on the fast track for a general's star and could not exchange loyalties.

When asked about his lack of dating, Krech unapologetically stated to questioners that an opportunity of upward mobility during an outbreak of worldwide war seemed to outweigh any other personal considerations. That pursuit required long hours and a single mind. He deemed it a moral pursuit and anyone that didn't appreciate his prerogative could go to hell. The truth be told, Krech simply just didn't seem to have the kind of demeanor to sustain relationships of the heart. He was like a refugee from the Land of Oz, with an integral emotional quotient missing. Instead of being charming, he'd be particular. Instead of being minimally sensitive, he came off as analytical. But even with all that, civilian female staffers were still interested in him. After all, men, in general, were in short supply.

They liked his thick, coal black hair and pool-blue eyes. The restrained dimples at the corners of his mouth. They liked the cut of his uniform on him and his air of lean assuredness. But for all those qualities he might as well have been a friar training to become a monk, regardless of him being Jewish. To his mother's chagrin, August Krech never saw a date more than twice. He never could see himself regularly calling upon a woman friend. Never could see a woman being anything other than a friend to him. And yet, at the same token, would never deny he was heterosexual. He just wasn't a consistently practicing one, at the moment.

On the Sunday of the riot, he had gone to a White Sox game. Krech preferred the Cubs to the Sox, especially since that nasty betting business, but the Cubbies weren't at home that week, so the only choice for the baseball aficionado was to go to the inferior Comiskey Park. Somehow, he'd also let himself get snookered into a blind date afterwards, later in the evening. Originally, it was to have been a double date, but his poker buddy flaked out after all the arrangements had been made. He really didn't expect to enjoy his time there, and to make up for what he knew would end up being a tortuous night; he'd gone to the game. Even though it was the Sox.

The woman that was his date, Betty Regoli, was a personnel assistant at the Headquarters. She lived on the West Side of the city, sharing an apartment with her mother and sister. Krech had met her once, in passing, and she was a pleasant enough girl, from what he could remember. Just nothing extraordinary to look at. Blonde, and Italian-Catholic, with thick thighs and shapely calves. He didn't know what she'd think about him being Jewish. Religion could be a chastity belt that no amount of assuaging and pleading could open. And the colonel could have used some release, though he'd never admit to it.

But as soon as he'd arrived, ten minutes early, problems came up. In the colonel's observations of the cramped tenement he found Betty wasn't ready, and that could be excused because he was early, after all. She quickly sashayed her way from the only bathroom in a slip, and with rollers still in her hair, hidden as much as possible by her well-meaning family. She promised, with a little embarrassment, that she would be ready in ten minutes. But that had been twenty minutes ago. The small talk he put with about the weather and his feigned interest in photo albums laid in his lap had pretty much run its course. Krech now had to enter into some sort of formal discussion and conversation with Betty's sister and mother. Something more intolerable to him, than unbearable.

For one thing, her sister had teeth spaced so far apart that she could no doubt eat her mother's spaghetti through a picket fence. Speaking of her mother, Krech uncomfortably noted that she had two detriments, a cyclopean eyebrow and a dark mustache. Because of their distracting appearances it took renewed concentration on his part each time he had to make responses to the mother's and daughter's inane questions. Did he have medals? How many Nazis had he captured? Were there any other boys in his family? What diocese did he belong to? Had he ever been engaged? And dinner conversation with Betty present hadn't been much better, even though the bistro they went to lent itself to familial repartee.

Betty's appearance did not require the dim lighting in the restaurant. Because she was the most appealing member of her family, the officer could keep engaged, but, as mentioned, the wizard hadn't given him his heart yet. True to his nature, Krech doubted he'd ever look in her direction again at work, let alone ask her out. They shook hands at the stoop of the seedy apartment building once the date was over and Krech appreciated and welcomed the manicured appearance of his shoreline neighborhood. He was sick of the whole idea of dating, for quite some time.

The colonel's antidote for the futile evening was listening to Tommy Dorsey and a succession of scotch. Halfway through the third drink, and almost a dozen cigarettes, Krech began to grow tired of Sinatra and called it a night, picking up the tone arm of his General Electric phonograph indelicately. He was not sober and it was just after midnight.

He fell asleep quickly, oblivious to the new morning, at first barely being able to hear the metered tock of his *Westclox* alarm clock on the bedroom chiffarobe, and then slipping into mercifully numbing silence and blackness. Three hours later a black military staff car slowly drove past his house, stopping halfway down the next block and then reversing itself. The driver, an army captain, wearing a short-sleeved uniform shirt, with matching khaki pants, leaned out of his car's opened window and glanced momentarily at the curb. The gears could be heard minimally crunching in the otherwise silent street, followed by the short acceleration of its motor. Then he decisively pulled up into the colonel's expansive cement driveway. Within moments he parked right alongside the colonel's Cadillac and stood at Krech's front door.

Once the colonel finally became conscious again, aware of someone at his door, he of course didn't know how long the captain had been ringing his chime. The bell's unrelenting and monotonous tone successfully pierced the cotton wadding of alcohol that had desensitized his brain, but common disorientation exacerbated the awakened officer's bewilderment more than it usually would. Rising quickly from his bed, he couldn't decide which was worse, his aching head or his parched, sore throat.

Ignoring the incessant bell, two glasses of water, a fumbling for aspirin and a suspect brushing of teeth didn't make Krech feel any better. But at least he wouldn't be answering the door with muddy breath and shellacked eyes. For a full fifteen minutes the knelling of the doorbell continued. When the colonel finally did come to the interior portal, the information he received when he opened it quickly caused the military messenger to be ushered in. Over cups of sobering, tepid, black coffee, Krech had the watch commander repeat his story. He couldn't afford to be acting under any assumptions.

"Now, let me get this straight," Krech said creasing the skin between his eyebrows. "You got all this information strictly from reliable law enforcement sources. And I'm not talking about beat reporters, I mean straight from the cops, no third party hearsay?"

"Sir, a platoon of MPs at the Detroit Police Headquarters saw it all for themselves. Beaubien Street was full of scout cars and jeeps. Rioters are filling up the city jail. They're even talking about turning loose inmates who have less than a month to serve on a prior sentence."

"Well, why didn't I hear about this until now, captain? When did this whole thing kick off? And why didn't the radio say anything about it?"

"Responsible journalism, I guess, Sir. All they'd be doing is reporting a riot, but not having any idea as to what caused it."

"And what did start this?"

"I don't know."

"When did you say this started up, again?"

"I didn't say yet, Sir. As far as we can tell it began about ten, last night."

Krech squinted at his watch, the corner of his mouth and lower lip drooping while he strained his eyes to see the watch hands. "That was five hours ago. You mean to tell me that within five hours of a major race riot the Michigan National Guard couldn't have been mustered up for duty?"

"Not for what's being requested, Sir. At least, to my understanding of the situation, Sir."

"And pray tell, what could that be?" Krech grimaced, shelving his pomaded black hair over his fingertips as he gripped his forehead with his widened hand. The aspirin had little effect on his headache, now. In fact, the only success it had was in souring his stomach.

"According to the Officer-of-the-Day, at Headquarters, this is command decision to be made by the Service Division. You being the first in that command—"

"Dammit all to hell," Krech groaned, leaning back into the stiff, low pro-file chair and folding the flesh of his jowls between his hands. "Start talking sense, to me man. What is Command being called for?"

"Sir," the captain went on, "Commissioner Witherspoon and Mayor Jeffries want to meet with you, personally, as soon as possible."

"Well, they could have called me for that."

"Sir, they're requesting implementation of something called 'Emergency Plan White', and only you could be talked to about it—in person, not over landline."

Krech had arisen to pour more coffee, upset that he had to begin deal-ing with this apparently growing crisis under conditions of sleep deprivation and a slowly receding fog of inebriation, but the code name "Emergency Plan White" brought everything into sobering focus that no amount of cof-fee could. The colonel reached for his robe's belt instead of the percolator, unfastening its loose wrap and then undoing the buttons on his pajama top. Now he understood why there'd been no phone call, and why the Michigan National Guard would not have the resources needed to act. "Has Michi-gan's governor been in touch with Mayor Jeffries, at all?" Krech asked in a somber and level tone.

"He's believed to be in Ohio, Sir. A governor's conference, I believe."

The colonel returned to his bedroom and in moments came out fastening the last two buttons on his uniform shirt. "Well, that's just dandy. I'll lay you odds he doesn't know a rat's ass about what's going on." Krech disappeared again into his room, coming back wearing unzipped pants over his boxers, and a pair of black socks over his right shoulder to put on his bare feet. He tucked his shirttail into his trouser's waist and hopped about momentarily while he put on his socks. Sitting down on his sofa, he found his shoes and began putting them on. "Here's what we're going to do, Captain."

"Sir?"

"Call the Provost's Office in Washington, okay? I need to speak to them, yesterday would have been fine."

"Will there be anyone there, Sir?"

"There's always someone manning that office, Captain."

Krech got up and opened his entry closet, taking out a heavy suitcase and some clean uniforms. "Have you been back to Headquarters? Does anyone else on Command Staff know about this?"

"You're the first and only, at the moment, Sir."

"After you get Washington for me on this line, go in the bedroom there and call General Aurand for me."

"The general, Sir?"

"Yes, the general. You get in there and tell him to meet me downtown, where I'll brief him. Just let him know he's going to have to call the president."

"What?"

"The president."

Krech brought in underclothes; so white they must have just been torn from their package, and threw them in over his folded uniforms. "You heard me, didn't you?"

"What on earth could be so important to have the president being awakened in the middle of the night for?"

"Roosevelt's the only person who can call federal troops into an occupying force within the United States, Captain. And that's what's being asked to be done." Krech picked some balls of black lint he'd noticed off of a shirt. "There's a good possibility that the jerrys have caused some sort of insurgence within our borders. I don't particularly like Hawaiian surprises, Captain. Do you?"

CHAPTER EIGHT
Downtown Detroit, 1943

For the most part, the downtown area of Detroit spawned groups basically made up of white rioters. Directly below the city hall building about a thousand of those rabble-rousers clogged the streets. Their infestation was so complete within the thoroughfare that approaching trolley cars had to slow down, for fear of running over civilians standing in their paths. Once the rioters saw that they couldn't stop the forward progress of the transit vehicle they vacated the tracks. All the while threatening to overrun it.

One instigator, a thug who was one of the first to remove himself from the rails, became livid that nobody had the courage to support him in trying to hijack the car. Incensed that it passed unmolested, he climbed on top of a street lamp's base. "Come on guys," he pleaded, "what are you waiting for? That conductor was a nigger, for Chrissakes. That was fresh meat, dammit!"

"Damn right, fresh meat!" a drunk roared, waving a crowbar. And then, almost on cue, another car rounded the corner in less than two minutes. "All together now, here we go," the inebriated thug encouraged. This time there was no hesitation. En masse, the mob blockaded the rails, stopping the trolley. This time there would be no stepping aside. Screams could be heard from within the immobile, cramped car as the drunk and others beat on its closed doors.

"Any niggers in there?" the chant rose, bellowing above the screams as the trolley entry began to succumb. Well within the coach, away from the windows, a middle-aged Negro gentleman ducked down and quickly retreated to the rear of the car, even though he was wearing a fine looking suit of clothes. Several passengers attempted to hide him underneath their seats, crowding around the innocent prey when they saw the agitators would soon enter.

"Hey! I think I see one," someone yelled from outside. A revived clamor of anger rose up as the multitude converged on the stopped street car as its opening gave way. The anguish of the passengers drastically spiraled as members of the horde made their way inside. The Negro, fearing the worse now, came out of hiding and ran desperately out the streetcar's back exit. He made it as far as the boulevard's trolley safety zone when two reports of gunfire silenced the frenzied hysteria in the street.

The intended victim from the train ducked these shots, but a third round ended up finding its mark. Lodging itself high in his left shoulder and breaking his collarbone, the force of the blast drove the wounded man's face onto the asphalt. Looking up in pain and fear, the Negro only felt true relief fall upon him when he saw two police officers standing near their scout car. He couldn't gather why they hadn't seemed to notice him, but nearing the point of passing out from stress and blood loss, he nonetheless began crawling towards them.

What at first seemed to be inattention, however, soon seemed to be an oblivious indifference to the man and his grave condition. The officers leaned their backsides against their car's closed doors and crossed their legs, folding their arms with nonplussed looks. One of them picked at his nose while the other snorted and turned his head to spit in the direction of the shooting victim. "Help me," the man was able to shriek, "I've been shot!" In concert, the peace officers turned their heads to see the wounded and prostrate civilian crawling, but they made no move to meet him. "What's the matter with you?" the wounded man sobbed. "Can't you see? For God's sake, help me! Please, I've been shot!"

One of the officers casually adjusted the position of his Sam Browne belt on his hip and spat out more of his sputum from the back of his throat. Then he stepped on the cigarette he discarded on the avenue. Together, these upholders of the law finally walked away from the curb they were watching from, and grabbed the man on either arm. He shrieked so loudly that the hubbub on the streets was overcome by the intensity of the cry. But the officers paid no heed to the protests or physical condition of the Negro.

"You're under arrest for disturbing the peace," the spitting officer said.

"Arrest?"

"That's right."

"But, I'm shot!" The grips on the arms of the frightened Negro tightened and he started kicking when he saw several men approaching from the crowd where his assailant was hidden. "Don't let them at me! Oh my God—

please, no!" And then his antagonists set upon him anew. About nine of them. Each one walked up to the dumbstruck captive and struck blows while the officers looked to either side of the street. For the officials watching from above, in City Hall, they'd seen enough. Reverend White was the first to turn from the window.

The indignation on his face was apparent while the visages of Mayor Jeffries, Commissioner Witherspoon, and Colonel Krech were blank and observant. The reverend turned to look at all of them, he being the only person of color in the room, and was not dismayed that he could not read any reaction from a single man. Mayor Jeffries just loosened the button of his pinstriped jacket and sat down at the conference table, quite away from the scene of disturbance. He ran the palm of his right hand along his thin, white hair, where the sweat had created a cowlick. Commissioner Witherspoon, with his short wavy red hair and pockmarked neck took a drag off the cigarette in the corner of his mouth and then exhaled from the other side, just staring. "Holy Mother of Christ," he said, and spit out a piece of tobacco that had stuck to the tip of his tongue. The last witness, the military adviser, Colonel Krech, simply shook his head in wonderment.

The minister faced them all as they now sunk back to the interior of the room, and they couldn't help but see his pained expression because the white clerical collar he wore seemed to underscore his face. "Now," he said, "now will you get us some help, or not, Mr. Mayor?"

The city's chief executive paid no attention to the icy edge on the holy man's voice. "Commissioner Witherspoon," the mayor began, looking up from the table, "get me the names of those two officers, if you please."

"Right away, Sir." Witherspoon crossed the room to place a phone call and pulled out another cigarette once his line had been connected. Reverend White didn't take his eyes away from Mayor Jeffries, however. The large ears and bulbous nose of the politician, mixed with his laissez faire attitude, irked the man of faith to no end.

"Mayor Jeffries, we'll not take this kind of injury without some recourse, I'll guarantee you that, sir. The colored community of your city is being put at risk by the very power that is supposed to be pledged to protect it."

"Please, Reverend," the mayor placated. "We're seeking to get all of our available resources to meet this crisis. I agree we need to come up with a solution to the dire problem we face. But what must be stressed to you, here and now, is that it is the solution we must keep focused on, not the problem."

"Regretfully, Mr. Jeffries," White replied sanctimoniously, "we coloreds here feel the need for more than just the guarantee of another white man's solution. We've had it up to here with such solutions."

"Now, see here, Reverend White—" the mayor began to demur, before Witherspoon got involved in the fracas.

"What's he doing here, anyway, Mayor?"

"I came up here trying to find out why your men arrested two hundred civilians—" the preacher reiterated when Witherspoon rolled his eyes. "Two hundred, Commissioner. Red Cross volunteers. How can you explain that?"

"That's easy. They had to be doing something, or they wouldn't have been arrested."

"They were trying to quell a riot in their community."

"Well, that's laudable, Reverend. But the last I heard, that was still a job for the police. They must have gotten in the way of some of our officers carrying out their duties."

"Like the ones outside here were doing, just now? Yes, I see. Quite a fine job, indeed."

Witherspoon turned from the trio at the table. "I don't have to take this," he muttered through partially clenched teeth.

Krech remained quiet during all the sniping, swiveling his head more and more, trying to keep up with the polemic's momentum. He could see objectivity was disintegrating in rapid fashion, and he cleared his throat loudly because they all needed to get back to the heart of why he was there. "Mayor Jeffries," he finally broke in, "I'm rather out of the loop on all this. As a matter of fact, I haven't even been introduced to this gentleman you're about to throw out."

"He's not official," Witherspoon objected.

Jeffries ignored the hostility. "Colonel Krech. This is the Reverend Alvin White. He heads a colored Episcopalian church in the Paradise Valley area. An outer community."

"I see," Krech said with a direct look at White, shaking his hand. They pumped their clasp once; the colonel noting that the minister's hand was firm, but smoother than his own. "How do you do, Reverend?"

"Not at all well, at the moment, Colonel. Not at all well," White answered without smiling.

The formal introduction having ended with White's curt rejection of familiarity, tension once again came back to the surface. It was almost palpable, at the back of their throats it stuck like some glandular refuse.

Witherspoon decided to take actions into his own authority and gently as he could possibly manage, placed his left hand behind the reverend's elbow and his right hand at the small of the preacher's back.

"Now, if you don't mind, Reverend. We need to—"

"Remove your hands from me!" demanded White.

"What did you just say to me?" Witherspoon incredulously asked the glaring Episcopalian.

"Withdraw your hands from me, Commissioner." Reverend White pulled away his right arm with as little physical commotion as he could muster, rebuffing the attempt to escort him out of the office. "Frankly," he continued, "I find it rather disconcerting that there's going to be a meeting here, concerning the use of federal troops on colored citizens, and you not having one Negro being privy to the discussion."

To say that the mayor, colonel, and police commissioner were shocked by the defiance was understatement. None of the power holders there could immediately respond to the minister's logical declaration and objection. It was like he'd dowsed them all with glasses of ice water.

"That's a well-taken point, actually," Krech had to concur. He appreciated that the maligned citizen was the one to bring up his own defense. But, it was the objection of a colored man, as far as Jeffries and Witherspoon were concerned.

"This is strictly government business here, Reverend," the mayor cautioned.

"Yeah," added Witherspoon, "you know what interfering with government business can get you. Besides—church and state business are on two separate sides of the aisle."

"And what kind of aisle are we talking about, Commissioner?" White asked.

"One that's covered with the authority of law over everyone. This ain't the place for meekness," said Witherspoon.

"With all respect, Commissioner," Krech interrupted again, "by the looks of things below, I think we'll need both influences here, in order to clear the air."

"It's just too irregular," Jeffries complained.

"Well, I for one don't want the press to make a judgment call on what happens here," Krech speculated. "I say, let him stay." Looking to Witherspoon and Krech for support, and to the reverend for capitulation, Jeffries turned his head first to one man, then the other. White stood stoically resolute. The police executive, however, shut down, thumbing cigarette ash to the floor, plainly in disgust. Krech finally took command of the situation. "Let's take our seats, shall we?"

They all four sat at the empty conference table, sitting opposite one another, the mayor not taking the chair at the head of the table, another symbolic capitulation. Krech was the first to speak after scribbling on a yellow legal pad hurriedly. "What's our official status?" he asked.

"At this time," Witherspoon began, "both the city and the colored neighborhood of Paradise Valley have been quieted, for the most part."

"You sure you want to maintain that analysis after seeing what just occurred down on the boulevard?" Krech asked, as if almost in behalf of Reverend White, sitting next to him.

"Well, Colonel, let's say, up until this point, I'd stand by the accounts I've received," said Witherspoon.

"And again, Mr. Commissioner, and Mr. Mayor," Reverend White interrupted, "can your eyes be so deceived by what you read, or more by what they see?"

Witherspoon didn't attack when he got the value of the flippant response from the preacher. He sighed, pausing to maintain his composure. "Reverend White," he said finally, "I'll grant you that there are still isolated, and mind you, I said isolated scuffles occurring here and abouts. But it's nowhere near the level of activity we had earlier."

"But who is it that makes up the majority of those arrested, Commissioner?"

Mayor Jeffries raised a silencing hand at that point, checking the natural tendency of his commissioner to become involved in a gambit with the savvy civilian of color. Jeffries picked up a small pile of papers next to him. "I've got reports from incidents here, Reverend. Reports of incidents that say there are just as many instances of coloreds committing atrocities as there are of whites."

"Truth be told," Witherspoon interjected, "your own kind ain't even safe amongst themselves when a hullabaloo breaks out. Why, I understand some colored boys threw a brick through a nigra gal's car window. A woman by the name of Rosa Hackworth, if I'm not mistaken. She was minding her own business, driving out to her sister's, or something. Probably going to check on her safety."

"Please, Mr. Witherspoon," the preacher sighed, "I already—"

"That brick thrown by them colored boys—your people, crushed the right side of her head in. Caved it in like it was a tin ball."

"Commissioner, please. I—"

"She bled to death, right in her own car."

"It was a case of mistaken identity, Commissioner."

"How can that be, Reverend?"

"Mrs. Hackworth was a member of my church. She was very light in complexion. From far away they could have thought—well, who knows what they were thinking. But one thing I do know. She'll be greatly missed in our community, and by her little baby."

"My God, my God," Krech thought as he listened. "What the hell have I gotten myself into, here?"

CHAPTER NINE
Fort Custer

A young Negro private by the name of August James Martin finished walking yet another fire watch tour at the army base named for that woebegone warrior, slaughtered by his supposed lesser. While the late night debate in Detroit's City Hall began to flare, all Martin knew was that he had just completed his fifth patrol, and needed to relieve himself of some diuretic. He looked at his watch on his left wrist as he passed a post lamp on the way to the nearest latrine. He had no idea that there was an officer with his same first name following orders in Detroit, just like he was doing.

Unlike the colonel, Martin's tour of duty tonight had little to fire the imagination. His one highlight had been witnessing a standoff between an opossum and a raccoon over the contents of an overturned garbage can. Martin was in no position to having to make life and death decisions unless it was about which of the two marsupials should live. When it came down to it, everything was all it ever could be expected to have been. August Martin was a bottom-feeder, a black noncom, whereas August Krech was a seasoned officer of high rank. And white. Militarily, there was no way you could make a comparison, but on a purely human level one would think that there could be some sort of interconnection. If there was any objectivity in life, if the Declaration of Independence really hadn't been more than a hyperbolic defense for the right to keep a slave, then a person could have seen some values in both men. But even giving liberal discernment to the perceptions of the men, the differences still striated into divisions, on so many levels of their humanity. They were so divergent that one could find it easy to question the English literary tenet that "a rose by any other name would smell as sweet".

In this case, the flowers might have the same name, but the one flower, the one rose so red it could be mistaken for black, that one would leave one believing it had been ill-named. It had no fragrance recognized by the masses as being rose-like. Some, due to it being so intensely colored, might even look upon it as being a weedy daffodil instead of a reigning flower. But as was mentioned, August Martin knew nothing of August Krech, and vice versa. All Private Martin was concerned about in the early morning and poor light was keeping spots of urine from landing on the tips of his boots while he stood up to the urinal trough.

August Krech manifested his first name. He was marked by majestic dignity and grandeur. The man inside of the uniform would have commanded attention even in threadbare clothes. His family came from old money, of Jewish-German ancestry, but immigrating well before the First World War. Krech's father, Dominic, had established a modest trust for his son that had helped to pay his way to West Point. There would have been more had a broker not embezzled hundreds of thousands of dollars from him in 1929. The audacious pilfering caused the old man to commit suicide. August was handed his first command position at the time, but was remarkably resilient upon hearing the news. His mother was not surprised at all by the response he showed to his father's passing. She knew her son would do well in life because it was inbred in the sinews that covered his bones. His father came from nothing and made something of himself and never dared to look back. August was the same. As a youngster, he grew up knowing what amount of money was needed to only make whatever he wanted to become a reality. While August Martin, on the other hand, knew only how to make do with his minimal understanding of worldly reality. And how little money he had to do anything.

When Private Martin had left his home to join the service his mother could only give him a sandwich to eat on the train, some prayers, and that was about it. Gus had had more schooling than either his father or mother, from what he could recollect, but he was no match for the neoclassical scholarship that Krech had been taught. Now, there would always be conservatives with bootstrap delusions who would say that this younger man had the advantage of time to work out a future prosperity. But Gus Martin would never make it onto the same playing field where the August Krechs of the world swung a bat. And he was smart enough to know that.

Martin walked around the headquarters once more, noting how the distant cicadas gave undertones to the winged rubbings of the ones in the trees nearby him. After a yawn he felt ready to stomach his fourth cup of coffee at the barracks. Turning back, he saw cigarette butts strewn about the colonial brick steps and he decided to police the area before going in. Taking the time to put things in order now, rather than risking it to be found out in the morning, would save him and his company much castigation.

Inside the foyer, there was a private sitting at a desk directly in line with the doorway, seemingly engrossed in one of several *National Geographic* magazines stacked nearby him. He only looked up from the pictorial when he heard the coffee swirling into Martin's cup as he held it up to the thirty-cup, shiny metal urn that sat upon a small table near the wooden stairs. The magazine reader didn't move a muscle; save for his eyes inspecting his fellow soldier from the bottom of the boots to the top of the fatigue cap he wore. He didn't seem to have good feelings for Martin, but his eyes were the only things that showed his contempt. "Are you Private Martin?" he asked.

"Yeah," Gus responded after a big swallow of the tepid coffee.

"Well, which one are you? August or Joe?"

"Gus. I'm Gus, Joe's my older brother."

"How much older, kid?"

Kid, Gus thought. His interrogator wasn't much older than he was. "Two years, if it matters." The private put the magazine in his lap, closing it, and pushed the fulcrum chair back from the white ash desk. The wheels of the chair made a sound like a heavy drawer being slid open. Three to four feet back from the desk, the seated private pitched his head back and then forward as he lifted his legs. The heels of his highly polished black boots tapped down on the desktop and he interlocked his fingers over the *National Geographic* with a small grunt.

"I don't know if I care for the tone you're carrying there," said the private.

"Could say the same about you."

"Do you realize this is where the sarge usually sits?"

"Yeah. So?"

"Sarge had to go home, sick."

"You relieved him?"

"That's a fact, junior. And I'm cadre for the watch, now. And I'm telling you again that I don't like the way you're talking to me."

"Don't take it personal. I'm tired."

"An excuse and a cup of coffee only go as far as a piss. Save it. I need you to go upstairs and get your brother up. That's why I asked who you were."

"Why am I doing that?"

"I can't do guard duty and be the cadre, all at the same time, now can I? I'm supposed to relieve you and your brother was supposed to relieve me. Everybody's been bumped up. Go get him up for fire watch."

"How about I stay down here and you go get him?"

The temporarily promoted soldier opened his magazine again without further comment. Gus considered the matter between them settled and blew at the steam rising from the brimming cup in his hands. "Martin—now."

Gus set the cup down and looked at the bossy private, and couldn't help tightening his lips; he drilled holes into the skull of the provocateur with his eyes. Gus was now the face from a picture. He knew his eyes, nose, and high cheekbones showed a configuration of there being some Indian blood. Though he was unmistakably a Negro; his great-grandmother was a Blackfoot and had had the spirit of a warrior. His mother used to tell him stories about how she would babysit for him and Joe when they were very little. She couldn't walk very well then and used a bullwhip she'd flick at them. The leather snake would lightly wrap around their ankles or wrists and she would pull them back to her. She wouldn't break the skin, or even leave a bruise. But defenseless, she was not. She once demonstrated how easy it was to crack a melon open with it. Gus remembered the solitary unsmiling picture of his Native American matriarch. He was thankful that she loved him and Joe, because under the dark veneer of her blank facade he could see that her anger was not a thing anyone would willingly want to encounter. And it was this part of her, surfacing through him now, that made him all the more threatening as he glared at his antagonist behind the desk.

"The longer we wait, the more messed up the schedule gets—longer it takes before you get to bed," said the reading private, blunting his earlier air of superiority. He was not as sure of himself now. Gus saw he couldn't look him in the eye and passed by without another word as he went by and up the stairs to the pitch-black sleeping quarters.

Sounds and smells were the only things he could accurately sense as he made his way down the aisle between the bunks, which could barely be discerned after he adjusted his eyes to the inky blackness of the room. Only snores validated that each bed was occupied, except for his own. The diverse pitches sometimes reached a common meter, a momentary unison that eventually syncopated itself into a discordant cacophony. The occasional squeaking of bedsprings only bridged the nasal symphony. Passing one bunk, Gus could smell where somebody had used way too much cologne after showering. Passing another, he could make out the unmistakable, musky, sweaty scent of a man relieved of confined desires. Gus smiled and shook his head. He wondered if the discharge had been honorable or dishonorable. Planned or involuntary. So much for the limits of saltpeter.

He and his brother's bunk took thirty-five steps to reach from the quarter's entry. They were on the right side of the room. Kneeling, Gus shook Joe softly.

"Joe, hey—Joe, come on. Wake up. C'mon, I ain't playing around." Gus flinched as his brother tossed from his back to his side.

"What you want, niggah?" Joe hissed back, his eyes not even opened. Most people when awakened from a sound sleep could be loud, or they might even scream, but not someone in the armed forces. There, you didn't talk loud after lights out. And it was nothing that was taught or drilled into you; everyone just exerted that kind of self-control. It could be something life-saving if you were in combat at night. Honestly, Joe had been startled at first, but once he recognized who the shadowy outline was by his bed he was really irritated. "Oh, it's your sorry butt. Go to bed and leave me alone."

"Joe, don't go back to sleep," Gus persisted. "You got to take the last watch."

"Kiss my ass. No, I don't."

"Listen, the sarge went home sick and my relief has replaced him. You got to take his watch." Just then, all of the Martin brothers' respect for the sleep of their fellows, signified by the decorum of their lowered voices, all went to naught.

A commotion arose in the building, coming from the bottom of the barracks stairwell. They were heavy footsteps and could be heard running up to the dorm, causing Gus to rise immediately and Joe to swing his feet onto the cool linoleum. A corridor of light blared forth from the area of the stairs where Gus had just come from. "Get up, you all," an excited soldier repeatedly pleaded. "Get up, y'all, and I mean right now! It's time to get to getting, around here!" And he pushed on the dormitory lights as if to punctuate the cry further. Gus was surprised because he thought for sure that everyone had been in the barracks.

Three sweating and gasping GI's stood halfway down the aisle of the quarters. Their eyes were crazed, charged with emotion. Each man in his bunk thought there must have been some catastrophic event. Maybe another Pearl Harbor type of attack. Maybe there was an invasion happening, right now. A very dark serviceman, with a sedentary physique from being middle-aged, sat up on his elbows in his bunk, situating his sheets over his protuberant girth. "What's the hell the matter with you youngsters?" he barked.

"They is killing niggers in Detroit, man! Shooting us right where we stand!"

"You're drunk," the old soldier said, dismissing them with a wave of his hand and laying back down in his bed, bringing the sheets back up to his neck. "Smashed as hell."

"We just come back from there, fool!" the second soldier said.

"Go to bed, you're all drunk," the old troop chastised. "And I damn sure ain't nobody's fool, youngun. I'll pin your ears back and eat you whole in one bite."

"About ten o' clock, last night it started. Some crackers threw a colored woman and her baby right off the Belle Island Bridge," the first soldier rebutted.

And that was what changed things. Southern whites had always found justification for holding back the numbers of black men, but not so much in the North. But now it sounded like they were practically accomplishing the massacre in the crib, according to the soldier. Almost as bad as shooting fish in a barrel. Where there once had been silent assessment of what had been said, a void of inattention, now agitated murmurings began to fill the air. Even the old soldier sat up in his bunk again, throwing back his sheets to get pants.

Joe pushed past his brother, hurriedly putting on his own trousers and leaping to the middle of the dormitory corridor in his bare feet. He waved his arms frantically, trying to quiet the rising anxiety and voices. He almost appeared to be attempting to take flight; so earnest he was in trying to get the attention of his peers.

"Hold it down," he pleaded. "C'mon, y'all. Listen to me. Be quiet!" The barracks finally settled for a moment and Joe quickly turned to the newly arrived alarmists. "Did any of you happen to see any of this going on? Well, did you?"

"Ah—uh, no. But there were some brothers over at the Forrest Club sure did."

"And did they tell this to you? Or did you hear this from a friend of a friend?"

"What are you getting at, Joe?"

"Think, brother. You ain't checked nothing out. And you up here wanting to get us all into a civil war, or something."

"Well, I'll tell you what I know. I know they brought two empty busses there, trying to get help. And if that ain't enough proof, I don't know what is."

That affirmation rejuvenated the entire clamor, then. It brought the immobile to their feet, compelling them to don their fatigues. Joe grimaced as he saw the irrationality sweep through the dorm. Now even the old service man was pulling on his boots. Gus saw Joe's eyes began to blink frequently, a telltale sign of impending anger getting ready to explode. "Wait a minute!" Joe exclaimed. "What you doing? Would you all just hold on for a second! Think a minute, here."

"Man, what's your problem," retorted one of the instigators.

"So, everybody's all riled up now, huh? Okay, so what the hell do you all plan on doing? Huh? What can we do, really? Are we civilians? Can we just run out of here because we feel like it?"

"I don't know about you, brother. We're going to go kick some ass."

"And with what?" Gus asked, supporting Joe.

"What do you think?"

Joe then stepped up to the initiator and grabbed him by the shoulders, looking him squarely in the eyes. Joe's raised eyebrow told the GI not to be surly.

"Did those busses—did the people on those busses—did they have guns?"

"I don't know. I didn't see if they did."

"Don't y'all see how crazy this is? Just where you think you can go from here?" And there were no answers from anyone. "I want to know just where you think you guys are going." Joe restated.

"To get us some M-1's and a couple of deuce trucks," the sizzling hiss of a reply came back. "And if you're half the colored man you claim to be, you'll get on board."

"I'm telling you," Joe began to warn, "If you do this, you're going to end up like the thirteen of us they strung up in Houston."

"This ain't gonna be no Houston, naw suh. Ain't gonna be no such a thing, Martin."

"It will be just like that. Just like Houston."

"There comes a time, Martin," one of the instigants resolved, "when following orders takes away from being an independent man. From being strong. Can't you see that?"

"They'll line you up and shoot you—they won't even wait to put a rope to your necks!"

"Who are these 'they' you're talking about, Martin? Captain Charlie? The Big Boss Man? Well, some of us don't need a white man to tell us what we should be fighting over. Okay?"

Still batting his eyes in irritation, Joe parted his way back to his bunk, cleaving his way through the consternation of activity all about him. Gus joined him, having turned his back to the fracas, also. Many footlockers were being opened on both sides of the room, now. Joe sat back down on his lower bunk and glanced at his brother.

"Ain't you gonna go?"

"Naw, Joe. You know I heard you. But what we gonna do?"

"Hightail it on outta here, Gus. Get a hold of the commander before they can see you slip out. I mean it. Hurry up. Before many of these fools get out of here. And get us all killed." And so, the younger brother slipped out without so much as an inquiry from the dressing troops as to where he was going, and he double-timed towards the night CO's office. If the Army got involved, all hell would be breaking loose.

CHAPTER TEN
Second Guessing

Some people would say that the plans being made by the rogues at Fort Custer, rushing out in the pre-dawn light, were as misguided as the resolutions being proposed by the government coalition in Detroit City Hall. A paucity of good sense, or misplaced bravado, on the part of either civilian or military forces heightened with each hour of the approaching day. As far as the Fort Custer anarchists were concerned, some felt what they attempted was commendable. If you happened to live in Paradise Valley, that is. But the citizens residing off of Woodard Avenue would not be as forgiving for such treason. The lines of opposition could not be any more distinct, and this was exemplified dramatically when Reverend White was dismissed from the town hall meeting, not long after Col. Krech arrived.

As well-intentioned and fair-minded as Krech was to the minister, he had to finally admit that the continued presence of the clergyman made for continual one-sided diatribe from both sides of the riot issue. It wasn't conducive to the matter at hand, no matter how morally correct it was to have the reverend there. The focus of all negotiations had to be the matter-at-hand, not whether a disgruntled citizen couldn't be at the table. Both Witherspoon and the mayor had reminded him, that the focus of the officials being there was supposed to be bringing about the eradication of the city's unrest. Therefore, with as much ceremonious propitiation as possible, Colonel Krech had to ask Reverend White to step outside the room. Even though it chagrined him to do so.

Now a new cast of characters found themselves in Mayor Jeffries' office by the ten o' clock hour. Freshened by a much-needed catnap on a leather seatee in an adjoining room while waiting for the cavalry to arrive, Krech's judgment had been honed anew and he held dubious predilections as to the capacities of the advisors surrounding him. The colonel sat at the head of the table once again, this time flanked on the right and left by Witherspoon and two empty chairs, one of those meant for the mayor. Joining them were the local commanders of the Air Force, Navy, Marines, and the Coast Guard and their aides. What made Krech uneasy about the men wasn't so much what they said, but rather the insignificance of their mumblings that undermined the colonel's confidence. Their small talk consisted of mundane and superfluous observations, punctuated by thumping of cigars and cigarettes into large, thick, glass ashtrays on the long table, only occupied by half its length. Because they were waiting for Governor Kelly to arrive the conversation had relaxed, with Krech being out of the room. Feeling camaraderie in numbers, they didn't bother changing their tone any once he returned. The comments they made were mostly inappropriate, too self-assured, and highly unmindful of the realities happening about them. That was what made Colonel Krech consider them with such disfavor. Their hubris sickened him, somewhat.

Mayor Jeffries reappeared by a quarter after the hour, opening the door for a man as tall as he, but of considerably more girth. Even with his decided limp, the waxing middle-aged politician captivated the room's attention. Everyone stood. Although, the truth be told, Krech didn't recognize him by sight, like the others did. The colonel moved to his right, sitting in the chair next to Witherspoon as the meeting convened. The governor took the chair at the head of the table without any homily to the mayor and directed a pointed stare towards Witherspoon and Krech. "I need an update, Commissioner. An accurate one."

"From about six, to seven-thirty, or thereabouts, things were fairly calm here in the city. Then all hell started breaking out from the west side of town,and that in turn got things hot downtown again. We've mobilized for twelve-hour shifts. Now, that should give us maximum coverage, but I just can't say for how long. As you can see," and here Witherspoon nodded at Krech while exhaling smoke taken from a final inhaling of a freshly stomped out butt, "we have the armed services here. They have ideas about how they want to run things."

"I see." Kelly eyed Colonel Krech like they each held a poker hand. "Colonel, I thank you for coming." The governor cleared his throat and Krech knew that he was going to hear a scripted speech. With the commissioner's assessment out of the way, Governor Kelly began throwing his authority against the weight of any idea that he wasn't the one in charge. "I'm prepared, gentlemen, to call for a state-of-emergency in the tri-county area around Detroit. The vitality of this city, and all it procures for Michigan, and the nation, cannot be jeopardized by the hands of a few hundred malcontents."

"Isn't that a little conservative, Governor?" Krech asked. "I would agree, and happily, that a majority of Detroit's citizens are staid and law-abiding. But what you have now is closer to a thousand on the march. And the numbers seem to be rising."

"Excuse me, Colonel," said the governor. "Is the army getting better intelligence than me and my people? I realize what you have in mind and I just don't feel it's warranted, at present. I'm having your Command stand down, for the moment until we've exhausted all our resources. Then we can reassess, if need be."

"Governor," Krech complained, "I don't think you understand. I didn't just show up here, getting out of bed in the middle of the night for some lark. I was sent here on orders, orders that come from the Secretary of War's Office. Mayor Jeffries, I thought you were leaving here to get the governor's authorization. What happened?"

"You shouldn't be so eager, Colonel," the governor said calmly. "You haven't been betrayed—merely usurped, is all. Mayor Jeffries did well to alert you, but it's my inclination to hold off on military action, at this point."

"Governor, the police are just spread too thin. There's an insurgency going on here, and has been one for the past twelve hours, with no end in sight. People continue to be in fear for their lives—"

"As is expected when there are rioters in the streets, Colonel." The Service Commanders from the Michigan reserves looked smugly at Krech. He hadn't endeared himself to them, allowing for only the most cursory of interactions. But the colonel wasn't so easily put aside.

"Your people, as you call them, are missing-in-action, Governor. The combined resources of your state troop units are roughly that of two thousand men. Between all these men—these officers, here, they can only account for thirty-three men. Thirty-three, Governor! And that includes them."

"I must admit, Colonel," Mayor Jeffries broke in, "that I'm at somewhat of a juxtaposition here. On the one hand, I was indeed relieved by you coming. But that was before I was aware that you were planning to initiate martial law. On the other hand, it's also true that we're up against it pretty well, here. I'm afraid what things will become like if we do go martial, and I can't imagine what will occur if we don't. But Governor, I know we're going to have to have heavy patrols throughout the day and night. There's no getting around it. If we don't, there won't be much city left to protect. That's my concern.

That's what I'm trying to prevent." The governor looked towards Wither-spoon again.

"Commissioner, when exactly did your men lose the handle on this thing? Why couldn't it be contained? You know, you don't take laudanum for a toothache when the pain gets to be unbearable, you take it before. Couldn't you see the direction things were going?"

"Sir, if you're asking me when I knew things were going to hell in a hand basket, I'd have to say I really couldn't. The thing seemed to take on a life of its own, almost like it erupted from the middle and then the fringes of the city caught on. From the onset, my scout cars incurred sniper fire on the East Side. Whites left their jobs at the plants to mass together in places. We can't locate the snipers in the colored sections, and there's no law against the work stoppage."

"But aren't we really only talking about a half a day having past, gentlemen? Since the initial calls went out to all your men, hasn't that been the time?"

"That's correct, Sir."

"Well then, redouble your efforts in getting your men, commanders." All the energy that Colonel Krech felt invigorated by from his nap seemed to quickly drain from his face. It was time to cut to the heart of the matter. Agitated by the inadvertent cog of disapproval from Kelly, he had to struggle mightily not to lose his composure while he talked through his position.

"Governor Kelly, why are you so hesitant to ask for federal assistance?"

"I'm really not objecting to that, Colonel. Tell me why the government wants to have it all-or-nothing. Can't you muster men without declaring martial law?"

"We don't know whether this is fueled by local factions, or our enemies abroad. The federal government wants to err on the side of prudence and not get caught with all our fish in a barrel, Governor."

"And this sends all the wrong kind of messages to the rest of the world, Colonel. You federalize troops and it will make us look just as bad as having storm troopers walking down the boulevard. I would hate to have the country and the rest of the world think that things are so bad here that I have to call in the United States Army."

"What? You mean to tell me that this is all about your pride?"

"Public relations have to be considered, Colonel, even when there's a war going on. It's not a matter of pride. Any politician would be reticent to have martial law go into effect in their city, in their state. Good God, man. That's a constitutional premise we're talking about enacting. You know as well as me, you couldn't just lend me your soldiers without implementing martial law. Don't patronize me with your suppositions about invasion theories. I hardly think you really believe that to be the case, here."

"But Governor Kelly, you have—"

"All laws—civil and state are suspended. Courts are closed; city councils are sequestered, police deactivated." Kelly drew a breath and held up a large paw of a hand to stem Krech from attempting a protest. "In fact—Colonel Krech, tell me if I'm not correct, but you—the Army Commander, in charge, exclusively rules. Don't you? In all respects. Is that correct, Colonel Krech?"

"The army's intent is not to—"

"I know how things happen, Colonel. People out there didn't intend for this thing to get so ugly, either. But it did."

"Governor, when federal troops are used to quell a domestic uprising, the people placed in to custody by the military are turned over to the proper civilian authorities."

"After the fact."

"Prosecution and punishment still rests with the civilian powers, not the army."

"After the fact, Colonel. And I'll not give you license to shoot citizens down on the spot. That's what happens when curfews are broken. And you don't give anyone a trial. Now, that's a little bit too much in the pioneer spirit, for my taste." Kelly smiled and pushed his chair back, pulling a cigar from an inner pocket of his suit coat. He bit off the rolled end of the Havana and lit the other with a matchstick struck along the inseam of his thigh. "Get me your boss, Mr. Colonel. Seems we have some issues to negotiate, so I can ease my mind."

"While your city burns."

"Was burning before I got here. In public relations, Colonel, you don't make a rush into a judgment. You end up second-guessing yourself. There's always time enough to make the right decision."

CHAPTER ELEVEN
Following the Code

What happened to the rogue soldiers at Fort Custer who were, in their minds, on their way to liberating the Belle Island belligerents was serendipitous; in light of what happened shortly after their aborted enterprise. In fact, most would have deemed it quite ironic. Troops of black soldiers did end up in Detroit, but not to wreak further havoc on the city. The miscreant troops never even left the base, so ill prepared were they for the swift censure that came from the commanding officer. By the early morning hours of June 21, 1943 the two dozen unenlisted saviors sat on their butts on well-manicured grass. There they sat back to back, supporting one another like human lean-tos because the tight handcuffs on their wrists didn't allow for one to balance his position as they sat. It was still outside of the armory, where they'd been detained for forty-five minutes, or thereabouts. One of the marauders complained that his wrists were getting numb. That was the older soldier from the barracks, the dark-skinned one with the gray at his temples and the slightly protuberant abdomen. He pleaded momentary insanity for his part in the foray, and tried to mitigate further with saying, "I tried to tell these damn fools they was out they minds! Did my best, to turn 'em back. Shoah, did. And this—this is what I get for my service?"

"Was that what you was doing, Pappy?" one of the military police indirectly asked, not expecting any further response. But the portly soldier didn't understand he was being ridiculed because of his overt acts in the botched break.

"You are damn, Skippy, son. Damn Skippy. Practically had to put hands—"

"Aw, shut your mulberry-looking ass up," another detainee shouted out, embarrassed for the unsophisticated bloke—No one laughed at the capping. They were too worried. Many more now had become more complacent, less confrontational, with each passing moment, and with anyone they spoke to. Upon reconsideration of their action, it was now known collectively that they were on the road to perdition. The punishment was beginning. First, they make you physically uncomfortable, withholding food and the possibility to relieve yourself. By now it had gone well past the time for breakfast. The gurgling of the knotted stomachs of the captives readily attested to their being mindful of that fact, and their pressing bladders threatened to burst. Bur they somehow came to accept that they were not going to get any morning chow— and some rued that the lunch they'd be assured to get might end being their last one, as well. A few even gave up asking for permission to urinate in a privy, and sat in puddles of urine.

No shots were fired during the ill-advised coupe but that was mostly due to the number of white military police brought to the area; a force more than enough to stop the insubordinate upheaval. History proved that racial incursion had always been dealt with in such a fashion. The officers, once alerted, were advised that a small group of mutineers secreted themselves behind a munitions dump. That close to the armory, the schemers knew a diversion would be needed in order to divert the armory watch. A flashbang grenade created just such an opportunity, and soon they were on their way to bludgeoning the guards using a further surreptitious ruse.

The protesting, dark as a blueberry quartermaster (who now couldn't believe he'd gotten himself into such a fix) wasn't suspect at all for being on the immediate grounds in the early morning hours. He supplied a charge from right off of the stock shelf, and made sure there was an especially concerted interaction with the armory cadre while rifles were being discreetly pilfered. But, laying in wait were the service police, and they made sure the revolt died without so much as a whimper. The insurrectionists were caught in the midst of their absconding with the weaponry, and were summarily arrested a half-hour before the rise of the sun.

Lt. Sackett noticed the gnashing of teeth the repentant soldiers displayed. He, however, dismissed the pleas he heard from them, as the sun grew hotter in the humid morning. He placed his sunglasses on his creamy coffee-colored face and deferred to no one as he stepped forth. He wore a thin mustache that was molded handsomely above his upper lip, and he neither smiled nor spoke when he got the list of detainees delivered to him. Not a bead of sweat glistened off of him while he stepped into the sunlight, in front of the arrestees.

"Lieutenant, let us go!" one of the men yelled out, "You got to. It's them or us, Sir. And you know I'm right."

Sackett continued to ignore the blubber and examined the field report more intensely. He wanted to say what he thought; that the soldier was saying an overstatement he'd heard many times before. One that he'd been guilty of thinking himself, at some level. But he didn't believe every black man's problem came about through the filtered oppression of a white man's agenda. He felt he knew better. "They're fighting out there, Sir." The arrestee continued, "Fighting with their own two hands. Now, what kind of justice they gonna get? Don't our people need an army to protect them?"

"Sergeant, get these fools out of here," Sackett said, signing the report and handing the clipboard over. "I don't know what makes me sicker, their stench, or their ignorance."

"Yes, Sir. They're as good as gone."

With a sweep of the sergeant's hand, the rebels began to be roughly loaded up into the back of an awaiting deuce-and-half, canvassed truck. Sackett looked at his watch and turned his back on the whole process, negotiating a bad taste that developed on either side of his tongue. He craved an orange soda. Folding his hands behind him, he started to make his way up the road, returning to the standard operations of the headquarter building, so discordant with the procedure and duty he had just supervised.

Tan dust eddied and plumed at his heels. Heading west, and coming to a crossroad, less than an eighth of a mile from the armory, he noticed an approaching figure running towards him. After a matter of a half a minute, or so, the officer could see that it was a young private, the one from the watch.

"Sir—sir. Private Martin, reporting as ordered." The skinny, out-of-breath soldier blurted out, trying to catch a breath at the same time. Once coming to a stop, he had really wanted to forget all decorum and just rest both his hands on his knees and without embarrassment or harassment just be allowed to suck in all the air he could. He would have sucked in air from the bottom of his feet if he could have. But wisely and obediently he instead snapped a dutiful salute, his chest and cheeks billowing.

Sackett whipped a returning salute from off his brow like he was a farmer raking down wheat with a scythe. "At ease, private." Now Gus bent forward unapologetically, to catch his breath. He'd been running at a good pace.

"Looks like you got yourself into quite a state, running out her, private."

"Yea—Yea-has, Sir."

"You're either a man on a mission, or a fool. Which is it, private?"

"Neither, Sir. Just a man told to see you ASAP. They pointed me in the direction you was bearing—and told me to hightail it out to you."

"Then, stand corrected, private. Because you are a fool to run all this way when I was coming back to the base directly, anyway. In fact, you could have waited for me outside the office door."

"But then, Sir. I'da been liable to being court-martialed. If I'da sat down and waited for you. Them corporals is awful mean, Sir. I'da have hell to pay if I'da done that."

"You're wise in your generation, private. That's the reason I asked for you. The reason why I wanted to meet you was to thank you for your diligence last night and this morning. It was an outstanding display of valor, given the situation. Had this been overseas, in a time of imminent battle, you could have been commended for a bronze star."

"Is that a fact, Sir?"

"That it is."

"Well—I, ah, never. Ah, Sir. Could I have your permission to speak freely?"

"Speak to me, Private."

"The fellows in the unit—"

"They're giving you some hard flack, are they?"

"Nah, I can handle that all right. But they do say things, Sir, that—well, maybe it isn't right for me to say."

"If there is any residual from what happened in that battery, I want to know about it. You came to your superiors with valuable information that guaranteed the safety of our base. I'm disappointed, however, that their plan got as far as it did. In fact, it's my understanding you stood in the barracks doing nothing but listening to those drunk soldiers plotting to overrun a federal armory on a government base."

Private Martin grew perplexed by the turn of the officer's intent. "Beg pardon, Sir. But I don't understand. As soon as I found out about what was happening in Detroit, and what they wanted to do, I came to you."

"Private, you were making a relief for the final guard duty. Those men came on base at a point on your perimeter, quite sometime before you came back to the company hall."

"But, Sir. I swear I didn't see anyone."

"It's lucky for us that you came forward when you did. But what if we'd been five minutes late finding this out? It's a good thing, indeed, that things turned out as they did. The PFC downstairs, at the time, he said that he had to take your brother's watch because you were so long in returning. That left the hall office open for intruders. Why did it take you so long to let me know there was trouble? You know right from wrong, don't you?"

"Sir, all I can say, truthfully, is that it didn't take me no time, at all, really, to know that what they wanted to do was wrong. On the one hand, I knew I had to report them. But on the other, I couldn't say I totally disagreed with the purpose of what they wanted to bring about."

"What do you understand that purpose to be, private?"

"Well—ah, I guess I'd have to say it was the fact of the baby being killed—"

"But that's not true—simply, not."

"Whether it was, or was not, Sir. Didn't seem to matter. Everybody heard what they wanted to. It was a little frightening. I'd never seen a colored lynching mob before; I mean, a group of blacks having that kind of mindset going around amongst them. Let me tell you, that was pretty unnerving."

"Indeed. What do you think would have been the worse possible outcome, had they succeeded?"

"The killing of citizens, Sir."

"Is that an admirable thing? Is it something to think highly of, private? That's what your friends were aiming to do. You, yourself, said that their aim was to take guns from the base and have a shootout. Am I right?"

"But, Sir—what's happening out there in Detroit is just as bad. Civilians are killing other civilians. All because of the skin. Our brothers and sisters are outmanned."

"That battle isn't ours to join, soldier. It doesn't follow the code. An army does not raise its arms against the country it's pledged to defend."

"Yes, Sir."

"And be further advised that had you not reported this, and they'd been successful, you'd be in the same boat with them. Do you understand?"

"Sir—Yes, Sir."

"Come, private. Walk with me."

Gus didn't respond with a verbal acknowledgement, for this was not a request. He walked along slightly behind the officer's right side. As the two backtracked over the road that Gus just came from, the private couldn't help but be further intimidated. Further driven to silence. A bumblebee flew near the lieutenant's shoulder and didn't even make him flinch; his head remained angled to the ground, hands crossed behind his back. The bee finished its inspection of the non-flower and veered off towards some scattered purple wild flowers, indispersed among a stand of foxtails. "You know, Pvt. Martin, those arrested are faced with some very serious disciplinary action. We're at war, and you should be familiar what the code requires in cases like these. This was tantamount to an act of desertion."

"Would they really kill them, Sir?"

Sackett stopped walking and turned to his right. He looked Gus directly in the eye and blinked once before asking him what really was on his mind.

Gus was strangely at ease. "Private Martin, tell me. Was this thing that happened last night some unplanned lark, or are their others seeking to try further outbreaks?"

"Sir, I think many of the men would say that if those men are killed, they'd have died for trying to protect they own when no one else would. If you call it desertion, Sir, well, you would know that better than me, but there are more than a few who'd say they'd deserted their people before they ever did the Army."

"Explain your meaning."

"Sir, they had to make a decision, the way I see it, over being who they are—or just being what others want them to be. I can't say they're wrong. What would you do, in their case?"

Gus felt that he had struck a plumb line with the officer. Sackett seemed taken aback momentarily; parallel creases of flesh on his forehead pinched together in agitation. "Am I going to have any further problems with you, or anyone else in your company?" Sackett restated.

"Naw, Sir—they ain't itching to get themselves in the pokey. But them also not knowing what's going on in the city, well, that does make for some hard feelings, Sir. A lot of the men expect to hear something from Command, seeing that most of them can't get any word from home."

They started waking again, but this time now shoulder to shoulder. "Very well," Sackett weighed his reply, "I'll make it a point to speak to that."

"I'm sure that would calm down many of the men, Sir."

"Acknowledged. Are you from there?"

"Indirectly, Sir. My momma raised me in Detroit, but I was born in Gary, Indiana. Most of my people are there." Lt. Sackett didn't say anything more, just slowly nodded his head a few times as he continued a walk that had now turned into a stroll.

"You're lucky to know that, at least," he said.

"Sir?"

"I lived most of my life in Kansas, Private Martin. My old man was a machinist, from the South."

"Bet he's proud of you, Sir."

"Wouldn't know that, Private. Hadn't seen the man since I was going on thirteen. I went back there last year to see my aunt. It was around the time of the State Fair, in Topeka. Say what you want, but Kansas is a place of innovation. I tried some new snack they've invented. They take a frankfur—I mean, they take a hot dog and they put it on a stick and then they dip it in a corn batter. Deep fry it, and they give it the name of a 'corn dog.' You put some mustard on it, some ketchup. It's nice eating. Different. Something you wouldn't expect from where I came from."

Gus's stomach howled loudly as he thought about the confection. Imagining it probably smelled like doughnuts being fried. And that made his stomach become even more boisterous. He wished he could control the gastric tones he emitted, but they were persistent now. The lieutenant didn't seem to take any notice of the intrusion, and that saved Gus some embarrassment, but he figured he'd better change the subject. "I don't get back as often, Sir. And I'm a lot closer to home than you."

"I see," Sackett said, compassion welling. They stopped in the road again and the officer placed the opaque glasses back on his face. "I'll make some arrangements for you to contact your family this evening, if possible."

Gus brightened. "Oh, that would be quite fine and gracious on your part, Sir. Quite fine." For a moment he considered whether it would be wise for him to put in a word for Joe, but he didn't want to push this opportunity. Depending on where he could place the call, maybe Joe could come along with him. But then again, Gus really didn't believe there'd be much chance of that happening, anyway. There wouldn't be much of a conversation between Joe and his mother. Their war was almost as entrenched as the country's.

CHAPTER TWELVE
A Proposition

Mayor Jeffries and Governor Kelly both knew, before Monday afternoon could turn into evening that the measures proposed for reigning in the chaos had to be explained to the citizens, directly. Besides preventing unnecessary casualties, the commoners also needed to know that the "garden," as it were, was still being tended to. The ruff that threatened to spoil the plot was going to be eradicated. On the way to a room in City Hall that had been haphazardly set up for a news conference, Colonel Krech pulled both men aside. "Governor, can you give me a moment, please?"

"Colonel—we're in the midst of—"

"Governor—please. General Gunther is back in Chicago after attending a meeting of the Joint Chiefs. He should be arriving here within the hour. Can't you delay this broadcast until you've at least talked to him?"

Kelly shook his head without any hesitation. "Too much time has passed. Why, the whole country is waiting to hear how we're going to stem this terrible tragedy."

"But, Governor—if you'll only—"

"When your general gets here, Colonel, we'll talk. But now, if you'll excuse me. I have a radio announcement to make." And with that, Kelly opened the door where Colonel Krech could see a few rows of metal chairs placed in front of a long table with several microphones.

"Mayor Jeffries, Governor—"an aide beckoned. A condescending stare from the governor let Krech know further entreaties would be senseless. His mind was definitely made up. Kelly and Jeffries left him standing in the hallway, watching newspaper reporters converge on them. Down below, on the streets, on the still writhing boulevards of Detroit, a police car maintained its rolling patrol as the address began.

Instead of hearing the governor minimizing the situation, they heard their dispatcher's flat voice, numbed by double-time duty, ordering two equally tired veteran cops to a Hastings Street address. A robbery was in progress.

"I know where that is," the older officer said.

"Tailor shop, isn't it?"

"Yeah, my brother gets his clothes from there, all the time. Tell base that we'll take that."

As the sirens began to wail on the way to the crime scene, the junior officer noticed several other misdemeanors and even felonies occurring right before his eyes. As they sped along, charred building exteriors, just as any destroyed along the European Front, blurred into sooted images. Sometimes a rat, dog, or cat climbed through or out of a frame that used to be a home's window. These creatures sought the shadows, fleeing the insanity the humans were perpetrating among themselves, and the scout car's wailing assail drove them even further into hiding.

Approximately one block away from the haberdashery the siren was extinguished, though the echoes of others still whined in the distance. The engine of the black-and-white was turned off and it was placed into neutral, coasting to the curb. As they exited the vehicle, weapons drawn and held close to their hip, each policeman could hear the loud voices.

Voices that betrayed everything that they were doing. The riot was just an opportunity for just this kind of thievery to manifest itself in the broad daylight, instead of by the cover of night. It seemed whomever it was doing it, didn't fear any repercussions.

"Did you hear that? They're in there, all right."

"Yeah. Come on." The older officer nodded his head away from the store entry. Approaching alongside the building, in tandem, one crouched and the other stood behind him; they both drew short breaths, and listened, anticipated.

Inside the shop seven Negro looters had just rifled through the cash register and were now in the process of plying their arms full of double-breasted suits. Their plundering contained no attempt in discretion. A large, sweaty looter, turning from beside one of the store's glass display cabinets, set down his collected items on a counter with folded and undisturbed dress shirts. Nearby was a handsaw that they'd used to cut away some of the boards nailed to the store's façade.

"Are y'all 'bout ready? I'm fittin' ta go."

Everyone else seemed to be still too caught up in their burglary. A tall, and very dark-skinned man brought over some boxes of shoes and set them near the questioner. "There's still plenty left here, fool. We can set things up that we want, and come on back for what we can't carry."

"I don't know, Jimmy," the sweating bandit pondered, "ain't nothing in here big enough to fit me. I'll have to end up selling all mine's."

"Hey—hey, y'all," a younger voice yelled from the storage area of the store, "look at what I found in here." A teenager came out from the back with his interlocked arms filled with brightly-hued zoot suits and feathered hats.

"Now, that's what I'm talking about, nigga."

"Let me give you a hand with that, Dime."

Two of the burglars unburdened some of the spoils off of the young criminal, revealing a face that was integral to all that had been occurring for the past twenty hours. Diatomaceous Thurgood Dolomite. "These are nice," Jimmy commented as he set a load down and rubbed the material lightly. "Where did you say the rest was at?"

"Through there. About five tall boxes full."

"Imah get me some of those," the portly robber declared.

"Naw, it's like you said," Diatomaceous refuted. "Ain't none back there big enough for you." That brought about some laughter from everyone but the signified target. His eyes grew small in his head with contempt.

"Least I got a righteous name, youngster. What kinda name is Dimeataceous for a nigger?"

"Yeah, Dime. How did your moms name you that?"

"It ain't Dimeataceous, nigga. Di—atomaceous is how you say it."

"Well, how did you come up with that 50-cent name?"

"My momma had a year a college and that was a word that she remembered from one of her classes. Some science bullshit, I don't know."

"It's from geology," Dime's Uncle Jimmy confirmed as he came back with two armloads of suits. He threw them on top of his other booty. "Diatoms were the supposed to be like the first form of life on earth. One celled rocks."

"But how could they be alive if they was rocks?"

"Well, they are rock like in appearance and texture, I guess. How do I know niggah? My sister took the class, not me."

"So she named Dime for a rock?"

"It symbolizes what she wanted for him," Jimmy said in all seriousness. "She got pregnant with him when she was messing around at some colored fraternity party. Had to drop her classes because of the shame. But she named him that because not only is diatoms the first life forms, they're crushed down into a powder and used as a water filter. Water's what life is all about. She wanted her son to be a filter to purify everything that was bad in life for we colored people. She wanted him to be a leader."

"Not with no name like that, you ain't gone be no leader." More chuckles. "So, what your momma think about you now, Dime. Up here stealing shit and things."

"His momma's dead," Jimmy said flatly and matter-of-factly. "She was shot by an old boyfriend, knew her before she got all those ideas to educate herself. He figured she went to college and got to acting wild, and that was how she ended up pregnant. He didn't know about what happened to her. He shot her, and then killed himself. Was gonna try to kill Dime, too. But he was with his granny when it happened."

"Hey, Dime. I'm sorry, man. I wouldn't have said nothing if I'da known before."

"Don't let it bother you. It don't me."

"What about your last name, Dime. Where'd that come from?"

"The boy's father was Creole," Jimmy further explained, "Had French blood, and the last name of Dolomieu. We just changed a few letters, to make it more American."

"All right, you boys!" came the shout. "Drop the merchandise and put up your hands." The police entering as planned caught the thieves with an appreciable degree of surprise. Everyone in the store jumped and were transfixed, but the tactic used by the lawmen was not a sound one. They had cleared their way too far into the room, passing the front door and exposing themselves.

The large thief, the one standing near the doorway's left side, couldn't sneak behind the cops, but he could see that he was practically behind them. He picked up the handsaw and swung it violently at the nearest officer's head standing closest to him, grazing the young man with its crosscut edge over his eye, through his ear. When he screamed in agony, dropping his gun to grab his ear, all the thieves threw the clothes bundles they had at the other cop. There was a mad scramble, and all the looters made a dash.

Finding his weapon, the young and wounded officer began firing it, soon joined by his partner. They emptied all twelve of their combined chambers but no one but the assailant had been hit. A single shot to his lardy and squat neck felled him.

Lying on his side now, mortally wounded, the blood spurted from the bullet puncture in a burgundy red arcing fountain. It landed almost two feet away, with wet splopping sounds. In a short time the wound began acting like a new orifice, with a life of its own, for what time was left. Its small bloody mouth made slight flatulent noises while his body vainly attempted to suck in air. The cops weren't there to administer any aid because they had given chase to the others. When they returned, the wounded had become the deceased. Now, murder charges could be added on to each suspect, even though it was the police who had killed him. And they would be found, eventually. One person could now be positively identified. They were somewhere downtown.

And miles away from downtown, and the Hastings Street tailor's shop, gangs of white citizens blocked the advance of any squad cars attempting to respond to the Paradise Valley area. These people established barricades made of automobiles strung across the road, several cars deep. The police had to disembark from their vehicles and walk into ambushes if they had any desire to get through. Desire that equivocated to imprudence, for the agitation was high beyond the borders the mob had set. The law was not being respected.

Splinter factions of the same crowd threw bricks and stones through the windows of houses and the Negro occupants would toss them right back at the hatemongers. This went on, back and forth for a long time, hours, and the Negroes inside the dwellings would keep to inner rooms, staying low. Eventually, the more dangerous elements in the pack tired of the cat-and-mouse and decided to gather newspaper and cardboard, dried grass, kerosene-soaked burlap, and any other combustible and to place them at points along house exteriors.

There were about four places they were attacking and the physical act of igniting the points outside the shanties required no courage. To them, it was like setting fire to a den of vermin. The homes were lit simultaneously, and quickly the choked screams inside the rapidly conflagrated homes gave rise to the mob's own triumphant cheers. A warped set of collective values, so degenerated by hate, turned the vicious crime of arson into an occasion for celebration. When the Negro inhabitants would run out, willing to face the crowds instead of burning to death, they were set upon viciously.

In another instance, further past the borders of Paradise Valley, near the Vernor Highway, a lone colored man ran out into the street and fired his deer rifle over the heads of an approaching throng. Fear of the defending Negro was soon overcome, however, with a general concurrence, an astute awareness. They outnumbered the solitary gunman; he couldn't shoot all of them. Almost acting as an individual, they turned and charged him. Immediately seeing the change of attitude, the Negro flung his weapon aside and ran away into safer enclaves.

All these incidents, and more, occurred during the Emergency Address taking place at the Detroit City Hall. Governor Kelly, now in his shirt-sleeves and opened collar, who could only guess at the nature of all the specific cruelties happening in the streets. But he alluded to the listening public that he had a general idea what was going on, and that the conditions in the city were indeed becoming dire. It was time for him to pronounce his plan of action.

"Therefore," he solemnly began, "in light of this situation, I am declaring a state-of-emergency, not only for Wayne County and Detroit, but also for Oakland and Macomb counties, to the north of the city, as well. In these affected areas a ten p.m. curfew is in effect for all persons not having important business or if they are going to and from work."

Colonel Krech, sitting in a faraway corner, leaned forward in his chair and put his forearms and elbows on his thighs. He shook his head and pulled a drag off his cigarette. He could see Mayor Jeffries—the good farmer now turned into lap dog, swabbing at his face with a handkerchief. Krech was disgusted with the curfew limits. He'd tried to get the governor to clear the streets of all people, leaving only police and military personnel on any given roadway. But of course, true-to-form, there was no backing down from the governor. It was almost like there was no plan.

"In addition," Kelly continued to advise, "the sale of all liquor is banned during as such time as the unrest continues." Now that action actually surprised Krech. Not the prohibition, but that the governor would implement such a measure. "All public amusement places are ordered to close, to be effective immediately. There is to be no unauthorized gathering or crowds in the streets. And now, for further words, I give you Hizzoner, Mayor Jeffries."

Jeffries took one more swipe at his brow before lowering his mouth to the bank of microphones. Krech left as soon as the mayor adjusted the media props and seemed to be reflecting on what he was going to say. The politician realized before starting that his written script was only repeating things that the governor had already covered. He decided it better not to recapitulate. He went on extemporaneously, setting aside his prescribed address. "One thing that should be remembered and paramount in all our minds," he said, "is that this day—this anarchy is doing a great harm to our beloved commonwealth. We should all be aware that the continued disruption of our city not only jeopardizes our common good, but in essence, the world's. We are a major artery of supply in this nation's war effort, and our enemies could not have accomplished as much against us if they had committed a full-scale bombing raid. I appeal to you, the good citizens of Detroit, to keep off of the streets. To stay in your homes, or at your workplace. Don't allow yourselves to be added to this vicious foolheartedness, and make this disruption an irreparable blight on our nation's war effort. Let our strength instead be a combined strength, one of goodwill and brotherhood. And may God help us all."

Krech found the hallway he stepped into eerily quiet, considering the activity three stories below on the streets, and also within the city hall building.

There was no one else in the hall with him. Lighting his fourth consecutive cigarette, he leaned his shoulder against its wall for support. The lights had been turned off in an attempt to keep the corridors from becoming too warm. At least, that is what Krech had surmised. Although it may have also been that someone just forgot to turn them on. Or didn't care. Whatever the reason, the effect was more pleasant, especially for the emotionally drained colonel.

He slid himself along the passageway for a few feet, having grown too tired to stand up straight. His head was disintegrating, the whole area of his forehead, lobotomized through a lack of sleep. He plodded his way towards Commissioner Witherspoon's office and he knew that it would be empty. Because everyone was in the process of obediently listening to the governor's flawed assessment. But Krech only wanted solitude now, a chance to enliven himself.

He felt like a lawyer who, after hoofing it around the criminal justice system all day for a client on death row, found out his client could not gain clemency. It seemed all together hopeless to him that Emergency Plan White would never be enacted. And while there was no reprieve for the federal plan, neither was there any reprieve from the alternating throbbing and aches in either of the officer's legs. They emanated from the arches of his feet, to stiff ankles, and then around to tired Achilles tendons.

He opened Witherspoon's office door and admitted himself, a beat and spent warrior. Now the small of his back further punctuated his ineffectiveness and flared with discomfort. But before retiring, Krech thought it better to forsake a comfortable chair and to instead covet a final cup of coffee from an urn across the room. It wasn't until after taking the acrid brew down his throat that he noticed his superior, General Gunther.

Apparently, he followed Krech directly into the room by not more than twenty seconds. As he turned to collapse in the lap of a chair he fancied when he first came in, it was the exact same moment he saw the general come to the open doorway. Krech made a delayed movement, a disjointed improvisation of a salute with a cup of coffee.

"At ease, Colonel," Gunther said softly.

"Forgive the appearance, Sir. How was Washington?"

"A futile hearing, but notwithstanding, I'm rather chipper. Had I been in your shoes the past fourteen hours, though, I assure you that I'd be no better for the wear, either. So, tell me. Just what the hell do you mean the governor is refusing our assistance?"

"Just that, Sir. Based on what I've seen and heard we have the preamble of a turkey shoot. Not only does Kelly not want to federalize, he has no explanation as to how he's going to get the handful of state troops he has to the riot sites."

"Hmmm—what are the commanders like in the state forces, August? Do they have a perspective that we're not seeing?

"Begging pardon, Sir. These men aren't fit to command National Guard. I can't say this overview applies to the majority of men, but I overheard one to say that he was going to order his men to shoot anything that is black and moves."

"I see. I see, most unfortunate." The general began to consider his options and thought deeply, lightly stroking his gray mustache. Thumb and index finger pinching together under his nose, at the upper lip's cleft, and then fanning their separate ways out to the corners of his mouth. "I don't want to have to push."

"There seems to be quite a bit of polarization on the race issue, Sir. With the Negroes, as well as the white. I frankly don't understand why Kelly's being so bullheaded. He's like Nero, watching Rome fall."

"What did he say his reasoning was?"

"He mentioned that he was concerned that private citizens would be put under arrest by the military without full privilege of due process. He's worried that doors would be battered down, people dragged from their homes."

"Then it's simply a matter of politics, is it?"

"It is?"

"Yes, I'm afraid so, Auggie. The Republicans have had it up to here with Roosevelt. The fact of the matter is, if the president saves the day, here, and wins the war, the Republicans will have quite a road to plow in the coming elections. FDR will have kept domestic peace and economic stability, plus rid the world of three despots. Kind of hard to beat, if you ask me."

"So, we have to find a way to let us take over the essential operations before our defense plants are destroyed."

"Correct. Let me tell you, Colonel. The Joint Chiefs and Secretary Stimson are really only concerned with those plants. First concerns have to be for any inherent danger to logistical manufacturing and supplies. They've said that civilian loss is acceptable if the federal government must move in to protect its interests."

Unspoken to the general was that Krech no longer felt so consigned to that framework, and that change came about once he had to look Reverend White into his eyes the other night. When the preacher had turned away from the upper floor window, aghast at what was being allowed to happen to his people, the lament caused a growing paradox in the colonel's values as to what was right or wrong in this matter. He was still coming to terms with that. And not only were military views being strongly called into a question. His own personal beliefs about equality were now circumspect.

"General, here's a thought. Now, say we do end up deploying our men. And say we're sending our white troops, into a Negro neighborhood. And there's killing. The colored press would surely put a bad light on that. If blacks see that the government is not going to do anything on their behalf, then an even worse outcome could happen if things really start to get out of control. It could get the whole country going."

"Why do you think that, Colonel?"

"I've practically been assured of that. It came straight from the proverbial horse's mouth, Sir. We need to make it seem that we're doing our utmost to ease tensions here."

"What are you suggesting then? Sending colored troops into parts of Detroit? What if a bunch of them decide to switch over to the cause of the insurgents? It's been known to happen."

"White troops are just as susceptible. With all due respect, Sir. There are police down there who have nonetheless switched over to mob mentality. Let there be no doubt about that, Sir. I think it would speak volumes to our intent if white and colored soldiers are used together here."

"It's a great theory, Auggie. But unrealistic in practice. Don't you think?"

"In the past that may have been true, but if we qualify who's mobilized in the colored forces—"

"But there's not enough time."

"We don't need time, Sir. Half the work's already been done. A whole division has forwarded names of a hundred-and-thirty, top of the drawer, Negro troops."

"Where?"

"Fort Custer."

"Is that Peets you're talking about?"

"Yes, Sir. We just had him up to Headquarters."

"Oh, yes. The contingencies. Peets, yes, he's a good man. A good man, indeed. But I don't—" General Gunther began smoothing his mustache again, and included grazing fingers across the front of chin, also. "You say these are his handpicked?"

"Yes, Sir. Tentative inductees in the special training at Fort Benning, next year. Don't say no to this, General. It goes beyond what light the colored population will put on this. Think of it. The Nazis and the Japanese have propaganda machines at the ready to twist this mess into weaknesses."

"All right, Colonel. You've made your point."

"I believe so, General."

"I'll entertain this suggestion of yours, Krech. In light of the situation, I believe it has some merit."

"What's our next move then, Sir? We have the governor to deal with, shortly."

The general had hissed under his breath then because he hadn't considered how to crystallize a response. He couldn't make this decision by himself. "I'll have to fly it past General Aurand, first. If he agrees to it, then we can try to get the governor to work things our way. But Auggie, no one is to make a move until I know we have level-headed soldiers, and not some barrel of monkeys ready to be let loose on the city." And that's when Krech asked permission to fly to Fort Custer and talk to Colonel Peets, himself.

CHAPTER THIRTEEN
Mixed Messages

Krech did not dream, though he slept deeply while enroute to Fort Custer on an army transport plane. His body preferred he lapsed into a momentary coma. Ordinarily, the residual energy used in freeing his subconscious thought in order to rest would never have taxed him so. But the squabbling he'd negotiated had drained the colonel. On the one hand, it seemed a matter of self-preservation; him shutting his mind down completely for the seventy minutes it would take to fly to the airfield in Michigan. While, on the other hand, he hadn't intended taking the respite. Prior to leaving though, he'd had a chance to shave, take a sponge bath, and change his uniform. A soldier loves the comfort of a clean pair of socks and with cleanliness came relaxation, and his present blanket of oblivion. Before succumbing to his exhaustion, however, the colonel had replayed his and Gunther's resolution once more. "*And be sure to tell him I'm counting on him*", Aurand reminded the colonel. "*There's no room for a fuck up, on this. You get me?*"

A screeching skirt of the plane's wheels on the ground and a slight jolt brought the colonel back to the stupor of the freshly awakened. He lifted his head from the small white pillow and was embarrassed to find he had spittle draining on it from the corner of his mouth. He stood while the plane taxied and passed his right hand along the side of his head to smooth his rumpled hair; simultaneously daubing away the saliva with a handkerchief he held in his other. Outside, the dusk just began filtering the horizon. The characteristically flat horizon was leveled by glaciers, eons ago, and made the farmland under it seem even more immense and beautiful.

Colonel Krech stepped onto the landing of the air ramp and couldn't help but to take a deep breath. He did this while noticing the quirky but pleasant contrast between the azure heavens and the cotton candy hues of the fanning alto-cirrus clouds. The sight combined with the silence of the evening was mesmerizing. Then a weak recording of "Day is Done," the serviceman's reverie, played over a loudspeaker at the strip. Even the birds seemed to stop chirping.

The colonel, like every soldier on the tarmac, faced west and stood at attention. Maybe he was tired, or just one of a minority of patriots given to sentimentality, but the ritual tonight caused him to swallow a little harder than usual as he heard it. A slight trembling of his lower lip and a mist across his eyes reaffirmed to him that he must be very tired to have his emotions running so close to the surface. He remembered the wettened eyes of Reverend White staring at him, when he had been dismissed. He felt that burden of barely being able to keep your anger in check.

A car and driver met Krech at the tarmac and took the colonel along a perimeter road that would lead to the fort. The driver assured him he wasn't being taken on a tour, though they passed several miles of cyclone fence before coming near the entrance. Fawning blue spruce trees loomed over and around the immediate entrance of the base, which had a pair of stone turrets. When the car turned the corner there, the officer could barely discern that the entrance wall was made of massive country rock boulders because night barely had overcome the twilight. Twenty-five feet beyond that gate was the guard shack, manned by an officious corporal.

"Good evening, Sir," the corporal greeted Krech, not acknowledging the driver who had pulled the driver's window past the shack doorway. Krech returned the salute.

"Give me the directions to the residence of Colonel Peets, if you please." The corporal's head cocked to the side slightly and then backwards, as if astonished by the inquiry.

"Beg pardon, Sir, are you sure it's Peets that you want?"

"Your concern should be, corporal, is that I get the directions I asked for."

"Well, yes, of course, Sir. It's just that, well, you might not be aware that Colonel Peets is a colored officer, Sir."

"Is that a fact? Well, glad to hear of it, and he has a house on this base, does he not?"

"Yes, Sir."

"Then, kindly phone the man and let him know I'm coming."

"Yessir. Continue on here, straight for a half-mile, and then take the left fork. Shortly thereafter, you'll see a sign. It will say, 'Negro Officer Quarters.' You turn in there and his house is the third on the right."

"Third on the right."

"Yes, Sir."

Following the directions wasn't actually necessary. Krech could see it was evident he'd come to the colored portion of the base when the car passed a line of black men waiting for the use of a common outdoor shower. Illuminated by a solitary lamp above the stall's entrance, the deep gold in the shoulders of the first few men in line could be made out. Krech looked with disdain at the assemblage because an outhouse was just up above the hill from the shower. Spillage from that ill-planned privy was finding its way into a recess near the shower. The men were living in conditions common to swine. The colonel turned forward so as not to gawk.

At about the same time that Colonel Krech arrived at the front gate, Colonel Peets was in his residence, involved in an argument over a bowl of chicken soup. The disagreement he was having actually wasn't over the soup; rather he was having a debate while eating it. The dispute was over the renegade soldiers, and Lt. Sackett was in the commander's kitchen, calling for official sanctions to be handed down immediately. But every time he produced a thoughtful rationale to go ahead with discipline the colonel would slurp on his tablespoon full of tepid noodles and salty broth. Colonel Peet's arbitrary nature was both infuriating and endearing at the same time to Lt. Sackett. The junior officer actually found the tactful disdain admirable, and wished he could show such a demonstrable obstinacy, but his would only be a pale imitation to this wizened warrior who'd mastered the art of nonchalance. Having a conversation with someone who responded to everything with ironic flair was unsettling, intimidating. In the dead of winter Colonel Peets kept a pitcher of ice water on his desk. Now, in the summer's swampish humidity, he ate hot soup or drank steamy coffee. Peets was contrary to the very marrow of his being it seemed, and no one could predict him.

"If we don't follow through on this, Colonel—we may as well give up on having any reason for the men to follow any order we give them."

"No, Frank," Peets said almost imperceptibly between sips of soup. "I don't want articles put on any of them. Not a one. Do you understand?"

"But, Colonel, I must insist."

"I'm set about this, Frank. No assaults took place, and only fifteen men were even involved. Case is closed as far as I'm concerned. Give them three weeks in the stockade. Nothing more."

"Is it me, Sir? Do you think I might have some problem with handling the first-level of hearings? Is that what this is really about?"

"Frank, please. You know better than that. You should, least ways. I've shared information with you that I wouldn't trust to many other souls on this base. Hell, even on the face of the planet. Do you think that I'd misjudged your mettle? I know you have some compassion. These men shouldn't die for being stupid, Frank, should they?"

The last statement of the colonel made Sackett revive the mask of reticence he'd had on his face earlier, back when he was with Pvt. Martin. It was if some indiscretion of his own past might throw an unwelcome shadow over him at any moment. Everyone had skeletons, he thought, things they would not like known about them, out in the bright day. But he also knew that some people couldn't rely on the shade of day to hide their taboos, either. He knew that some people were just as haunted by shadows perceived in the daylight. But before any register of concern could flicker for more than a moment in his eyes, the telephone rang and he escaped more scrutiny. He crossed to the wall phone. "Take it in the front room, please," the colonel asked, and Sackett gratefully followed that imperative.

The lieutenant rushed to the small, but handsome, cherry wood table that the too-large phone was set upon. The wood's veneer, once beautiful, was now abused and further obscured by an ugly lamp. He picked up the black receiver on the fourth ring. "Colonel Peets' residence; this is Lt. Sackett, speaking." A span of thirty seconds passed and Sackett cupped his hand over the phone's mouthpiece. "Colonel, I think you might want to get in here."

Peets came from the kitchen and set his bowl of soup on the corner of the dining room table, still non-plussed until he heard differently. He watched Sackett take his hand back from the mouthpiece and press for answers to questions. "That was who? What? And how long ago was this? I see—no. No, thank you corporal. No, that's all." Sackett hung up the phone softly and his face lost its tone. "That was the guard gate; Colonel Krech is here from Division Headquarters."

"What!"

"Yes, he's on base. On his way here, in fact. He'll be here any minute. You think that Headquarters knows about what happened, Sir."

"Of course, they know," Peets said flatly, as he threw his spoon down into the unfinished bowl of soup and quickly swiped at his mouth with a napkin. "And we can just kiss that special assignment goodbye, too. I can tell you that." Sackett could see the colonel tensing. "Now, do you understand why I didn't want to charge any of those men? It only makes the case for the War Department. Why should they give us more responsibility? We'll just fuck it off, anyway.

That's what they'll think, you know. 'Let them just keep on shoveling our shit and setting up our mess tents.' That's how they want it."

"Sir, what if he's here to extradite them back to Chicago for court-martial?"

"What if he is? What choice would you or I have in the matter? I'd have to give them over to him. If I don't, my tongue could get stretched as long as theirs." Peets slammed his meaty fist on the table so hard that it caused some of the soup to spill. "Dammit! So close. So close. Those poor, stupid, pathetic niggers. Couldn't they have thought one minute about what they were doing? It's out of my hands."

"How do we know that's what he's here about, Colonel? I mean, how could they even know. We haven't placed an incident report. We haven't called the—"

"Phones have mouths, Frank. Walls have ears."

"You think some white officers might have said something?"

"I don't know. If they did—you can bet I'll be finding out. And when I do, the low-down, side-winding—"

A trio of knocks on the front door suspended the vitriolic moment and stopped all movement in the room. The two black officers held their glances at the entry door. "Want me to answer it?" Sackett whispered.

Peets picked up the half-eaten bowl of soup from the cherry wood table's corner and handed it almost roughly to Sackett. "No, don't bother. Put this in the kitchen."

Peets cinched his shirt further into his beltline as the lieutenant vacated to the house scullery. He pressed what residual pomade he had left in his hair closer to his temples, and then he rubbed his palms to see if they were greasy, too greasy for a handshake. Satisfied, he walked casually to the door after a cleansing breath and opened it.

"Colonel Krech, I thought I told you three months ago that I have no intention of giving up my command to you," said Peets loudly in welcome. He extended his large hand and Krech firmly clasped what was offered, and grinned.

"Oh, Anderson, I think I'd be hardpressed to fill your most able shoes."

"Of course you would, my feet are too big. Come on in." Peets stepped aside and allowed his guest to cross the threshold, but Krech didn't go any further than a few feet inside. There was a hesitancy and wariness that he felt, and it very well came from both sides, Krech surmised. They both felt threatened in trusting each other. Even through their smiles.

"Well, I know you didn't come all the way from Chicago just to stand in my doorway. Come and take a seat, man. Have you a little sit-down," said Peets.

Krech let himself be ushered into a high-backed and overly padded chair that Colonel Peets usually deigned for himself, only relinquishing it when company came. Part of the chair's back winged its way forward in a splayed protrusion at its crest, coming along either side of a seated occupant's head. Colonel Krech crossed his legs in seeming comfort, but really didn't care to have his peripheral vision obfuscated.

"You look like you've taken to my chair," Peets noted, "but for the record, if I go—it goes."

"It's a well known fact that possession is nine-tenths of the law, Anderson. So, I don't think you'll have to get a judge advocate to keep it," Krech replied with a trace of a grin. "But, I must say, your home is nicely put together."

"It's all right for government issue. Anyway, before we go on, I want you to meet someone. Lieutenant, could you come in here, please."

The appearance of Sackett in the room visibly distracted Krech from the matter at hand. He stood to meet the junior officer. "Good evening, Sir," Sackett said, saluting first and then offering his hand. "I'm Lt. Franklin Sackett, at your service."

"He'd been back there in the kitchen doing dishes," Peets joked, "and I didn't want him to feel compelled to keep an apron on."

"Understood, Anderson. Hello, Lieutenant."

"I hope you had a pleasant trip in getting here, Sir. I'll be on my way."

Krech raised a hand to banish the thought and moved around to the back of the chair, alternately rubbing and kneading its shoulders. He was really uncomfortable in it, so he was glad to have had a reason for standing, yet hoping to appear at ease by still being in close proximity of the offered seat. The caressing of the shoulders that were like blinders was an added touch. "Don't run off on my account," Krech said with thinly veiled assurance, "Is he one of your staff members, Anderson?" Sackett wanted to desperately be far removed from the place and couldn't help but look grim when Colonel Peets squeezed him atop of the shoulder.

"We can speak freely. Sackett's my adjutant. If you can say it in front of me, you can repeat it to him with nary a quibble on my part. He has my highest confidence, Colonel." Peets' voice was tighter now, belying the casual assertion he made. The sociological poker was intense.

Krech usually was a good judge in personal assessments, or character, if you will. He was aware of the expectancy in the room, an apprehension, to put it more precisely, but he could not identify what was causing that, for the moment. He just continuously kept monitoring the immediate surroundings, trying not to let a single moment pass that could unlock the reason behind the sometimes—ambiguous behavior in his hosts.

He had learned early on that the deeds of a man speak the truth, more than his words. And he loved to read the way things sometimes played in between the lines of what a person would profess and what they would actually do. Actions configured somewhere at the intersections of thoughts and manifestation. Then putting himself in Peet's shoes, he figured out that there indeed was enough reason for them both to be wary of one another. At least, for the time being. But such suspicion could not carry on for too much longer, for there was an objective of greater concerns that needed to be met. And met expeditiously.

"Very well, then. I'll be candid with you simply because I don't have the pleasure of time in this matter. We need to talk directly about the situation that's been developing in Detroit, as of last night."

At first Sackett had thought that for someone who wanted to waste no time, Krech seemed to pontificate, but when he mentioned Detroit—all ears came open. It seemed anxiety blocked the airway in Colonel Peets' throat for a moment. The urge to swallow overcame any other command or response. Seeing Peets' momentary inability to speak coherently, Sackett took over the supplication of a rebuttal. And he did that with a rhetorical question of his own. "Sir—do you mind if we may ask, is the inquiry from your own initiative, or is it aligned with some kind of Command process?"

Krech noticed that there were beads of sweat on the foreheads of both the men in front of him, but then again, it was summer in Michigan and he himself probably had slight grease to his face, too. He replied in a way not to show any offense for the question. "I was authorized to come here by General Gunther—therefore, yes, this is an official visitation."

"Concerning?"

"Are your men exhibiting any undue anxiety about the circumstances occurring—the things that may lie at the core of what is happening? In a few words, have your men been 'jumpy', lately?"

"I guess that depends on what you consider being 'jumpy' is, Colonel," said Sackett.

"At ease, Lieutenant," Peets forcefully reproached, finally finding his voice, for which Sackett was thankful.

"Relax, Anderson. I'm sure the lieutenant didn't mean any disrespect. But this thing has been going on now for two days. To put it plainly, I think we're going to need your support from here."

"Oh, we got extra culinary staff. We can give you a whole mess company, maybe two—no problem at all. You expect to be there for some duration?"

"Anderson, please—you just don't seem to understand. I'm not looking for cooks and mess boys."

"You're not?"

"No, I'm ready to give you and your men a rare opportunity. Anderson, you've been through this, and more. But that can't be said for most of your men, here. For them, what I'm asking for would be an initiation by fire, but that's the way I think any real soldier would rather have it. Do you think your men are prepared for an initiation by fire?"

Now it was Sackett joining Peets in looking confounded. There were sardonic, indelible grins tattooed on their faces. It was strange because moments ago they had been so sullen; like they had been sure the Grim Reaper followed Krech directly into the house. But now, their faces seemed more relaxed, relieved even. Peets and Sackett rediscovered the pleasure of being able to smile genuinely, and even though pressure still existed. The smiles they gave were broad. Peets finally sucked in a deep breath and eschewed it out of his ballast lungs with a whoosh.

"Well, come on now. Time's wasting." Krech teased the officers, now that he'd bowled them over. "Speak, man. You know, Lt. Sackett, I thought I'd never see the day when Anderson Peets wouldn't have something to say. Have you some information, some opinion?"

"Our best marksmen have been undergoing training for the last sixty days, Sir," Sackett said with dignified delight, "and under my direct supervision, if I may be so bold."

"Outstanding. And tell me this, Lieutenant. Now, how can I put this so as not to offend?"

"Right now, there ain't a thing you could say that could disturb me. Go ahead and ask away, Sir."

"All right, then. How comfortable are you with your mens' level of restraint, shall we say?"

"The answer to that, Colonel, is that they are simply trained to be soldiers in a context of war. They are mostly cool under fire."

"Glad to hear that, Sackett."

Peets inwardly flinched with Sackett's intransitive analysis. Him saying most of the men were compliant was a flag. He felt he needed to deflect Krech's attention, quickly.

"I have a question, August," Peets said. "The governor. It doesn't sound like to me that he'd ever sign off on such a thing. Does he have any idea about what's being planned?"

"By the time he does we'll be deployed and mobilized. He'll have no input whatsoever as to who makes up our troops," Krech chuckled; the tip of his tongue sticking through his slightly parted teeth.

Peets couldn't believe the scene playing out before him. The manic discourse they'd been involved in earlier was almost dizzying in the heights and depths of the dramatic events turned upon them. Now, mercifully, it truly looked like the sun would rise again to see another day. "Something told me I liked your style, Krech," Peets lauded. "What unit will we be teaming with?"

"The 701st, a police unit."

"Now, that's what I'm talking about," Sackett hooted.

"You must stay for some imbibement, Colonel," Peets offered, holding up a bottle retrieved from a hutch. "Please say you'll stay for a drink."

"Oh no," Krech refused, remembering the hangover he'd had, "I must get back directly."

"Auggie," Peets said familiarly, "this is eighteen year-old single malt scotch."

"Well—ah, oh, well," Krech stammered while looking at the label. "I guess one for the road, huh? Wouldn't hurt us much now would it?"

"No, Sir," Sackett agreed. "I'll go get some glasses."

"There's some next to that bottle of gin, Frank"

"Oh, why bother with glasses, gentlemen." Krech took the bottle from out of Peets' hands and pulled the cork, again causing a moment of shock for his hosts. He extended the bottle to Sackett, "Junior officers first."

The least ranking officer hefted the two-thirds full bottle of amber liquor and timidly brought it to his lips. He considered just how much he should take, being that he was the first at the well and didn't want to appear to be a lush in front of senior staff. With more than a slight feeling of self-conscious-ness, he took a small mouthful, being careful not to leave excess spittle. Fin-ished, and with his eyes misting from the spirit vapors he'd just ingested, he handed the bottle back to Krech. Sackett was not given much to drinking, truth be told. But this was an order, subliminally enforced. Colonel Krech re-ceived the liquor but still did not bring it to his lips, even then. He offered the bottle to Colonel Peets, who took the scotch with a broad smile on his face again. The significance of what Krech was doing was not, altogether, not touching. Peets now knew that Krech intended to be the very last man to drink from the bottle. Sensing that, Peets was not nearly as contrite about locking hold of the neck of the bottle to his mouth as Sackett had been. He took a long, hard swallow. Followed by two bobs of his barely discernible Adam's apple. Brusquely, almost as a challenge, he jutted forth his arm with the bottle towards Krech. Peet's lower lip still glistened with the liquid spirits upon it.

Krech raised the clear glass stem of the bottle to his lips. The eyes of the Negro officers being on him didn't seem to cause Krech any unsettling feel-ings, though. As it had been said, actions speak louder than words. That could be why he didn't draw a hand over the tall neck of the bottle to wipe off saliva from the other imbibers. Krech intended that his draught would have to be the longest, and Peets had taken a considerable swig. Colonel Krech threw his head backwards and made the bottle go perpendicular to his chin. Two air bubbles rose to the inverted base as a large amount of scotch cleared his palate. When he brought the bottle to rest in front of him, Krech's eyes bulged and teared. His eyebrows also lifted high onto his forehead, a circumspect denial of the blend's potency that beguiled no one in the room. Including him.

"It's a lot smoother than what I'm used to, Anderson." The alcohol was still expanding beyond Krech's esophagus as he sat the bottle down on an end table.

"When should I have my men assembled?" Peets asked.

"As far as I'm concerned, gentlemen, you can start coordinating things with the 701st right now. With the slight caveat, of course, that it's still on stand-by status until the ball is officially rolled your way. You understand?"

"Of course."

"Good. Now, I have the pleasure of going back to call Detroit and informing General Gunther of our good news, eh?" Krech saluted Peets and Sackett. "Anderson, Lieutenant—" he shook one pair of hands and then the other, "it's indeed been a pleasure. More than you could know." Business concluded, Colonel Krech left the government-issued dwelling with a great sense of accomplishment.

Now Peets picked up the abandoned scotch bottle and wiped the top of the bottle's neck with the fleshy web between his thumb and index finger, the part where the flesh divided and was praline colored, on the palm side. He didn't feel a hypocrite to Krech's demonstrated philosophy on working together, for Peets simply couldn't abide drinking directly after anybody. He had been willing to make the sacrifice for this occasion, only.

"Ah yes, Lieutenant—or should I be saying Captain?"

"Captain?"

"It's what I promised, didn't I? Captain Sackett. But don't let that go to your nappy head too quickly. I seem to remember you wanting to be contrary and filing all kinds of charges." Peets swallowed three more gulps of the tea-colored potent spirits. "Something about court martials, and such?"

Sackett took the bottle from his commander and in seconds had his mouth bulging with quaffed scotch. He could only laugh in his good fortune.

Peets took the bottle back and shook it momentarily at Sackett. "Let's finish this off then. Here's to your promotion, Captain."

"No, Sir. Here's to the end of the world. Because it could only mean the end of the world when a colored man ever got a good wind at his back."

CHAPTER FOURTEEN
POUGHKEEPSIE 6-5000

And while Colonel Anderson Peets commiserated to Captain Sackett about how he was sure if Krech continued letting loose of his senses that they all would invariably be seeing dogs and cats bedding down together for the night.

A thousand miles to the east, and an hour later in the evening, a dinner party was also breaking up with brandy being served.

It was on O Street, in the nation's capitol. Brownstones of various sizes there lined both sides of the avenue. Green shaded maples, amber hued by the street lamps, were being buffeted about by occasional bursts of warm wind. A passerby could look directly into the first floor of Henry L. Stimson's home. At the moment, the Secretary of War wildly gesticulated his arms, almost like a crane stretching out its long wings.

He wore a dark turquoise smoking jacket with red-patterned, embroidered cuffs and collar. He was all of seventy-nine years old. Born two years after Lincoln's assassination, he had served the United States government at its highest levels for five presidents. Had been a Secretary of State to the present president's cousin. And Secretary of War for Taft. He had been a presidential envoy to Nicaragua and squelched the hot revolution there with a Latin American policy he spearheaded. He once held position as governor-general in the Philippines. In many ways, he had significantly helped to shape the foreign policy in the country for the past twenty-five years. Belying his frail appearance now, nonetheless, he still stood before his guests, a formidable individual. Still sharp of wit, though ailing lately. In fact, even at the moment suffering from a case of gout, and midway up his left thigh, almost to the hip, arthritis, his complaints were never about his person.

So then, what was this intelligent, visionary of a man doing flailing his arms about him? A behavior surely not given to a gentleman of any sort. The reasons for the antics were because Stimson wasn't talking about anything purposeful at the moment. He was recanting to his guests, a brigadier general and a major general, a story about a ploy he happened to accomplish upon some hapless Negro grounds person, earlier in the day. He always had a mean streak to his tricks.

"Well, gentlemen," he said, "When they ran out of the paint I was just a-hoppin'. I was so mad. They surely should have been able to at least cipher out the square footage of the windows. I tell you, poor excuses for workers."

"Maybe, they were trying to use up some reserves they had. In fact, Henry, you could argue that they were quite efficient, maybe more; maybe they were over-efficient. They used up all the paint before their supervisor could return with more to finish," General McNarney countered.

"No, you could argue that. Not me——Well, sir, here comes this darkie up to the French doors. Beauregard was on an errand, so I answered. This young buck, maybe thirty years old, asks to use the phone. I say, 'Whatya need a phone for?' he said, 'I need it to call my boss and tell him we need more paint." Now, I haven't opened the door any wider than this, you see. And Stimson held apart his hands about five inches. I tell him I don't have a phone. That threw him for a loop. He stands there for a minute, and almost starts scratching his head. I start to laughing, and I said, 'Come on in, boy.' So, I open the door about two feet, or so, so he'd have to turn sideways to enter. Now he's got to be really careful, you see, because the doorjambs just been painted. So he's coming through with his back to me. And what do you think I do?"

"Let him use your phone, I assume," said General Somervell.

"No, Sir. I took this cane here in my hand. And I cracked it across his backside"

Somervell and McNarney were both stunned with the admission. They'd known of his predilections but not to the extent he talked of, now. "You struck him, Sir?"

"I surely did. And what happened afterwards proves my point I'm trying to make to you two."

"What did happen, Mr. Secretary?"

"Nothing, absolutely nothing. That big black fool just stood sandwiched between the door, and me, turned his damn fool head at me and looked me right in the eye. And didn't say a word. I tell you, here I am with gout, and an old man, and I could still put a licking to a nigger."

"Mr. Secretary," McNarney interrupted, "I think there's several things you haven't considered as to what the response you desired would have cost. Both to you, and the young man."

"If he had struck you back, Sir. And let me put this plainly, that was a fool-hardy thing to do. You're lucky he had some sense."

"Shows he had no sense at all. What man, what real man would let another man kick him, or crack him in the ass and not do a thing about it? You or me, we wouldn't bat an eye and have defended ourselves."

"But that's just the point, Sir," Somervell argued, "You're talking about a man who has been conditioned to not even look at a white man. Him glaring at you could be about as much as you could expect. To do anything else would have put him in the can, for sure. And no doubt he has a family to feed. I'd have taken it too, Mr. Stimson. Given those odds."

"It's thinking like that, Mr. Somervell, which ruined many a poor white during Reconstruction here, and in Maryland. I saw it happening all around me while I was growing up."

"Well, one thing's for sure," General McNarney said, "the coloreds in Detroit aren't in the least bit timid, at the moment."

Six metallic notes chimed in ascending and then descending toned intervals outside of the room. "Are we expecting someone else?" Somervell asked.

The sliding doors of the drawing room were opened noisily, like heavy slabs of rock being grated against one another. Parting them about five feet was accomplished through the effort of a stubby Negro butler, replete in evening coat even though it was now near the midnight hour. He walked into the foyer and deposited himself directly in front of Secretary Stimson.

"Judge-Advocate, Major General Cramer here to see you, Sir."

"Wonder what the devil he could want?"

"Should I send for him?"

"Yes, Beauregard, send him on in. And then close the doors after you."

"Yes, Sir."

The butler waved the officer into the room and departed as directed; making the doors create as little sound as possible but still resembling something akin to the sounds of an entombment, as he shut them.

"General Cramer," Stimson greeted, "You appear to have some important documents within that large folder, I gather. But what I want to know is, for what?"

"I'm sorry to interrupt your evening, gentlemen."

"You all know each other here, don't you?" Stimson asked.

A round robin of handshaking and murmured introductions stop-gapped the meeting, momentarily. Giving Stimson time to light a Cuban cigar. "All right, enough with the chitter, what's in the bag?"

Cramer reached in the leather duffel and produced a two-page document to hand to the Secretary. "This is a presidential proclamation authorizing federal troops in Detroit."

"Oh, I see," Stimson said, looking over the page. "But what's this here about the Sixth Command?"

"Sir?"

"Read it aloud, from here."

"'Be it further deemed and authorized that the Sixth Service Command and its agents will have full jurisdiction as to what troop numbers and troop make up will be utilized to quell said insurrection.' Is that the clause you're talking about, Sir?"

"It is. Doesn't that seem a little odd, that wording there?"

"No, Sir. To be honest, I can't find anything out of place."

"It's a small, possibly innocuous addition to the clause and how it's usually written. Usually it only states that the Command in the region takes charge of the number of men used. This seems to sound like to me that they might be dickering with the kind of men used."

"There is that talk, Sir, that Negro troops might be, used in contiguous deployment with the National Guard units."

"Segregated?"

"One company of blacks would be embedded with a white police unit in certain areas of the city."

The displeasure on the Secretary of War's face was evident. The room grew as still and quiet as the lit chandelier or the plush red satin curtains pulled back from the street-side windows. The dark green carpeting of the room seemed to grow marshy, causing the men to sink in its pile from the weight of the brewing diatribe that was about to explode. Plainly, Stimson had no idea that this was in the offing.

"It's that Boston Yankee bitch, Eleanor. I know it is. It's just the kind of thing she'd do."

"What's the problem, Sir? It's just a company of men out of a whole battalion."

"One man in one platoon is problem enough, far as I'm concerned, General Cramer. It breaks not only military law, but also civil law. What are you flinching for, McNarney? Trying to figure out what I'm thinking, are you? Why the hell I keep you on as my Deputy Chief? I'll be damned to know. Can't I even trust you to take care of informing me about these things being concocted right under our very noses?"

"To be honest, Mr. Secretary, I had no knowledge."

With a hobbled quarter turn to his right, Stimson was now barking into the face of General Somervell. "And what's your excuse, eh? Are you color-blind? Huh? Bah!"

"We were trying to break the news, but in actuality they haven't been sent for as of yet. For now, it's only an idea. As far as I know it's only a contingency. They are not—"

"And as long as I'm War Secretary, they daren't. Not put side-by-side with whites, they won't. Not in *this* man's army, and certainly not in a race riot."

Somervell didn't retreat, however. "You know, these are extenuating times, Sir. Sixth Service Command points out, and yes—yes, I do concur, that Negroes have just as much to lose or contribute to getting this situation under control. They have as much right as any white citizen of Detroit to help in defending it and frankly, I'm ashamed—"

"Ashamed?"

"Yes—ashamed that you make me feel I need to apologize for saying so."

"Oh, you do, do you?"

"Yes, Mr. Stimson, I do."

"Well that's where you're wrong, Somervell. A Negro will never be in a position, within our society, to contribute as much as a white man. Whose war is it anyway, Somervell? Think about it a minute. As far as the Negro goes, let them dwell on praying in their churches if they want to be of any help. Let them pray that their white protectors will come through and save the day for them. Their prayers will be appreciated, as far as prayers go, and they'll also be given the additional blessing of some feeling of equality whilst there."

"A feeling of equality?" McNarney pondered aloud.

"Church?" Somervell questioned, equally as incredulous.

"That's why they like going to church so much—which by the way brings up a joke. Why is it that niggers have to be in church for so long? Because they have a lot more to ask God for."

There were polite chortles.

"It's not rocket science, gentlemen. Ask any German."

"But, Sir? We're seriously talking about soldiers, here. Not a bunch of church deacons."

"Gentlemen, gentlemen—don't you see? It is only under the benign and all-loving, all-knowing, all-powerful eye of God that they—the Negro—can feel the love that only God can give a human. In the afterlife they'll get their true freedom, but to acquire it now on Earth would only be a lynchpin to their people's demise. It's all the same, believe me. The Bible says all men are created equal, and I'll buy that. As it is written, so let it be said. But you all know, and I know that all men can't be treated the same. And in the end, they're not. And why? The Negro, gentlemen, likes being in the Army the same way he likes belonging to their church. It gives him a sense of belonging, a sense of belonging that he'd only ever felt similarly in the darkie church. Now, it's been said, theoretically, that it's in the Armed Services that the Negro comes closest to equality with whites. Again, in theory, only, mind you. Plessey doesn't mean shit. Nigras like things separate. They don't want no part of marching with white soldiers. No more than our boys want to have to fight alongside of them. Colored people don't want to be just like us. The enjoyment they get out of life is seeing how close they can get to be white, without being white, because they know they can't. But if they ever did get that way, they'd truly be unhappy. They don't know what displeasure comes from having the world nipping at your heels all the time. The White Man's Burden has been a heavy one, indeed."

The generals were astounded by the deviation in this political giant's philosophy, but Stimson had gone back to studying the proclamation. "And I'm to sign this?"

"Yes, Sir. There's a signature block for you and the Secretary of State, along with the President's."

"Is he back from Hyde Park?"

"No, Sir. He's still with the party from—"

"Yes," Stimson cut off, "The Queen from Netherlands, I believe. Well, she could be the Queen of Neanderthals for all I care, if she is taking the President away from his duties during a time of total anarchy in his country. What's the President's Hyde Park number, Cramer?"

"POughkeepsie 6-5000, but Mr. Secretary—"

Stimson waved an irritated hand towards the general and picked up the phone receiver in his liver spotted right hand. "I'll not be submarined by that woman again, and I do mean Miss Eleanor." Stimson dialed for an operator. "Hello, operator—yes, get me POughkeepsie 6-5000, please." His left hand covered the mouthpiece of the receiver as he talked to the generals. "I've been Secretary of State for one president and Secretary of War for two, but I have never—in my life, seen such a fly-by night administration of a country."

It was apparent that Secretary Stimson still held a bad taste in his mouth for FDR; after all, he hadn't been a Secretary in the Cabinet for the first two administrations. He hadn't been the first choice by the president. And he'd never said anything about it per se, but he was a little perturbed by the oversight. Though in the president's mind, none had occurred.

The reality of the predicament they were in, and facing, still showed Emergency Plan White's preparation to be a sound one. It was a contingency plan for just the sort of situation that was occurring in Detroit. After the Pearl Harbor attacks the administration knew that the possibility for internal

espionage could increase. Emergency Plan White was outlined shortly thereafter, and to hear Stimson tell it, only his direction could be attributive to any
success it reaped.

"Hello, this is Secretary of War Stimson. With whom am I speaking?"

"Good evening, Mr. Secretary. This is Grace Tully." She spoke with a clear
and soothing modulation. A voice quite suitable for selling products on the
General Electric Hour. She even used seamless protocol by referring to the time
of the call as being in the late evening rather than the truth of the matter, that
it was now approaching one in the morning.

"Tully? The President's secretary?"

"Yes, Sir. That's correct." She really couldn't stand the man, truth be told.
She disliked him for his barking, braying personality. Stimson, on the other
hand, had a doggish analogy for her personality as well. He thought of her
being like the president's dog, *Fallah*. A nervous and over-protective terrier.
Constantly screening out calls that the Chief of Staff should have been directed
to, or if need be, the President.

"Well," Stimson miffed, "It doesn't sound like you. Must be the connection we have. Anyway, I needs speaks with the President."

"One moment please, Mr. Stimson."

Stimson covered the mouthpiece again and muttered something to the
generals and then had one of them call Beauregard in to freshen their brandies.
"I knew this thing would happen, one day I knew I'd see it come to pass. Two
years ago, when he caved in to that nigra fellow—that Randolph. Desegregat-
ing the entire defense plant jobs or they were threatening to go and march
hundreds of darkies down the avenue. And Eleanor made him overreact."

"Hello, Mr. Secretary. And how are we this evening?" It was a young man's
voice on the other end. Stimson felt he'd be handed over to a teenager soon if
he didn't put a stop to it.

"How I'm doing is really immaterial to you, young man. No man in his
right mind would be calling the president at this time of night unless it was very
important. Now, for the second time—I needs speaks with the president."

"One moment, please."

Stimson scowled in disgust and lowered himself into a nearby chair. His
leg was beginning to throb with more concerted pain. Another man's voice
came over the phone. "Hello, Mr. Secretary—"

"Yes, yes, yes, yes, yes, who is this now?"

"This is Will Haslett, an aide to the President, and at your service, Sir."

"Well, that's all very well and good, but I believe I told that Tully woman
I wanted to have a word with the President. And that's what I intend to do.
Do we have an understanding?"

"But Mr. Secretary, President Roosevelt is presently in the company of the Queen of the Netherlands, at the moment. He cannot be dis—"

"Get the President on this phone, now."

General McNarney, Somervell, and Cramer were anticipatory as to how the conversation would go that they were going to witness. Stimson sat up in his chair when he thought he heard the phone in Hyde Park being handled. "Henry, I hear you're in rare form, this evening," President Roosevelt chided. "What can I do for you, my good man?"

"Forgive the interruption Mr. President, but I needed some clarification from you before signing some papers here."

"Is that what's got you all hopped up?"

"Well, they are highly irregular, Sir. I wanted to know if Governor Kelly actually even called for our troops to be activated."

"There were no calls made to the White House. But I was covering the events in Detroit and had Miss Tully transcribe a copy of the proclamation."

"So, you've read it, then?"

"Yes."

"And you want me to sign this, as it is?"

"Henry—I have guests, please—"

"Mr. President, before you or I sign this blamed thing, I think you might want to know some things that your people may not be aware of."

"Oh—and what is that?"

"There's a bit of a sticky-widget here, Mr. President. General Aurand of the Sixth Command has already put units in place."

"Well, Henry, we can call it an activation by proxy. I'll delegate the authority for him to respond on my behalf, in this situation."

"But, you don't understand, Mr. President. He's got colored and white soldiers together."

Stimson could hear FDR pause and inhale thoughtfully on his cigarette, "How many?" the president asked.

"A company I'm told. But there could be more."

Another pause. Longer this time. "Well, Henry, I'm sure Aurand's got his reasons for doing what he is there. You know, you and I are probably too far removed from the action to really know what is needed. We should avoid making snap judgments, if we can."

"Doesn't take much brains to know that the Negro soldier is not capable of taking a leadership role in a race riot. They have no self-control in great numbers. Are easily swayed."

"I know you're feelings, Henry. But I believe this is a diplomatic representation being made to the public. I don't see where it will be needed that they'll be put at any of the points of crisis. Colored officers will not be supervising white soldiers."

"Franklin, you know their record. It's something that just isn't embedded in their race as of yet, Mr. President. To try and pool them together with white troops, in any kind of a battle situation, will only work a disaster to both factions, I'm afraid. You mark my words."

"I appreciate your candor, Henry. I count on your opinion tremendously in making decisions concerning the war. But the fact of the matter is that our role in Washington isn't the same as the role for Service divisions. Here is the one point where state's rights should have pre-eminence. We should be on the stand-by, and provide whatever logistical assistance is needed when the Service Command requests it."

"Yes, but—"

"We don't want to be tying down a commander with our directives as to how to deploy his own people in an emergency situation—"

"But, Mr.—"

"Because as soon as we do, Henry, we'll furnish him with a first-class alibi if anything goes wrong. And you know, as well as I do, how wrong these things can get. He should be left a free hand. Until he asks for something, we say nothing. And when he does, we should be at-the-ready to give it to him. Very promptly. Understood? Henry, do you hear what I'm saying to you?"

"Yes, Mr. President," Stimson said resignedly.

"Oh, by the way," FDR continued, "I didn't think to have the need for it this weekend, so I didn't seem to have the presidential seal with me for the proclamation. Left the damn thing in Washington. I gather it's still legal though, I have witnesses."

"Foreign witnesses, Mr. President?"

"I meant my staff, Henry."

"I see. Yes, Mr. President. A good night to you, Sir, and the Missus." Stimson placed the receiver back upon its phone base cradle.

"You see there, gentlemen. This is what our country is coming to, nowadays. The days for the white race maintaining power are numbered. Mark my words. My leg hurts fiercely, generals. I think I'd like to go to bed, now. Goodnight, and see yourselves out."

CHAPTER FIFTEEN
The Cup of Trembling

"You're serious about promoting me, aren't you?" Sackett asked Peets while he awaited the colonel's return from the bathroom.

"Why sound so incredulous—hasn't everything happened just about the way I said it would?" Peets asked as he closed the bathroom door when he exited.

"But to be honest, Sir. You didn't know any more than I did whether Krech was here to handcuff us, or hire us. I saw how worried you were—couldn't get nary a word out."

"Yes, we dodged a bullet, and a big one it was, too."

"Like a 50 millimeter."

"But now is not the time to become a shrinking violet. We have to seize the moment of initiative here. Seize it."

The telephone rang and Sackett answered. He was then immediately placed on hold. "Who is it?" Peets inquired.

"Major from the 701st. Got me on hold."

Colonel Peets drew close to Sackett, so as to almost hover over him, occasionally pressing a large index finger in front of the subordinate officer's face, or gently prodding him in the chest. All the while building up the ideal conception he desired to see come about through the medium of Sackett, and the vessel of his commission. In politics, a tall, up-and-coming Texas congressman used the same kind of tactic to effect persuasion on some of his stubborn colleagues. But this wasn't the floor of the House, and it was Sackett whom stood feeling quite ill at ease, cornered by Colonel Peets and simultaneously trying to navigate through a conversation with a white officer.

"Colonel," Sackett said, "With all respect. I'm honored that you consider me worthy of such an endeavor, really I am, but I don't think it's ethical, to my way of understanding."

"Why not let me worry about that. I'm the one signing the orders, and—"

Sackett waved his hand rapidly to quiet Peets, shushing him with a furrowed brow and indirect glance. "Yes, Major Carpenter—that's right, Fort Custer. We're giving you two companies. What? No, Sir—two units. I can— yes, I'll hold."

Peets resumed his harangue, but Sackett resisted. "Sir, it's my ass on the line if I'm caught. Not yours —" The major came back on the line. "Yes, hello, Major. Yes, that's fine. They'll be briefed and ready. Yes, within the hour. Goodbye." Sackett hung up.

"We upgraded to go, yet?" Peets took another shot.

"Still on standby." Sackett was now growing a little concerned. For one, he was completely caught off-guard by the colonel's demand for him to pose as a noncommissioned officer at some future date. And secondly, Colonel Peets seemed to be, well—drunk. Sackett thought that it might not be such a good idea to have the colonel address the men before they left. The lieutenant tried not to flinch from the high alcoholic content in Peet's breath as he continued giving Frank the treatment.

"You can't have it both ways, Frank," said Peets. "You've been sitting on that fence for too long."

"You can't tell me that there aren't some risks involved, Colonel. Risks that a reasonable man wouldn't take. Why should I?"

"I've taken certain measures already. There's a personnel file, a persona created, and all you have to do is to fill in the blank, to make him manifest. You're asking me for a sure thing in a time of war, and no soldier could give you claim to knowing that."

Sackett stepped back from Peet's jabbing finger. He looked down at his shoes, conflicted as to how he should respond. Then Peets did a wonderfully strange thing. The hand he'd been using to taunt Sackett was still extended towards him, but then Peets turned his palm upwards and opened his hand. Two pairs of silver paired-bars were in the center.

"I got them out from the bathroom," Peets said.

"Sir, are you sure you haven't had a little too much to drink?"

"You'll need these when you go to Detroit."

Hesitantly, Frank reached his right hand towards Peets', but then withdrew the arm again. "I can't," he said.

"Go ahead and try them on," Peets encouraged, "They're my old pair." Peets took the lieutenant's hand and firmly placed the captain's insignia into it. "These are meant as a down payment, a down payment on an acknowledged risk."

Now it was all over. It was why Frank avoided even looking at the bars, at first. For he knew that if he held them for any amount of time he'd follow his inclination to seek out more power for himself. That self-interest could get out of balance, and that concerned Frank, considerably. With more power one becomes less insulated from being judged. And Frank knew there was certainly a judgment coming his way. Complacent with cronyism and its affluence, he would probably be caught unawares when a time of reckoning actually would draw near. But he held the bars, now. And they felt very nice. There was no letting go, now.

"That's all that old insurance sales experience coming out of you," Sackett said with a trace of a smile. "Thank you. I'll wear them with honor."

"But not when you're incognito, of course."

Sackett smiled warmly. "Rather ironic," he said.

Peets took another shot as the telephone rang again. Setting aside his new accoutrements, Sackett answered it with aplomb confidence. "Colonel Peets' residence, and *Captain* Sackett—speaking." Silence. "Thank—thank you, Lieutenant. No, that's all been taken care of—yes. Right, well, we're on our way." Sackett looked at his red-eyed superior as he hung up the phone. The colonel was grinning at him like a proud parent, caught gawking at their favorite child.

"Don't worry about me, Frank. I'm all right. It's not the liquor that's gone to tipping me, if anything, it's the booze that dulls the exuberance. Otherwise, I'd be going around like a complete blithering idiot. I'm so happy."

"You do have a certain aspect, Sir."

"I know what you're thinking. But you're wrong, Frank. Ah, Sackett. How can I get you to understand the magnitude of what is just about to occur? If you could only really know and appreciate where this places us in military and American history. It just makes me feel—I don't know how to put it—I think one way to describe it would be that it feels I've gone up to Mt. Sinai and been allowed to drink from the cup of trembling."

"Yeah, but to anyone else it will look like eighty proof trembling, Sir."

Peets grinned. "Guess you better make me some coffee in the time we have left."

"Just need to put a fire under it." Then Sackett hesitated to leave, "You know, it's funny you mention Mt. Sinai. I remember in Leviticus that two of Moses' nephews were burnt to a crisp for making an unholy offering there."

"But their father, Aaron, worked things out to keep the other two alive, didn't he? Just make the coffee, Captain."

CHAPTER SIXTEEN
Double Duty

In the barracks, lights out would occur in less than an hour and its soldiers were therefore finishing making their final toilet runs, and preparing for the next day. Activity in the living quarters is concentrated in those last few minutes. In the military efficiency is the keyword, and it is maintained, or a general lack of preparation is exposed as being self-evident. Something insufferable. For when the lights were turned out, you had better be squared away. More work and less yapping, was the motto. That didn't mean that there couldn't be pleasant exchanges and banter between the troops while they prepared to retire. What it meant was that a man being mouthy could not be tolerated for tying up another man's hands from doing what they're supposed to be doing. A soldier had to be able to do several things, and oftentimes simultaneously. You therefore, invariably, teamed up with a friend to cut the chore's time. Siblings are natural partners for just such enterprise in an institution like the Army, and so Gus and Joe Martin huddled together over their unpolished boots by their bunk area. Joe sat on a milking stool and Gus used his brother's lower bunk. "Not one. Not one, thank you," Joe complained.

"Leave it go, Joe."

"I mean, they didn't even beg for the calls. You just went up and asked for them all, and didn't anyone say scat."

Joe reached across to the bunk and retrieved three cotton balls, next to his brother on the gray, scratchy wool blanket. He dipped the large ball into an inverted boot polish lid, with a skimming of water in it and began making quick circles over the newly-waxed boot's toe.

"Momma was all right," Gus said.

"You got through to her, huh?"

"Yeah. She misses you."

"Oh-kay."

"Joe, you know—you're really no better than the other guys around here that you're so put up about. At least they made a call. Here you had the chance, and wouldn't even bother. Now I may be younger, but I don't think our mother should be treated like that."

"Stow that, junior. Tell me what she's doing for her security, the hell with sentiment. Was she feeling safe?"

"I told her that if things get dicey around there, for her to take Daddy's old shotgun out of the cabinet in the basement and stay down there."

"She goin' to do it?"

"You know Momma ain't touching no part of no gun, but I think if push comes to shove, she might."

"That broad a lot tougher than you give her credit for, Gus. She been through some stuff, believe me. And I ain't just talking about Daddy, neither. Hold on a minute, we need some more cotton." Joe leaned back on the stool and yelled out, "Hey! Who out there has some cotton and boot black to spare?"

The response that came was readily given, flippant in its tone and denigrating in its civility, one soldier said behind some cover, "Don't tell me you Toms over there done run out of cotton!" Somebody else then added, "I hear them two niggas got the market cornered. What they doing without some cotton?" There was a good deal of yucking going on around them after that comment. That is, there was until Joe went to the middle of the aisle in the dorm, his eyes flashing like struck flint.

"I know whoever said that has got nuts heavy enough to back that up to my face. Because if he ain't, he's damn sure going to end up sucking on mine." Joe's eyes twitched with anger as he scanned up and down the aisles with his eyes, and in between the rows of beds. "That's what I thought."

"I said it—And what if I did?" a lone and defiant private proclaimed as he too stepped into the aisle.

"Now—prepare to wear your nuts for earrings, motherfucker," Joe said stepping towards him.

"Private Martin!" the sergeant's call bellowed through the dorm, putting in end to the bellicose inertia between the two antagonists. In fact, he was at the bottom of the stairs, and didn't even have to be present in order to be a deterrent. They all knew how alert he was. And he kept his shirtsleeves rolled up over his considerable large, shiny and dark brown biceps. They were arms like a boxer, like a blacksmith. No one wanted any part of him if it came down to breaking up a squabble.

"Yessuh," Joe snapped, not taking his eyes off his adversary.

"You and your brother, front and center at the armory and check out your full gear."

Now, Joe *did* take his eyes off his rival, and placed them squarely on Gus, who was just as bewildered by the order. "I didn't mean tomorrow, ladies— get your fucking asses sashaying down to that goddam armory double-time, you maggoty shits!"

They didn't know where they were going to, or what was going to happen, but both Joe and Gus knew that there had only been a cessation in the tensions within the room between some of the men and them. It frustrated Gus to no end that some who didn't even know them, really—had them pegged out for being a couple of house niggers. They resented the brothers for their part in making sure their insurrection never got off the ground. Many believed that if you would report fellow blacks for insubordination, that you then were not as 'cullud' as them. For it was the white board of justice that dispensed all sentences. And if you helped them to mete out punishment on a fellow black, then you were felt to be duplicit with the aims and strategies of the exploiter—the one whom you reported to, and in the end, were really no better than.

Now, Joe and Gus knew that their fellows had looked upon them with new eyes ever since the first night of the riot. Looked at them with the same lack of trust many blacks had on their faces when dealing with unsavory whites. They'd thought they'd overhead some muttering before. But now it was out of the bag, for it was the very first time that they'd actually been confronted about it, to their face. And if it hadn't been for the sergeant being there, there could have been some real damage done to the both of them. And that was unsettling for them, they had to admit.

Those feelings were the converse of how they felt once they joined the other one hundred and twenty-eight men at the gymnasium. For all of them seemed to be above the politics of the moment and simply wanted a chance to serve with honor, and planned service, not insurrection. Some of the men had an idea what was going on from the time they'd picked up their bolt-action M-1 rifles at the armory. At the quartermaster's window, loading magazines into their .45's, more immature members in their party practically swaggered with self-assuredness. Equivocating the weapon to their identity and personality. The more seasoned men, however, didn't feel a need to act with such brashness or audacity.

They were aware of the timeline, the chronology, and history of the Negro soldier's service in the United States. For them, they were simply proud knowing they'd probably have some place set aside for them in a small niche of oral tradition they were shortly about to contribute to.

Apparently, some had been made aware what was happening through a few ranking non-comms, although that hadn't been the case for Joe and Gus. All that those two knew was that they were being sent out armed, into a city, during a call-out for National Guard federalization. This was not the special weekend training they'd been having to attend—that went above and beyond their regular assignments. And they actually didn't know the purpose for that time allocation anymore than they understood why they were selected for the deployment. They definitely had no idea that they'd ever be called upon to demonstrate their untapped potential. But now that that potential was indeed about to be unfurled, whether America was ready for it, or not, they began to recognize how powerful they actually were. Standing next to one another in that gym, they all couldn't help at point or another to stop and just gawk at the bronzed soldiers' assemblage.

In the semi-lit gym, darkened while the lights were warming up, where all that was really left to do was to receive the word to go, there was a palpable force of spirit weaving through it. Staging here would be momentary, at best, having done most of the logistical workload at the armory. So, while awaiting the command, the troops checked one another for soundproofing.

Soldiers need to maintain a degree of stealth, and having paraphernalia jostling about while you moved was not conducive to that end. Canteens needed to be kept full, mess kits secured, and all magazine clips bound with black electrician's tape. Gus and Joe helped one another, taping down adjusted belts on their provided web gear.

In the gymnasium foyer, to the east of where the troops were gathering, Colonel Peets came out of the restroom and approached Captain Sackett as the senior officer patted his breast pocket. "Better now. Brushed my teeth. Got rid of some of that trembling breath," he said. Sackett smiled because he knew the importance of appearances when you administrated. Peets was indeed in control of himself and the situation around him. "Now, let's get out there and open up a new page of history for the blockhouse, shall we?"

In the gym, Gus passed Joe a stick of chewing gum. But he declined, having an aversion to the licorice laden *Blackjack* brand of gum. "Fine. More for me, then," Gus said. "Hey, Joe, bet them fools in the stockade are really kicking themselves in the ass right about now, you think?"

"Just because we're going to Detroit doesn't mean we all should start singing spirituals. This here ain't about nothing, really. It's not what this war, this country, or Detroit, is really all about. In fact, before it's over, we might end up wanting to kick each other in the ass for getting caught up in it."

"You honestly think that?"

"I know so—little brother. I know."

"Well—you can hold your breath if you want to."

"Sorry to deflate your joy, little one."

The double doors swung open. "AATTEN-HUH!" The bark of the sergeant's demand cut through all chatter between the brothers and it echoed up to the steel channel in the rafters. A thunderous clap of boot heels, coming together in automaton unity immediately followed the command. Hands slapped down to sides of fatigue pants with a crack. It was immediate. It was precision. It was glorious. They moved as one, and "many" as "one" is an enemy's worst fear. Be they military, or civilian.

Looking left, the entourage watched Colonel Peets' barrel chest visibly swell as he took in a deep breath, along with a long stare outward upon the assemblage. He felt each man's eyes on him, exulted in it, but even more, he admired the cut and gibe of the men before him. About to represent everything he held dearly.

The north end of the gym had a partially extended bleachers that jutted out from a large bank of lacquered raisers. Peets crossed to the sectioned dais, and his footsteps seemed to be the only sound that emanated in the hall. With surprising grace for a man of his size, Colonel Peets stretched his right leg up and hoisted himself atop the platform by pushing off firmly from his left leg and tow-heading his way forward. Momentarily, with his back still towards the gathering, he struggled a little to right himself after the climb. He went so far as to straighten his coat after his effort. All was definitely going right with him at the moment in this little section of the world. Peets let loose a little bit of a smile as he turned around to face his troops. Simultaneously, and silently, he asked forgiveness from God, for thanking Him for the riot. For it had opened opportunities that wouldn't have existed, otherwise.

"At ease, men. Now, we don't have much time before you need to get leave of the base, so I'll be specific. You all know, or should know, by now, that you're going to riot areas in the city of Detroit. That's understood. But what you have to appreciate is that you won't be doing this in a colored unit. Aiding in the federalization autonomously. No, this time you're to be liaison with white troops, specifically the 701st and 728th MP units." Peets let the news give vent to some mutterings, for he knew this would raise the anxiety level of everyone. After a couple minutes he resumed. "Basically, you will be utilized, to my understanding, as perimeter teams. Keeping citizens from committing crimes to life and property, while the assault teams of MPs move on undesirables and clear buildings. Now that's a very tenuous situation, men, because we're not cops. You must think, therefore. Be aware at all times of where you are, and who you are. For those of you whom it hasn't passed over, this is a historic preclusion to the Negro effort in the war; it's not just a domestic insurrection. This is the dawn of a new beginning, if you'll pardon the cliché. But one person can undermine all the potential for this new threshold being honored. So, do not be the one to undermine our perceived goodwill. If you do—if any of you bring discredit to your unit, be prepared to bear the full weight of my displeasure. I want you to use the maximum level of restraint in your civil and military dealings. I should not have to remind you of that which you already know so well, and that is that you will be judged on a double standard. And while that may be true, you should also know that you ultimately can only be evaluated on your singular performance, regardless. The enthusiasm and interest in the training you've been receiving thus far has been exemplary, not only from the invective of the select few among you, but the entire regiment. That dedication assures me that you can, and will, do any and everything that is properly required of you to prove us a credit to the United States Army, the State of Illinois, and the Negro citizens of America. Honestly, the truth of this is very real to me. And very personal, as well. This day, I am as proud of you as a father would be sending his children off to college for the first time. So, now I must send you forth, but only with you knowing that you go with my blessings, each and every one of you. And I order you to return safely, as new men, with new vision and pride, rekindled by a job well done."

The reaction to Colonel Peets' send-off was loud and long because it had been more derivative of a pep rally than the conclusion of a military address. No one, not even Captain Sackett, attempted to quiet the men in showing their feelings for Peets, who, for most of them, epitomized the regiment. It was the colonel's moment and all the leaders knew it was. It was the closest he would come to being a part of this historic force, and he deserved it. The spontaneous hurrahs and whistling flushed the crowd's emotions towards him.

Joe, however, held his jubilation in check. In his mind's eye he saw a vision of what could eventually turn their glee into so many gnashing of teeth. It was the flip side of bravura that Joe Martin saw on the horizon. All-show and no-go. No one knew how whites were going to react to their being there, even if this group was authorized. That's why he was smirking as the others howled around him. That's why he didn't get emotional over the rhetoric in the commander's "orders". Forget all the flag-waving. Joe was going to save his own ass—period. All that hoo-rah-rah wasn't about shit, to him.

In Detroit, at the same hour a police scout car slowed its forward progress. The neighborhood it approached was Negro, and predominated by a six story tall brick building called the Frazer Hotel. It was not far at all from where the officers where at, near the intersection of Brush Street and Vernor Highway. The common sounds of urban life that would usually be there this time of night were not evident in the streets as the police neared the rooming house. A place designated for coloreds should have all sorts of commotion going on. Inside the building, though where there was an absence of lights in the windows, and a lack of radios playing—an eerie cessation of all domestic squabbles further troubled the officers; this was a truly uncommon setting they were coming upon.

Increased anxiety also came from hearing the dispatcher's radio traffic. They knew that in certain areas of Paradise Valley, many homes were ablaze or being harassed with persistent gunfire. In this three-block area, however, the population was strangely removed from all of the surrounding conflagration. And it made the short hairs on the napes of both the officer's necks begin to stiffen. The creeping sensation caused both of them to shudder involuntarily. With more than a little unease, they parked their car in the unseemly, and oh so dark night. "Looks like they busted out all the street lights," the older officer said.

"What are we gonna do?" said the younger cop.

"Well, I can tell you one thing. I don't like this."

"Let's call for some help."

The thick arm of the senior cop stayed his partner from picking up the radio mic. "Buddy boy, like it or not, I'm afraid we got to go check things out." He explained that he thought it best to leave the relative safety of their car and to approach the Frazer. Outside, a circadian fugue, inspired by nature, interluded the officer's debate as they mulled over the situation. The metallic chirps of the crickets, and the nasal, elongated duck call of cicadas made them all the more anxious. A third man in the area, however, a black man, found the insect cacophony to be more of a serenade.

He was in between some abandoned cars, partially covered with some large debris that was also stacked near the garbage dumpsters by the fringe of the asphalt parking lot. He finished quietly opening his sixth can of beer with his can opener as he crouched in the shadows. Then, after chugging half the can down, he took his gun off safety, and waited.

And despite the urging of the junior officer to stay put, the veteran cautiously opened the scout car's door, so as not to alert anyone of the pairs' position. They didn't close their doors shut, in part, for that same logic. That's how serenely quiet the night was. Moving warily, prudently, they stopped when they noticed the bugs screeching ceased. The cops looked around, just in case it was someone else who frightened the insects into the silence. But apparently, it was only the officers to have made the creepy-crawlies quit calling out. After some tense moments, inevitably, the crickets began rubbing their legs again. The cicadas rubbing their wings. The cops approached the curb as the dusky watcher in their midst wiped his sweaty forehead with the back of his hand. The high dew-point of the summer night moistened the steel blue barrel of his gun.

The police were still in line of his sight. And if he could see them, then he knew that if they were lucky, they too could see him. And that was reason enough to make anybody sweat. Yet and still, the sniper appreciated the sense of disaster building in front of him. It gave him a heightened sense of being. Though outmanned, two-to-one, he believed the odds were in his favor. The lead officer placed his foot on the sidewalk, and the officers were south of the hotel entrance. The sniper didn't bother taking aim because a deluge of small caliber weapon fire spewed from the front windows. Rounds scattered as they bounced off the pavement and the patrolmen then knew they had greatly underestimated the firepower of their quarry. One round yelped as it ricocheted off its course on the concrete.

Immediately retreating and scattering back to their car, the young officer felt an impromptu wave of nausea sweep over him; the out-of-shape, veteran officer heaved rough exhalations, and found it increasingly difficult for him not to keep from passing out. He was on the floor of their car and his partner flung himself upon the front seat once he'd retched at the door. He grabbed the microphone.

"We have—we have shots fired! Shots fired! Scout 9-1-4 reporting snipers at Vernor and Brush. Think it's called the Frazer Hotel."

"Scout 9-1-4 that's roger, tango-alpha, code three," the dispatcher replied without a trace of alarm. Just perfunctory acknowledgement and training to set in motion resources to assist them. The second patrolman, the older fellow, moved suddenly. It was as if he was now completely recovered.

"What are you doing?" cautioned the young cop.

"I'm going to the dumpster there; see if we can set a crossfire."

"No. Let's wait for the boys. They're on their way. Let's hold here."

"I'm going, you hear me? And you better give me some cover fire. Them sonsabitches are playing our song, and I'll be damned if I won't dance a little with 'em. Kid, we can't let them get the upperhand, here. Can't let them think for a minute that they can get away with something that is so fundamentally wrong. What's the matter with you? Are you crazy? Turning into a nigger lover, or something?"

The old veteran flatfoot broke out, if one could call it that, with a rapid but wobbling jog that was just shy of being a sprint. The Negro sniper, a trained sportsman, had drawn the shotgun up to his cheek the moment he saw the fat cop break from cover. Minimal aiming was needed as following the law man's flight was not a challenge. Even in the dark. The trigger tension was light and it almost made the assassin pull his shot because of its premature detonation. Through the blue smoke of the rifle's discharge, the sniper could see the effect on the shadow of the officer as the blast found meaty marks.

The officer's legs scissored in the air as he fell forward while smashing his chin to the ground. Normally, one would have braced for such a fall with outstretched arms, but this officer's hands were driven through painful necessity to an area below his waist. He lay shrieking on the asphalt with shreds of the flesh from his testicles squeezing through his fingers. The night became even stiller about him, it seemed. As if only to magnify his agony. But in reality, he was beginning to die. The tongue of the assailant protruded between his own toothy smile as he appreciated his work, and he chuckled with a soft sigh. "That little piggy will get none," he said to himself.

"Man down! Man down!" the young cop wailed. "Jesus H. Christ! They're blasting the hell out of us."

The dispatcher responded and tried reassuring the field officer that help was on the way. And it was then that the junior officer saw the gunman for the first time. The timing of the revelation was fortunate for him because the Negro had repositioned himself from off of the white siding of the building. Wearing a white tee shirt, he had been practically invisible standing in the shadows of a mulberry tree. But now the surviving officer saw the shotgun barrel now being leveled towards him. And great alarm almost left him immobilized, like a transfixed deer caught unawares.

But then, in true Saturday matinee "Tom Mix" fashion, the young man with a badge flashed his right hand down to his revolver and immediately brought the bead in upon the bad guy. He fired his service revolver before another half-second passed, for to have done so any later probably would have meant ill for him. Though the officer had discharged his weapon reflexively into the air from a prone position, his mark was true. The perpetrator of his partner's demise had his pure white shirt suddenly, and starkly, burst forth with a crimson ink stain of spreading blood.

When his knees touched the pavement it was the exact moment that fifty scout cars arrived, from the combined public safety agencies of the City of Detroit and the Michigan State Police. They were prepared to turn the Frazer into a shooting gallery. They brought out deer rifles, shot guns, machine guns, semi-automatic guns, and .38 service pistols. The Negroes inside the hotel were using revolvers and .22 caliber rifles, for the most part. It was a weak defense, but apparently a provident one, up until then.

Their initial gunplay made the police overreact and a bravado of artillery was now being leased upon the structure; some reported to say there having been 750 rounds expended by some accounts. And all during this time of being barraged, the inhabitants of the hotel just went about reloading what weapons they had. They put up another short-lived affront, but the tide had clearly turned.

For good measure, the officials fired another 300 rounds of ammo even when the tenants began coming out after a cease fire was called. Miraculously, there was only one casualty, and that was to the mortally wounded gunman in the driveway. Lined up against the hotel's brick façade, the Frazer lessees were given brusque treatment. Every man, woman, and child were made to undress in front of one another, and the police. They were all also probed before being allowed to put their belongings back on. The men were not given as thorough a treatment as the women and girls. They were brutalized in the shadows with rough gropings.

Unconscious, but alive for two more days, the old bull placed his bloodied hand on his partner's shoulder before passing out. "That's how it is with 'em, kid." he said, "It's like jabbing at a dog in a corner--whenever it gets hungry. Sooner or later," he groaned. He had to close his eyes and tighten his eyelids in a grimace. After a moment he whispered, "Better believe—one day, it will bite your fucking hand off." His partner could see him struggling to stay conscious just a bit more. Long enough to curse. " Goddam fudge bastards."

CHAPTER SEVENTEEN
A Call for Help

No place in the city was outside of the reach of the rabid hatred that was expressing itself within its boundaries. Areas commonly held to be staid and provincial were full of skirmishes and conflagrations. Governor Kelly finally realized that assessment now as he continued monitoring events from Detroit City Hall. The fever was too virulent. Huddled together with General Gunther and Commissioner Witherspoon, only the lower half of Kelly's suit was illuminated by the desk light in the Police Commissioner's Office. It was the only light on and it barely lit up the walls in the room, and not without good reason. Snipers on the ground were shooting up into the high rises, so it was prudent to be as obsequious as possible. The three men didn't say a word for several long minutes when suddenly a roar came up from streets.

"My God," said Kelly, "there must be ten thousand people down there. Even with all the gunfire."

Gunther didn't bother replying or giving an assessment. He had given ample warning before to the politician and hadn't been heeded. Not one to gloat over misfortune for the sake of a plaudit, the general could only shake his head mildly when Kelly all of a sudden sounded awed by the accrued circumstances. The general simply reached into his uniform coat pocket for a comforting smoke, effectively turning his back from both the governor and the window he was looking out of.

Kelly stood in silhouette against the burnt-orange backdrop of adobe colored buildings across the street. The many fires in the streets caused this harvest aura; in congruency with the screams, some of which were muffled, and some that were painfully explicit. It all resonated upward to the fourth floor window observation perch, and to the ears of the governor. The howls had a mixture of anger and agony that was heart wrenching to him and the wails were punctuated by gunfire or smashing glass. An explosion, followed by a flash of high-yellow luminosity revealed that Kelly was dripping sweat.

"My God. Sweet mother of Jesus, it's got to be ten thousand, at least."

"More like twenty," Gunther finally appraised, through with letting him stew in his juices. Kelly seemed such a smaller man when he had been at the window a moment ago, despite his hulking bulk. Gunther offered him a cigarette but Kelly refused. He just used both his large and doughy hands to wipe the perspiration from his face. The mayor came in and didn't look optimistic.

"We're losing it, Mr. Governor," Jeffries finally got out. "It's as plain and simple as that. There's a huge mob on Woodard. It's almost out of control."

"We have to drop back behind barricades in some places where whites are making incursion into colored areas. We got officers under fire from Negro snipers, too." Witherspoon said.

"We need manpower, Governor," Jeffries pleaded. "It can't get any plainer. Listen to reason." All eyes drew upon the figurative and literal man-in-the-middle, Governor Kelly. He swiped at the sweat on his forearms and then on his cheeks. Placing his hands before him, he even looked like he was seriously contemplating prayer. It was time to fish or cut bait, and the governor never liked hooking his own bait. Though cries played out to him from the streets below, he still couldn't let go of his stewardship.

"The dilemma is clear, gentlemen. But I wondered if the general would care to know what really bothers me about this whole scheme—"

"Now, Governor—"

"It's not too far flung an objective, General," Kelly said, "That is truly the only reason why you are here. Those people down there that I'm about to set you upon have given me their confidence as governor of this great state. I ran on law and order, not just for whites, but for the coloreds too. I pledged to each and every man, woman, and child in this state that they would have security in their persons. Taken out of my prevue, there can no longer be such a guarantee. The army will have full authorization to barge down their doors, or shoot them on sight. That is a complete betrayal of what I ran my election on. I have betrayed my mandate, today."

General Gunther sincerely felt the anxiety with which those words were spoken, and believed he'd been a little too judgmental about this man. "Governor Kelly, my role in your city was initially to assess the situation and to assist you. I hope you believe that. The next thing I'd like to say, Sir, is that during the course of my initial deployment new orders arrived that have to be carried out. That happens, as you know, to soldiers. It should be no surprise that a contingency plan hadn't already been arrived at prior to my leaving Chicago. The need for that contingency has arisen. I admire what you do for the war effort in this great state, I really do. But we do have to move ahead now, so that tomorrow we can say, together, there will be a Detroit standing when this is all over. When everything is said and done, that's really what it's all about, Sir."

"I'll make sure you're quoted as saying that in the papers, General" Kelly sighed, a resigned and beaten man.

With the voice of assent given, Gunther quickly contacted Colonel Krech at the train depot. And he, upon getting the go-ahead, waved down his two lieutenant commanders, a major and a captain. They were double-checking inventories newly received from their quartermasters, and were just about to run consignments on some removed pallets. Once hearing Krech's piercing whistle, they brushed past the communications site on the dock, with its easels and graphs. A topographical map of Detroit, supported by sawhorses, was to the right of an engaged soldier who finished receiving a phone message. Everything was in full operational mode and the major wanted his police battalions to get going. The captain, on the other hand was in charge of logistics, and was only going to get satisfaction out of how well this theater operated. He wasn't going anywhere.

"Gentlemen," Krech called to them. "Just got word that we're to begin moving into positions."

"I'm locked and loaded, Colonel," said the major.

"The command center is satisfactory and functional," the captain reported.

"Good. Now, let's revisit the Cadillac Square deployment. Major, I can't release three more companies to the downtown."

"Colonel, we've been hearing things over the wire and I tell you a hundred men are not going to be able to control about 14,000 people."

Krech pointed out red and blue pins on the topographical map and then looked back at the major. "Blue and red, city troops and unincorporated area controls, pretty much evenly divided. Where would you have me pull those companies from, Bill?"

"Why don't we stagger the deployment, sweeping outward from the city to the outer lying areas?"

"Too much chance of incursion. It's got to go down the way I planned it, fellas. The attack in the colored community there must be coordinated with the simultaneous maneuver in the downtown area. Otherwise, we'll be running back and forth between the two and frankly, I'm not getting into that kind of game, gentlemen."

"But Sir, I'm still short. Now that we're deploying fully, the 175 men I gave up to auxiliary support could sure be used here," the captain objected.

"Everybody's going to be short, Captain."

"Yes, Sir."

"No more complaining about it, get me?"

"Understood," the major capitulated. "Just tell me what you want me to do, Colonel."

Krech looked at his watch. "All right, Major. Fall back here until the Fort Custer contingent arrives—which should be in the next fifteen minutes, or so. Place them in your units and rendezvous with Delta Company in Paradise Valley."

"But I thought—"

Krech looked up from the clipboard he was going over and stopped the major's contrary rebuttal—cold. "Captain, go and conduct theater radio check, if you please." Krech's eyes didn't leave staring at the major fully while he returned the captain's salute. "Are we having a little breakdown in morale, Major? Because if we are, you need to tell me any and all reservations you may have about the assignment. I need to know particulars, now. It's not like you to be so close-to-the-vest."

"Well—fact of the matter is, Sir, it's probably not what you'd think it'd be. It's true, I ain't had the experience dealing with colored troops, the way Drummond has. In fact, it actually bewilders me why he doesn't head up the Paradise detail, but be that as it may. The issue isn't about the color of the skin of my men. Deep down in my heart of hearts I really feel that. It's just that, I'm not so sure my units will get to see any real action given the clean-up role we'll more than likely be playing. And that doesn't sit well."

"So, you believe you are being kept in the margins?"

"A day ain't ever come when I lace up my boots that I'm not ready for full head-on battle, Colonel. I don't cotton to pulling a sweep-and-weep detail, but, so be it. I just think it's a poor utilization of resources."

"So, it's the action you're craving?"

"Hell, yes."

"What's make you so sure you won't be seeing any?"

"Not like there will be downtown. And when have there ever been a bunch of coloreds put in the middle of any real tactical maneuvering? No, Sir. I can see the writing on the wall. And it's got me on the outside looking in."

"And you don't like that, do you? Bill, take solitude in the fact that as long as there are a predominant number of whites who feel as you do, you can pretty much count on having this kind of thing happening every couple of decades, or thereabouts. So, if you'll allow me to act in your interests, maybe I'll just put your name at the head of the list for action in 1964, okay? Would that suit you?"

The major looked at Krech with not a little bit of derision after the commanding officer turned away. Social psychology was not his strong suit.

At the beginning of the end for the downturn mobs, they were oblivious as to how Emergency Plan White was about to be unleashed. The teeming mischief makers were too exultant in their anarchic reverie to hear the approach of the armed services transport trucks' engines. The actual numbers of rioters in Cadillac Square were only a few hundred, or so. The white spectators there, however, numbered in the thousands. And they only added to the confusion as they watched the smaller wrecking crews continue to do damage to life and property on Woodard Avenue.

The far end of the boulevard was a screen of obscuring, greasy black smoke and flames from burning cars. This tactically advantageous position further obliterated the view of the far-off deuce-and-a-half trucks and the troops that had just disembarked from them, and from the eyes of the disorganized throng. So caught up in the disobedience of their collective moment, they failed to notice three hundred fifty soldiers forming by the canvassed vehicles. Without warning and with stealth expediency, the regiment took positions that lined across the breadth of the avenue.

"Bayonets, Sergeant," the major ordered, "arms at high port."

"Yessir." The sergeant, baggy-lidded and of a slightly squinted eye, took his chewed stubby out of his mouth. He was a caricature of a barrel-chested noncom, fit for the newest *Warner Bros.* cartoon and a *Daffy Duck* episode. His bottom lip wore the distended seer he seemed to have stamped onto his face. He threw the cigar remnant away right in front of the officer's jeep and turned to his company.

"All right, boys. Get them pig stickers on those weapons," he commanded as tobacco juice drooled from the corner of his mouth.

The federal troops affixed their bayonets on their rifles with imprecise alacrity and awaited the next command.

"Port shoulder! Arms!

At this command all the enlisted men brought their weapons to bear in front of their chests with a loud slap of unity that disintegrated any ambivalence as to the job they were about to do. To a man, each soldier felt the same way, as if he was gearing up for a battle with an enemy on foreign soil. This was in stark contrast to the civilians who were on this side of Woodard. For they were sure the troops had come there to protect them from black agitants. The more observant and cautious onlookers, however, decided now was the time for them to head to their homes.

"Citizens of Detroit! Clear the area," the major ordered, using a bullhorn by his side. "This city is now under federal law. You are ordered to disperse and observe curfew."

There were many still standing in the way, yet. And the major shook his head, but it wasn't from sadness. "All right, Sarge. Let's move them out."

With an arcing sweep of his right arm from behind him to in front of him, the sergeant obliged. "Forward! Harch!"

The left-footed step-off of the militia, all carrying their rifles from hip to shoulder in front of them, all wearing identical stoic masks of dispassion, looked like some nickelodeon propaganda films that both the Germans and Americans were guilty of producing. But this was happening in America.

As they moved north, sweeping the rabble-rousers before them, it became apparent to official and unofficial observers that the rampage in Detroit's downtown was finally going to come to an end. But for the men working on the outskirts of the metropolis, success wasn't as clearly distinguished. Houses darkened in the distance, with pitch black silhouettes and roofs afire were the first sight the Fort Custer entourage saw. Flames stretching along the Vernor Highway appeared to some like orange hair was at the base of the horizon, buffeted by a wind that was increased in its volume by the heat it produced. The GI's bodies instinctively reacted, and autonomic chemistry pulsated with adrenaline numbing overdrive as they prepared to expend themselves in this Darwinian struggle.

A file of jeeps downshifted as they passed Joe and Gus. They were two out of sixty-two Negro troops embedded among the columns of white foot soldiers. Two of the soldiers ahead of the Martin brothers, one them Gus believed to be the platoon leader, spoke casually to his friend, as if Joe or Gus didn't exist. "Oops!" one of them said, taking full advantage of being within earshot of the nearby colored soldiers, and causing some other whites to look their way. "Ooops, it's starting to get a little spooky around here, isn't it?" No one bothered saying anything, but that didn't stop him.

Three more jeeps just passed the company then and Gus appreciated the timing because Joe's expletives were drowned out in the process. Captain Sackett was in the rear of the last jeep, and looking to his left, he thought he recognized some of his men. He tried harder to identify one especially, whom he'd heard cursing as the command jeep passed. Eventually he turned around, though, and they traveled farther north, in the direction of the glowing fireball of crisped buildings.

"Hey," the instigating white soldier said to his marching counterpart, "Ain't that the 728?"

"Could be."

148

"Man, I wouldn't mind riding in a jeep, about now."

"Why?"

"Beats walking. That's all." Then he looked over his shoulder, directly at Joe. "But nowadays, they'd probably make us ride 'nigger', anyways."

A white buck sergeant, who had been running up to the front of the marching formation overheard some of the derision festering in the ranks. "You put a cork in it, right now, mister," the sergeant chastised as he double-timed past.

Once far enough ahead, the noncom brought the company to a halt and had them squat down alongside the road. Some took off their helmets, sitting on them and rolling cigarettes with practiced speed and coordination between hands, teeth, and paper and tobacco. The wisecracking service man, the one the sergeant just stuffed, attempted to groom an unruly tuft of his brown hair from off his forehead after taking off his helmet.

"Listen up, and pass this along," the sergeant went on. "The 728th has cleared and secured downtown, now it's our turn to shine. D company, from the 728th, will rendezvous with us at the Frazer. It's a hotel, about a half click up the road."

"What are we looking at, Sarge?" one the permanent troops asked.

"Just like we practiced it, boys," the sergeant explained. "As we approach cross streets up here, look for whites with clubs, bricks, and rocks—"

A few cowboy whoops pealed out.

"As you were!" The sergeant waited for anyone else to make light of the situation, and after a half minute and a reproachful glance, continued, "They are picking up anything and everything they can find to use as weapons as they try to break through into the colored section of town, here."

"This been happening anyplace else, yet?"

"Several instances," the sergeant confirmed. "Inside the area, groups of whites are beating up coloreds and setting fires to their homes."

Joe and Gus could almost physically feel the stares directed at them, hailing down upon them, and on all the other colored troops gathered there with them. A silence, combined with concerted stares from underneath the brims of some of the pot helmets seemed to ask the unasked question, "What do think about that?" Individuality and self-determination become lost when one is cloaked in otherness. The white troops looked for cracks of weakness, or uppityness, in the bronzed visages amongst them.

"A main concern, also, gentlemen, is the report of both colored and white sniper nests in the vicinity. So, y'all look sharp—mind the p's and q's, boys."

"Stop it, Sarge. You're making me thirsty." The crack broke the tension for a few seconds and then the conversation plunged back into its intended objective, and obvious anxieties.

"What's our response to be when we come into contact with these hostilities?" There was complete silence, for a long time, and Gus wish he'd never had said anything just then. Joe was gawking directly at him, his eyes warning his little brother. The silence was agonizingly long.

"Feets don't fail me, now," the towheaded soldier teased, attempting to break the tension as his fellow had, but failing miserably at it. But he snickered anyway.

"What's that?" the sergeant testily asked.

"Well, Sarge," the towhead began to counter, "if these boys here act anything like the 92nd did in the first war, we'll—"

"This ain't the first war! What you know about the first war, anyhow? Since it was over five years before your redneck ass was born." But the sergeant's honorable defense of the Negro soldiers fell short of being a vote of confidence because the damage had already been inflicted. The mention of the 92nd Division's infamous service in World War I had commingled anew with all the suspicions and unreasonable notions many of the white troops felt about being deployed with Joe and Gus, and all the others. Ill-equipped, and undertrained, a Negro division had been easily run off of the front by the Germans. No matter how much the sergeant honored them, most of the white soldiers began wondering seriously if they'd be able to count on the colored platoons forced upon them. But there seemed to be no doubt in the sergeant's mind and he had a directive to carry out. He turned to face Gus and gave him an earnest and respectful reply.

"You all got a couple canisters of CS gas. It was developed 15 years ago, and the initials stand for cock sucker." Guffaws and shrieks of laughter. The sergeant smirked, and let the commotion die down. "If we have a mass of people to disperse," he continued, "we'll use those first and sweep through. They won't want to hang around with this CS crawling up their noses. And if they do bolt towards us, drive 'em back with the butts of your gun."

"So, no shootin'?" the towhead questioned. "That's one helluva way to have a coon hunt."

Joe's eyes became almost blacked out slits as he stared across at his nemesis. The smoke from Joe's cigarette plumed forcefully from out of his nose, screening his face somewhat. He flicked the smoldering butt across the way, like a mortar, at the towhead's boots, who quietly glanced at it, and then back at Joe. The sergeant didn't see what happened between them.

The towhead leaned over to whisper to a white troop who was nearby and witnessed the uppity response. In barely a sotto voice the agitator said, "Well, now. Seems to me that I should consider myself fired upon, shouldn't I?"

"Pass what I said along," the sergeant said rising, "and let's get moving, gentlemen."

Everyone had to stretch out little hitches in their muscles, especially their backs, and as Gus arranged his pack he gave his brother a wary eye and he could see that a switch had gone off in Joe. One that could be seen activated by the look in his eyes. And it made Gus more than a little nervous, given Joe's prior history in failing to control anger and impulsivity.

"Well, Joe," Gus said. "I guess we can't complain too much about doing just a little more walking, can we? At least we got dry socks."

Joe cinched up his web gear. Still staring at the towhead that had his bucket on top of his head, now. "Joe? You hear me?"

"I've just about had it with that hillbilly, over there."

"C'mon, Joe. He was only trying to get a rise outcha."

"Might rise up something better left kept asleep, if he ain't careful."

"You don't mean none of that."

"Hell I don't. Watch."

"Joe?"

"Yeah," he replied, grunting as he adjusted his backpack so his spade didn't dig into his hip.

"You ain't scared, are you?" Gus asked softly.

"Scared? Naw, man. I'm not scared."

'Me neither, really, but all the same, between you and me and the devil on the hill—keep an eye out for me, okay?" Gus watched Joe turn to look his way and give him a paternal look. For a moment, with the half-closed eyes and a slant of smile, Gus saw his daddy, juxtaposed with a hint of their mother's high cheekbones. At that moment it was all the reassurance he needed.

"Yeah, Auggie, you do the same for me, okay?"

"I'ma hold you to that, now"

They began walking.

"Uh-huh."

"So, you can't do that sittin' in the brig."

"I told you, I got you. Leave it alone."

As the company approached a bend, with a dark road shouldered by tall grass and thick, dark trees, everyone could feel the potential for a skirmish coming up. Then the popping started. The rioters didn't have many weapons, in comparison to the military, but what deer weaponry and shotguns they did possess, they brandished with a defiance that split the company apart as they ran for cover.

The GI's lobbed four tear gas grenades along both sides of the tree line; where the sniper fire was closest to them, and because of the opulent and full moon's light, and the gas's grey-blue veneer of smoke, ghostly figures momentarily defined themselves. A voice shouted out from the quirky scene, cursing the irritating smog, and then a well heard remark followed. "Hey, look at this!" came the phantom civilian's exclamation. It had to have been a civilian because it was clearly understood and all the army personnel had on masks. "Hey, they got colored G.I.'s with 'em!"

"Nigger lovers!"

"Well, if that—that don't beat all. Let's let 'em have it!"

Instantaneously, it seemed a fusillade of stones and bricks began flying through the air as the skirmish became invigorated by the kerosene of renewed prejudice flung on the embers of the mob's angry focus. There was a tympanic thumping of flesh, and alarmed grunts from the troops as bruises were inflicted. The soldier's held muster, however, and inundated the area with even more gas, driving away the culprits. It looked like there was a fog near the ground, the concentration of the CS was so pervasive in the area.

Just as the soldiers began to give chase the sergeant collared the towheaded soldier's friend as he ran past him. "Platoon leader, take your unit up the road for a full click and get it cleared for us, you understand me?"

"Yeah, Sarge. But do you think you got a handle on this yet?"

"We'll be all right, but we got to get down the road. We're pulling 'em back, here."

The corporal looked to his left and saw Joe and Gus double-teaming a trio of rioters with the butts of their rifles.

"Hey, you two," the corporal yelled at them. "We gotta move out. Sarge says, now."

The civilians who were being chased saw the distraction as the perfect opportunity for dropping their stones in their hands and high-stepping out of the vicinity. "Where are we going?" Gus asked. By this time the towheaded soldier had joined the platoon leader and felt it necessary to add his demand to the situation.

"Martins! Both of you get your black asses moving and boy I mean, right now! You hear?" And justifiably so, the towheaded soldier was summarily knocked to the grass by a well-placed stone being thrown. Gus smirked, but Joe laughed. They went over to give what help they could, but were less than earnest in mitigating the towhead's discomfort.

"It was some dad-blame coon-shit! I saw him," the towhead winced, grabbing at his ear, blood in thin rivulets around his knuckles. The platoon leader assisted his buddy to a stooped position when the eyes of the wounded peckerwood widened in alarm as he looked past Gus's shoulder. Simultaneously turning their heads in the direction of Joe, the platoon leader and Gus could see Joe placing the butt of his rifle into the pocket of his shoulder.

"Joe! No," Gus pleaded.

The towhead's mouth gaped wide in anxiety, in a silent scream as his eyes scrunched closed, not willing to look at the death coming his way. The report of the shot replayed upon the static night's air, and everyone cracked their necks to see what had happened.

Gus was relieved when he didn't see the towhead's head or chest erupt into slushy hamburger, and he was still standing. He knew Joe wasn't that bad of a shot, and if he'd wanted to shoot him, that peckerwood would have been dead. And while Gus was confounded the towhead was elated. Shrieks of his laughter, upon realizing he was still alive, were punctuated by the heavy fall of a body to the ground.

The deceased was a young Negro, a boy of about seventeen, maybe, and he had a deer rifle by him. The stock partially covered with his downed bulk. He was large for his age, and probably a little too clumsy and slow to play the role of an assassin.

The towhead couldn't believe the shot that had been made. And Joe didn't speak a word until he came eyeball to eyeball with the soldier he just saved.

"Well, boss," Joe glowered, "Seems to me, my aim must work near as good as my feet. Wouldn't you say?"

Joe slung his rifle over his shoulder and walked past both of the perplexed white soldiers, and Gus followed shortly, walking backwards for a few feet to make sure they wouldn't be stopped by warranted or unwarranted surprise. They headed further down the road to Paradise Valley.

CHAPTER EIGHTEEN
The Visit

All the lights east of the south end of Woodward Avenue were extinguished, for the most part, but there was evidence some people had still stayed behind. Either that or they simply made a flimsy attempt at appearances of being home to ward off the looters and interlopers. Serving notice that whoever came up the walkway was going to be watched. The cicadas—those metallic sounding, clarion calling insects, heralded the approach and arrival of the soldiers to the neighborhood with on again, off again, rapports to each other. Gus heard them rubbing their wings again just as soon as he broke off from his file, which now patrolled in another neighborhood a few blocks over. Joe was in that group, and he didn't know exactly when Gus suddenly was not by his side any longer, but Joe wasn't worried he'd gone. Neither was Gus. For good reason. Beaubien Street was all too familiar to him.

Radios were on, some with their music, or some tuned in to *The King Biscuit Hour* or the eerie *Inner Sanctum*. The sounds perked up Gus's ear as he passed the homes in the first block, or so. Not too many were resting inside, he guessed, and an occasional gunshot in the distance reminded the civilians that it was best for only soldiers to be tramping around, yet. On some houses, therefore—those with the lights off, and no sign of anyone at home, Gus softly jiggled the doorknobs to see if they were secured. Satisfied with one, he moved on to the next.

A moist gale of air receded the sounds of the music and broadcasts from the areas ahead of him in the upcoming block, and cooled the brow on Gus's sweat-dampened face, and the nape of his neck. Falling into the background of his hearing were the running commentaries, and descriptions of the atrocities that blame laid out, quickly being overcome by the increasing din of the cicadas; "The pastor of Paradise Valley's Presbyterian Church then led over two-hundred rioters through the—" the announcer erroneously droned, to be replaced with the mayor's speech, heard coming out of another house, and his pointed analogy, "The enemy couldn't have accomplished more if they had completed an all-out attack—"

In this block there were no radios on. And only one house with its porch lit. And that was the one Gus stood planted in front of, with a strange mixture of relief and apprehension. The porch of the dark house had warped floor boards and a familiar construction. The house itself was only a single story patchwork, an amalgamation of diverse building materials, mostly covered with tar paper in layers over the exterior frame of boards, to block out chill winds and field mice. Moving past the broken fence and unmowed grass as he walked down the buckled and cracked concrete path to the house, Gus cautiously placed first one foot and then the other lightly on the skeltered porch. With stealthy moves, he sidled up next to the front door, but a floorboard creaked underneath him from him shifting his weight as he tried to economize the number of steps he'd taken. He stood motionless. And he heard a click from inside.

"I don't know who you is," a muffled, strong, but frightened woman's voice spoke up, "but I gotta shotgun in here, pointed right t' the door. You hear me?"

Gus took a further step to the left, but didn't draw his weapon. "Now, ain't no need to shoot, ma'am," Gus calmly declared. "Ain't anybody out here but some nappy-headed fool tryin' not to look like I'm a motherless child."

"Baby?" the woman screamed. And Gus heard the thud of the weapon being set aside and a fugue of locks being fumbled open. "Is that my baby out there, come for his Momma?" Gus couldn't hold back his smile.

"Yes—Ma'am!"

The door opened to reveal a lightly complexioned Negro woman wearing a white terry cloth robe. In the profile of light from the porch, she appeared to be in her latter years of the thirties. Her hair appeared relaxed, but it wasn't. The dark brown waves tendriled in loose curls on her shoulders and framed a face that was distinctly of mixed heritage. She joyously pulled Gus inside with a pull that almost toppled him, and shut the door. Then there was a spontaneous embrace, so physical in its veracity that it concluded with his mother jumping into his arms and wrapping her legs around his waist.

She flung off his helmet and began planting loud and smacking kisses all over the top of his head, and Gus twirled her around in happiness. "I'm so glad you're all right," Gus said.

Between kisses Mrs. Martin replied, "I heard on the radio—*mmuah*, that they was calling out, *mmuah*, *mmuah*, the National Guard, but I never—*mmuah*, in my wildest thought I'd end up seeing you here!"

Had this been a public display some people might have been a little disturbed at seeing this rapture between them. The two looked more like young lovers, than mother and son. In fact, for one moment, some unease did cross Gus's mind as he noted his mother's shapely legs because it was his mother's custom to not wear any underwear when she was in her bed clothes. He gently lowered her to the floor, within arm's reach of the forewarned shotgun. "Just look at my baby boy," she squealed. "You so grown up, and handsome. And such a—" She grabbed Gus by his shoulders and looked him in the eyes; "You ain't AWOL, is you?"

"Momma!"

"Sorry—"

"But I guess technically—"

"Gus!"

"We're patrolling, so I'm on duty. But, Momma, I had to come check up on you. You can understand that, can't you?"

"Well—we all do what we's got to sometimes, honey." Mrs. Martin said coyly. That allusion let Gus know his mother didn't condemn him. She had to bend the rules herself, at times. That's how she got the job downtown at Davenport's department store working at the cosmetic counter instead of scrubbing toilets, passing herself off as white. In fact, a white confidant had let her use their West side address and claimed her as a tenant in order for his mom to complete the ruse. So, she understood what necessity dictated to be done, and why consequences be damned, sometimes. Gus moved the shotgun.

"I can't stay long. Joe's out here, too," he said softly.

His mother's response was a mixture of emotion, almost as commingled as her ethnicity. She looked up to her taller, darker son, and a wave of concern deepened and gave way to pained misgivings. "How is your brother?" she asked, trying to force a detachment of any feeling, one way or the other.

"Oh, you know Joe, Momma. He takes care of himself."

"That's what worries me."

"He's about five blocks away," Gus said and gave his mother another hug. There was tightness in his throat that spread down to his chest as he inhaled, struggling over how to tell his mother what had happened. Even he himself didn't know what would come of it. "Momma, Joe ended up shooting somebody."

She placed a light hand on Gus' left shoulder and her eyebrows arched in surprise, "A white man?" she asked.

"No'm. Colored, but he was drawing down on one of us."

"One of who? What's that crazy niggah doing shooting at his own kind for?"

"I told you, Momma. The guy was fitting to shoot a white soldier. Oh, momma, I really got no time to explain, but I'm here right now. And I got to get back to my unit, soon."

Mrs. Martin affectionately held Gus's chin in her two cool and silky hands, and gently pulled his face down towards hers, so she could look him in the eyes. She then kissed him on the forehead again and ran her fingers alongside his head. "Thank you, Jesus. Yes, yes, baby." She pumped out gratefully. "You hungry?" she asked, and started to walk across the room to the kitchen before even getting an answer. "Lemme make you a nice sandwich before you go."

"Momma, I really—"

"You got time to get something to eat," she said. "Ain't but three steps over to the ice box." And that was more than apparent. There was not even space for a formal dining table to eat at, and no door to separate the cooking area from the rest of the compact dwelling. "And I ain't had ice brought here for two days and I don't want this ham to turn before what I have melts."

Gus's mother took a couple of steps to her right, opening a small pantry and pulling out a half loaf of bread. Before opening and releasing the brass handle on the wooden *White Clad*, she reached for a cigarette on top of the rectangular appliance, and a blue-tipped wooden match from a small cardboard box. The match head popped, and made a little flower of fire when Mrs. Martin ran it quickly against the grain of the ice box. Gus could see her hands shake as she tried lighting the rolled tobacco.

"You'd think I had the trembles, the way I'm shaking. All this damn coffee I been drinking." The cigarette stopped seesawing up and down in her pinched mouth once she finished talking, and there was a half smile of embarrassment. Gus knew that his mother sometimes would go on a tear with some gin, every now and then. Ever since his father's death, but he would have known if she had been drinking. And he was sure she hadn't. Finally lighting her smoke.

She took the ham butt portion out of the refrigerator after she exhaled a plume of smoke, set the plate on her counter next to the bread, and then got out a small jar of mustard, and a block of cheese.

"Thank the Lord it weren't no white man your brother killed," she said, in the way of an interrupted reflection.

"I don't know if he was dead, Momma. He just shot the man, is all."

Puffs of smoke rose in small billows over his mother's right shoulder as she deftly cut thin slices of the ham, and the perforated Swiss cheese, putting them in layers on the open-faced bread to her right. Gus's heart beat with invigorated love for her as he watched. His mother always went through the extra effort to make sure she cut Gus's meat portions for his sandwiches in finely sheared carvings, unlike Joe who liked the assurance of getting hefty servings on demand. She was making several of the snacks. "That may be, Gus. But all I know for sure is," and here she turned her head towards Gus for emphasis, squinting from the smoke getting in her right eye. "Your brother's got a shootin' type of mind about him. So, I ain't surprised." She turned her attention back to applying some mustard on the delicatessen manufacturing line she had going.

Gus received the sandwiches for him by giving his mother a kiss on her cheek and he sat down at the small table. Once she saw him imbibing from his canteen and taking large bites from the meal she made, Mrs. Martin then sat down on her couch by the draped window and put her feet up on the matching hassock and took small bites from her own.

"Momma?"

"What, baby?"

"Do you know how this all got started?"

"Now, don't go asking me nothing I ain't got the answer to, Sugar." And Mrs. Martin swiveled her hips on the davenport and brought her feet quickly to the floor. In one swift moment she was up and walking back into the kitchen and pulling two coffee mugs out of a cabinet. "Where did it start? Where does it always start?" She poured the steaming cups and brought one over to her son, who was now mauling his second sandwich. "But I tell you one thing. I sure know where it ended up. Yessuh, right here in my front yard."

She sipped her coffee and looked over the rim of her cup at her son. "White mens and polices comes through here, like the world had come to an end, for two days now. They be shootin' niggahs right and left. And what's worse, to me least ways, is we got our own fightin', robbin' one another. And that's why I'm a little disgusted with Joseph."

Gus glanced back over at the shotgun, and then back to his mother who had a chewy piece of gristle stuck near an incisor that she was trying to get loose without being indelicate. Eventually she took her uplifted pinky finger to work at the sinew, "Pardon me," she said. She was an enigma, indeed. Here at home she dropped the façade of whiteness she kept up to keep her job, and let her language sway lazily. But then, at the most unexpected moment she would act genteel. Gus grinned, for to him, she was the epitome of beauty and grace, and he could never imagine her to be someone to be disgusted or embarrassed by.

Gus cleared his throat. "Uhm, how did you get up the nerve to—uh? Y'-know?"

"To what?" she asked, and then caught his askance look. "Oh, how did I pick up your daddy's gun? You know, I never could get rid of it. Even after the 'accident'. Something told me to hold on to it. Couldn't stand to look at it, even dust it off, but I keep holding on to it."

"I'm surprised. I know Joe would be."

"I bet he would, too."

"But why, Momma?"

The small firecracker popping of another match, and she lit another cigarette after she finished her coffee.

"Why? Because I had two boys to raise without a man around the house, that's why. I figured one day, I'd have to use it to either protect my family. Or, in your brother's case, to protect me. I knew when the time came, if I needed to, I could pick that damn thing up. And use it, too. Lord, help me."

"I gotta go, Momma." Gus took the last bites of his sandwich and gulped down what was left of the now lukewarm coffee in his mug.

She reached over to him as he rose from his chair and touched his face and stroked the arms of the uniform, fawning over her soon to be departed child, but she didn't feel all that anxious. "I want you to write me, hear?" she admonished.

"Yes'm."

She pulled a white handkerchief out of a drawer in the kitchen and wrapped two chunky ham sandwiches in it, and put them into Gus's hands.

"You give these to your brother."

Gus carefully put them into a cargo pocket alongside his fatigue's lower leg. They hugged one last time and she held on to his arm as Gus crossed his way to the front door.

"August?"

He turned.

"You tell Joey—tell him that no matter what's happened—well, what's passed has passed. The past stays in the past, that's what you say to him, okay? And you tell him—"

"Yes, Momma?"

"You tell him his momma still loves him. Do that, okay?"

Gus pressed his lips for the last time that night against her moist, and soft as dough, cheek. "I love you, Momma," Gus whispered in her ear. Opening the door.

"I know you do, baby. Come see me soon, too. Y'hear?"

And then he looked back at his mother in the doorway, before he stepped away from the porch landing. He badly wanted to sound encouraging, but instead only could come up with a feeble response.

"I'll try, Momma. I'll try." And he was gone. The night taking him back again, as silently as it had delivered him.

CHAPTER NINETEEN
Months Later

At Fort Custer, Captain Sackett's staff car negotiated the slush piled along the curbs and streets in white and gray boulders of snow. The vehicle behaved well in the inclement conditions, mechanically impervious and driving steady.

"Steady and ready", he thought to himself, looking out the back seat window. Like most colored officers, Frank filled his hours of underutilization with personal activities when he wasn't involved in some quaint custom, or downright futile project that could be classified as: busy work. His promotion had not elevated him to any heights of daring, and he hadn't expected it to, but he didn't want to get into the self-fulfilling mindset too common amongst his peers. For many, hoping they could do something meaningful in the war had become something of a waning fervor. They were relegated to being perennial service bridesmaids, and they knew it. A bridesmaid was the only thing you could compare them to, for a best man is a supportive equal. No, bridesmaids were accurate because of the emasculated roles the colored commanders played. They were not entered into the equation for winning, and probably never would be. Officers like Sackett came to understand how the Army admired someone looking like they were doing something, even when it meant there was nothing at all being done. You had to think about staying busy in this war because every moment counted, you were told. Sackett wiped the condensation from his car window. "Counted for what?" Sackett almost said aloud.

And the snow began falling. It came up suddenly and soon the only differentiating characteristic of the landscape horizon was that at times one could make out the slightly darker gray of the skyline amidst the whipping snow. Otherwise, buildings, weaponry, parked vehicles, all of them became subsumed in the perspective warping of the storm. It was beginning to look like everything was being erased by all the white.

A fitting sentiment, maybe, for the time of year. The Army, as the rest of Americans, rejoiced especially at the hope a new year could bring. It was around the holidays, especially, when the repeated absence of a peace brokerage filled even the most stoic with a brimming sentimentality, every now and then. To the men overseas it might seem as God and the rest of the world had cast them all aside, but a new year allowed for some hope; a hope that the Nazis would get to a point where they would finally capitulate, and get on with being civilized again. After all, you could only fight a losing battle for so long, but it seemed the jerry troopers were holding fast. They knew where the line was weakest, and believed they had the advantage in time and manpower. The battles now came so fast and fierce, so hard fought, and on both fronts of the axis, that many an American foot soldier simply wished the enemies were getting as sick of the slaughter as they were. That they felt the same way.

It was December 31, 1943, Sackett mused, and the United States Army was just as strapped to the limits for a want of men, as they had ever been. But they still refused induction of Negro troops into the European Theater.

In the rumple seat at the back of the car, Sackett was distracted from that quandary as he could only marginally recognize the areas he passed now. And that was due, in no small part, by him remembering certain familiar tree formations that were along the way of their travel. Relatively aware of his surroundings, the young captain became entranced by the maelstrom of nothingness in the white and gray blizzard outside of the car's warm interior. And he analyzed the immediate situation at hand.

Americans were growing aggrieved and belabored of all the killing from the war. Heavy casualties in Europe and the South Pacific had weighed upon the society in increasing numbers and the toll scratched at the vitals of the nation's progeny. Two out of every five families had men serving, and these were God-fearing men, for the most part. And every year their families and brethren asked the Almighty to renew their faith by making a lasting peace, but the unilateral agreements for tranquility never seemed to take hold. It was a marathon, not a foot race.

Supplying men, weapons, and technology, and lying them at the portal of the forces that time held sway over, seemed to be the only way to hopefully bringing the pendulum of chaos nearer to a standstill. The American industrial front proved that it could manufacture itself out of almost anything, and had created a veritable military-industrial revolution. It led the world in manufacturing. But how much would be needed to end the terror and domination? Would we have to produce a weapon so awful that only it could stalemate the German juggernaut? And what could an alternate plan be?

Sackett's reverie soon gave way to guilty feelings as he speculated about himself and his men. Here he had a whole division of men, and they sat here in America stomaching first a Thanksgiving dinner, and then a Christmas feast, and now the New Year's respite, without having fired a shot at the enemy. Even worse, he thought of the condition the men were in being returned; many with morbid detachments of limbs, drumsticks or wings absent. As carved up as a turkey or a ham on laden tables. At what cost did Americans know how they were able to enjoy their blood red cranberry sauce, at what benefit was their Christmas gravy they sopped up with Parker House rolls?

How could they ever fill the seat left empty for years?

And the melancholy Sackett felt upon that reflection was more than enough self-pity than anything else. He acknowledged how awfully solitary his life was, at this moment. He wished there was someone waiting for him today. Someone back at Thanksgiving to care whether or not his footsteps were coming to their door. And the guilt and pity were bookends to the depression he felt each time the holidays came around. Every time they came around, for years now.

But he had to brighten up. The service had become his family, and married to the mission was his betrothal. Sackett wondered if he was becoming as clichéd as the saying, and joined to the hip with the rest of the hackneyed service men who had spent their entire adult lives in the military. The men who were really heroic, in his mind were the ones who fought in spite of having families wishing them out of harm's way. They adamantly believed, in the vault of their will, that the mission at hand was only second to that of doing God's work in battle, and their families occupied the third rung of the ladder. Sackett looked in the rear view mirror, then to his right, and back again to the window nearest him.

"Everyone did something to contribute", he decided, and as long as you were ready to answer the call when it came, you could hold your head high. There was the larger goal, which was so large you didn't even understand all its components, but it had a moral authority and thereby achieved its congregate validity. To play a part, or to be a part in a good thing, no matter how tedious, is certainly more honorable than to being soiled in one singular and quick misstep.

Which is what he wanted to avoid. What could possess the colonel to holding him to honor the sordid barter he'd made last summer? That Sackett achieved becoming a commissioned officer, in the first place, was above and beyond anything he had ever dreamed of. And that was the main reason Colonel Peets' delusion about him masquerading as a service man was simply too distasteful for him to even entertain. But, upon further reflection, for the pure joy it seemed to bring into the elder man's sandstone colored eyes, well, Sackett now wished he'd patronized his commander more. Sackett blamed himself for not being more observant. What else but dementia from miniscule strokes could have accounted for the Fort Benning scheme that Peets had thought up? And Sackett remembered how prideful the colonel looked at him as they drank the scotch whiskey with Colonel Krech. It was a sanctimonious gaze, not unlike that of a father to a son. Sackett felt a physical tug below his heart. Peets'body was failing him. To witness the slow moving, but sum-total rejection of a person's will upon their body—an individual who seemed to be the only—family. "Oh, my," Sackett said to himself. His former comparisons of duty and honor and family were wrapped around his new awareness now, and inside, it made him weep. His eyes misted for moment, but he knew he could not let the driver see his turmoil, and he looked at the rear view mirror again, to be assured he wasn't being stared at.

Peets had no immediate family either, his wife and son were killed in a car accident a dozen years ago. Peets had been the captain's surrogate father, and he his son. And as such—now it was clearer, Sackett realized that he had been promoted within the service, but demoted to the third rung of the ladder of priorities to the bigger thing. The thing that mattered. The thing he could not fully—"Oh, my", and Sackett began backstepping through the events of the last few months.

The City of Detroit and Washington D.C. could not come up to the task of really figuring out what happened in the riots last summer. The independent commissions that both governments convened seemed to agree on one thing, however, and that was, to a man, that the blame was all pointed at "colored agitators" who had attempted squatter's rights over portions of Belle Island. By the time the contagion of rebellion had peaked, for some unknown and sundry reason, these people thought that they should, and could, take over as much of Detroit as they could possibly lay their hand to.

It was felt by both commissions that the force whites exerted to squash the uprising was necessary at the time, although it was not written in those terms. Who made up the police, after all? And the army? They were the ones who were exerting said force, and they were overwhelmingly white. But they were also judged by other whites to have used lethal force judiciously, and suc-cessfully kept the peace at a time when it had been endangered. Case closed.

Sackett switched the black leather gloves he held in his right hand to his left and then rubbed his cheek for a moment, continuing staring out at the winter landscape. He looked down and began to inspect the veined wrinkles in the hide of his gloves.

"This was called a riot," he thought. But he knew that once upon a time there had been colonists once on the east coast of the continent who'd had a "party" of sorts to rebel against the oppression of an imposing government. One that did nothing to sustain them but to tax them. That party was an honorable and patriotic thing, at the time, let there be no doubt. And Sackett couldn't get that un-military thought out of his subconscious. Somewhere inside of him an ember of individuality began to glow where the smoke of his agitation had previously smoldered. "But," he thought, and Sackett crinkled up his nose as he forcefully exhaled out of both his nostrils, "Let some niggers get uppity because they ain't getting what they feel they got coming, and well—hell, that's a riot." And Sackett slapped the gloves against his palm.

"We're here, Sir."

For the first time in the whole trip Sackett saw more than the white hair in the back of the driver's head. He had a white mustache to match, and looked as iconic as a character on a box of hot cereal.

The chauffeured military carrier pulled into a roundabout drive, recently cleared of piles upon piles of wet snow by frostbit service men. The car parked squarely in front of the base hospital, far away from the curb. "I'll be getting the door for you, Sir," the driver, a first sergeant, said.

But Captain Sackett jumped out quickly as soon as the car stopped, and didn't wait for the driver to open the door. As if he'd grown impatient from all the sitting he'd endured. He stood outside with a fixed deliberation, and adjusted his coat collar in order to keep the cold, blustering wind from accumulating snow quickly about his neck. Before tightening his Class A hat more firmly down upon his forehead, Sackett looked up and squinted to keep the snowflakes from covering his view. He looked up at an upper floor window, momentarily, and with a solemn countenance.

Then he adjusted the hat both front and back, and walked under the medical center's vestibule. He was prepared to begin ringing in the New Year.

Making his way through the antiseptically stringent air of the inner corridors of the hospital, Sackett failed to notice the moribund attempt at cheer that the seasonal decorations and war bond posters gave the interior as he made his up to the Negro ward. He didn't pass anyone as he familiarly made his way down the highly waxed aisles in the ward. In fact, he saw not enough staff, until he reached the area of the nurses' desk and removed his hat and overcoat.

He deposited the hat and pinned it under his left arm and folded, and then draped the coat over his forearm.

The now familiar nurse hadn't been visible to him as he approached because she'd been bent over small white paper aperitif cups that she was filling with medications. Sackett caught himself appreciating the lieutenant's shining, relaxed hair that rested on her shoulders, underneath her starch-stiff cap, as she worked. He wondered if she had to even use the chemical relaxers that were becoming popular. Both colored men and women used it to straighten their naturally coiled hair. She had good hair, though, and might have been able to just use an iron on it; it was so sheened—bluish black. Whatever process she used to get her hair to lay the way it did, the captain appreciated the end result.

"Excuse me," he said, trying to politely gain her attention, "I'm here to see the Colonel."

But she didn't even look up at him. Her mouth silently kept a count as she filtered in blue pills into five cups, and then went on to another color. Pointing at the dispensed meds with her pen and then scribbling on a nearby clipboard.

"Nurse?"

"Captain," she said, and continued counting and then writing, "you know the rules. You've been here enough times to know we don't allow visits after four"

"But this is New Years."

She put her pen down and stood fully erect behind the counter, her almond colored arms akimbo and her hands firmly on her hips, the care provider raised her whip of an eyebrow and tilted her head as she pursed her lips before speaking.

"Regulations don't change jes' because it's a holiday that you decide to show up on. Captain."

"Oh, uh-huh, and you don't either," Sackett said smiling.

"I don't what?"

"Change just because it's the holidays. You still just the most fussy and contrary woman I've come across in this man's army."

She relaxed her hard stare, and let a smirk cross her face that betrayed her intentions. Captain Sackett just kept grinning at her, and she couldn't pretend otherwise. "All right, all right," she said. "I guess I've been teasing you long enough. You know he told me to give you a hard time, and he outranks you."

"Yeah, and I outrank you."

"Not on my floor you don't. Get on in there before I change my mind."

"Yes, ma'am."

And Sackett took one step towards the room and turned back. "What are you doing for New Year's?" he asked.

"Something that doesn't concern, or have anything to do with you. Now get."

"Thank you, Nurse Nightingale."

Sackett whirled around to the room as the beginnings of a full grin replaced the smirk on her face. The lieutenant was a purveyor of humility, but not a bad sort. She had been one of the first to congratulate him on his double bars.

The door to the colonel's room was slightly ajar, so Sackett peeked in and saw him in the bed that was parallel to the big window. His back towards him. He was sleeping in the lumbar supported position, upper-body elevated, so he could breathe easier and have less likelihood of choking as he swallowed. He'd been told that aspiration was a big problem, and it had happened once already. Suction procedures were now needed on a rotating basis.

The colonel's breathing came in shallow exertions, and somewhat un-evenly, Sackett noticed. In the rasping of air, Captain Sackett could hear how laborious the act of living had become for his superior. A chart with a graph hung near the foot of the bed, containing some sort of neurological data, Sack-ett believed, and was partially obscured by the thin clear and light-blue plastic tubing running from an oxygen tank to the colonel's nostrils. The unaffected side of the face, the left, was turned into the pillows behind Colonel Peets' head; away from the entry and out towards the window.

As he entered inside the room, Captain Sackett quietly set his hat and coat down in a nearby chair and then crept towards the colonel, so as not to awaken him.

Peets' right arm and hand, more like a bird's, now. An appendage that had the curled lameness of a maimed eagle's. It seemed to be attached to him as a foreign thing, like a botched procedure from a mad scientist. The claw or talon of what used to be a hand was turned upwards on the pillows, and it was tucked closely, almost protectively, by his face. The left arm occasionally twitched seemingly on its own accord, at times. Deciphering misplaced impulses from misfiring nerve connections. What a pitiful hulk Colonel Peets had become.

The whole right side of his body was under siege of the stroke; not only was his arm and hand affected by the deficits but the mouth and eyelid on that side drooped and refused to cooperate. In the weeks, now months he had been there, Colonel Peets made it clear to Sackett that he didn't care for the total incapacity he suffered; it only exacerbated the melancholy he had from not being fit to run his division any longer. For Peets, a reason to go on was getting hard to come by, at times. When disgust for what the situation presented to him grew to be too much for him, Colonel Peets let his general malaise blanket him in forgetful sleep. It would take a lot of rest to get any better, he felt.

The glottis muscle, at the top of his throat, clicked whenever he swallowed the small pools of saliva that dammed over into the well of his mouth. When awoke he exerted some control over when he did swallow, because it took too much effort to do it as often as a healthy man, but in his sleep the autonomic scheduling took over and Sackett saw a rivulet of dribble begin to run down from the corner of Colonel Peets' distended lower lip.

Sackett drew himself closer, extracting a white handkerchief from an inner coat pocket, and lightly dabbed at the spittle. He couldn't tell if he was awake or not because his eyes were half-opened. Peets didn't feel the cloth on his jaw, but he could sense motion coming by his left side, and when he awakened it startled the captain.

"Ath—you— were," Peets said, finally.

Sackett did his best not to seem ill-at-ease in front of the colonel, but he was embarrassed at his show of over-familiarity, and being caught trying to dote on his superior officer's personage. "How are we doing today, Sir?" he asked softly. And he pressed the white cloth of surrender into Peets' left hand as the invalid maneuvered himself in his bed.

Peets rolled, pushed, shifted his hips, and used his left limbs to turn onto his back in the bed. And it took some doing, but when he had finished the colonel let his right hand flop to the covers, accompanied with a feeble and abbreviated sigh of satisfaction.

"You—don't—need—to—be here," the colonel blurted. The speech would come out in halted fashion at first, but eventually he'd build up a head of steam and would be able to have a fairly comprehensible dialogue, with some effort and frustration. Peets had a hard time trying to calibrate his breathing and the mechanics of vocalizing, yet. His phrasing came out choppy, strained, and unevenly loud at times. If he grew too excited, as he was now, facial muscles would begin to twitch, or his tongue would spasm against the interior of his cheek; eventually it would roll out of his mouth and make him feel like he looked as bad as some lazy dog at a kennel.

Captain Sackett was patient and tried to make sure he didn't show concern over what he witnessed, or heaven forbid, his repulsion. But as the struggle continued, Sackett had to stand even firmer in his conviction in order to not look aside. He valiantly tried appearing unperturbed. But he failed. The colonel's eyes and his met. And it was through their eyes alone that the encroaching paralysis was realized to be as terrifying to Peets, as it was Sackett.

Then, almost as unexpectedly as it had begun, the quivering subsided. Another rivulet of drool got the captain to reach for the damp handkerchief Peets retained in his good hand, as if to prove he wasn't being deterred.

"No!" Peets vehemently shouted, jerking the hand away.

"Colonel? Why won't you let me help?"

"Like eating thoup in the thummer, huh? Maketh thense to me, even if it don't nobody elth."

His voice was thick in its modulation, but he could be understood. Sackett took a step back and walked to the end of the bed so he could look directly at Peets.

"I never athked no one to help me, never my whole life. Or have them clean up after me when I'd metthed up. I'm fruthrated, and yeah, kinda thamed in thome wayth, too. When I get people looking at me the way you did. I just as thoon not bother."

"I apologize, Sir. I didn't mean to gawk, but I'm not—not comfortable with hospitals. Especially ones where friends are at. I hope you understand, that I meant to be here, in spite of how these places make me feel."

"You feel thallowed up inthide of them, don't you?"

"Not claustrophobia, but what it is—well, I really can't put words to it. I guess it's just to say that it's nerve wracking for me to be somewhere where I have no function, no understanding of anything going on around me. But it should go to my credit that in spite of all that, I made it here to see you."

"What day ith it?"

"New Year's Eve."

Peets eyes looked to his left and a stenographers pad and pen on a meal table.

"You want this?"

Peets shook his head, "Just thlow me down while talking, but at leatht I still can write. Heh, heh."

Sackett smiled.

"Thith day," Peets continued, "ith a day to put away old bithnett. It time to ring in the new. Where you headed to?"

"Ah, I, uh, was thinking of stepping out later on at the Officer's Club, for just a bit."

"Man," the colonel mused, "I bet they got cornbread, all hot—buttered, thize of hay baleths. Greenths, collardths, turnip, muthtard. Catfith in corn meal, a big pot of gumbo."

"You better slow down, Colonel. I only brought one handkerchief for you. It ain't all that much."

"Hell it ain't. Boy—you juth don't know."

"Well, they are going through some tomfoolery to make it extra special, I guess."

"Tell me."

"From what I hear, they got tomatoes fit for slicing up and putting them right alongside of the fish."

"Ith the middle of winter."

"They grow 'em in a greenhouse, I guess."

"That be fine."

"Yassuh, and they got King Crab to put in the gumbo."

"Flown in?"

"Came on train. They got a way to refrigerate a whole train car and not use nary a bit of ice. And guess who invented it? A black man, now ain't that beat all?"

Peets became quiet and reflective. The thing about the train cars was interesting because of what it could do for military logistics, as well as commodities. But hearing about the food caused lament. Even if he could have attended, Peets knew he would not have been a partaker of those victuals. Oh, maybe the hothouse tomatoes, or some celery. But over the many years of libations one could have, on and off holidays, when you're a diabetic, and enjoy a high-fat diet, and drinking not meant to slack thirst,—well, those factors all played no small part in his intracerebral hemorrhaging, and the colonel knew he would not see their like on any plate meant for him. Peets sighed again, but Sackett thought that meant he should continue.

"They tell me they're trying something new, too. Pig snout in a wine sauce. Can you beat that?"

"Ith that right""

"Yassuh, got 'em wrapped in grape leaves and everything. Just like the Greeks be doing it."

Peets started doodling on the writing tablet.

"You all right, Colonel? What's the matter?"

"I hate the food here, Thackett. Hate the food even more than being in here. They give me all the clear liquidths, when they know I can't even hold a pot for me to pithth in—I hate being tho powerleth."

"Your illness is not what you are, Sir. You hear? Just run into a bad stretch, that's all." Peets just stared, sighed.

"How the trooth doing, with the combat?" he finally asked.

"The quartermaster has been troubled by some of the logistics on some requisitions he put in. We been doing what we can."

"If anybody geth hardheadth 'bout it, you thend 'em to Krecth, hear?

"Yes, Sir."

Peets throat clicked with a slow swallow.

"Frank?"

"Sir?" Sackett replied, bending his ear closer.

"What about my plan? You thought about it?"

"Request explanation, Sir, about said 'plan'."

"Frank—"

"Oh, all right, Colonel. But when you took ill I thought it would be in the best interest for me to fully engage with the command duties. I'm sure that's what you'd have preferred, Sir."

"I'm 'fraid my getting ill ain't the worsth thing for you."

"What do you mean? The Ft. Benning training?"

"I mean it ain't juth me that ith forthing your hand."

"Sir?"

"I had thome people thee me, Frank. People from Thicago, with the Inthpector Genralth' Offith and they had a lot of quethions about you."

"About me? Aw—go on, Colonel. What could they possibly want to know about—?"

"Kanthath."

"Kansas? What about it?"

"Quethionth about—You really from Kanthah, or not."

Sackett didn't move or change his expression; he was a mask of dispassionate indifference, on the outside. But looking into his eyes, Peets could see he'd struck to the core of what the official inquiry had alleged.

"Are you?" Peets asked again with a level stare.

"Am I what?"

"You're not really from Kanthath, are you, Frank?"

Sackett's arms folded up in front of him like jack knives closing across his chest, one over the other. He shook his head slowly as he rubbed one hand over his face several times. Sighing, he couldn't seem to speak any words at the moment. He only could massage the planes of his features.

"Is this off-the-record, Sir?"

"Don't bother. I think I already know."

"Then I guess it's too late to say that it's all probably some kind of mistake or that it's the first I've heard of anyone being asked?"

"No, I don't think any of that would matter, now."

"I don't know what to tell you, Sir."

"You don't have to tell me anything, Frank. I'm not the one who wanth to know. You been a damn good tholdier for me, and you know I ain't above breaking thome ruleth."

"Do you think I should just go and commit a court-martial offense, now? Under an added suspicion?"

"Like I thaid, I ain't the one wanth to know. Better if I didn't. But I do know one thing. It'd be a hell of a lot harder to find you on the front, than here."

Sackett turned around in place and tried to look through the ceiling for guidance as he deliberated. "You know how crazy this is? I could risk either a formal Army inquiry, or end up being Nazi fodder, all based on the hearsay of a man, who's—begging the Colonel's pardon—probably suffering dementia, or worse, under medication!"

Peets chuckled heavily. "Yeah, ith a helluva pickle."

"And how am I supposed to be mustered up out-of-the-blue as a private?"

"All ready cut the orderth. Did it while you wath in Detroi' lath thummer. That ith the lath time I had to thubmit the training rothter. Didn't make you a buck, though. Private firth-clatth."

"Wouldn't it be a little strange to have the commanding officer's name and details being the same as a non-com's?"

"It can happen, Frank. Hath happened, before."

"I still have to think about it."

"What the hell ith there to think about!" Peets erupted in anger. "Either you got the fire in your gut for war, or you don't."

"I got—"

"You got nothing!" Peets boomed, "Nothing but them inthigniath on your neck that ain't worth a damn here. You won't have 'em over there, I know. But you won't be without 'em and in the brig, to boot. Think about it. What you'll be part of—no rank can be given for it. You will be legendary."

"Oh, I'm that, all right, Sir."

"Huh?"

"Nothing. And how do I get my commission back when the time comes and I'm fortunate enough to still be alive?"

"The key for the pull-out drawer, the locked one. It ith underneath the drawer, towardth the front."

"I wondered why Davies couldn't find that."

"You will find the orderth, and a theparate letter in an envelope. That one thayth that you acted on my orderth to deploy incognito and you have all righth and privilege of your rank."

"That would get me off the hook, but throw you into the fire, wouldn't it?"

"Don't think that would matter much, now. Prob'bly even less then."

Sackett retreated back one step from the colonel's bedside and saluted his commander. Peets flinched his left hand up, at the wrist.

"Will you be back before midnight?"

"If they'll let me. Besides that, it's pretty nasty out." Sackett answered tersely, feeling the weight of a new burden draped on him.

"I'll leave word. Y'know, Frank, ith funny."

"What is, Sir?"

"The white folk put the colored ward near the top of the hothpital, tho they ain't got to be by uth," and as his voice trailed off, into a tired drone, said, "but our roomth got the betht viewth." And Peets yawned; making a canyon out of his mouth and then drawing it shut as he closed his eyes and lapsed into a new round of congested snoring.

When he left, Sackett noticed more spittle forming at the corner of Peets' mouth again. He decided to leave the dampened white hanky gripped in Peets' good hand, rising and falling as his chest arched, in meter with each breath the colonel could muster. When he woke, Sackett hoped he would think of him, leaving a tool of simple, civilized society, a handkerchief, in his grasp. Even if it was only to give him enough dignity to being able to swab spit from his own cheek. As if laying it down would be like giving up the very flag of surrender.

CHAPTER TWENTY
The NCO Club

There happened to be going on that same night another kind of surrender. And it was as mirthful a one as Colonel Peets' was a resigned defeat. The dance floor of the NCO Club contained many ladies lined up and ready to surrender some time for a good dance, and maybe a good time. Anything to relieve the absences that this war had made so apparent, that is, if someone could casually observe the gathering for what is was. The men were outnumbered, three-to-one.

Fortunately, the heavy flurries had stopped around eight o'clock that evening, just before the doors opened and the awaiting, white-shoulderd and snowdusted first-comers began checking in their heavy coats and men's oversized galoshes.

The warm, wet tongue of a young woman gave a dewy flick on the cheek of a soldier as they danced. And his reaction was one of pleasure mixed with repulsion, almost as an afterthought. He straightened his back, withdrawing from their close embrace but still clasping both of her hands.

"Aw, girl. I told you; don't be acting like that, now." And then he rubbed the moistness from his cheek with the back of his coffee bean colored hand. "Shhoot, whatcha hafta go an' do that for? What did I tell you?"

"Oh, shut up," she said, giggling and snuggling closer to the man who had grown less urgent in his retreat. She looked up from his chest and flicked the tip of her index finger against the fatty part of his broad nose.

"Look, here," he said. "If I was looking to get mahself shot, I'd have signed up for overseas. Not act a fool with a man's wife in public."

The music abruptly switched to a livelier tune and the coupled rolled to their left as the girl laughed and continued dancing. The cuckold maker now positioning himself squarely into the midst of the dance floor, amongst a group of sixty, or so non-coms. Each man had women of varying degrees of comeliness as well as skin tone. There was every shade of brown imaginable under the roof in the nightclub. The only difference being was that this juke wasn't a club at all; it was the base's armory gym which had been recomfitted for the New Year's festivities.

It was a mélange of Negro soldiers and their wives, girlfriends, mistresses, and lovers. All of them cavorting about in one sense of the word, or the other, depending on the multitudinous reasons to deign their inhibitions to the wayside as the night wore on. The women, long-legged or dimple kneed, pigeon toed, or hammered, also had the various dimensions you could imagine in a vast array of flirtatious females; some with ham-sized calves, while others had delicate ankles and Cinderella feet. But each had a partner who escorted them with pride, on their arm and on their faces. They were all strutting about, in stark contrast to the sober behavior of the women who were managing the party.

These were mostly white women. They manned coffee pots and kept sugar and gingerbread cookies coming, as well as taking stock of when the egg nog supply was dwindling. These social workers had scourged through the tri-counties in Michigan, like bloodhounds on a chase the past few months, searching for a great assortment and variety of female companionship that they wanted to introduce to the black troops. With the good planning, the potential for a turnout was supposed to be good, but by that night, with the blizzard conditions outside, even the auxiliary women agreed the weather would surely cut down the numbers of those attending. But whoever braved the elements to come, they would do their best to seeing he or she had a good ol' time.

Fast-paced dervishes played by the band, a jazz ensemble made up of sweating and multi-talented enlistees, found their tunes creating a pulse in the bodies undulating on the floor as they danced. The dancers were as agile as gymnasts; over here you could see a man jump above the crowd and touch his toes momentarily as he split his legs apart in the air, and then lightly touch ground. At another part of the floor a soldier would be spinning around on one leg, the other extended straight out, and his date jumping over and then ducking under the leg as he twirled. Yes, there was some dancing going on that night. And when the song finished and the band took its break it was almost ten. A jukebox started to play and the seams on the hosiery of the women were not as straight as they'd been when they'd first gotten there.

Pitchers of beer got passed over the heads of the partygoers on the edge of the dance floor area, enroute to long, red-and-white checkered, plastic table-clothed tables plied with all sorts of food and holiday ornamentation. One of the soldiers by a wall stood up on a folding chair to intercept one of the clear plastic urns on its way over to a table, looking like he wanted to sing an ode to the hijacked beer container, as he drew it close to him and secured it. His comrades at the table broke out in an uproarious din upon bearing witness to the thief's wiles. It seemed almost a serendipity that everything seemed to be working out well as it was. And the year was bound to go out on a celebratory and promising note, after all.

Further to the rear of the hall, Joe Martin sat at an empty card table; empty save for three empty beer pitchers and his sober, attendant, and dutiful brother. Joe was earnestly putting himself into the pursuit of finding his cheer in the holiday celebration. He grinned and then sneered at an imagined antagonist of some sort, which was apparently just across from him. That Gus was there, sober and concerned, didn't enter into Joe's mind or have any effect on his behavior. There was a sudden musical flourish and the band's emcee came back to the microphone and spotlight.

The baton carrying leader of the ensemble bowed curtly and thanked the crowd for their enthusiasm. "We're gonna slow things down a little for you, so you'll have something in the tank for when the New Year starts in less than three hours." The paper horns and hand clackers filled the pause. "This one's for all our guys and gals overseas, it's called 'Don't Get Around Much Anymore'." Joe called a waitress over to the table and tried to make some small talk before he ordered more beer. All the while, the distinctive Duke Ellington signature riffs on the piano belied the indecorous things Joe said to the woman who attempted to serve him.

Suddenly she became agitated and stepped away from the table, yanking her arm away from his attempted grab. Gus felt embarrassed for both himself and the server. "Sure," Joe said in a tone that was between a slur and a belch, "sure, you can say that now." And he started his dry, nasally cackling, "But come midnight, you know where you want to be. And I'll be right here, too. Waitin'." The waitress looked at him like she had something bad-tasting raise up in the back of her mouth. She looked over at Gus.

"Do us both a favor, and get him to hold his breath until then, okay?"

"There's only one thing I need you to hold, girl. Ain't that right, Gus? Huh?" And Joe once again reached for her arm.

"Hey! You scratched me!"

"Joe," Gus cautioned and pushed his brother back in his chair. "Stop it, Joe."

Joe muttered something under his breath and enfolded the beer pitcher in his arms and rested his forehead against the brim of the sweating plastic ewer. Seeing that he wasn't able to pay for it, the waitress asked.

"Are you paying for this?"

Gus pulled out a dollar bill and set it on the table, not wanting to even appear to be making a furtive movement. "I'm sorry, ma'am. He's—well, keep the change. Okay?"

The waitress' eyes widened and she smiled when she picked up the money, but then scowled back at Joe with pursed lips. "Thanks," she said to Gus. Then she gave him an approving look and a raised eyebrow. "You kinda cute. Why don't you lose him? He's a creep." The girl turned and departed, her pert breasts jutting upward and outward as she walked, looking this way, and then that for other tables that needed orders filled. Gus had been too ashamed to answer, or even look at her. He didn't want to acknowledge the truth many all ready felt about his brother.

Gus knew that when drinking, his brother's personality could become exceptionally boorish on occasion, and chronically abrasive. When he was sober the caustic barbs only came every so often, but when he drank—there was little of anything left worth redeeming in Joe Martin. He looked at him, staring at the piano player in the band like a dead fish.

Joe didn't like that "piano playing nigger", he said to himself. He nimbly played the sheet music, but he didn't have the artistic expression that Duke conveyed, Joe thought. There was the sensuality in the melody that Ellington wrote; that could not be masked. But what he heard tonight lacked something. Joe kept watching, unimpressed. The piano player, upon Joe's further reflection, was much darker-skinned than Duke Ellington, and to Joe he seemed to be playing the music a little too arrogantly. He had the mechanics of the composition, but none of the clarity and brilliance—lightness—that the Duke gave the music. In fact, in Joe's mind, the dusky sergeant's muddy skin tones could only produce a lesser quality performance. And he listened even more closely to the playing, and then declared to himself that he wasn't even sure if it was that close, really. He half-stepped his way through the scales that the master had composed. Everyone else's memory filled in what was missing. Everyone, that is, but him.

"Joe?" Gus called.

"Hmm—Oh, hell, that girl there ain't nothin' but a floozy, that's all she is." Joe thickly muttered.

"You're not going to make it to twelve, the rate you're going. Let's get you some coffee, Joe."

"Nah."

"C'mon, Joe. Please."

"I don't want it."

"But it's not what you want, Joe. It's what you need."

"I don't want any fuckin' coffee," Joe growled at his sibling, like an alpha wolf warning a beta that its attention is becoming unwanted. "I don't *need* any fuckin' coffee. You 'stand me?" His voice growing louder started drawing attention. "I don't *need* your sorry ass tellin' me what I gots to do."

"Joe, please—"

"Joe, nothing—I'll fuck you up, Junior. Y'hear me, understand what I'm sayin'? Huh?"

"You don't mean that, Joe." Gus' voice amplified in passion where Joe's boomed from inebriation, yet together they were making a scene. "You're pissing people off, and I'm trying to keep things calm. All right?"

Joe lolled his head to the side and looked at the gawking passersby and waved a limp-wristed hand of dismissal at his brother and them. He swiveled in his seat to begin pouring another beer. Strangely enough, the moment Joe had waved off everyone, the band stopped playing. Joe was too concerned with leveling the head of his beer to be conscious of Captain Sackett walking up to the raiser and taking possession of the band's microphone. He hadn't removed his coat, and the snow was still visible as it melted, but he did take off his hat and smooth the pomade into his hair before speaking.

"Good evening. May I have your attention, please? And please, stay at-ease."

The hubbub of voices and activity lowered quickly, and the clinking of knives and forks against plates abated, as well.

"I hate to break up the festivities, and I apologize for the interruption, but as most of you all know—Colonel Peets is still hospitalized…"

Joe grabbed Gus by the arm. "What the hell does he think he's doing here?"

"The colonel left specific instruction for me to convey, on his behalf, all the command's best wishes for the holiday. He extends that to each and every one of you. And I might add—"

"Yeah," Joe loudly interrupted. "You can sure follow some orders, Capt'n, Suh!" The nasal cackle followed the disparagement echoed hollowly from the back of the room, where Gus had to struggle from spitting out a mouthful of beer.

Sackett maintained his composure because he knew all eyes were on him, and he had to discount the inebriated soldier, whoever it was. "I might add, in that spirit, that I, too want to let each and everyone of you know how much your efforts here are appreciated and—"

"Yeah, Cap'n?" Joe shouted incredulously, "Wha' about all them niggas you got up in the stockades for six munts, huh? You 'preciate them, too? Helluva way to show it."

"Shut up, Joe!" Gus hissed, and grabbed Joe by the collars.

Nervous talk began to heighten the suspense where heretofore there had only been empty silence. Some began to castigate Joe for his inappropriate manner, and disrespect. But Joe's belligerence had been lit and would take no quarter, only its full portion. He went on with his diatribe.

"What about them, Cap'n? You gonna wish them a Happy New Year too, down at the brig?"

Sackett forced a smile and thought to himself that the best way to cover his embarrassment would be to leave the stage as quickly and graciously as possible. He put his hat back on his head. "You all enjoy the last couple of hours 1943 has to offer to you." And he made a hasty retreat off the dais.

Indecisive applause was given the announcement's conclusion. Those people who clapped probably did so more to bring the feeling of celebration back to the context of the night's activities. Joe's tirade had made them all feel vulnerable, naked, in a sense. The music came back softly and food began to be eaten once more, recreating the subsumed clatter. But anybody who thought, or rather, hoped that the officer was going to just leave without an explanation being given to him, knew better, and kept their eyes to the back of the room as Sackett made a bee-line to Joe's and Gus' table.

Gus stood and saluted before the captain got within six feet of the corner table, and Sackett looked past him and glowered at the stupored Joe.

"Pardon my brother, Sir," Gus pleaded. "He's had a little too much—"

Sackett ordered the younger Martin to be quiet with a curt swipe of his raised hand. "I'd order you to your feet, soldier," Sackett said, "but I know they won't support you."

Joe rocked his head up from his folded arms.

"You got a beef with me?" asked Sackett.

And Joe just stared into his mug of beer while his head wobbled over it.

"I *said*," Sackett emphasized, "do you have something to say to me, soldier?"

Joe cast a lazy glaze at the captain, took a deep breath and spoke. "Last summer," he began, "you went and rounded up all of them brothers, on their way to Detroit, didn't you? And you know, Cap'n, at first I thought you done what had to be done. But now—*Sir*, six months done gone by and ain't nobody from they unit seen hide no hair of 'em. Did they deserve that, Cap'n?"

"Who are you to question what the command deems fit to incur on malcontents?"

"He's just drunk, Sir. He don't mean anything—"

But Sackett held up an abeyant hand at Gus again. "I'm not talking to you soldier..." The captain squatted down to get eye level with Joe. "You're lucky I have some holiday spirit in me, private. Otherwise you'd be on report and you could spend your New Year's counting the hairs on your friend's backs. Is that what you want?"

Joe turned his gaze.

"You're too kind, Captain," Gus said. And Sackett stood up and turned to look at him.

"Don't I know you?"

"Private August Martin, Sir. I was the man who notified you about the, ah, the, ah, uprising."

Joe harrumphed loudly and swelled his cheeks with a large swallow of beer.

"Get him sobered up," Sackett ordered, "before he gets hurt and I have him on report for insubordination to an officer."

"Yes, Sir." And here Gus saluted, as the captain turned his well-polished heels on the Martins and left out a side exit. Gus felt a wave of relief overcome him, as if the weight of a whole man had been taken off of his chest. He was holding his breath and hoping that Joe wouldn't make any parting comment to further infuriate Sackett. Thank God it's New Years, he thought. He sighed audibly and slouched himself down in the nearest chair, mentally and physically spent.

"Good riddance," Joe said in a delayed response.

"What would cause you to go and make a scene like that for, Joe? Huh? Are you out of your mind? That was a damn officer you were talking to, fool!"

But Gus' inquiries were not heard by his brother, or the officer he'd offended. Captain Sackett turned his collar up outside in the night, and adjusted the black scarf worn underneath his coat. The driver had the car parked at the end of a wet, but snow-free sidewalk that led to the gymnasium door Sackett came out of. A light snow had begun, and it was disappearing into the blue-gray fog of his staff car's exhaust. Sackett had told the driver to keep it running. Seeing his charge heading in the direction, the driver got out of the car and opened the passenger door for Sackett. The fumes from the exhaust rubbed around his pant leg and ankles like a fawning cat.

"Get me the hell away from here and go downtown to the Officer's Club," Sackett snapped at the innocent driver.

"Yes, Sir," came the old soldier's slightly bewildered reply. He tried imagining what had happened to turn the captain's mood, so quickly, but knew he should not delay. And before five minutes passed the car was crunching its way past the perimeter gate of Fort Custer. Passenger and driver silent. Only the sound of snow and ice being crunched by cold tires.

Back inside the gymnasium the music was lively, once again, but Joe had had enough of his little brother's staunch badgering. "Look," he said, "I told you. I 'jes don't like the sonbitch, okay? Is that enough for you? Cuz' if it ain't, that's too damn bad."

181

"Okay, Joe. Damn those men—what about you? What did Captain Sackett ever do to you for you to be so disrespectful? And from what I remember, it was you who told me to notify him that the men were going off. So, he did what he had to do. If they been in there for so long, who's really the cause behind that? Not you, not him, or me—you tried to tell 'em what would happen. They wouldn't listen."

"I don't care. I jes' don't like the sonbitch. There's something about him, Gus. I can't put—but the way he looks. All high-yaller. Yeah, he could be that bastard, all right."

"What in the world you talking about? You trying to make it seem like you knew the captain before we even got into the army."

"Maybe I did, Gus. You such a mister-knows-it-all, but maybe I know something you don't. Maybe I did know him."

"He had no idea who you were, Joe. Wouldn't he have—"

"You know why I left momma's?"

"Well, yeah. Everybody in the family knows what happened."

"No," Joe said, slowly shaking his head, "you were around after all the commotion, but you have no idea what set it off. What got the whole thing started, that you know nothing about."

"I heard that—"

"You only heard second hand, from Aunt Jo Pearl. Y'see, while you was spending the summer with her, in Chicago, I had to find work. Pay off taxes Daddy left. I came home one day to the house, and the screen door was unlocked. Saw Momma on the couch with a nigga that looked 'jes like your dear Cap'n. Grinding on top of her like he was a dog locked up with a bitch."

"Are you sure?"

"Pretty sure. I runned him off. Told Momma to put some clothes on, an' he comes back. That's when we tussled, an' Momma got in it."

"And you grabbed Daddy's shotgun."

"Yeah, an' you know the rest."

"What you mean, I know?"

"By her way of telling, I was aiming to shoot her."

"What do you expect, Joe? She saw Daddy blow his head off with that gun. Do you even think about what it took for her to step in between you two?"

"Shouldn't *she* have thought about what I'd do if I ended up finding her like that?

"But Daddy's dead, Joe. Shouldn't she have the right to find a new man? A right to love somebody?"

"If Daddy hadn't been so sloppy drunk from her flirting ways with men, maybe he wouldn't been as careless when he was cleaning that damn shotgun, Gus. Y'ever thought about that?"

"How could I, Joe. You, yourself, said I didn't know half about her."

"That weren't nothing you would have had to dug up. That was too obvious."

"Joe—y'know, sometimes I would just as soon call you a sonuvabitch, but I wouldn't talk that way about my mother."

"Suit yourself. Wouldn't bother me, none."

"You are as ornery as a catfish in a washtub, Joe. You won't give her a good word, a good thought, no matter what she do. Remember how she made you those sandwiches last summer? You wouldn't touch 'em. Those were peace offerings, Joe. But you just don't get it."

"A woman'll do that. Try to make you forget by filling your gut. Sandwich can't make up for what she did, Gus."

CHAPTER TWENTY-ONE
The Feel of Command

"Don't seem to be you're night, Sir. If you don't mind me saying," the driver opined as he switched his attention from between the road in front of him and the officer viewable in the car rear view mirror. There was a long pause.

"What's that?" a distracted Sackett asked.

"Are you all right, Sir?"

"Hmm? Oh—I—I—ah, just got through talking to a guy back there that I should have thrown into the pokey, is all. I would have, too."

"Drunk, Sir?"

"Hammered. And smelt like a skunk, there was so much beer sweating off of him."

"Got a little loud, did he?"

"Worse. Insubordinate."

"Well, then. Sir, I'd say you've about got yourself used to the feel of your command, I guess."

"Not by the way I acted back there."

"For what it's worth, Sir, and you can only take it from being a non-com, but I've seen many commanders come and go in my days. Now, a real leader looks at the regs and still pull back the full weight of his hand. If'n he sees fit to. He don't let the regulations dictate his every move, he uses 'em to complement his own decisions."

"There's only one way to ride a horse, private."

"But you can't make it go if'n it don't want to. A horse won't go where it's liable to break a leg. There are times the rider's got to trust the animal. And when he does that, well, that horse will then go about anywhere he wants him to. That's how it is with officers and foot troops, Sir."

"So, I should kill him with kindness, private? Is that what you're saying?"

"Far be from me to tell you. I'm just making an observation, Sir."

"With a guy like that, though. He won't be reasoned to, that way. I should have tossed him."

"Want me to turn back?"

"No—if I was going to have him arrested I should have done it then."

"Begging pardon for asking, Sir. Then why didn't you?"

"Oh, I don't know. It kind of had a feeling to it, a little strangeness about the whole thing, like something I had experienced before but can't quite remember, exactly."

"That's déjà vu, Captain. When I was a young'un and driving a wagon back in Missouri, one time in a county just outside of Morgan. I seen this barn out in a field near a county road crossing that went to Benson. Now, I'd never been there before, but that barn looked so familiar to me. I remembered from seeing it in my dreams, and there was a storm. Turned out I was talking to my mother one day before she passed and she described that very place. Turned out she was working at a farm near there when she was pregnant with me and a tornado passed between it and her at the other place. She almost lost me. So, I reckon I got the memory of that from her. Could be you knows him through somebody, if not directly yourself. I'm tellin' you, stranger things have happened."

"Hmmm."

"Maybe somebody the Colonel had dealings with sometime."

"How long have you worked for Colonel Peets, soldier?"

"Oh, nigh on to fifteen years, Sir."

"You've been a staff driver for all that time?"

"Yes, Sir."

"And never got higher in rank than an E3?"

"That's how come I can say what I did about your decision to leave that man alone...Y'know, Sir, things got their way of happening. I was Sergeant Major once upon a time, but I ended up having to take care of a bad man who liked to put hands on my daughter whenever he took a liking to. Usually after drinking. And you understand, I couldn't have that. Broke her leg in two places one night, and I sent him to Jesus. Happened on base. The Colonel, well, he had mercy on me. Took me on when anyone else was going to throw away the key. I can never get them chevrons and rockers back, Sir. That was part of my deal. But Colonel Peets saw to it that I'd be under his direct supervision. So, I did no time. He took me on, and I ain't ever given him no reason t'evah let me go, neither. That's how come I said you wear your command well."

"Do you have other family?"

"Just the gal. She with her momma. Walks with a cane."

"That's a shame."

"Well, I feel all right because, leastways I got satisfaction knowing that he ain't walkin' at all. Maybe that was the storm I saw a comin' in my dreams when I were young. Who knows?"

"Interesting story."

"Not story, Sir. Fact."

"That's pretty trusting of you to divulge that kind of information. I mean, not knowing how I might react."

"I figure if the colonel were fine with it, you should be too, Sir."

"Private?"

"Sir?"

Captain Sackett felt the rear wheels fishtail slightly under him, but he wasn't duly concerned. To him, the back seat felt encompassing and protecting and the driver had everything under control. Sackett remained quiet a little longer, listening to the whir of the heater and the oscillating swish of the windshield wipers. The driver looked again in the rearview at his charge.

"Sir, you wanted to ask me something?"

"Ah, yes. I don't plan on staying long at the club."

"No, Sir," the driver affirmed, as if he had assisted the captain in making that decision.

"And, ah—I was planning on stopping back at the hospital, to see the colonel."

The driver made no comment and kept his eyes ahead on the white road; screened on either side in blackness, save for the lights from the heavy car's beams.

"I was wondering, private."

"Sir?"

"Would you care to join me for that visit?"

The old soldier snapped his head to the right, and would have spun it around completely to stare Captain Sackett in the face, if he could. The rear of the car slid more, and the driver momentarily struggled to get the vehicle and himself back under control. "That would be right fine, Suh! Right fine, indeed."

"Well, stay sharp and be careful, then. We got to make it to the club first."

"Yes, Sir!" The elder turned to the side again grinning and then smiling broadly as he gained control of the situation, revealing a gum line that over time had receded simultaneously with his hair. "Thank you, Captain!"

"Not a word to anyone."

"No, Sir. Nary a word."

"All right, then. Why don't you come in for a spell once we get——"

"Oh, no, Sir. Begging pardon—I'll be fine. Liquor was a big part of what got me busted down. I got me a thermos of coffee I might fill up, but that's about all. I jes' be waitin' outside for ya."

Sackett could see the outer limits of the city, and the night's lights framing the buildings that they emitted out of. None of the conflagration from six months earlier, though the night hid the most prominent scars of that time. This was Sackett's first time back there, actually. And it seemed such a long time ago. For several minutes, the captain lost himself in thought.

He wondered what exactly the colonel had been told, how much he had been asked, and how much he really knew about him. And what would he do about it? It had to be pretty bad for Peets to suggest he literally get out of Dodge before the sun set. So, he pretty well must know just about all there could be to know. Lacking a total confession. And he wasn't going to give anyone that, freely. He had asked him where he'd been from. It was direct and accusatory. Sadly, even moreso, Captain Frank Sackett could not dismiss the inquiry because unfortunately his was not a clear conscience. And Sackett really felt the need for that drink, now.

"Well, here we is, Suh."

But the driver was only alerting the captain of their approach. Eventually, he turned the staff car to the left, onto a dead-end side street, near Detroit's downtown. He then parallel parked it in a loading zone by Davenport's department store. The mannequins in the windows blindly looked out, over the roof of the cars, and towards the east. Towards the black shell of the burnt out haberdashery across the street that some looters had pilfered. The snow covered much of the riot damage that still hadn't been rebuilt or dozed over. And left ugly skeletons with memories of bloodied noise and silent ghosts.

The driver stepped out and opened Captain Sackett's door with all the air of importance as if it happened in front of witnesses. As he stepped out into the crisp dry air, a flashing neon beer sign that was situated above a doorway at the bottom of a street level stairway pointed the direction the officer had to go.

"Make sure you come down and get more coffee if you need it, hear?"

"Yes, Sir. Enjoy your stay."

The captain returned the salute and walked to the building's stairwell with renewed buoyancy, a spring in his step despite his previous misgivings in the car. As he drew nearer the door the muffled commotion from within hastened his imminent arrival. The ceiling was low in there, so low that one had to figure that this was an establishment barely up to city code. From where he stood at the landing, if a glass floor had extended, he could have walked over the heads of all the partygoers. Lord help them if a fire ever broke out, he thought. From this vantage point, a person could scan the half of the retail space in the store basement that had been leased to the Negro officers and their guests.

They might very well have not had a live band, as promised, but they did have a full bar. And unlike the NCO Club's party, held in the larger armory for logistical purposes, here there were no folding chairs and plastic table cloths. Here you found plump, cherry red, upholstered booths that surrounded shiny, dark tables. And these tables weren't closed off by a standing-room only crowd of beer hijacking grunts. On the contrary, whatever soldier you found here, this night, was wearing his Class A formal attire. Or if not that, a resplendent tuxedo.

But the façade wore thin for Sackett quickly, though. He sighed heavily and shook his head ever so slightly with a mild perturbance. It was difficult for him to juxtapose in his mind the sight of well-groomed men in tails chewing on pig knuckles with extended pinky fingers in the air. But they showed no shame in doing so; in fact, they looked like they were partaking of Mediterranean caviar on crackers made in France. And their bourgeoisie dates, in their gowns, also played up their parts in the high society imaginings.

Now, a closer inspection revealed some details of the true dichotomy in the setting, intentionally removed from the environments where real debutantes would be gathered on such a night. The tuxes that at first glance looked uncommonly good were actually second hand, and low-scale rentals. And the cuisine they nibbled on like it was a cultured delicacy was typical fare actually at most family gatherings for colored people on any given Sunday. All this forced show, in a store's basement, saddened Captain Sackett a little.

But, what of it, he thought. These are my people. Some countries cook snails, from the land and the sea, and rave over it. So, why can't pig intestines, and ox tails, and other parts of cloven-hoofed animals be just as celebrated? Besides, it did smell good, and he was suddenly hungry. He went down into the crowd.

Over a period of time since the riots the club had become a cult place for liberal and moderate whites to go "slumming". There were around twenty such couples Sackett noticed as he made his way to the coat check, after imbibing a few tasty hors de voeurs. These whites, more than a few of them Jewish, didn't bother pondering political associating or reprisals from enjoying their friends of color. The Jewish partiers abstained from eating non-kosher food offerings, but the rest were piling on collard and mustard greens and chicken on plates like everybody else, using the same utensils. After last summer many whites didn't want it to be said of them that all whites were intolerant, and couldn't or wouldn't intermingle freely among Negroes. And there were others who were beyond the politics and just plain enjoyed being around blacks; probably who grew up around Negro tenements in the South, and were at ease with the culture. Yes, in fact, many of those whites felt their freer moments of expression were when they were in the company of a group of rollicking black neighbors, having a good time. Still, there was something about it that gave Sackett the feeling that it wasn't as genuine as it appeared.

They might duck down back in the alley with Black Sally, but they weren't going to take her home to meet they momma and daddy. You could bet on that. They were the ones you'd call *honkeys* because they'd wait in their cars and honk their horns at all the black girls they saw pass, when they wanted something a little strange. Happened more than some people knew. Now, the white women and black men, well they had to handle such interest entirely different, or risk a lynching for him and a beating for her. The honkeys would be right along side watching, too, if they were found out. Watch and not say a word. Because they knew it was taboo. "They just couldn't help they self", Sackett thought.

It was crowded near the booths and Sackett had already begun taking off his outer wrap and his hat as he finally got closer to the counter. A very attractive young woman exchanging coats for tickets caught Sackett's eye. Her dark auburn hair was relaxed and swept back in a perfect bob cut, without any trace of a hair being out of place. Her large eyes had lashes that were as long as a spider's legs it seemed and she had just the cutest pyramid of nose. Her lips were full, and moist with red lipstick, that drew attention to how light her skin really was when she ribboned out a flash of white teeth. Sackett suddenly became preoccupied and didn't know she was smiling at him as he set his coat down and began rifling through its pockets, and the ones on his uniform.

"Can I help you, Captain?"

"Can't seem to find my watch piece."

Then Sackett looked into her eyes for the first time since being at the counter and they were the color of bleached turquoise stones. She didn't blink, but let her eyes look full and long into the officer's. He was mesmerized.

"I got a quarter to eleven. Happy New Year."

"Ah, yeah—same to you. Same to you."

He turned away and almost stepped onto someone toes behind him, so that rattled him even more to make a quick exit. But before five steps were taken, the coat check girl called after him. "Hey, you forgot your ticket!"

Sackett patted his pants pocket as he returned to the stand's counter. Almost grateful for his hurried departure when he returned to see that wonderful smile, he held out his hand and she put the slip of paper into his palm and rolled his fingers around it. But she didn't remove her hands, instead, she wrapped her fingers lightly over his fist.

"Don't want to lose anything, do you?"

"Certainly not. I guess I should make my resolution right now."

"What would that be?"

Sackett gently pulled back, his fingertips lingering as they dragged across her palm, and held up the ticket.

"Pay better attention."

"I hope you do, Captain."

And once again she watched him walk away again, now her toothy smile biting somewhat into her lower lip. For all his talk about being more attentive, she thought, it seemed he was becoming even more unaware. She wasn't looking for any overt reaction from him, but if the broad shouldered captain, with his coal black pomaded hair would just read her mind, the night could be something so much more for them both. He hadn't looked yet, and probably wouldn't, she thought, as she saw him walking towards the bar. "Men—soldiers," she sighed.

The pub section was on the west side of the basement, far from the stair entry and coat check area. The massive, thirty-foot wooden length was baroquely embellished with sculpted pomegranates and urns, wreaths and ribbons. It was made of cherry wood and always had the smell of aged barrels on a hot summer day. A mirror behind it, which ran the entire length, made the size of the club area appear twice as large as it actually was. Sackett took a stool at the bar, towards the short side, that was slightly removed from the other imbibers. He reached into his rear pocket for his wallet and placed it and the coat ticket next to it on the counter.

"Your pleasure, Sir?" the bartender asked.

"Gimme a cognac, on the rocks. And put that in a bucket please."

The bartender had a jovial disposition. He was light-skinned and wide of girth and had a moustache too small for his moon-sized face. "A bucket, huh? Want it with a mop, or a sponge?" The bartender's jowls began to vibrate from the intensity of his smile and his self-appreciation for gibing his customer.

All cleverness aside, the captain only mutely stared ahead, past the barkeep, to the lines of liquor adorning the display under the mirror. Waiting for a response from Sackett only caused the service provider's jaws to slightly ache from freezing the grin on his face, though.

"Make it a double," Sackett quietly said.

The façade vanished, and the drink master muttered to himself and picked up the bill Sackett left for his tab. With a shrug and rolling of his eyes in exasperation, the bartender turned away to prepare the simple order.

Sackett looked down the bar's length and indifferently surmised the people there. Seemed like everyone had a date for the night, and were having a good time, as well. Maybe that was why he was thinking maybe it had been a mistake to come. At some point, earlier, he thought he could have enjoyed some cat-and-mouse foreplay with interested parties here; and he had felt a strong urge to talk about something else but the war. A sincere exchange, about pleasant things. Not just the absent-minded banter offered by the ebullient bartender. But that motivation had died, passed by after considering the mess he was in with his superiors. The camaraderie, all the effusive cheer, it all seemed so forced, as if by will if not by design, and Sackett did not want to be part of such a deceit anymore.

He looked back the other way and gazed at the coat check girl again, hoping to rekindle his initial desire, or to get the courage up to just leave. She was laughing at something one of her co-workers whispered to her. Her smile was like a ribbon of white enamel across her light almond-colored face. She tossed her head elegantly to the side as she laughed. Sackett thought to himself, how could he have been so self-absorbed in all his issues to not want to pursue getting to know her better? The other woman left, and it seemed the checker knew that the captain had been watching them, staring at them perhaps. She confidently turned towards him and smiled again, a banner acknowledgement this time, instead of a common ribbon. But Sackett turned his head back to the bar with a rueful grin just as soon as he realized he'd been found out, and simultaneously his drink arrived.

"Here's your cognac, and change," the bartender said, setting the coins down beside the coat check stub.

When Sackett looked, to pick up his coins he realized the ticket had writing on it. The handwriting was looping and decidedly flourished with femininity; it said, "Let's dance." Sackett smiled for the first time since he'd been in the club.

While still delighting in the revealed attention he'd gotten, Sackett began to turn and look back over his shoulder, but thought better of it and instead got the attention of the bartender with a friendly wave of his hand. Seeing that the officer had a different outlook made all the difference in the world to the tavern manager.

"Yassuh, Capt'n."

"Hey, do me a favor would you?"

"I'm your man."

"You got champagne, right?"

"Sweating cold and in buckets. Y' wants one?"

"As a matter of fact I do. Leave out the mop, but I'll take a towel."

The bartender gave Sackett a quizzical glance and then his face flashed in humor-filled recognition at the satire played on him. "There you go, dude! That's all right!"

"Lemme get one," Sackett said, extracting a five dollar bill from his wallet. "And I'd like it set down right over there, by the coat check. And make sure I got two flutes, okay?"

"For you and who else, Champ?"

"Not that it's any of your business," Sackett informed the bartender with slight agitation, "but it's for me and that lovely cinnamon looking donut over there—"

The bartender's left eyebrow arced and he slammed his meaty palms face down on the bar top, his arms wide, and leaned into Sackett's face. "That's my sister, man."

Sackett's spine straightened quickly as he began sputtering an apology. "I'm, I—I'm sorry. No offense intended, believe—"

And then the bartender let go a bellowing whoop of laughter as if all the guffaws he'd been suppressing had finally been released. The merriment of the large man startled Sackett as much as if it were yet a threat. Surely, the man was mentally unhinged.

"She's not my sister, man!" the bartender shrieked. "But I had you, didn't I? Didn't I?"

Sackett's head slumped between his shoulders and his chin practically reached his chest as he collapsed his elbows in relief. He thought for sure that the bartender was going to take one of those arms, arms worthy of a blacksmith, and careen it down upon him. Instead, thankfully, he was slamming them rapidly on the bar top. His stomach hitching spasmodically as he reveled in his gag. It was almost starting to get embarrassing for Sackett.

"Yassuh—I sho' 'nuff got you there," the bartender exclaimed, pointing at Sackett's lowered head. "Sho' 'nuff!" And he snapped a hand towel in the air for emphasis.

Sackett could only get out a pained, nervous smile.

"Look," said the bartender as he offered a hand of truce, "let me get you another drink on the house, and you go on over there. I'll get that bubbly for you, di-rectly."

"Thanks," Sackett barely whispered.

The cognac Sackett got in turn was neat, and in a shot glass. After downing it in one quick gulp Sackett felt composed enough to saunter over to the coat checker's place of business.

"How do you do?" Sackett said, peeking around the corner.

"Well, hullo," she replied, in a dulcet voice that had the singe of habitual cigarette use to it.

"I'm Frank Sackett," he said, "and I was wondering if your job wasn't too demanding, and I also was likewise wondering that if it wasn't, would you care to dance with an admiring gentleman?

The banner reappeared inside the booth.

"If'n he's a gentleman, I guess I can," she said, and opened the waist-high gate to join the pleased captain.

Outside, the solitary driver was just getting back to the staff car after relieving himself by making some yellow water on a grimy snow pile about ten yards from his post when he saw a canopied military police jeep go past the store's alley.

Once inside the car, he looked over to his left into the side view mirror and saw the MP unit skid a little upon braking, and then backing up and turning into the dead end, coming directly up alongside the staff car. The driver put aside his fresh cup of coffee and partially rolled down the car window.

"Are you the driver for Captain Sackett, of the 184th?"

"Yes, can I help you?"

The news the driver received was so riveting and catastrophic, he had to eject himself from the car and grab hold of the jeep's door and get confirmation of the message. Then almost as quickly as they had come, the police departed, leaving the old PFC adrift, buckled against the left front quarter of the car. But his anguish soon turned into a desperate vitality, maybe borne from indecision, or panic. Possibly measures of both. And he quickly grew confused, literally running circles around the car and pumping his arms skyward, speaking but not saying anything intelligible.

A gust of wind came up just then and swirled in a new dusting of snow from the main thoroughfare. The old soldier ran into the club, in spite of decorum and protocol, because his only objective now was to find Captain Sackett.

Once inside the darkened subterranean venue, standing atop the stairway, the driver tried to focus his weak eyes. Scanning right and left did him no good because klieg lights blotted out periphery. He grabbed a hold of the iron railing and walked down the stairs, halfway, and looked again. But it was just too dark, and an Ella Fitzgerald tune, one ideal for a slow dance, caused the illumination to be even further diminished. The driver was quickly becoming exasperated, and the anxiousness caused him to clench and unclench his fists as he stretched his neck first to the left and to the right, on tip-toe for added effort, but to no avail. Ella's voice rippled, completely oblivious to the private's imperative.

Meantime, Frank Sackett was thankful to be finally oblivious about everything else but the five-foot, four inch woman he sidestepped with, rolling her

to his side and dipping her lithe frame momentarily. The small of her back a̲.
ing and her breasts artistically protruding forward against his chest was a furthe̲.
inducement. He purposefully moved her towards the middle of the dance floor
so the crowds might force them to have to even draw more closely together, and
disallow any ready avenues of escape. But the girl he was with had nothing like
that in mind. Sackett gently kissed the neck of the club worker and she smiled,
lightly bit her lower lip, seductively, and tried her best to entice.

The driver finally spotted them after numerous peerings and began to call
out for Sackett, but soon thought better of it. He was hesitant to draw undue
attention to himself or the captain. This was the case even though his business
was of the direst importance. He thought it better to instead try attempting to
cross the floor and make his way indirectly towards the amorously engrossed
officer.

Navigating the dancers proved intrepid, as they physically rebuked him from
encroaching his way past them. And then, before the old man could get half way
to the couple, the song ended and the two were off to the far side of the room,
somehow finding a path of egress in the dancing amalgamation of partiers.

Seeing chances of gaining Sackett's attention quickly growing for the
worse, the elderly aide dismissed protocol and attempted to hail the captain.
But his voice was never a loud one, more like a hoarse whisper in regular conversation; it carried no weight to be heard above the din of the crowd, and
their vibrant applauding. And now a livelier tune began to play and the driver
was being crushed between even more dancers entering the dance space and
others leaving it. For a half minute, it seemed, he couldn't move forward an
inch from where he started. Resigned to the impossibility, he retreated and
tried to find access along the walls, but the place was packed tight. And he was
at a complete standstill.

He sagged against the stairs, winded and frustrated by the impotence of
his attempt. He found it getting difficult to breathe down there, as well, so he
morosely climbed the stairs and made his way to the door. But the private had
difficulty doing that even because of the late-comers who were still trying to
get in, simultaneously with him leaving. It only stood to reason, though. It was
almost midnight.

As the coat checker let Captain Sackett escort her back to her job site
she held on to his right-angled arm, wrapping both of her hands around the
bicep area.

He opened the gate for her with a little flourish, bowing to her as she released his arm and then entered the storage area; with a dancer's grace, a grace
heightened by no small sense of satisfaction that illumined her smile. She
turned to him and let both hands rest softly down upon the counter and she
pointed her chin up to him expectantly.

But Frank Sackett did the unexpected, just then, and reached around the corner of the check area and pulled a silver bucket with thin chrome legs over to the counter area. A magnum bottle of *Moët Chandon* and two flutes nestled deeply in the ice reserves were at his disposal to serve.

He hadn't heard the gasp or noticed the coat check girl's mouth dropping open slightly from his gesture because his head had turned to the side for the moment, but she was totally caught off guard; however, she did not want to seem overly impressed. Because her momma raised her right. Even though, after all, well—the man had brought a whole bottle. Not just one glass. He was working hard for her, she thought, and then she wondered how her mother would have handled this.

"Now waittaminute," she giggled, "I said I'd dance with you—just dance, okay. What's all this here?"

"But I know you worked up a powerful thirst out there," Frank chided the cautious employee. "And you been working all night, to boot." He popped the cork then, not waiting for an answer. The bottle's foaming volcano spilling a portion into the spigot.

"Hold up, I bet you don't even remember my name."

"Yes, I do." And Sackett comically rolled his eyes in false concentration, "It's Sugar, ain't it?"

They both laughed as he tilted and poured into first one flute and then the other. The captain's charm was making him hard to put off. But her momma always said that the devil was a good looking man. "Please, Bernice," he said. "Before the year runs out."

Quaffing the sparkling wine with its cold effervescent bubbles made both of their taste buds harden. Berniece was having a similar affect upon her aureoles and nipples. And they kissed, long and deep, their tongues feeling somewhat pleasantly rough and cold, not unlike a cat's tongue when it licks your face. At least, that was Bernice's assessment as she ran her hand over and over the nape of Frank's neck.

Captain Sackett was not into making such speculations, however, for he just knew what he liked. And for this moment, at this time, he had no worries to think about.

By the time the couple in the club had finished with their embrace, the driver had exited back out into what had now become a whirling maelstrom of snow. He paced around his parked vehicle like an animal on the prowl, wringing his hands, and sometimes flapping his arms around his chest as he tried to entrap what little body heat he could.

But that stopped after awhile. With exhaustion came resignation, and he sat on the running board of the staff car, oblivious it seemed of the hawkish winds that sent ice shears of cold from one side to the other. Snow piling atop his coat and hat. This most forlorn figure just sat there, with his broad, squatty fingers gouging up the flesh of his jowls and waited. Waited like an obedient, but whipped, dog. A dog waiting for an inattentive master to take it home.

The driver didn't bother to pull his collar close about his neck, even. Cupping his chin in his hands, now, he simply accepted that inches of snow were piling on top of his service cap and the shoulders of his dark green coat, and he didn't care. Not any more.

Inside the club, the object of the driver's pursuit, poured a third glass of champagne for him and his companion and had nearly emptied the bottle. In one half hour the celebrating would begin in earnest and activity in the club was elevating; increased by jubilant and libidinous attendees at the soiree, now unraveling their manners and inhibitions, delighting in the excuse for hedonism. It seemed that everything and everyone had been shrunk down to their essence and capsulated into a suspension these last few minutes of the year of our Lord, 1943. The world had surely been mad enough lately to be fit to end that night, some had said. None even suspected that such power existed.

The music blaring out into the crowd from the large speakers had giggling runs of clarinet ripples. Sustained squeals taking the listener ever onward on a roller coaster of cleft notes. It seemed the idiom for this level of frivolity was appropriate; the place was jumping, as the saying went, and nobody could have stopped it if they had wanted to.

For such was the plight of the service aide outside in the cold night, now looking almost like a halfway-created snow man sitting at the side of the car. His lips curled inward with humiliation as he bared his teeth in a silent moaning. Tears welled up like hot little globs of oil in his eyes, but the air dried them before the wetness could touch his cheek. He failed and hated to admit it to himself that he couldn't have tried a little harder. Maybe gone a little further.

Occasionally, little hitches of crying would come out, followed by sighs so piteous that one most assuredly would think he'd lost his soul. Clear viscous snot started flowing out from his nose, which he at least took the time to wipe off his upper lip with his coat sleeve. What was the use, he thought. And then for some reason he looked up and over to the saloon stairwell, and wonder upon wonders, there was Captain Sackett. Weaving drunkenly by the railing, he was trying to put his arm into his coat.

"Whatcha stan—whatcha stannin' there——oh. Y'ain't stannin'. You's sittin'."

Sackett tottered a few steps.

"Whatcha sittin' there, fer?" He giggled. "Can't you see I need a little— little help?"

The old soldier got up and walked over in quiet deliberation to assist the officer, now blowing his nose into his white handkerchief, and all the while listening to the captain sputter on.

Sackett realized he hadn't eaten. He'd been hungry earlier, but hadn't had anything to eat and that was why he was so drunk. It was not his intention to be slovenly, but he was no superior, at this moment. "My gosh, man," he said, "How did I let time go by like this?"

The aide simply sniffled deeply and dutifully adjusted the captain's coat collar, squaring the service hat, and gently but firmly gripping the younger man's shoulders to straighten him up. He looked into Frank's eyes with full emotion.

"You needn't be in such a hurry, Suh. You needn't be."

"No, come—c'mon we can still get—"

The driver leaned close. "They ain't no place to get to if it's the hospital you talking 'bout, Suh. The colonel—the colonel, he dead."

Hearing those words spoken so softly in his ear drained all the alcohol out of Sackett's blood. Legs straightened that moments ago had been rubbery, and his wandering gaze now became riveted. But he grabbed hold of the old man's arm still, for strength to deal with the shock.

"What are you saying?"

"I waited and waited. I even came down to fetch you twice," the driver explained, crying unashamedly now, like a child expecting some bitter punishment, "but it's de truf—he sho' nuff gone, now."

Frank felt like someone had just yanked off layers of skin from his chest. A raw pain replacing it, and a low groan began to resonate in the back of his throat. But it got choked off somehow before passing his tonsils. All he could do was sink to the ground, but the old man, who now seemed amazingly strong, wouldn't let him. Both men now had tears in their eyes as they looked at each other, and neither cared.

"I lubbed that ol' man, Suh," the driver lamented. "With all me, I surely did. And you must forgive me for speaking so, but I got to tell you. It ain't right. It ain't right that you go on an' get my 'spectations so high, and then not be mindful to keep 'em from getting' stomped on—Colonel Peets and me, Suh. We was more than just two soldiers. He were like family ta me. Y'hear? Family. And I never got my chance to say goodbye, proper. So, I hope you'll 'scuse me if I'm amight perturbed with you."

Sackett felt like he'd been admonished by a stern father. Probably what, more or less, his own father had been. Somewhere in Alabama. Years and degrees of Fahrenheit-warmed breezes away from where he stood now. Frank now turned away, too. Ashamed to rebuke the non-com for being so bold. He had been properly chastened and also knew that just he needed to be silent, and take that medicine.

The reverence accorded the news of the colonel's death became palpable with three successive blasts of Arctic like winds that threatened to unseat Frank's hat. He pulled it closer over his brow, turned his collar up and thrust his hands deep into the wells of his coat pockets, finding his gloves at the bottom, and started to walk out of the alley.

"Where you going to, Suh?"

"Just go on home, soldier," Sackett replied. "Go home."

The officer cinched his coat tighter about him as he turned, and the driver could hear the wail of "Oh, my!" ring back to his ears on the tracks of a howling wind. The snow swirled all around Sackett in a glowing ball, beneath a streetlamp he passed in the alley way. Walking nowhere in the cold particularly, and similarly, with no purpose... until he could find a place to rest for what was left of the terrible night.

PART II

CHAPTER TWENTY-TWO
Another Day

Jim Martin had been astounded by all the intricacies of the detail last night's visit by Franklin Sackett had revealed to him. For one, he could not discount the appearance of any lack in vigor that the old man might have conveyed. Even though he was retelling a story that a writer had researched and connected the events for, Sackett himself held an extraordinary sense of authenticity in the story being told to the son of August Martin, even for his age. He had a sustained energy that did not waiver. Not until the hours turned into the early morning, and upon agreement that they would continue the following day, did the old man yawn and decide to call it a day. Sackett promised, and Jim knew, that there was a great deal more to be unearthed about his father.

This man who mysteriously came into Jim's life was making his father become real to the son, and no longer just the speechless and pathetic shell of a figure he'd despised all of his adult life. Jim remembered a little about his grandmother, Cleo, but now that Sackett had placed a whole new picture of her in the frame of Jim's understanding, of who she really was, and what Jim knew she had allowed taking place in order for him to be sired in such a strange and horrible awakening, of innocence destroying innocence. Well, it was like reading a story backwards. But the elements still needed analyzing. Just like Franklin Sackett felt his hamburger needed more seasoning. Giving his apologies to Lorraine.

"It's probably my medicine," he said.

"You sure you should be having all that salt, though?"

"What's the use of eating something if you can't taste it, Mrs. Martin? But what you've laid out for me here is fine, Ma'am. Right fine."

"Could I have some of that salt, Franklin?"

Sackett crossed it over the table to Jim.

"I been telling her ever since I knew her that she seasons things too lightly."

"That's a relief," Sackett said. "Otherwise I would be thinking something else just done petered out on me, here. Seems to happen every other day."

Brad's legs begin to kick back and forth slightly as he rocked in his chair. He pushed back his lunch plate. "Momma—we gonna be late."

"What time the tournament start?" Jim asked, scooping his fork in a shoveling maneuver to pick up some baked beans.

"The game starts at 2:00, but coach wants us there early."

"Bernadette, where's your outfit?"

"I'll get it."

Lorraine rose and stacked hers and the children's plates.

"Excuse me, get your bag Brad," she said.

Sackett's raised eyebrows at all the commotion around him. "You're not staying?" he asked.

"They got a church league game. Brad's a forward and Bea is on the pep squad," Jim explained, wiping the corners of his mouth with a paper napkin.

"Besides," Lorraine said, "you two got a private conversation going on at the moment, anyway."

"Oh, I'm sorry," Frank apologized sincerely, but Lorraine waved her hand dismissively.

"You don't understand, Franklin. It's all right. Jimmy fills me in after the fact, so I'm not left out, in the least. But you two have to fend for yourselves for dinner. *We* are going to be at the *Pizza Hut* after the game."

"Why don't you bring us back some, then?" Jim suggested, trying to get out of foraging, if he could.

"Uh, don't think so." And Lorraine backed her way into the kitchen's swinging door with her load, and disappeared.

"We'll go out," Jim assured Frank. "Want a cigarette?"

"Thanks, don't mind if I do."

Halfway through the caustic but pleasant inhalations and exhalations, Jim tamped a long ash cylinder on the lip of the glass ashtray. He'd thought about how to ask Sackett this question for quite some time before he was finally able to get asleep the other night. "I'm not going to have police come knocking on my door because of you being here, am I, Mr. Sackett?"

"I would do no such thing as to bring my troubles to your door, if I believed that to be the case, Jim. And I can appreciate your nervous indulgence. But let me just say that the next few segments of the telling will explain all the mystery about me. But that's really just a subplot as to what the heart of the matter is behind me coming."

"All right, let me see. Colonel Peets passed away and you left—going where?"

"Somewhere not close to the place I had to eventually return and move forward from. I was rudderless, and for the first time without a mentor to provide me any guidance. I had to feel the earth underneath me again, find my center."

• • •

When Captain Sackett finally contacted the division headquarters as to his whereabouts, changes were already under way to allow for his leave.

"Now whatever you do," warned the newly promoted Sergeant Major Davies, "don't process that requisition any further, until you can verify those last two signatures." And for emphasis he displayed two separated fingers in front of the face of the taller buck sergeant he lectured.

"I see," he said, adjusting his collar and matching khaki tie. His shirt seemed a size too small for this orientee, and this was especially true because of the malfunctioning steam heater in the office common area.

Davies was a zealous noncom, Sgt. Pintor thought, especially for only being the acting commander for a week. But then, he didn't fault him all that much because he too wanted to make a good impression on the captain once he returned. So, this new buck sergeant, who looked so lean and muscular, almost West Indian in appearance, let Davies feel his oats without showing his annoyance outwardly.

Davies crossed the office with an undeserving swagger of authority and addressed Pintor in a tone of confidence. "Don't worry," he assured him. "It may take a little while but you'll get the hang of it, soon enough. But I'll be your direct supervisor. Any questions you have, any at all. I'm right here. But of course, you have the prerogative to run common duties as you see fit. Every man's got their particular style of leadership, don't they?"

My thoughts exactly, Pintor thought, but he managed to begin his next sentence with making clarifications about a regulation instead. Something to show Davies he'd been paying attention, and to test his new supervisor's acumen, as well. "What was that you said before about how intelligence general ops could be countermanded regarding an inspector general audit?" But a worker coming in the foyer interrupted the flow of one-way conversation.

"Hey, Sergeant Major, can you sign me off on this here door? I'm all finished."

"How wet is the paint?" Davies inquired, while he and Pintor walked over to examine the job.

"As long as no one goes touching it in the middle of the glass, we'll be in business. Had some touch up done, there."

And he pushed the door to and fro using the posterior fingers of his right hand on the door's edge. The outer door no longer scuttled across the entry way in the headquarter building. It had been planed down, and even the arc of the scuff marks it left in the hallway had been obliterated with a flawless refinishing. So now there was no auditory alarm for restive soldiers if a superior should happen to be coming through. Not even so much as the small shriek of a door's hinge. Davies, Pintor, and the corporal admired the finished work, while the corporal ran cheesecloth around the wood, removing any last traces of dust.

"Is that how many non-coms it takes to open one door?"

It was Sackett.

"ATTEN-HUT."

The men formed a barrier that obfuscated the door from the captain's eyes, but that didn't keep him from curiously trying to peek past them. "Welcome back, Captain," Davies greeted, "How was your stay in Harlem, Sir?"

"What's this? Sergeant Davies," Sackett inquired, the question asked, ignored. "Congratulations are in order, I guess. You're a master, now? And who's this?"

Sgt. Pintor saluted and offered his hand, "Sergeant Pintor, Sir. New office adjutant."

"Welcome aboard, Sergeant," a bewildered Sackett said.

"Thank you, Captain. It will be a pleasure to serve."

"At ease, men."

The trio of Sackett's attendants stepped back to reveal the door to him and Frank's eyes darted over the pane from left to right, reading the declarative, and then furrowing his brow as he tilted his head in the direction of Davies.

"It is correct, isn't it?" Davies asked.

"As far as spelling, but who gave—"

"We wanted to get it done before you got back from your trip. How was it, Sir? Did it go as you planned? Did you get to the Apollo like you wanted?"

Sackett had silently stepped past the men, taking off his hat and overcoat placing them over his arm almost as if he was in a trance. He entered into the main office slowly, hesitantly, as if he was considering turning back around, and then he saw Davies' name on his old office door. Seeing that change solidified the new context of the bureau and he saw that his name, CAPTAIN FRANKLIN SACKETT was indeed arced over the frosted pane to Colonel Peets' former place of work, just like it had been done on the outer door. Underneath the spanning gold and black-trimmed homage were the solid black block letters, 184TH FIELD ARTILLERY. And under the division designation was the final honorarium. The word, "COMMANDER".

He took a quarter turn to his right and mouth slightly agape stared at Davies in a perplexity that could not be accounted for, yet he had no words to ask how all these changes happened so quickly without him knowing. Davies smiled and took Sackett's wraps and hung them.

"Bet you can't believe we got on so swell without you, in order to do this," Davies said, "but by jingo—we done it, all right. Didn't we, Sir? Just over two weeks and here we are."

"Who's the new man, again?"

"Buck Sergeant, Pintor, Sir. Trying him on for size in my old job, now that I'm your, ah, ah—"

"Administrative adjutant, Sarge. Is that what you're trying to say?"

"Right, right, that's it." Davies pulled out a pack of cigarettes, partially extracting a smoke, but then reconsidered the propriety of lighting up at the moment and put the tobacco back into the pack. "I keep forgetting that. All this time and I never knew that was your actually your designation, Sir. Thought it just was sub-commander.

Sackett didn't take any notice of the gaffe that embarrassed the new master sergeant because he was too preoccupied with opening the door to Peets' office. And his hand was now on the doorknob. "What's it like inside?" Sackett asked.

"Cherry, Sir. I think you'll find it quite suitable."

Sackett wondered if Davies might have been inferring to the fact he had needed to take three weeks' bereavement leave after the colonel passed, or that he was still experiencing delayed emotional pangs, and guilt. He wondered if Davies had said that to let him know that he understood and that they all had done everything possible to uplift his spirits upon his return. Suitable, Sackett thought to himself. It was a subjective word. He didn't ask if all of Peet's accoutrements had been moved out. "No calls, please," Sackett ordered.

"As you wish, Sir," Davies said in a reassuring and understanding tone. A tone that Sackett felt was well-intended but just a might too patronizing.

And then within a moment, Davies was nowhere in the vicinity. Sackett turned, rooted it seemed at the office door, but he prepared himself. Hand still on the knob, but not having turned it yet. He closed his eyes so he could be impacted with the full effect of the hoped for transformation that he needed to see in the room. He didn't want to be reminded of dead warriors, today. Eyes still closed, he stepped inside.

When he opened his eyes he was surprised, in a way, to find that all changes had been simplistic. The biggest modification happened to be a new carpet and there was a different desk in front of the venetian blind window. The flags of the states of Michigan, Wisconsin, and Illinois had been taken off the walls and staved. The Illinois and Wisconsin flags were at either side. Behind the desk, on the left side of the window was the American flag, and to its right, the Michigan state flag.

The wooden blazonry of the 184th's field colors were still on the wall opposite, but under it, Sackett noticed a new piece of furniture. It was a slick-finished, cherry wood rocker, with two inch-high, burnt-orange velvet upholstery on the seat and the arms, and at the head rest. Sackett recognized the chair and slowly moved towards it, seeing a note lain on the seat. Coming closer yet, Sackett also recognized the handwriting on the note. It was from Davies, and it read:

Dear Captain,

The wife thought this rocker you had your eye on would occupy a more useful space in your office than in our attic. In other words, I got stuck cleaning last weekend. So, enjoy it. And it is a pleasure to say, welcome back.

Master Sergeant Davies

Not only had Sergeant Davies taken it out from his house, but the captain could see that he'd had it refinished, as well. It was a thoughtful act and caught Frank off-guard with the compassion expressed. He'd underestimated the soldier's depth of complexity. His heart. It made the captain feel ashamed of the way he treated him earlier in the outer office. Finishing off the setting were a tall parlor lamp and a throw rug neatly placed on the hardwood floor in front of the furniture. And on the side of the chair was a small table. A telephone covered up about two-thirds of its polished surface. Then five feet away was a well padded, cushiony love seat that had compact curves of elegance and style. It would be a perfect accommodation for a guest when an informal conference was appropriate. Sackett was pleased and also knew he had found a place for doing his reading at times when he needed a change of location within the office. When he needed to get away from being behind his desk, in order to gain perspective.

Sackett turned on the lamp, sat down in the rocker, and ran his fingers over the phone's receiver. He drummed his fingers over the plastic and then found himself picking the thing up and dialing a number. No operator came on the line, for it was a direct communication. On a secured line.

"Colonel August Krech, please," Sackett requested.

"One moment," the respondent in Chicago said.

In the moments he found himself waiting, Sackett pushed back in the rocker a few times, and luxuriated in his new setting, making a mental note to have Davies come out some night for a steak dinner. And he looked up at the blazonry for a moment. All for one, he thought to himself, remembering the ex-officio motto that the unit gave itself. Then there was a click on the phone at the other end, like the sound of the thumb-clacking toy would make from a box of *Cracker Jacks*. Then Captain Sackett heard the Colonel breathe heavily into the phone, as if he were interrupted in mid-thought.

"This is Colonel Krech, may I help you?"

"Colonel, this is Captain Sackett at the 184th, Fort Custer. We met at Colonel Peets' last summer, remember?"

"Oh, yes, Captain. I remember, very well. My condolences to you on the passing of Anderson, by the way. He was a credit to your people." Your people, Sackett heard Krech's word echo in his thought.

Tried to not let his tension get the better of him when he heard that, and he rolled his eyes as they smarted from the misting of tears he fought from experiencing. Tears of anger, not grief. The sting of emotions Krech's well-meant eulogy triggered was almost suffocating. It was getting difficult to prepare to talk as he listened to more vapid platitudes, but he grit his molars and put on a mask in order to hide his feelings. "Yes, he was a great warrior, Sir. I dare say it will be hard to find someone to replace—"

"Oh, quite right, Captain—quite right. Who could even think of trying to *replace* him? We can't replace, Captain. We can only renew his legacy." Colonel Krech discontinued further verbal meandering, however, and finally asked, "So, you had a question, Captain?"

"Well, Sir, yes I do. They've seem to have gotten my name painted on a door up here, and I know I don't rate command ranking, so I was calling to inquire, exactly—"

"Oh, that's interim," Krech explained, "but for how long I can't really say. We'll find someone, eventually. But until then, considering the fact that we've had to muster you boys—well, I think it might be wise to have consistency in play there. Your experience is invaluable, at the moment."

"I appreciate the vote of confidence, Sir."

"But of course," Krech assured, "I've had nothing but good things said about you since Detroit, last summer."

"Thank you, Sir. But actually, that's another matter that I'd like to speak to you about."

"You've read the reports, haven't you?"

"Not as of yet, Colonel. But this isn't really about fact-finding, or investigations or anything about what caused or didn't cause the riot, Sir. What I want to know from you is about my soldiers, here, and how they will be used in the coming movement. Now, Colonel Peets made it known to me that we had men chosen for special training—"

"Uh-huh."

"What I need to know, Colonel Krech, is whether that training is on stand-down status, or what?"

There was silence. Sackett wanted to be sure that he had his flank covered, given what Colonel Peets had told him before he died. "Colonel?" Sackett mildly persisted.

"Oh, I—I should, ah, be getting some word from Washington any time now, Captain," Krech responded. "But the troop movement hasn't been released by the Department, yet, you see? So, I would be premature and maybe speculative, at best, if I were to say how things stand. One way or the other. You and your men's patience have reason to be thin, though. And I recognize your position, but hang tough with me, okay?"

"Well, I guess that's fine. I mean, as long as we're both hanging, there isn't too much room for me to complain. Is there, Colonel?" And Sackett realized he may have breached the lines of familiarity with a superior, but didn't apologize.

Colonel Krech chuckled into the phone at the slight indiscretion. "Keep that sharp wit, Captain. You'll see your way clear in that matter, I'm sure."

"Thank you, Sir." But Sackett sensed that Krech's retort was thinly edged with some irritation. But probably because he was being kept from other pressing matters, maybe.

"Good day to you, then. Commander Sackett." And the colonel hung up the phone on his end of the line. But Sackett did not feel at ease with what transpired in the conversation and his hackles were up. It felt like he was being played along.

Sackett knew what they were trying to do, that by placing him in a position of command, and moreso, a command that was in line with an investigation about discrepancies from the riots, that they then could have a subterfuge to perpetrate a further investigation on him, simultaneously. Putting him in an acting-status of command would lend itself to applying closer scrutiny to him without denoting their true suspicions. He felt they were beginning to tighten a noose, and it surely wasn't a rope that was being shared in a society of mutual admiration, as Krech implied. It was a rope that was squarely placed around only one man's neck that he knew of—his.

Just then, there were three very short cursory raps on the office door, before Sgt. Davies entered. "Begging pardon, Sir, but—"

"Baxter," Sackett scolded. "This can't be like ol' times around here, anymore. You understand? I said no interruptions—not interruptions when you feel convenienced to make them."

"But I wouldn't be so bold, Sir. I just thought you'd want to know that I had to hire a new driver for you."

When Sackett looked at Davies' shame and hurt, he'd wished he hadn't reacted as he did. "What happened to Colonel Peets' driver?" he asked.

"Put in for voluntary transfer, Sir. After you'd gone. I got the new guy outside if you want to check him out."

"Couldn't that wait?"

"How'd you expect to get home tonight, Sir? Just take a gander at him and spit him out if you don't want him."

"Oh—all right. Send him in."

"Yassuh," Davies said turning to leave.

"And Baxter?"

Davies turned at the door.

"Thanks for all you have done for me, here. It hasn't all gone unnoticed. I guess, I'm just—"

"Don't even think about it," Davies assured the captain. He opened the door to the outer office then, changing his demeanor. "I'll send him in directly, Sir."

Davies stood with his back to the door's jamb way and waved the potential driver inside, while Captain Sackett had returned to his desk and was searching through some drawers for his pipe tobacco. There had been a meticulous transfer of seemingly all his property from his previous desk but not that. Sackett then looked between some folders and saw it.

Finding the tobacco, he picked up the pipe, which he was still trying to acquire a taste for, so he could try to cut down on his chain-smoking. He took a pinch of the moist and pungent, shredded leaves and filled the bottom of the blackened bowl. His back to the door. As he lit the pipe with four sharp and rapid intakes, a dull thud of heels clapping together brought the officer to turn and appraise the soldier standing before him.

"Private Martin, reporting for duty, Sir."

The skin shone brightly on the young man's face, more chance than not from having had a recent scrubbing. And the smile on his face could not have even been remotely interpreted or characterized to be sardonic, or confused with being an affixed enamel badge. Gus Martin stood in the captain's office completely enthralled at the opportunity to be considered for this prestigious job. To him, it seemed everything he could have hoped for; a short term accomplishment that could only help his military career. The angled arm, frozen at the saluting position, revealed a hand that was not dry and ashy, but moist from lotion; his fingernails were clean and trimmed and his right thumb was cocked like the hammer of a gun.

"At ease," Sackett directed.

Gus took a parade rest stance, looking right nor left, just trying to appear militarily-relaxed, but hoping to imply, or give the impression, that a quarter mile run would not be out of the question for him if called upon to do so. Sackett set his pipe down and let it smolder in his desk ashtray. He leaned forward, putting the tips of his fingers on the desktop and keeping them there as he sat down, still looking Gus over.

"You look very familiar to me, private."

"We've had some occasions, Sir."

"Refresh my memory."

"Well, Sir—the riot. I alerted you about the uprising on the base. And then I was on the team that deployed in Detroit. And—ah, ah, more recently at the NCO Club—New Years."

"What are you talking about?"

"My brother, Sir. He was the drunk you talked to that night."

"Humph, I wouldn't be too anxious to remind me about that kinship, private."

"Just trying to clarify for you, Captain. It's not a matter of pride, I assure you."

Sackett picked up the pipe and leaned back in his chair, applying a flame to the bowl and puffing a chimney of smoke out of it. He seemed to appear older to Gus than he remembered when he smoked the pipe, and more intimidating. "You the same type of apple?" Sackett asked.

"Sir?"

"Are you two similar? Because I don't need someone who has no sense of protocol or decorum when driving me around. There could be high-level people riding alongside me, and I would not countenance lightly being embarrassed."

"No, Sir."

"I also don't need someone who can't mind their business. There has to be complete confidentiality maintained, nothing ever repeated."

"No, Sir."

"Humph."

There he went again, Gus thought, with that grunt of dissatisfaction. And he keeps staring at me with that hard look, too. Gus thought for sure then that

Joe had submarined this whole thing for him. Damn him.

"I dunno, Martin. I don't think I can use a private for a driver."

Sackett thought he could see the kid's eyes begin to swell with tears. And Gus swallowed hard to keep himself stoic. Sensing the conversation and inquiry now being over, he snapped to attention and saluted. Sackett stood slowly and saluted him back with a lackadaisical motion, and then said, "But go on down to the PX and get some corporal insignia, and report back here to Sgt. Pintor to get my car ready by four o' clock."

"Thank you, Sir!" Gus erupted, "Whoop!" he almost screeched. "Thank you, Sir. Oh, thank you. You won't ever be sorry for this. I swear to you."

Between hand pumps and balancing his pipe from spilling from the energetic adulation, Sackett still found moments in the interaction amusing to him, chuckling at times between all the effusive behaviors.

"All you got to do is show me how you open doors, boy. I can't say I want you to prove you can shake my arm off."

"Yes, Sir. Sorry, Sir."

"You're dismissed."

There was a hyphenated salute and a jumble of olive drab uniform and leather soled boots running out of the office. Sackett closed the door and heard the newly promoted corporal give out another yelp of indiscretion. That was followed quickly by Sgt. Davies.

"Martin! Act like you got some sense boy!"

"Sorry, Sergeant! Yes, Sergeant!"

Then he could hear the commotion of someone tripping.

Sackett grinned. Not caring that his pipe had gone out.

CHAPTER TWENTY-THREE
Rank and Privilege

Gus concentrated, so as not to stick his index finger as he punched through the canvas of the khaki shirt. The needle went in with a deft insertion, right alongside his thumbnail as Gus held the cloth insignia firmly in place. Notwithstanding the pins he used to square the stripe and rocker on the shoulders of his uniform. Drawing the needle out, his right arm spanned wide and his eyes followed the straightening of the thread.

This occasion was so special for Gus, and he was relieved, delighted in fact, that sharing his good fortune within the barracks would not be necessary; not until he had the new rank on his sleeve. Indisputably in place, and none of the naysayers could give him any flack. Sitting there on his bunk, in his t-shirt and pants, Gus just hummed to himself as he worked. Joe was on his bunk, but he was turned away from Gus's direction. Now he had just finished his second-to-the-last shirt. He hung it up from the upper bunk's frame, alongside two other finished shirts. Tailored for display. Now, he wouldn't mind some passerbys to coming down the barrack's aisle. He'd love to explain the developments.

As he worked on his final shirt, Gus not only hummed but would whistle every now and then, lost in a personal reverie of high expectations. As he sewed, he began to imagine the various functions he would have to accompany Captain Sackett to. The ideas started at the realm of plausibility but soon rocketed to stratospheric proportions.

He saw himself having to drive Captain Sackett on secret missions, with flashes of mortar fire beaconing in the night. He saw himself passing off documents and weapons to the captain, as well. And his whistling became louder as he grew more excited by his imaginings, and all the while the needle continued to punch through the cloth, first in, and then out—in, and then out...

"Hey!"

It was Joe.

"How can a niggah sleep around here while you got all that 'Gimme-cracked-corn-and-I-don't-care' bullshit you been whistling going on? What you all so fired up and happy about?"

Gus didn't answer. Stopping both sewing and whistling for a moment, he turned his head, giving Joe a blank stare. After a dramatic pause he put his attention back to finishing the work at hand.

"Oh," Joe huffed, "so I'm just supposed to figure it out for myself, huh? Is that it? Well, I wasn't born without a brain, Gus. I see the stripes on them shirts, and whoever's paying you to put them on for him is a fool."

"No, I'm not," Gus said.

"What you talking about, niggah?"

"These are mine, Joe."

"How'd you get jumped up two pay grades?"

"I'm a staff driver now, Joe."

"Who'd be fool enough to let you in the driver's pool?"

"Somebody did, Joe. All I know is I got chosen."

"By who?"

"The captain."

"Well, you go on back and thank him for the consideration and then resign, y'hear."

"Joe!"

"You heard what I told you about him and Momma."

"You couldn't even be sure it was him."

"I'm sure enough." Joe got a gleam in his eye that made Gus's flights of fancy seem trite. "And he knows he did it, too. He knows I know. And that's why he picked you. Because he knew it would drive me out my fuckin' mind if I found out. The bastard. I hate that sonuvabitch."

"First momma, and now you. Better watch your backsides, junior."

"Joe!"

"She hates me, Gus. Hates me. Y'know that? All because of him, and his tomcat ways. All because her itch became more important to her than the memory of our daddy, Gus. And when I laid her straight about how things should be—she wanted nothing more to do with me. No, suh. Don't put anything past that niggah."

"You're being silly."

"Oh, I'm the one being silly, now?"

"Joe, you got it sounding like he's got making your life miserable more of a military agenda for him than keeping Hitler out of London. Like, he'd really do that."

"What makes you think he wouldn't?"

"Wouldn't what?"

"Have you make a choice—like Momma did."

"He's an officer, Joe. Be serious."

"No, he's just a man. Officer be damned."

"Joe, what about the code of ethics?"

Joe cackled dryly, wringing his hands lightly, with a self-assuredness that almost seemed he was making a prescient analysis.

"You think that commission means anything? That commission he wears don't give him angel's wings, boy. Colored officers ain't about shit. The niggers they's in charge of don't trust 'em. And the white man who trains 'em don't want him, and won't give him no kinda respect. And you want to go 'round washing the feet of this made-up nigger Jesus? You want to be his disciple? Son, let me tell you something. He'll throw you down to walk over a puddle as soon as talk to you. But he can't, if you don't let him, Gus. Not if you don't let him."

Gus thought for a moment to say something, but he knew that nothing he could say would ever sway Joe's convictions. And those always were so pessimistic. There never was an upside to anyone or anything. But Gus became numb to it, by now. It's how he was. Maybe they were already growing apart, without Sackett's mingling. In this time of celebration and satisfaction, Gus didn't feel like he even had a brother. His response to Joe's pleas was to purse his lips, and test the air for the proper tone, as he started whistling once again. Whistling about cracked corn and blue-tailed flies.

Several weeks later, new developments were occurring in Chicago, as well. Though on a much higher level. And on matters so important that the division commanders of the Sixth Command had to forego a early season baseball game involving the Cubs and visiting Brooklyn Dodgers. The service command had lovely box seats at Wrigley, and the spring afternoon was perfect for taking in a game, but it was not meant to be. Colonel Krech, General Gunther, and General Henry Aurand, the Commanding General, all gathered in Krech's cramped office, shared *Blatz* beer and passed around a bowl of peanuts as they listened to a radio broadcast and checked the teletype occasionally.

"Isn't this about the time that if we'd been at Wrigley you'd have a staffer calling for you, Henry?"

The general smirked, "I am solely dissimilar from the characterization of that remark—" and he joined everyone else in the guffaws over his attempted self-deprecation. All things humorous are always tinged with some truth, though, and when the 7th inning stretch came around the general hadn't bought as near as many hot dogs and beers as his subordinates.

There was a knock on the door then and when he opened it Krech could not believe the timeliness of what happened next; a fresh-faced lieutenant, one of Aurand's aides, held out a sack of polish dogs and another cold six-pack. "You all owe me many apologies," Aurand chided them, and laughed again.

"You're a damn fine man, Henry," Gunther said, taking two of the passed treats. "I don't care what Auggie says about you."

Krech's wide-eyed double take when he heard the disparagement about him got the whole group roaring again. They genuinely liked one another a great deal, regardless of their ranks. And as quickly as their jocularity began, a unified groan came forth as it was announced two more Dodgers scored off of another infield error.

"Dammit!" Aurand bellowed, shoving the torn end of his polish sausage and bun to the side of his mouth. He quickly wiped some excess mustard with a napkin. "That's two this inning! Why don't they put in York?"

"Inexcusable," Krech said.

"I'm gonna go and take a look at the tape," Gunther informed the gathering. "I could use some air."

"Yeah, nobody could be as bad as Leonard Murello," Aurand said.

"York's rock steady, usually, so what gives? What do we got to do to get a decent shortstop, here?" Krech wondered.

"Maybe it was gnats?" Aurand joked. The bugs were known to be overly amorous when humidity and heat got up there along waterfronts, and that could cause pockets of swarm clouds.

"Gnats? It's barely spring."

"Yeah—you're right. I'd blame it on Murello, too."

"Too many mental breakdowns, probably," Krech opined. "They are definitely not on the same page today."

The radio announcer said that Bob Chipman was finishing the inning as the Cubs pitcher. He'd walked his first man, giving the Dodgers two on-base, and he had one strike and three balls on Brooklyn's Goody Rosen. "*Chippy looks off the runner on first,*" The broadcaster said. "*And he holds up the steal...and now here's the wind-up, and the pitch. Rosen couldn't check swing on the pitch, low to the outside, and somehow he got a hit. It's a hopper to the left—Murello has got to hustle!*"

Gunther re-entered the office and Aurand and Krech looked at him like dramatic theater masks as they howled their shared displeasure in his direction. "Well, if that's the way you two feel about me, gentlemen—" Gunther playfully chided.

"Nothing personal, Gunny," General Aurand apologized. "Another muck up, by Murello, is all."

"What did he do now?"

"Murello missed a skipping ground ball between 2nd and 3rd. Dallesandro brings it in from left field, but he missed the pick up, too."

"Don't tell me," Gunther pleaded.

"They missed tagging the man on third and had to throw for home but, you know, Dallesandro ain't got the strongest arm."

"Two more runs—Dodgers, end of story."

"How many outs?"

"One!" Krech and Aurand said together.

"Doesn't sound like anything a beer can't cure, boys," Gunther said, grabbing fresh ones from the cooler.

General Aurand took his and then reached over to turn the radio off, "My apologies, fellas. But I figger it's just better to get drunk than listen to the rest of that game."

More laughs.

"Did the wire come in yet, general?" Krech asked.

"That can wait...Hey, any of you two ever see any colored baseball?"

"What the hell you bringing that up for, Gunny?"

"Well, we were listening to a game, weren't we?"

"Yeah, but it sure weren't no nigra baseball," Aurand retorted. "What are you getting at, any way?"

"Let's look at what just happened, for a minute." Gunther turned his chair around and straddled it. "As I see it, that man responsible for the error could have said he missed the hop because he caught a reflection from the sun in his eyes, or from off the ball. Now, do you think a colored ball player would miss the same ball under those conditions? Think about it."

"Oh, he might be able to field it," Aurand said, "but his throw would probably cause another error. Split-second decision making is not their particular strong suit, Gunny."

Though Krech genuinely liked both his superior officers, there was one thing he didn't share in common with them. And that was his disapproval of unsubstantiated ethnic notions. He was fairly aghast, though hiding it, that he was hearing both of the generals applying Darwinism to modern sports in such a cavalier fashion. And knew they probably would not have done the same out in public, but that was even more discouraging to him, in a sense. Krech thought he'd seen some change in General Gunther since the integrated deployment in Detroit, but he guessed he must have been mistaken.

"You guys shoulda seen some Negro League baseball, if you wanted to see some slick playmaking," Gunther went on. "I saw some smokers while I was at the Pentagon that I'll never forget. Got a chance to see Buck Leonard over at Griffith Stadium. Guy was phenomenal, had a .459 batting average."

"Gunny, it's pretty easy to get an average that high when you're batting against mediocre pitching."

"Oh, I dunno, Henry. I wouldn't call Satchel Paige a limp wrist in any league, would you Auggie?"

"I've heard that claim. But I can't really say, having not seen the man play."

"Well, it's not just hearsay," Gunther confirmed. "Take it from someone who has. He'd give the Babe Ruth hell, I tellya."

"That'll be one of the great unanswered sport questions for all time," General Aurand sighed, disturbing the thin head of his beer as he brought it to his lips.

"The Babe against Paige," Krech mused.

"Never happen," Aurand said.

"But why not, Hank?" Gunther questioned, "I mean, not specifically, but in principle why couldn't it happen one day? Look at today's game. That fielder, whoever it was—"

"Dallesandro," Aurand filled in.

"Okay, Dallesandro. Well, he didn't seem to have much on the ball today, now did he? Are you going to sit there and tell me it was because he's Italian?"

"I wouldn't be the first," Aurand joked.

Krech was flummoxed by Gunther's change in trajectory, for he knew the man was not a staunch advocate of integration, to his knowledge. But the general speaking as he had made Colonel Krech braver in speaking up. "Hey, if you look at the Dodgers—they are on some kind of streak and they have coloreds on their farm teams. Maybe they had some of them working with the "A" club during the off-season. Rumor has it they may even sign one to the majors, soon."

"It will never happen," General Aurand resolutely denounced. "For one thing it'd be too expensive."

"How?" Gunther asked.

"They'd have to double their training facilities, and traveling would be a nightmare for logistics. *Plessy v. Ferguson* is the law of the land. Not even the Dodgers can change that."

"That may be changing, Hank."

General Aurand looked Gunther in the eye, caught unawares by the orchestrated drama his second-in-command unfurled through the subterfuge of baseball. "What the hell you talking about, Gunny?"

"When I first read the teletype I was surprised, to say the least, so I put in a call to Washington for confirmation. There will be no colored quota in troop basis selection for the coming year. They are doing away with it."

"Wha—?"

"Seems so, Hank. From here on out, we take the turnip right off the truck. Just as they are. No digging around for the whitest ones, anymore."

"I'm more taken with rutabaga, General," Krech teased.

"This is going to bring about some very complicated movements in the service, Gunny. Hmmm." Aurand thoughtfully stroked his chin. "Did that include infantry?"

"I'd imagine so, Hank. Looks to be an across the board policy going into effect."

With no further thought, General Aurand began to spell out what needed to be done, given the new circumstances. "Krech, I want to proceed then with the specialized training detail, immediately. Contact HQ at Benning to articulate the logistics. Find out what kind of orders we need to cut."

"Yes, Sir."

"I understand you had some experience putting together mixed troops in the recent past," Aurand continued. "That insight will be invaluable in communicating what our Negro troops are gonna need down there."

"I don't think it'll be anything more than feeding them and pointing to 'em which way the fight is, Hank," Gunther surmised, "no need for treating 'em like they're some kind of phenomenon, or something. They'll do fine. Won't they Colonel?"

"If Supreme Command is putting the kibosh on quotas, I'll lay odds that we're about to see a major offensive. Probably in multiple theaters. Given the chance, I think they'll prove admirable. But that means really giving them the chance."

"I never thought I'd see the day," Aurand said. "But, I can follow orders, and that's what we'll do."

"Auggie?" Gunther called softly, hesitant to bring up unpleasantness, "I understand that you were fairly high on the idea of the mixed deployment in Detroit. And it played well for the service, politically—but, there are some nagging concerns that really were not fully laid to rest. Given that we are now going to use these troops from Custer, I want to put to rest any possibility of those soldiers getting uppity. Especially down in Georgia."

"Are you talking about the little insurrection that happened there?"

"Yes. I understand that it was handled internally."

"They were given time to cool their heels, General. And no other instances of insubordinate behavior have come up, since."

"But that's not merely insubordination, Colonel. And you know it. Those men should have been fully charged."

CHAPTER TWENTY-FOUR
A Change of Plans

The sash to the Fort Custer Artillery Headquarters office window was forced open by Sergeant Pintor's extended efforts. Its wood having swollen somewhat from the past winter's invasion upon it. An intermittent breeze came through the bug impacted screen, allowing for some ventilation in the humid interior. Captain Sackett, the Master Sergeant, and Pintor each had handfuls of files that they'd been in the process of purging. The Sixth Command's directives required that all details involving training should have all ready been worked out, but there were many loose ends in Sackett's office because of the change over from losing the Colonel. So, now the three soldiers were doing their level best to rectify the situation, and it was hard work. They had to examine records for unnecessary duplication and missing artifacts.

Pintor gathered a new stack of folders and brought them to his desk and began the classifying of the records by evaluated completeness. One stack for files with missing documents, one with missing orders, and a third for folders with redundant materials. Then he would have to find the missing pieces, if lucky, in boxes of non-alphabetized papers. It was tedious work, work that demanded concentration, and that's why he'd opened the window. To let some coolness and fresh air not only revive them, but take the staleness out of the air, as well. A mustiness from all of the aged papers exhumed in the room. And it was effective, for the smell was getting better. And they weren't sneezing as much, either. But the opening of the window also came with a price. A nearby sycamore tree, not far from their building, housed several families of bickering sparrows this afternoon.

Occasionally their fighting for the limited nesting grounds in the trees went on with such a concentrated chatter that it would cause more than a little distraction. Sometimes, the men would have to raise voices to be heard. It was proving to be an untenable situation. But the breeze was so welcomed.

"Captain, I swear, if you'll let me just take out one or two of 'em," the buck sergeant pleaded, "they'll all get the message and get on away from here."

"Now, sergeant. What would it look like to have you out there taking pot shots at birds outside this building?"

Sgt. Davies grinned and nodded his head, imagining the scenario Sackett conjured. "Yeah, Captain, but y'can't always judge how good a road is by the number of cars on it."

"They'll quiet down, sooner or later."

"I got these all in order, Captain," Davies said, pointing to several tall stacks of file folders. "I'm gonna start putting' 'em away."

"Thanks, Sgt. Davies," Sackett concurred in an inattentive way, himself reading over documents from two different files. "We're about due for a break then, I think."

"Sounds good to me," Pintor said.

Someone running in the outer hall cut through the din of bird calls and metal drawers slamming. His arms and legs akimbo as he slid to a stop while passing through the cramped office's doorway, Corporal Martin gulped in lungful after lungful of air, like a thirsty man drinking water, before he could finally get the words he needed to say out of his mouth. "Sarge! Sarge, look here! I got it," Martin yelled, holding up a set of papers.

"Corporal!"

"Oh!"

Martin, with still heaving chest, saluted Captain Sackett with all the decorum his rank commanded. "Beg pardon, Sir."

"As you were," Sackett said with disinterest, for he was so immersed in his work. "Sgt. Davies, see what's got that boy all in a tizzy."

Davies took the documents out of the Corporal Martin's hands and gave them a cursory inspection before slowly turning towards the commissioned officer. "Capt'n. You better have a look at these."

Sackett took some time to read the first page, and Martin could see his eyes scroll downward and then back up as the officer re-read certain clauses. Then, moistening a thumb with his tongue before turning a page, Sackett cast a wary stare at the once private and newly-turned corporal he'd hired. As he turned and read the second and third pages there were several more moments when he gave Martin summative glances. "These are official papers, Corporal," Sackett pointedly said.

"Yes, Sir."

"They are reassignment orders."

"Yes, Sir."

"Orders not cut from here, do you understand what I'm saying?"

"Yes, Sir."

"How did you get orders not coming from out of our office?"

"Some white fellas gave 'em to me. Said they were from Service Command, y'know, Chicago. They were in a jeep and saw me while I was washing the car at the motor pool."

"What the hell we doing all this for then, Captain?" Davies asked.

"Do you think somebody's falsifying documents?" Pintor asked.

Sackett flipped through the pages again and shrugged. His eyebrows momentarily arched. "Dunno, Sarge. Come into my office, Martin," the captain softly ordered.

Dutifully following into the commander's workplace, Gus shut the door behind him, extinguishing all the sounds of the outer bureau's commotion. No birds, slamming file drawers. Captain Sackett didn't go to his informal chair, near the door; instead he'd crossed the room and sat behind his large desk. He centered the papers on his blotter, framing around the edges with his fingers. "Have a seat, Martin." Sackett pointed to the chair in front of him and Gus didn't seem to have enough weight to sink down into it.

Feeling exposed and vulnerable, at this point, Martin gave a small, practically imperceptible gasp as he felt a stabbing pain shoot through his lower colon. His nervous stomach was reacting to his situation. How could there be anything wrong with what he did, he asked himself? He began to worry that there had been some misunderstanding on his part, one that he had no control over. Something he didn't see, or quite understand, in the design of how things played out in the Army way-of- life. And that inattention, he thought, could end up keeping him at Fort Custer. To Gus, that would be unforgiveable— not going overseas, well, that just seemed a military emasculation. It would be the quintessence of what being powerlessness amounted to.

"These orders say that you are eligible to transfer to Fort Benning, on a special duty."

"Yes, Sir. Everybody's that's been doing the combat training been getting one. I seen 'em, Sir. All twenty-four of us."

"I see." Sackett took off his wire-rimmed reading glasses, turning his head slightly one way and then the other as he removed the ear fasteners—so, as not to bend them. Still contemplating, he then cleaned the lenses before speaking again. "It also says the transfer is supposed to be a voluntary one. Do you understand the purpose of your detail's assignment?"

"Yes, Sir. They told me, front-line duty."

"With white soldiers, Martin. Not just white field officers supervising colored soldiers, private. We're talking complete integration."

"Oh," Martin intoned, not sure of what his reaction should have been to this information Sackett provided. He struggled to grasp all the layers of complexity.

"Those guys in that jeep didn't tell you that, but I'm telling you. Somebody should."

Corporal Martin pursed his lips momentarily and batted his eyes rapidly for a few seconds after he came to a conclusion. "Begging pardon, Captain, but how would this be any worse than what we did in Detroit?"

"That's a fair question. The difference is you were stateside, and I was involved in the chain-of-command for that deployment. You go to Europe. It's all your asses out there, and no net for me to throw."

"I understand," Martin said evenly. The resolve evidenced in his reply told the captain, without even having to ask, that there was nothing he could do to dissuade this soldier, and his driver. "I'll try to be a strong representative," the young man promised.

"Well, it seems like you have your mind made up."

"I do, Sir. But there is one regret."

"What's that?"

"Well, it's only that—that you have been so kind to—"

"Don't flatter yourself, soldier. We don't make decisions based on kindness." Sackett shot back at Gus, who was trying to retreat into the cushions of the chair to get away from the acerbic correction getting dished out to him. "I didn't hire you because I liked you. I hired you because I had a job I was willing to entrust you with. That trust, seemingly, was misplaced."

"Sorry, Sir."

"Don't apologize. My feelings are not assaulted, in the least, Corporal Martin. But you best prepare yourself for what you're getting into. The South is no joke. When you go down there, I guarantee you'll be finding that out, directly. Believe that, mister. You will find that out, sure enough."

"Yes, Sir."

"I wouldn't do it, myself," Sackett warned as he took out his pen to sign the document. "You'll all probably end being the first squad caught in a cross-fire—but I'll sign this for you. Seeing that it seems what you really want."

"Yes, Sir, it is."

"All right, then." Sackett's pen made the noise of a rodent scratching through a plaster wall as he put his signature to the paper, finishing with an indignant flourish. "You're not leaving that crazy-ass brother of yours here, are you?

"I wish I could speak for him, Sir. But I haven't had a chance to get his take on the plan." Gus knew he couldn't have made any kind of statement one way or the other about his brother. He couldn't manipulate Joe into doing anything he didn't care to do. He never could. If he wasn't interested, Gus knew not to even bother him. "But I imagine he would be up for the adventure."

"Adventure, huh? Boy, you got a lot to learn."

Several hours later that night, when the sounds of the multitudinous crickets had replaced the cacophonous warbling of the afternoon's birds, Gus had gotten an answer to Sackett's question. The insect night sirens kept emitting their unbroken chain of love calls, even as the lights in the barracks were extinguished and the metallic lullaby filling the air made all too real the images that one can believe to see in the pitch of night.

Gus found it too hard to sleep. He'd tried for hours, but the internal luminosity of his roving, excited, mind's eye would not allow rest. One thought ran past another, never completing the circuit of Gus's subconscious. "Joe?" he finally whispered. "Joe, you asleep? Joe, you awake?"

"You gettin' on my nerves, nigga, "Joe mumbled in a quiet but angry hiss. "First, I hear you turning every which away, and now this. What?"

"I was thinking, y'know. About the deployment. Joe, you don't have to go down there—not if you don't want to, I mean, not if it's just because I'm going."

"You let your head get any bigger and they won't have a helmet big enough to fit it. I don't give a rat's ass that you signed up first. That ain't why I'm going."

"What do you mean? Why are you going, Joe?"

"The way I figure it, I been itching to kill me something for a long time, now. One of our white boys say the wrong thing, at the wrong time—who know? Might end up mistaken for a jerry. Sounds like an honest mistake, you ask me."

"Don't say that, Joe."

"Shut up."

"It's not right."

"Hey, you two, simmer down," someone across the way aisle complained.

"Go to sleep, Gus," Joe ordered. And with that Gus had no choice but to roll over on his side again and do as he'd been told. But his mind kept pumping chemicals into his brain until he finally drifted off around three in the morning. His mind slipped into unconsciousness running, and that's where he took up his dreaming, in a place only known to his imagination:

It seemed he'd been running for hours on end but the night was not growing any lighter. There was a German bunker about a half mile from his position, a verdant open field between labyrinths of hedgerows. He was alone, and he had no idea how he was the only GI involved in the assault. He was a couple hundred yards away from the last enemy nest he'd destroyed, but it only seemed the structure was decimated.

With the alacrity of a fleeing deer. His weapon at high port-arms, he kept running towards the next bunker, far away, but close enough to lob artillery shells overhead. Creating bombastic clouds of explosive white against the black celestial sphere of night. Gus's exhalations fogged the air and he grunted out his panicked cries. He needed cover.

Emerging from a thin tree line, Gus stood at an open meadow that was about two-hundred feet wide. On the edges of the grass he could make out that there were more hedgerow and trees. And he'd make his run for them, but for now had to stop in his tracks. He could not take another step. His legs, now rooting to the ground, allowed some of the blood to balance within him and his lungs replenished the oxygen somewhat. At least he was no longer gasping for each breath.

Then he heard the laughing behind him, in the distance but drawing closer. And that was the only thing he needed to put an end to resting. He took off for the trees, not focusing on the seemingly endless, tall waves of grass he had to cross. Grass so tall he had to high step over it to keep from stumbling. His dewed, slippery rifle was so heavy in his sweating hands. He didn't know how much further he could go.

"Halten, schwarzen mann. Wir schaden nicht Sie," the Nazis ghostly and reassuring entreaty wafted through the foliage, several times. And though Gus didn't know the German language, he could sense by their tone that they wanted him to trust them. He might not be sure of what they were saying, but he did know that if he let them catch him there would be no niceties applied in his care. Then they began laughing as they called out, "Schwarzen mann? Schwarzen?"

The Nazis began firing at their weaving American prey, toying with him. Gus could hear the rounds whiz and zip past him, over him, around him, like heavy metallic bumblebees.

Reaching up to his right chest Gus snatched a hand grenade, stopping long enough to turn and throw the bomb in the direction of his pursuers. In seconds an orange fireball lit the night and Gus saw the three Nazis propelled by the initial concussion. Infused with chunks of dirt and grass the orange quickly turned to a haloed yellow debris cloud shrouded in a smoky, expanding ribbon. But to Gus's amazement he saw all three of the enemy troops landing on their feet, and beginning to continue their chase. Barely missing a step. They kept pursuing him to the tree line.

Now, their laughter had a crueler tinge and the gunfire was more earnest. A round found its mark and tore into Gus's right shoulder, unbalancing him momentarily, but not dropping him. Gus continued running and slung his weapon over his good arm, and then another shot cracked the night air. It was like the sound a huge chunk of ice makes when it's splitting from melting. That bullet entered Gus's left leg, in the hamstrings, successfully felling him.

There was no chance of escaping anymore. Muscles in the leg were severed and the bullet exited out of his lower thigh. Managing to wrestle himself to a sitting position, Gus drew his Colt Baretta by crossing over his body to unholster it with his left hand. He chambered a round with his right hand and set the hammer. Pointing it with bad intent at the oncoming fascists, he prepared for the worst.

But Gus couldn't fire. They stood over him, laughing and jeering, "Dumm schwarzen mann. Der Jude-Hunde sind mehr eine Übereinstimmung." Then they began spitting on him while they raised their rifles. Gus turned his head and closed his eyes, awaiting his inevitable demise but the moment didn't occur. Everything grew still. He wanted to open his eyes, hoping and wishing that it was all just a bad dream, but he dared not.

From the pain in his leg he knew he wasn't dreaming; and he could distinctly smell the wet grass—feel it dampening his uniform. And then reconsidering his plight, Gus opened his eyes, deciding to look his executioners in the face—defiant.

But the helmets silhouetted in the dark did not have the flared characteristics of the Nazi helmet's deflectors. The buckets on the three men, standing over him, were the same as his. "Coon hunt's over, boys," one of them said.

And the blast from the fired guns of the rogue soldiers' replayed over and over again in Gus's troubled sleep. He could smell the cordite and still saw a toothy smile masked by the blue smoke. The flash from that muzzle, somewhere deep in his subconscious, was the final light to be extinguished for Gus Martin.

CHAPTER TWENTY-FIVE
Georgia on my Mind

The Saturday morning light blinded Gus as its beam through a nearby window fell upon his shuttered eyelids and forced them to open simultaneously as he bolted upright in his bed with a faint gasp. The sheets on his bunk clung to his body because of the condensation real fear brings. Joe, meanwhile, was across the aisle from him and fully dressed. He looked over at his startled younger brother. The sounds of flies relentlessly dive-bombing the inhabitants of the barrack's sub-par interior seemed to be the only noise either of them heard. "You never used to have bad dreams when we were back in Michigan, Gus." And with that Joe picked up a push broom and a five-gallon bucket that was almost full of debris. Without a further word he walked outside. His head erect and his shoulders pulled back, Joe seemed to make everything he did deliberately dignified. It was the beginning of the third week of repairs to the bivouacs. The freshly incorporated men from Ft. Custer, as well as all the other black soldiers entered into the training, had to renovate their own living quarters. Inside and out.

Their nostrils were continually filled with the smell of rotted wood from the floorboards and wall beams they dismantled. The accumulated mustiness of earth, dust, and old tar paper heaped up on the grass outside their doors. The piles were picked up by trucks every three hours, or so. And the white drivers were not expected to help load the refuse, but to assure timeliness and productivity were maintained in the work schedule.

There were twelve wooden barracks to be recomfitted, and they were very old and on the other side of the base of the new brick and mortar housing wings. The colored soldiers had to maintain their own kitchen and latrine area, as well. But that was no matter. Because of the array of labor skills many of the men had, they needed no foreman in the construction. All they needed to be given were the tools to complete the work. And that was being done readily. By the coming week the worst-case structures would have all been gutted, and then the wood reinforcements and plastering could be done to start paving the way for housing assignments, outside of the tents. Joe and Gus's group were in one of only two barracks that were deemed habitable during the reconstruction.

Joe told Gus, once given the chore, that this clean-up assignment had been planned all along. He said that it was just some way to keep the two-hundred or so of them busy, while the commanders tried to figure out a way to get them trained and yet uphold Jim Crow values.

Gus jerked off the sheet covering his lap and went over to his footlocker to pull out a pair of pants. They could only shower every three days, so body odors congealed with the smell of the trash on the moist breeze. There was no smell of peaches or pine trees, only the laboring musk of sweating men.

Gus thought about his dream while he dressed and relegated its origin to having had to make three changes of location on the base in the two weeks they'd been there, and that he'd gotten a hold of some meat that was turning bad. They'd been shuffled around like a pea under a walnut shell for a good deal of their stay. As he put on his socks and his boots he considered whether this had been a well-advised exploit. He felt as if all the Negro transfers had to be constantly walking around with light feet because they dare not break the eggshells of Southern tradition. A tradition which stipulated that people of muddy color are to be seen only when they are expected to be seen, heard from only when asked to give an affirmative or not at all, and always—always, accepting whatever burden were to befall on them with a smile.

Other men began to return from morning chow and picked up the tools by their dirty bunk areas. Off in the distance, hammers could be heard thudding out an unintentional and likewise incomprehensible semaphore to every one within hearing distance—which was, the day's work had begun. Gus didn't put on his fatigue shirt because it was almost eighty degrees right now, with the sun having just transcended the sky's color from a palette of many hues to a singular, celestial, powder blue. He placed a white utility shirt on his left shoulder and sleepily went out to join the others, foregoing the greasy breakfast that his stomach would not have held within him, anyway. He grabbed two of the four buckets that Joe had filled near the steps and began to take them to the dump pile. But once he turned, facing east, he set down the garbage in his hands and tapped Joe on the arm.

About two-hundred yards from where they stood, the Martin brothers saw another group of Negro trainees not shackled into menial service. It was about the size of a whole company of them and they were getting some actual military training done, of a sort. And even though they weren't being made to do what Gus and Joe were, they had some of the same tools deployed to them while they practiced their drill formations. At first, Gus and Joe both were going to be dismissive and return back to their work. But then as they watched a little while longer, Joe could see that they were not being given any serious education in tactics, but were merely a bucket brigade made up to parade around for some white cadre soldier's amusements.

Three white noncoms had them performing close-order drills and the company did so, poorly, and all the worse for them. Part of their lackadaisical effect had to have been that they were carrying brooms, mops, and even small tree limbs instead of armory issue; that made it hard for them to take what they were doing as anything serious. And those that did have an earnest need to learn the maneuvers, due to the lack of proper training in the first place, were put off from learning by the disintegrating morale of the others. And the cadre wasn't making it any easier for them.

As the orders for splitting columns were barked, straw and horsehair broom heads slapped the anxious and wary company members in their faces and about their heads. Much to the amusement of the redneck men giving the insistent orders.

"Ah, whoa," guffawed one of them. "That's a goddam shame. You no-marchin' jungle bunnies. Don't let that weapon fall t' the ground. You hear me, boy?"

One of the more perplexed troops immediately became a target. "Who told you to put that weapon down, nigger?" the white agitator yelled.

"Where'd you learn to walk, boy? You some kind of barnyard animal, or somethin'?"

"Can't you walk a straight line, nigger?"

And on and on it went. Joe elbowed Gus and they picked up their buckets and headed back to their assignment with clenched jaws and hot eyes of contempt.

The cadre went up and down the motionless ranks and ridiculed many of the men so harshly that a collective nervousness set in even among the most disdainful of the group. Unbeknown to the cadre on the parade field, a jeep approached from a dirt road. It carried an officer and a driver on it, and it slowed down to a crawl as the executive officer witnessed the goings on, saw the ill-equipped men. His eyebrows raised appreciably as he heard the disparagements hurled at the black soldiers, as well. "Stop the jeep," he told the driver without a trace of rancor.

The trainers, such as they were, didn't even notice the high-ranking officer watching them over their shoulders. And they acted accordingly, continuing their harangue. One Negro soldier got tripped, another cuffed about the ears and dared by the assaulter to try and defend himself.

"Get me to my office, right now," the general practically whispered, his anger tightening his throat closed. His accent, even through his tight-lipped disgust, revealed the tenor of a man who knew what it was like to face a nor'easter.

"Suh?"

"I said my office, now please."

The driver had learned to understand the clipped cadence of the general, but it was difficult for him if the commander spoke too quickly or too softly.

The jeep leaped back to life and summarily charged up the road, making the distance between them and the harassed soldiers increase by the second. They had to veer to the left to clear the dumpster vehicles being loaded by Joe and Gus Martin's barrack. "Driver?"

"Suh?"

"When we get there I want you to get a hold of Lt. Colonel Deauville. Have him report to me, in my office. Directly and immediately, you understand?"

"Yessuh."

"Make sure he does, as well."

When General McClair had gone into his office, he didn't find himself with a lack of things to do in order to keep busy. Tracking items in a budget sheet on his desk informed the general of the logistics nightmare the assimilation became. It hadn't originally been thought to be problematic but after witnessing what he'd just seen, the general knew there were intangibles that hadn't been accounted for, as well as the larger omissions. The quartermaster had gotten requisitions for them, and he wondered what accounted for the colored men being so shabbily treated. Scrutinizing the data made for McClair passing the time until the junior officer showed. Unfortunately, the assimilation of the Negroes into the program was proving daunting, after all.

While turning yet another spreadsheet page, McClair noticed a stack of around a half of a ream of paper at the left corner of his desk and glanced at his watch. With a closed-mouth, nasal sigh, he set the other documents aside, and then immediately, in rapid fire succession, began scrawling his signature quickly at the bottom of each sheet drawn from the stack. Subsequently, depositing them neatly to another pile in front of him. McClair's eyes did not vary from their oscillating motion as he worked, nor did the speed of his hand slow when the expected knock on the door came. By that time he had finished signing twenty or so of the papers.

The knock came again, sounding a little impatient now, but still a confident knock. The general kept writing and his signatures were more scratch-like as he thought over how smug the man behind that door must be. He kept on writing.

"Come in." The door partially opened and a blond man stuck his head in.

"You wanted a word with me, General?"

"Please have a seat, Lieutenant Colonel."

His name was Deauville and he was tall, so tall he had to duck his head almost three inches to enter the room without injury. Like the general, he too wore a long-sleeved shirt even though the day was mercilessly hot and mucky. But no tie. Deauville had a straw-colored cowlick irrepressibly standing atop of his head; one that overall could have stood a trimming by General McClair's observation. Yet the junior colonel could not discern any such circumspect appraisal by the general because the man hadn't given him much more than a furtive look since his entrance. He hadn't even taken notice of the colonel giving him a salute. Deauville watched McClair continue signing at least four more documents before clearing his throat.

McClair passed one last paper aside as he looked up for the first time with undivided attention and waved off the salute with two of his fingers, the same way one would do when shooing a pesky fly. Their eyes met Deauville's cold, gray ones, and McClair's emerald pupils. McClair could see a hint of agitation, and there was. Deauville did not like to be ignored.

"You may be seated, Colonel."

Deauville dragged the nearest chair across the floorboards with a deliberate malaise and intentional scraping sound and plopped down into it. He scooted his backsides to the middle of the chair and reclined backwards, crossing his left leg over his right and sighing. "How can I help you, General?" He straightened his back in the chair after showing his initial contempt and let his wrists flap over the ends of the arm rests. "Evah-thing fine 'roun heah?" And after his Confederate tinged query Deauville pursed his lips and then sucked in his cheeks to get up some spit to wet his mouth.

"Are you the re-training officer?"

"Yassuh, that be me."

The general overlooked the informality in the answer. Perhaps because McClair found it so hard to take his eyes off of Deauville's Adam's apple. It was extraordinarily distracting, bobbing up and down each time he spoke, or even uttering a sound. Not wanting to judge him by appearances, but the sweaty collar, poor posture, and lack of earnestness, made it difficult for the commanding officer to admire any one thing about the man before him. He was the embodiment of hick. "It was my understanding," the general began, "that the colored men assigned here are to be incorporated into mainline field training with our white troops. Am I correct?"

"That's the requested policy, Suh."

"Then what, may I ask, was the rest of the battalion doing while I saw a company of Negro soldiers on the parade field this morning?"

"Those that aren't retro-fitting barracks were supposed to be on the firing line. That is, if I recollect rightly, Suh?"

"Then I have two questions; one: why weren't the colored soldiers on the line with them? And, two: why were the men on that parade field doing close order drill with brooms instead of rifles?"

With that gauntlet thrown down Deauville uncrossed his legs and removed his arms from their resting position. He jutted his aquiline nose and cleft chin forward, placing his elbows on his knees, and clasping his hands together as if about to begin a prayer. "There's three reasons for that, Suh," Deauville began, and he started to count them off on his fingers, "First of all, within the first week of their arrival, we found out that these darkies are not accustomed to company movements. Secondly, we just don't have the weapons—"

"Don't have the weapons?" McClair interrupted, finding a point of contention he'd follow up on.

"Not for a brigade, we don't. Far from it, Sir?"

"Go on, Colonel."

"Besides that. The way that they march, Suh. Well, if we had any guns to give 'em they'd have more than likely ended up shooting someone lame. And that brings up the third reason for delaying the training, Suh. We don't carry, shall we say, the proper auxiliary resources for training the culluds."

"Auxiliary resources?"

"Yassuh. You asked me about the ones building those bunkhouses, out there by Harmony. Well—that just goes to show how this here thang weren't well thought out. If'n you wanted those men to be instep with everbody else, don't you think it would have been advised to already have the quarters up for 'em afore hand? Those men doing that construction need training, but we using 'em for quartermaster duty, instead."

"Housing logistics, aside. What other resources aren't in supply? You said resources, in plural."

"Yes, I did."

"Well?"

"Suh, we ah—well. We ain't got plasma for nigras." Deauville saw McClair's eyebrows avalanche furrows and wrinkles of consternation.

"What do you mean, you don't have Negro plasma?"

"Ain't a pint to be had on the whole blamed base."

"Lieutenant, there's a whole battalion of colored paratroopers that have been training here since January. Where have they been quartered? What about medical supplies for them?"

"Oh, you talkin' 'bout them boys from the 555th?"

"Exactly."

"They come here with they own fixings—including medics and such. We just had to put them up in segregated quarters up on Kelley Hill."

"So, what's the problem, Deauville? You have plasma on base, then. You told me there wasn't."

"But that's specifically for them smokejumpers, Suh. I can't go and commandeer they supplies that was set up for them, now can I?"

"What about getting blood from the local coloreds?"

"Well—that's another problem, Suh."

"What? There aren't Negroes in Chattahoochee or Russell Counties?"

"Oh, no. We got 'em plenty, for shoah. But, ah."

"Go on."

"Well, they's a lot of 'em with bad blood. Can't go and be givin' our boys the syphilis now, can we? So that's why I'ma sayin' it's a plain fact, General. We got to hold off. If one of those boys got hurt on that field we wouldn't have any way to treat his mortal injury. And that would happen if we put those nigras on the firing line."

"Lieutenant Colonel Deauville," McClair sighed and shook his head. "I am shocked at the logic and excuses you are presenting to me."

"Well, General, what I meant to say was—"

"You've already said more than enough, Lieutenant. I have seen the ledgers and know for a fact that there are weapons here for those troops."

"We had to convert those to a battalion in 2nd Armored."

"On whose directive?"

"Base Command—said to send them directly to Sand Hill."

"Then if there aren't enough weapons for the firing line have the men share what we do have. If colored soldiers are in close-order, there damn well better be whites drilling with them, and the in the same way. Do I make myself clear, Lieutenant? Do you understand?"

"Beggin' the general's pardon, but I don't rightly believe it's me who don't know the lay of the land, here."

"We are under orders here, Lieutenant, and we will carry them out!" McClair railed, and then added, lowering his voice and his vehemence, giving atonement. "I know you didn't ask for this duty. Neither did I. But our Service Command has ordered it, and it will be carried out. And it will be carried out expeditiously."

"Permission to speak freely, Suh?"

"Granted."

Deauville rose to his full height, straightening his shirt into the waistline of his pants as he began to speak. "With all respect, *Sir*," he began cautiously, "you don't seem to understand. Probably it's from a number of reasons, but the main one is you ain't from the South. Y'see, not only on this base—but the towns around us, as well, are not ready for integrated training. Not no-way, not no-how. Y'see, there's been a problem with some of our niggers down here. And if the word gets out, and it will, a large part of Georgia will feel the North is once again undermining Southern society and the local custom. We don't need to deliberately add to our colored problem by having them nigras put in a position to get uppity on us. It will go badly for them if they do."

Now the shorter man stood, tossing his pen onto his blotter and looking intensely at Deauville as he leaned forward, his cheeks reddening. "Let me tell you about what I *deliberately* intend to do with the Negro troops here. The only thing, the *only* thing I try to do deliberately is to very much impress on them that we are always fair and that there is no possible discrimination going on here—"

"Excuse me, Sir—you misunderstand. I'm not implying it can't or won't be done. It's just that we need to study them more fully. We need to understand them better, is all I'm saying."

General McClair straightened his back and crossed his arms with a perturbed look still on his face. Then grew more contemplative. He brought his cupped left hand up to his face, rubbing his chin with his thumb and then crooking his index finger under his nose. He turned his back to Deauville and stared out of his window. "One thing we must never do, Lieutenant," he said, "is to attempt to 'study' them, as you put it. As if they were some sort of oddity of the human community. Nor should we, I feel, make any special effort to understand them." McClair now placed his hands behind his back and turned to confront Deauville again, but this time with an imploring gaze. "You see, Deauville, I believe that normally they do not want to be studied, understood, or uplifted in any way. They just want to be treated like men. Think and act towards them as soldiers among soldiers. If they misbehave, see that they are punished promptly and exactly, mind you, I said exactly as any white soldier would. If you treat them normally and casually they will not tend to get the idea in their head that you qualify them as a *problem*. It will go better for you."

"Yessuh," came the resigned and quiet reply, soured by the rhetoric used against him, "is that all, Suh?"

"Yes, Deauville," McClair sighed, seeing he couldn't impress his way of thinking past the bedrock of the southerner's prejudice. "You may go."

Deauville whisked his right hand to his coinciding brow and then smartly lowered his arm as General McClair flippantly returned the protocol and took his seat again.

Returning to his paperwork but not hearing the door close the general slowed his writing, eventually stopping. He looked up to see Deauville still immobile in front of him. "Sir?" the junior colonel interrupted.

"Yes, Lieutenant."

"I'll think you'll find that history supports what I've been saying, Sir."

"The history you allude to also has to do with me, doesn't it? Me and my Yankee roots? Well, I hope that men aren't doomed to be slaves to history, Deauville. Let's get about writing a new history, Lieutenant. Beginning now."

Deauville reached across to the corner of McClair's desk and picked up a classified document entitled *Leadership and the Negro Soldier* and waved it in front of McClair. "Then tell me, Sir, what's it to be?" he asked. "The Department of War seems to have felt a need to study this, and passed their conclusions along. Now you're telling me no such studying is needed and just to throw them into the batter. I'm sorry, Sir. I'm amight confused by that seeming contradiction."

The colonel tossed the stapled papers into the chair's lap that he'd been sitting in. Then he reached into his pocket and pulled out a hand-sized foil pouch and took out a quarter-sized dollop of chewing tobacco. He kept looking at McClair even though he'd gone back to signing the forms on his desk. Deauville's jaw tightened as the chew was mashed into his molars and an almost immediate seam of brown spittle began to brim over the corner of his mouth. Deauville wiped the excess with the back of his left hand before it began to run down his chin and left without speaking further.

After he'd gone, McClair had to admit even to himself that he was just as bewildered as the bigot he'd just tried dressing down. What in hell was this man's Army coming to?

CHAPTER TWENTY-SIX
More Than a Game

First Jim, and then Franklin extinguished their respective cigarettes in the bronze-colored glass ash tray between them on the *Formica* table. They'd been sipping on glasses of beer for some time, and the quart bottle was surrounded by the aluminum foil wrappings from two Italian beef sandwiches they'd enjoyed. "You tell a pretty compelling story, Mr. Sackett."

"I thank you, son."

"But in all of the places in the country to have training—"

"If you think about it, ain't much difference as far as how anybody felt about us—back then. No matter where you went. I think they decided on Benning just because most of the black population was still down South, at the time. I guess they felt we'd be comfortable."

"That shows how the minds of our leaders work, doesn't it?"

"One man's caviar is another man's bait, I guess."

Jim laughed heartily and stood, before he began to clear the table as the front door opened and Bernadette and Brad could be heard entering the home. But the voices they exchanged were not pleasantries.

Neither man who listened knew exactly what was being said exactly but the tone was harassing and Bernadette was the prevaricator. Brad came through the push door with such force he almost knocked it into his father's hip while he was emptying the table trash into the kitchen garbage pail.

"Hey!"

Brad, still in his uniform but wearing a jacket over the orange jersey top, whirled around with eye-widening dread after realizing he'd not seen his father. But he couldn't even muster an apology out. His eyes were almost spilling forth with tears and his chest was heaving. Jim cocked his head to the side quizzically. "How'd the game go, son?" The young boy looked first toward Mr. Sackett and then back to his father until his sibling tormentor followed him into the room.

"Can't miss—can't miss. Cry baby, can't miss."

"Shut up!" Brad screamed, his teeth gritted in anger that he couldn't express. He raised a hand as if he would strike his sister but stopped in mid-air because he realized what would be the consequence.

"Can't miss—can't miss."

"Hey, you two. Bernadette stop that noise, y'hear? Now, what the hell's goin' on?"

"I—I" Brad stammered.

"Well, did you win the game or not, boy?"

And with that question came, a wail followed. A wail of anguish that hit a note of high despair. It rose to a sustained pitch and then became hiccoughing sobs and hot tears. Then the emotionally wounded child ran out the kitchen and into his room with only short unintelligible bleating left in his wake. The wracked sobbing touched Frank to the core.

"What was that all about?" Jim asked Bea, but as she was about to answer, Lorraine came into the kitchen.

"Bernadette," she said, "I want you to go to bed now. Say goodnight to Mr. Sackett."

Looking almost like she was being cheated out of the joy of the retelling, Bernadette dejectedly bade a farewell to Sackett and exited the kitchen through the push door by her mother.

"Must have been some game," Sackett guessed.

"Did they win?" asked Jim.

"Yeah, but—"

"Then why is he moping around like it's the end of the damn world, or something?"

"Brad got embarrassed during the game."

"Somebody say something?"

"No. You know how hard he tries to play basketball as well as the other boys. I remember last week him telling me that he'd been improving so much that the coach was giving him a few minutes in the last three games."

"Pardon me," Sackett interrupted, "but is this grade school basketball?"

"No, it's church leagues," Jim replied. "We don't even go to the church whose team he's on, but he wanted it bad."

"Well, in today's game one of our players made a good defensive play and got the ball loose. Knocked it in the backcourt and it was fittin' to go out-of-bounds and Brad was the only Presbyterian player in the area."

"Presbyterian?" Sackett seemed surprised. "What was the other team?"

"Lutherans, I think. St. John's."

"Now they got some nice uniforms, too. White and gold. They look right smart. Brad picks a group that wears orange and black. Look like a bunch of jack o' lanterns."

"Stop that now, Jimmy. He'll hear you." Lorraine shushed.

"Okay, so what happened?"

"It seemed like the whole gym got quiet and all the eyes were on Brad. You have to understand, Mr. Sackett. I love the boy, but he's no basketball player. He shoots free throws underhanded, down by his knees and tosses it up towards the basket. He just can't get close any other way. Anyway, so there's this moment of truth. I think if he'd had his druthers, he wouldn't have had anything to do with that ball. But it rolled right up to his sneakers and he picked it up. He dribbled past the half-court line and stopped."

"He didn't go for a lay-up? Doesn't he know what a fast-break is?" Jim asked.

"I think he just got too excited to know what to do. He turned to look back and had stopped bouncing the ball so he couldn't go any further. It seemed like he wanted to pass it, but there was no one near. So, he threw up this big ol' air-ball that didn't even come close. Everyone in the crowd went from quiet to an almost simultaneous groan. The whistle blew and Brad was limping over to the sideline like he'd been hurt. But after the game he seemed fine...that's when Bernadette started in on him. The other girls on the cheer squad were giving her a hard time and she gave him her portion of that all the way home."

"So, he faked an injury?"

"Jim, if you could have seen how alone he looked."

"Yeah, but that ain't no reason for him to add deception to poor preparation. Ima go and talk to that, boy." And he turned, but Lorraine placed a firm hand on his arm to restrain him.

"Not tonight you don't need to. Not right now."

"Well—it serves him right wanting to play on that team, anyway."

"But our church doesn't have a team, Jimmy. And his best friend is on the Presbyterian team."

"Well, I don't like him faking."

"You ain't never been embarrassed playing sports, Jimmy?"

"I didn't play team sports. I boxed. And didn't nobody question my athleticism because I didn't do basketball, football or baseball, neither."

Lorraine rolled her eyes and gave a little sigh of exasperation, and Sackett rose to excuse himself. "I'll see myself out, Mr. and Mrs. Martin."

"You don't have to go."

"No—that's all right."

"I'm sorry for the entire squabble, tonight. Please—"

"It's all right. I'm about talked out for the night 'bout now, anyway. I think I'll leave the talking for you two."

"Can I give you a lift to the hotel?"

"Naw, I can still get a bus. Should I come back to finish, Jim? Sometime tomorrow?"

"I get home about six in the evening."

Sackett picked up his hat from the table and doffed it towards the Martins before putting it on his receding silver hair. "I need you to fill in some missing information for me about your grandmother, if you can."

"Sure."

"G'night." Sackett tipped his hat one more time before exiting through the swinging white door and out to the curb.

"I really like him," said Lorraine.

"Yeah. He's a little odd, but he can sure tell a story to paint a picture." And then Jim playfully grabbed his wife about the waist and tickled her gently. "And what you think you doing grabbing me by the arm? Woman, don't you know my hands are registered weapons."

"Yeah, and you want to keep them weapons you best let go of me. Now, stop Jimmy." Her husband continued to tickle her ribs despite the mirthful pleas until by happenstance they drew close, and completed the playful interlude with a kiss.

The next day, Brad had gone to the Boys Club not far from his school to play some ping pong and have some pop, if the Coke machine wasn't still broken. Around 4:30 that afternoon he walked with another boy for a couple of blocks on the way to the bus stop. Brad's friend, Everett Wilkins, was in the same boat he was, both parents working until 5:30 and no sitter with a car to come and get him. Except Everett lived closer. It was fine with Brad, though. He liked his forays into independence on the two days when he had to fend for himself. Bernadette wasn't the answer to this issue, however.

She had a routine worked out for her where she was doing homework with a friend on a semi-regular basis who lived in the opposite direction from their house; but they didn't mind driving her home, it seemed. Sometimes she even stayed for dinner there and would make it a point to brag about it to her brother. The family she visited was solidly middle-class with clear plastic covers over their living room furniture, and they didn't have any boys there to play with. Though Brad tried to work his way into the situation at his parent's insistence, it wasn't long before he had to make it known that he had to have some other arrangements.

If he needed to, if there were ever trouble, he knew where the Foucault's house was. And he knew he could get to some refuge there in a pinch, but that would only happen in a dire emergency. Being around his sister was like having too much of a good thing, he surmised.

Too much of anything can make you sick. For awhile Brad had gone on a little tear where he would commit to stealing *Hostess* Cherry Fruit Pies from a local convenience store. At first, the looted compote, with its glazed buttery crust was a delicious bounty to him and kept him coming back. But at the height of his deviancy, in one day, he'd stolen five of the pies in an afternoon and eaten each one. That night, a conscience and a stomachache set him on the path of the straight-and-narrow. He couldn't even walk by the store anymore after that night. And you couldn't get him to eat a slice of cherry pie, now. That's how it was with his sister. Brad loved her, but she being older wore on him with all of her petty embassies she'd put upon him. They simply needed their own space, and Mondays and Wednesdays were just the right intervals needed to keep them civil to one another as they grew up in their close quarters.

Everett tore half of his *Bazooka Gum* in two and handed a piece to Brad before he waved goodbye and headed for his house. Everett was a good friend, Brad thought. He was generous and he didn't talk badly about you. He had a lazy eye that his parent's were trying to have corrected by some glasses, though. Brad would help him with reading sometimes. If anybody started making comments about Everett around Brad, he'd just walk away from the group. Everett had been at the basketball game Saturday, and yet he didn't bring it up, or make fun of him. And for that, young Mr. Martin was indeed thankful. And for the gum, too.

"I'll see you tomorrow, Bumpo." That was Everett's nickname and it came about from his disability and his bumping into things unintentionally. He didn't mind being called that, though. His family was the ones to start it, anyway.

"Yeah—I'll beat you in ping pong tomorrow. Watch."

Brad smiled bemused and benevolent, "Okay."

Everett used ping pong to strengthen his hand-eye coordination and to exercise his ophthalmic muscles. His family doctor suggested it to the boy's parents. Sometimes he could get back some highly improbable shots because of the skewed perception he got on playing the ball. But mostly, Brad tried very hard just to keep the ball in play with Everett, never trying to actually beat him. It was always, truly, just a friendly game.

Brad found a stick with a rusty nail in it and as little boys are wont to do, had to pick it up. It was the heighth of a good walking stick so he took it along because there were several more blocks before he got to where he caught his bus. Sounds of the wood clanking against parking meters, or hydrants, or public trash bins followed Brad as he made his way down the street. His gum was still getting his salivary glands to react, but the artificial flavoring had faded. Almost at the same time when he'd grown tired of playing with the stick, a mean old dog threw all its weight against a high wooden fence to Brad's left and began snarling and barking. He'd jumped at first, of course, but then took it personally that he'd been frightened. That made him angry, even though the fence planking looked like it was barely containing the canine behind it. Brad turned towards the fence.

"Shut up!" he yelled back. And for emphasis he rapped several times on the wood with his scrap lumber, getting the dog riled up even further. "Stupid dog. I said shut up." He threw the stick over the top of the fence and it cleared it by a couple of feet, the dog's barking fading in the distance as it ran to retrieve what had made the trespass into its domain.

Brad smirked at the brute's lack of purpose, then put his hands in his pockets and began walking to the corner where he would have to turn. He tried to blow a bubble with his spent gum but hadn't acquired the expertise for that, yet. That, like becoming a good basketball player, had proven elusive to him. The gum ended up spat out on the pavement shortly afterwards.

Brad just continued walking the familiar trail to the bus, not particularly thinking about anything, or anyone, when he began to digest how his day had gone.

Today had been a day of vindication of sorts for him. Not every one knew about his debacle at the basketball game, but enough did to chide him about it. Fortunately, he'd developed a thicker skin by morning and had prepared himself for the onslaught. He only knew that he'd tried.

His dad wasn't the kind of father you'd see on television sitcoms, one who loosened his tie and rolled up his sleeves to shoot a few baskets with his son before dinner. That wasn't Jim Martin, at all. And that made it a little easier to not be so disappointed because they didn't have a house with a basketball hoop and backboard on their garage. They didn't even have a garage. More like a packed shed.

Their house was a rental and Brad could never remember ever seeing who it was that actually owned the place. He never fixed anything up, that was certain. The double sash window in his room, freed from years of painted layers, had to be propped up with a ruler. One time a thunderstorm blew through and knocked the stick out of the track while Brad was watching the squall line approaching. He was always mesmerized by weather events. His little fingers were curled over the sill unfortunately, and with a violent gust of wind, the full weight of the sash came down with great force on his fingers, breaking several. The slight bend in them now was a testament to his family being practicing Christian Scientists. They had a family doctor, but they didn't go to him any more than they had to. You'd have to be pretty bad off to get medical attention from a professional in the Martin house. Some kids joked that it was because his dad was just cheap. Brad couldn't figure it out, but he remembered praying through his tears for his hands to stop hurting for several weeks, though. It took so long for the pain to go away.

There also was a crescent-shaped keloid scar on Brad's right hand, just below the base of the thumb, which was evidence of another incident where the power of prayer had corrected spiritual error. Brad had cut it while doing dishes and jamming his hand down to the bottom of a glass with a dish rag, to clean it. He'd turned his wrist and shattered the brim, slicing open a couple layers of epidermis. Jim Martin nursed it until the bleeding stopped and then soaked some medical gauze in some *Listerine* and held that in place over the wound with more gauze and tape. Changing that dressing as needed. Truth be told, the cure was more painful than the initial injury. Because it had been too wide a gap, and no stitches administered, the keloid formed. Crooked fingers and scars. Brad fervently hoped that should he ever really need a doctor that he would be taken to one. His dad just kept on telling him, however, that "Your outside may get scarred, but your spirit will be unblemished." The attempt at solace did not reach its mark, however.

Halfway down the block now, Brad saw someone getting off the yellow line bus that made him start running. "Mr. Sackett! Hey, Mr. Sackett!" Within moments Brad was standing next to the now familiar visitor who'd been to his home, reaching him before the bus had even pulled away from the curb. Sackett was surprised to have heard some child calling out his name, and for a moment didn't seem to recognize who the boy was. But Brad prompted an exchange.

"It's me. Brad Martin."

"Oh, well—my. You are a long way from your house, son. What you doing all the way out here?"

"I go to school back over there," Brad pointed behind him. "Mondays and Wednesdays I take the red line home so Momma and Daddy can work late."

"I see."

"Where you headed to, Mr. Sackett? That was kinda neat to see you come out of nowhere."

"I'll take that as a compliment, young man. As a matter of fact, I am going to your house, as well. But I thought it was the blue line that took me out there?"

"Not on weekdays, it don't."

"Oh—so, you can show me which way to go. Would you do that?"

"Yeah, sure."

"It's amight warm today, ain't it?" Sackett commented, more than inquired as they approached a storefront with a soda machine outside.

"A little," Brad agreed, "I guess."

The old man reached into his overcoat pocket, which he carried over his arm, and pulled out his rubber change purse and handed Brad two quarters. "Here," he said, "Why don't you get us a couple soda pops out that machine there?"

One coin trickled its way down into the machine's cash bin and Brad opened the delivery door and pulled out the first bottle of *Coca-Cola*. He handed it to Franklin and then repeated the procedure to get his own, popping the cap off with the machine's attached bottle opener. "Want me to open yours?" the boy asked. Sackett shook his head and laid his coat down on top of the soda machine, momentarily. And then he walked over by the opened door of the store in a most matter-of-fact way. Brad curiously watched as the old gentleman placed the edge of the ridged bottle cap on top of the exposed strike plate from the door jamb and then raised the other arm and a clinched fist about seven or eight inches above the levered bottle. With a quick and de-liberate blow downward, the fleshy part of Sackett's hand dislodged the cap off the beverage container without breaking it or spilling a drop of soda.

"Wow!"

"Wow—indeed, young man. I guess I still got it."

Sackett pulled his coat off of the Coke machine and began walking away, taking his first draw on the bottle. He'd gone a few steps when Brad stopped being immobilized, looking first at his open bottle and then back to the store door, and then back again. The admiring youth looked up at Sackett. "How'd you do that? Magic?"

"You just have to able to improvise, son."

"Impro—what?"

"Improvise—finding alternative ways to accomplish common things."

"Huh?"

"Well, you opened your bottle in the conventional way, using a bottle opener. I, on the other hand, improvised. I just showed you there's more than one way to get things done. Same result, different tactics. You improvise, too."

"I do?"

"Yeah, when you shoot them free throws. Ain't nothing against the rules to shoot 'em the way you do, but you make points shooting 'em, don't you?"

Brad's mood and demeanor softened, "I guess so."

And then there was a long, long period of silence between the two. Maybe Mr. Sackett had been trying to cheer him up, Brad thought, but it had the opposite effect. "What's troubling you, son?" Sackett asked.

"I don't think I want to play basketball anymore."

"Because of one bad game—and not even a whole game, but just a busted play? Come on, Bradley. You just need to find out what you should have done and then practice it, so the next time you'll be better prepared."

"But they'll laugh. I know it."

"Just let 'em."

"Laugh at me?"

"It won't last for long. And if they see you playing better they'll stop even sooner. Think about it, Brad. If they really didn't like you, wouldn't they do more than just laugh?"

"I dunno."

"In the end it's your decision. But you think about it.

"My dad wouldn't mind."

"Your daddy wants you to do whatever you want to. He let you play in the first place didn't he?"

"Momma made him."

"Oh."

"Do you like my daddy, Mr. Sackett?"

"Of course I do, son. Shouldn't I?"

"I guess."

"You love him, don't you?"

"Sure, I do—it's just that. Sometimes he just—"

"He takes care of you. Doesn't he?"

"He gets rid of the cockroaches when they get into the bathroom. And one time there was a rat in the kitchen one morning when I got up, and he killed it." Frank grinned mildly at the child's innocent but tactless response to his inquiry.

"You might want to keep things like that to yourself, young one."

"Why? It's what he did."

"I know, but some people could hear that and think that maybe your house isn't clean, or your family might not be. And we don't want them to think that. Personal things about the family shouldn't be shared with just anybody."

"Are you family?"

"No—but I know your family. Very well."

"Do you think we have a clean house, Mr. Sackett?"

"Your house is fine, little man."

"But I got a hole in the roof of my bedroom."

"A small one?"

"No, it's big. And it's all dirty around it and you can't see what's in the blackness. It's like my roof has this mouth that hangs down over my bed. I'm scared sometimes that something will come out of there when I'm sleeping some night."

"Have you talked to your parents about that?"

"Daddy says he is going to ask the landlord about fixing it, but nothing has happened."

"Maybe he don't know how to fix it."

"He don't. And he ain't gonna pay somebody to fix something he shouldn't have to. That's what he says to me."

"Oh. But it really bothers you?"

"I'd like to have friends come over to my room, but—"

Sackett sighed, "I understand."

"Momma says you're here to talk about our ancestors, with my daddy."

"You could say that."

"Well, if you want to know about them, let me show you where they are."

Brad pointed at a cemetery that was midway down the cross street that they were walking towards. Its verdant carpet and isolated markers partially covered by a cement block wall and wrought iron fencing. "Who do you know that's in there?" Sackett asked, looking at the youngster with him at the corner.

"Just family."

They crossed the street, quickening their steps when the pedestrian warning signs on the light began to flash.

"But who, Brad?"

"Come on," the boy just patiently said. Offering no further explanation. They tossed their empty pop bottles in a trash bin by the curb before they came to the cemetery entry. Sackett read what was on the metal grillwork, aloud.

"Mt. Olivet Cemetery." Then he looked at Brad, "You sure you know where to go? Because we can't waste too much time here if we're going to get our bus."

"The red line bus comes right down there at the end of the block." Intrigued, Sackett nodded his assent and they entered.

It seemed the sounds of all the urban area receded once they stepped through the internment ingress. Save for the grounds men working with an almost silent backhoe in the distance, there were no other living things around, except for the birds chirping and the bicker back and forth of scampering squirrels.

"We need to go twenty-four rows down and twenty-three over," the boy said matter-of-factly.

"To our left or our right?" Sackett asked.

Brad hesitated a moment and did a quarter turn first to his right, and then his left, using a pointed arm like a fleshy divining rod. "That way," Brad said pointing across his body to his left instead of using his left hand. "I'll know for sure when we get there." Sackett smiled and began to follow as Brad unceremoniously ran down the gravel path counting the adjunct markers as he went past, "Six...seven...eight."

"Not too fast now. I don't want you to lose me."

"Okay!"

About a hundred yards down from where he was Sackett saw the energetic boy stop and turn back towards him. Pointing to his right with an outstretched arm and a proud grin, "It's right down here," he shouted.

"All right, hold on a minute so I can catch up."

During the few minutes it took the senior citizen to draw to within ten yards of the boy, Brad occupied himself by turning around in circles occasionally, and by picking up gravel from the path and throwing the pebbles at nearby trees. Sackett delighted at the child's exuberance in living. But at the same time saw the double paradox. The innocent vitality of the Martin boy in this place of sanctity, and his own rendezvous with time sweeping inescapably closer to him. In this setting, he could not help but almost hearing death whispering in his ear.

"Can I go now?"

"Yeah, you run on ahead. I can see you, now."

Turning to his left where Brad formerly had stood, Sackett could see the high-stepping run of the youth. The tan soles of his sneakers flashing back at him, and growing smaller as again more distance of separation occurred. "Where does all that energy go?" Sackett thought. He believed he heard an answer, maybe from Death, "I take it inside of you, so I can grow and work my will when the time comes. I'm part of you, from the moment you enter the world. And I drain your battery. Your soul force's energy until you can no longer eat. No longer sleep. Can't walk—can't talk. Or even smile."

But Sackett kept his eye trained on Brad, and walked onward. And what he had heard was the benevolent Death talking to him. When your life is taken too soon, from mishap or adventure, those passings are more painful, Sackett surmised. That is what is meant by the violence of death. It wasn't the how of the act that made it so horrific, though terrible it may be. What made homicides so painful was because some of death is killed along with the victim. And it is cheated from enjoying its daily victories. Victory that was at work in that little boy running ahead of him, just as battles were being won inside of his own shell. But one would be wrong if they thought that Franklin Sackett was afraid of dying. He knew it to be a bookend, and part of what would complete his existence as a human being. It takes your death to define what your living meant.

"Here they are, Mr. Sackett."

Brad scurried around three different sets of markers, picking off debris from the bases of the monuments. "This one is the grave of my great-grand-mother. She was named after Cleopatra." The granite of her stone was brown.

"I heard some people say she might have been as beautiful," Sackett said, looking at it from behind the still boy. She had been born in 1904. She died last year. Sackett shook his head, remembering Machiavelli once said tardiness often robs us opportunity. He'd wanted to see her again.

"Did you know her?"

Sackett didn't answer, and feigned interest in the other grave heads. Joe's grave was next to her's, showing he was born August 17, 1922 and died on December 26, 1944, and with it was an adjoining marker for August Martin. His birthday was January 12, 1926. "Why come there's no end date on his?" Brad asked.

"It's because your grandpa's still alive."

"Oh."

"My great grandma was old," Brad stated, "as old as you?"

"Naw, I got a few years on her." He lied...

"She even bought ones for my daddy and momma. They're over there." The twin grave was definitely ascribed with James and Lorraine Martin's names. But there was nothing other than their names engraved. "That was nice for her to do, I guess. Wish I could have known her, though. I didn't get to meet my grandmother, either."

"She buried here?"

"Uh-huh, over there." Brad pointed at a grayish-green granite tombstone about twenty feet from the others.

"She on your momma's side, or your daddy's?"

"She's my daddy's momma."

Sackett strolled over to the distant marker, it read: Imogene Troubles, September 26, 1934 – April 9, 1950. Beloved daughter, sister, and mother. "And not even sixteen," Sackett mumbled to himself, thoughtfully.

The grave was conspicuous in its solitary placement, for there were no other Troubles interred nearby. And apparently Cleo had gotten resting places for all her immediate family. And this one, seemingly, unexpected addition. Mr. Sackett looked back over his shoulder and saw Brad trying to sneak up on some chipmunks eating pine cone bits. "You wouldn't happen to know your father's birthday, would you?" Brad shrugged his shoulders and returned to his hunting. "Come on, then." Sackett ordered. "We don't want to miss our bus, now."

CHAPTER TWENTY-SEVEN
A Mother's Love

"**E**xcuse me gal," the words spoken so close to Cleo Martin surprised her out of her disconnected reverie inside the post office. Gus' mother was shocked to a point that she gave an involuntary shudder. She could feel the exhalation of the white man behind her on the nape of her neck, and smell the sour breath as she stood in front of the wall of post office boxes. She turned her head and saw the old man had a bulbous red nose with angry looking capillaries. "If you don't mind, missy. I got mah own mail t'get to, my own self, if you please. Thank you." Careful of being rude lest she draw attention to herself, especially in public areas, she stopped sifting through her mail and made a quick apology. With haste, she then walked out of the federal building and into the city's streets.

This was all part of her façade that she maintained in order to keep her job at Davenports. Just looking like you could pass for white wasn't enough. You had to live in the right place and take precautions to not be found out. A white girlfriend let her use her father's boarding house over by Bricktown as an address for her residency, but Cleo had all her mail sent to a post office box. And that meant collecting it once a week, after she got off of work, and headed back over to Paradise Valley and her real address, near the Sojourner Truth Housing Projects.

Paradise Valley was its own little enclave, just as much as Greektown was its own. Since 1920 the Negroes of Paradise Valley supported enough of a financial bedstream that they had amassed a movie house, a pawn shop, a grocery co-op, eight grocery stores, and a bank. Seventeen doctors, twenty-two attorneys, and enough barber shops for each one of the lawyers, too. Thirteen dentists had offices in Paradise, and you could go to almost a dozen restaurants. Also known as Black Bottom, Paradise Valley had six drug stores in it, five undertakers, four employment offices, about three car garages, and even a candy maker. When Jesse Owens came to visit and stayed at the *Gotham*, you'd never seen so many white people soaking up the local culture in Paradise. And Joe Louis' momma lived over on McDougall. But if you wanted to be passed off as white, for whatever reason—you'd better not let it out that Paradise Valley was where you laid your head.

Cleo began collating her mail again at the bottom of the concrete stairs when she immediately recognized the shaky inklings of her youngest son's hand. She looked up momentarily, to cross the busy street and once past the halfway point of her departure from the previous block she spied a dark-green enameled curbside bench. She sat down on it with an expectancy that brought a smile to her face as she did a closer examination of the envelope.

It was addressed to Mrs. Cleo Martin. Her father had named her Cleopatra but had only stayed in town long enough to do just that. This was just about as long as he'd been in residence to start his fatherhood, as well. Therefore, she carried the moniker placed upon her with as much grace as she could, but not willingly, and not long after she had mastered her own verbal skills she let it be known that she preferred the name shortened. If anyone wanted to spite her, she'd said later, they'll have put Cleopatra Martin on her headstone when she died. Anyone close to her would have known better.

Cleo's praline colored forehead clouded over as she looked more closely at the letter. A furrowed indentation borne out of curiosity indented the bridge of her nose. The return address was from Georgia. And she put her back to the bench's upper slats like someone had just pulled her legs out from under her. She'd had no idea that either of her sons were now a thousand miles away. It was the unexpectedness of the knowledge that created a burgeoning need to see her sons.

Closing her eyes for a long moment, trying to gain some inner strength, she set her other mail aside, fanning them out like a pinochle hand on the blistered wooden seat of the bench and then pinning them underneath her right thigh. Cleo pulled the pages out of the one solitary letter she held and unfolded the stationary. Only then did she open her eyes to begin reading:

Dear Momma,

Forgive me for not writing you any sooner, or for my not being able to get home to see you for the Holidays like I promised, but you know how promises go when you're in the Army. I hope you are doing well.

As you've probably guessed by now, I'm not in Michigan, anymore. But that's not the reason I didn't get back for Christmas, though. I just couldn't get a pass. And Joe, well, he didn't even make an attempt at trying, I'm sorry to say. Oh, by the way, he is here with me.

I can't tell you much about why we're here, but we are stationed at Fort Benning. We're into some pretty heavy training now, especially since we finally got the equipment we'd been waiting for.

Cleo resented the fact that her son felt a government's duty overrode her concerns. After all, she thought, she wasn't the one in the Army. And she definitely felt like she should have known about this. She continued with the letter:

Our barracks are set out a ways from the other buildings, out back by some old cemetery. I guess us colored boys are supposed to be the first line of defense against haunts, huh?

That made Cleo smile, in spite of herself.

Some of the boys, though, they ain't too keen on the idea. But I'd punch a ghost in the eye if it meant standing between me and getting a chance to do more than throwing out slop pails in this war.

You know what I miss, Momma? I really could go for a batch of them lemon sugar cookies that you used to make. I can almost taste them now and its got the corner of my mouth getting wet. Too bad you're so far...

The sound of the approaching trolley sounded like the distant roar of ocean waves beyond a wall of sand dunes. Putting her other letters into her purse, Cleo stood and soon found herself immersed in a crowd waiting to board the transport, just as well.

As it pulled up to the stop, Cleo figured she wouldn't have a chance to finish reading the letter while on board the trolley. It was looking to be pretty full, so she'd have to wait. But her mind remained trained on her boy, however, as she boarded.

She wanted to come up with some sort of a plan, a course of action, a recourse that could erase all the miles of separation. She wondered if the time was different in Georgia, or whether they were operating in the same dimension as the good people of Detroit. Good Lord, she thought. They down in the mouth of it. That was for sure.

But her baby wanted him some sugar cookies, and his momma damn sure wasn't going to stand and have him disappointed. She'd never taken any days off sick since she began working for the store. If ever a boy was asking to see his momma...

On that same day, at the same time, but an hour later from Detroit, Staff Sergeant Avery sat back in his solely occupied bus seat with a bemused eye. His window was half-opened and with a good deal of satisfaction the dusky soldier drew in a lungful of smoke from his short cigarette and exhaled it in that direction. The peach colored sunset, so appropriate for Georgia, still shone clearly through the window. It turned the blue haze of the smoke into an amber fume, and spiraled it upward and outward, sucking it out into the warm, moist air of Chattahoochee County.

"Hey, Sarge," one of Avery's black troops called, "how come we got to walk back to camp?"

"The bus don't run but two more trips back and forth after this one. We'll still be in the show."

"Dad-fetch it," the soldier complained to a seatmate. "I ain't trying to do anymore marching today."

"Then you shouldn't have come."

"You should have figured that we was walking back when he passed these out to us," and the soldier patted the holstered .45 at his side. "They've invested too much into our training to about now, than to go and get us into harm's way and have no way to protect ourselves.

"He's got something there, Twine."

"Shit," the first soldier said, "they ain't loaded. We ain't going to scare off no Klan with empty guns."

Avery didn't bother to intervene in their argument. They were all travelling off-base to catch an intermission from their training that had been well-earned. It was an opportunity that came about with some bartering, but they were on their way. And they would be prepared for any eventuality.

All of the magazines for the pistols were half-loaded and under command of the sergeant, in two ammo boxes he had under his boots.

During the training, a major one at that, Avery and twelve other Negro sergeants had been assigned as field marshals for the war games. Each of them had seen extensive duty during World War I. The first time Avery saw assault teams comprised of white and black men working together without so much as a double-take between them was a sight to behold. Each one of the black soldiers on the bus with him he did not know directly, but he witnessed splendid field execution from them over the last several days. Avery's pride was boundless.

There was a new day on the rise in military thinking and theory which Avery didn't quite understand how it came to be, but he welcomed it, nonetheless.

But the reality of the privileges that couldn't be earned still made itself known to the men who wanted to have their due. Everyone had gotten back from the exercises preparing to celebrate, even as tired as they were. They had gone two weeks without decent food, entertainment, or beer. Soon, a consensus among them came to be that they wanted to alleviate the cloistering of their natures during the bivouac.

A British film had arrived on the base and been playing to full houses. It dealt with the war, as many films of the time did, and it was called *The Yellow Canary*. It told the story of British aristocrat who involved herself with the Nazis before the war and how she tried to extricate herself from them once the axis formed. Cinematic images of gray-toned battlefields, beautiful women, and the promise of espionage had most of the men who'd been involved in the war maneuver ready to have a look at it. Word of mouth had spread that it was exceptionally good. Unfortunately, however, there was only one more show scheduled by the time the men got organized and arrived at the PX theater house.

When all the black troops arrived all the seats were already occupied. Some of them suggested that they just stand against the back wall, but that proved to be unfavorably held amongst those already inside. The colored troops, as it were, were simply without any further recourse. They just had to accept that they could not see the movie. On its surface appearance the denial wasn't a malicious one, such annoyances rarely are, but it nonetheless made all the Negro men outside the theater wonder as to how their eminence and esteem had faded from the short distance it took to walk from their bivouac area to the camp theater.

Avery, who had been making a purchase at the nearby commissary, noticed the accumulation of Negro troops, many vaguely familiar, and he heard the buzzing stir of discontent on the fringe of the crowd. He walked over to find out what the situation was and when told about it had a conference with the theater manager, thus quieting the soldiers for the moment. And they awaited his return outside.

When Avery came back he told the soldiers that he'd inspected the movie house's interior and that, indeed, there were no available seats. And he added that to place more men inside the building would be a violation of the law. But within moments of saying that, Avery came up with a consolatory proposal. He wouldn't tell them what he planned to do, but he did say he'd have to get permission from the company commander.

Avery had had the men wait outside of the commissary, telling them to relax, as he telephoned the officer-of-the-day. The minutes grew longer and longer and the men became more anxious. Finally, Avery returned to the awaiting soldiers and had them form ranks, whereupon he marched them to the armory to acquire sidearms.

Gus and Joe thought, as well as many of the others, that they had been given some extra-duty for being uppity and making a fuss. But when they saw Avery come out of the quartermaster's with two ammo boxes they knew something highly irregular was coming to light. Avery only half-heartedly suggested to the lieutenant that they have the weapons, but never in his wildest flights of imagination would he have thought permission would be granted.

As the last squad of men received their .45 weapon, a corporal called Avery over to a phone and gave him the receiver. Avery shook his head several times and thanked the officer for the assist, before turning to the assembly and explaining the plan.

A local bus company was coming to the base to pick up the fifty men and drive them into the nearest town for their night's entertainment. But that they would have to walk the five miles back. The lieutenant let them carry the weapons but insisted there be no drinking among the men, and that orders to arm would only come from the sergeant.

Some voiced their objections but the majority thought the special attention and trust given to them was worth just a little more sacrifice. And so they waited for the bus at the base gate and some noted how almost a year earlier they'd have ended up in the stockade for being outfitted as they were.

Gus was stopped by Joe as he was passing him by, "Hey, let me talk to you a minute."

"What's the matter?"

"Not really anything wrong, but do you realize we're all prepared to walk five miles in the dark, in Georgia, and not have any idea what movie it is we're going to see?"

"Well—it's, ah—dang, you got a point. Hey! Anybody know what's playing?" Gus asked.

No one bothered answering him, perhaps because they too realized they had acted on a perception of slight, rather than a reasoned act. "I'd sure hate to go all the way there and not like what's on the bill," said Joe, reaching for a cigarette out of his shirt pocket.

"I think it's an Alfred Hitchcock picture," someone said.

"Well, that cuts it down, don't it? Thanks for the tip," Joe said facetiously. "I guess truth of the matter is that it really doesn't matter to anybody standing here what's playing. Does it, Gus?"

"Yeah. I know. Just the fact that we're going, huh?"

"And that's a fact, junior. That is a fact."

It was early in the evening by the time the bus came.

So that was how Sgt. Avery came to be sitting next to the opened bus window, finishing his smoke and feeling so sanctimoniously proud of what had been organized; so proud that he could care less about the doubts of some men in the group. And he was not at all bothered that twilight had just begun to descend its curtain across the oncoming night's sky when the bus let the men out about a quarter of a mile away from the edge of the Chattahoochee River town of Seema.

Seema was one of several little offshoot communities that surrounded the larger Phoenix City and had nearly seven hundred inhabitants in it. People who'd mostly never gone further than Phoenix City for anything their entire lives were its native residents. Certainly inhabitants who participated in, or showed support for the Klan. Sgt. Avery seemed unmoved by that reality, however. With singular purpose, he made sure the soldiers walked for several hundred yards before he called them over to the side of the road. Well before they were at the edge of the town.

"All right, y'all now listen up," he said, the familiar country pattern in his speech not obfuscated for the sake of his authority. Avery set the metal boxes he'd been carrying on the ground and opened each one with something approaching reverence. "I'm fixin' to issue y'all some clips because I'll be damned if I'm carrying these all the way into town and back." The men all laughed at his flippancy. "But hear me, and hear me well, gentlemen." And Avery waited for the chatter to fade, so as to be sure to be heard. "Every one of you Swinging Richards better keep them goddam weapons holstered, understand?"

After he'd heard a few grunts of acknowledgement or plaintive voices, he started the arming process. "One clip to a man."

Avery passed out the magazines quickly, placing the containers into outstretched and mobile hands. He didn't bother looking up, knowing he could be assured that none of the soldiers would dare trying to covet another man's issue. Avery knew these weren't children and he would not treat them in such a manner, but he did look up when he heard more than the sound of the magazines being driven home. "No rounds in the chamber, gentlemen. I shouldn't have had to tell you that."

Moments later, some soldiers could be heard quietly reinserting their bullets back into their storage clips. Avery placed the empty ammo boxes behind a cropping of nearby rocks and then strutted up to the front of his company.

"Here's the ground rules, troops. The lay of the land, as it were—first, we stay together. Not one person going here and another goin' off t'another. Naw, naw, Nawsir. We are all going to one place—and that's the movie. When we are at that venue let me make it perfectly clear that we all sit together. And finally, it bears repeating, though I shouldn't have to say it—no one is to draw their weapon from a holster unless I give them a direct order to do so. If I see a man pull his gun out trying to impress somebody I will shoot him in the head my own damn self. Now, let's move lively, men. You can smoke 'em if you got 'em. Let's go into town, y'all."

They walked forward into the night towards the lights of Seema in two files, not by any military intent but just that it was the practice of movement in the Army. However, their regimentation didn't go so far as to all the men marching along in step. But even without that, the smooth and uniform manner in which these bronze-skinned soldiers made their way into the town caused a mild, unspoken, panic as they rounded the first corner into the main streets. Joe noticed how they were being espied by the townspeople. "Look at 'em, Sarge," he said. "They look like they just seen the Nazis come marching in."

Avery gave a casual nod to the older Martin's observation and kept the formation moving towards their neon-trimmed objective, the Majestic Theater. The cotton-candy pink walls and the baroque straw-colored fascia of the nickelodeon house reflected the red, blue, green, and white illuminescent trim from the lights. The movie house's name was in large block letters of yellow and orange pulsing lights, one stacked on top of the other above the picture show's portico. All of Avery's men purchased their tickets quietly from the flustered teenage box office employee, who had never so many Negroes concentrated in one place after the sun going down.

Towards the end of the line, while waiting to purchase their tickets, Joe noted that the film was indeed an Alfred Hitchcock affair. It was called *The Shadow of a Doubt* and it starred Joseph Cotten.

"Is that true what they say about him, Joe?" Gus asked.

"What?"

"That Joseph Cotten's got some colored blood?"

Joe considered it for "a moment, and yes, he'd heard others make some remarks to that effect. His tight, and wavy hair, and thick nose, along with the full lips could make for such an argument. That he had black blood in his family or that he might even be passing himself, but Joe didn't believe all the supposed hysteria. "He still looks whiter than, Momma," he said to Gus.

"Is it any good?"

"Is what any good?"

"What we've been talking about damn near half the night—the movie!"

"It's pretty good. At least, I'd go see it again. It's about this guy who runs away from Philadelphia because people think he's murdered someone there, and he starts a new life…Sound like anyone you know, junior?"

"Will you lay off about Captain Sackett? You got no reason to be bad-mouthing him now, hundreds of miles from you—and you still trying to stir up mess. Joe you ought to be ashamed for thinking like that. He ain't no murderer."

"And Joseph Cotten's not black, so let's move on."

The inside of the plush carpeted theater had romantic lighting, softening the hard edges of everything and everyone in the popcorn-smelling lobby. With all its gild framed larger-than-life posters. They all gave the nervous usher their whole tickets, who kept glancing at every soldier's sidearm and the protruding gun butts that extended out of the holsters, flustering him to a point he did not even bother to tear their tickets in half to give them their passes. Touching the palms of their hands would have almost made him more nervous than just their weapons being inside the building, but having to deal with both extreme situations at once seemed to be a bit much for the usher to handle. The men knew why they weren't being treated customarily and didn't hold up the line waiting for the insignificant article that was tossed aside into a waste can, rather than into their hand.

Sublimated by a pastel, dimmer lighting was a glass concession stand, to the right of the lobby's foyer. And it immediately began siphoning off customers, some of the soldiers included, who were going to purchase confections for the viewing. The distracted white customers did their best not to pay any attention to the service men interlopers who were clearly out-of-place in the segregated venue.

Sgt. Avery looked to his left and saw a burgundy velvet rope that had a sign attached to its sagging center where it spanned the first raisers of a carpet spiral stairway that disappeared behind the curvature of a rose-colored wall. Another partition sealed off the opposite entry to the balcony as well. The signs said the balcony was closed but Avery knew that usually there'd be another sign posted near the balcony way: "COLORED." Seeing that that option was not available as a way to diffuse the anxiety of the white patrons in the show, Avery turned to buy himself some popcorn. Almost immediately when doing so he was intercepted by a tall, double-chinned white man in a blazer. Avery immediately took him to be the manager of the theater and he was sweating profusely.

"Sergeant, can I help you?" he said with chagrin.

"No, thank you," Avery replied with curt demeanor and thin politeness. He knew that the manager didn't intend to offer him or his men any leeway or assistance in their outing. "I think I'll just buy me some popcorn and get situated for the show, if you don't mind. Is it starting on time?"

Some of Avery's men noticed that the sergeant spoke with precise vernacular now, and not the comfortable patois he used earlier in speaking with them. The roly-poly manager grabbed hold of the balcony rope. "Oh, you have about five minutes before it starts, Sergeant. I'll just open up the balcony for y'all."

"There's no need to bother," Avery assured him, ducking his head into the auditorium momentarily and then turning to face the manager again. "Looks to me to be plenty of seats in here for me and my men."

"But, you don't understand—"

"Don't understand what?"

The manager drew closer to Avery and tried to lower his voice, "We can't have y'all on the main floor. The reason why we have the balcony is for the colored. We are not segregated, here. We allow nigras. But we do have our rules."

"Then why is the balcony closed?" a private asked.

"As you were," Avery rebuked the soldier.

The manager had wiped his brow with his handkerchief and seen where he had duty to fulfill. "The reason we have it closed off, since you boys don't seem to be familiar with our ways here, is because after sundown we don't have our nigras into town. Now, we heard about you northerners coming down here to train, and have been accommodating. But y'all don't want to seem to understand the way we do things."

The change in the manager's attitude and cordiality was not wasted on the perceptive sergeant, who had already seen three police cars pull up to the curb of the theater. Five officers got out of each vehicle. The first cop on the scene inside the theater immediately asked the beleaguered businessman what problem he was having.

"Why, it's these here army niggers. That's the problem."

Avery began rubbing his face in exasperation and all the troops gathered around where he stood, but the theater owner had become braver now that the police arrived. "They come in here," the manager began to explain, "and refuse to obey our laws. Now I have a right to refuse service to anyone who is not law abiding, don't I?"

The officer turned to Avery. "The man sold you tickets, didn't he?"

"Yes, sir."

"And he offered you and your men seating, did he not?"

"Yes, sir."

"Well, all right then. Boy, what the hell is the problem?"

"Everyone who buys a ticket can sit where they want, officer. We simply want to do the same."

"You see what I mean, officer. They don't realize that a ticket only gives them a right to a seat in the theater, and that any decision as to who sits where is an arbitrary one on our part."

"That's a fact," the officer agreed, and then turned again to Sgt. Avery, "and you understand what he said, don't you boy?"

"Oh, I understand, sir." And both the officer and the theater owner began to breathe easier thinking they'd begun to get Avery to listen to reason, but that was short-lived. "I truly understand your position, and I regret you feel the way you do because we don't want trouble. Now, we've just finished with war maneuvers and wanted to watch a movie, that's all. And I realize this man may very well have the right to force seating in his establishment, but I also realize that you only have fifteen men here to enforce that so-called rule. I have forty men—and they're armed."

"Are you crazy, nigger?" the cop flummoxed, "Do you know that you've just made a threat to a police officer, boy? I could arrest all y'all fo' incitin' a riot!"

As much as the officer and manger were upset and bristling, Sgt. Avery was as calm. "Sir, I have not threatened you. I've merely said that we might respond to any aggression against us in kind, as any man would. Wouldn't you agree? My question to you, sir, is this. Is the matter of where we sit so important to you that you would rather fight about it at the point of a gun?"

"Seems to me, sergeant," the theater manager chimed in, "the same question applies to you."

"And I've stated my position on that, sir." Avery looked directly at the befuddled police officer and then back at the theater manager, weighing his next move for a split second and then acting upon his gut. "Now, if you'll excuse me gentlemen," he said, "Me and my men have a movie to watch."

And they all walked into the darkened theater, Sgt. Avery not letting out a sigh of relief until his anxiety could be concealed under the cover of darkness. On the other side of the doors the police officer gently pulled the exasperated business man away, terminating the confrontation. "We'll let the M.P.'s handle it," he said.

But instead of the military police reigning down punishment on the uppity patrons, one simply asked to speak with Avery. The men were made to hand over the ammunition they carried, passing the magazines down the aisle to a confiscating M.P.; to the indignation of theater operator and the bewilderment of the police, the Ft. Benning peacekeepers negotiated a stalemate concerning the incident.

Avery and his men could stay and watch the movie, and on the main floor, but the M.P.'s had to be on alert outside of the theater while the Negroes attended. The manager wanted assurance that each would be court-martialed but no commentary was made regarding that request. They only committed that a report would be given to the base and that there would be no future episodes akin to this one.

One of the reasons the military police were at a loss to satisfactorally answer the civilian question was for the very reason that new directives had been coming out of the base Headquarters. In times past, the colored soldiers would have been quickly, if not roughly, taken from the area. The difference now, however, was that there had been official government recommendation from the combined services about the needs and treatment of Negro soldiers.

Now, it was implicit that officers were to take into account how certain factors could lead to reactionary feelings both for the soldiers, and the civilian areas where they would be exposed. It was stressed to everyone in the chain-of-command that behaving towards Negro troops in an uncivil manner was not acceptable, especially in social contexts. And that was why Avery and his men were not harassed further; they had been the recipients of some of the first federal protections for Negroes in the country.

The administrative staffs, however, also knew that a balance needed to be struck as tolerance was pursued under a separate-but-equal ideology. The ramifications of the social integration in the South, though limited, still had not been fully analyzed as to what extent attitudes could be shifted.

The stance of the Army, according to the 1944 Troop Basis, was to foment liaisons between the communities and camp bases by monitoring planned outings in towns situated near them. Because of all this, the M.P.'s were ordered to stand down that night in Seema and not to arrest the soldiers involved. That is not to say there weren't repercussions after the men were driven back to the base.

The lieutenant, who had been the officer-of-the-day, had a stern and hyperbolic lecture given to him from Lt. Colonel Beauville as to his judgment made in allowing the Negro troops to be armed. The lieutenant said the men would be "sitting ducks" for Klansmen while they walked back to the base, and that was why he'd issued them sidearms. Plus, he said he had given specific instruction as to when and where they were to come into play. Beauville didn't want to hear the excuses.

The lieutenant, in turn, then chastised Sgt. Avery for behaving in a stubborn and insolent manner to local officials. But that was the extent of their punishment, not discounting the men having to stand at attention outside their barracks all night and guarding their own individually chosen rock.

That was the consequence, but the repercussions were more engrained. Within a fortnight, two weeks, of the incident, the high command at Ft. Benning ordered an immediate out-of-bounds directive that regarded the town of Seema. The order was to stay in effect until further notice and applied only to Negro soldiers. To punctuate the restriction, Negroes from Seema would not be allowed to visit the base, as well.

Up until that time the command had turned their heads when fleet-footed girls of the darker persuasion were smuggled into camp. At one point, they had grown so lackadaisical in regards to the impropriety that some known prostitutes didn't even have to concern themselves with showing identification at gates. But that all came to end, now.

Though it seemed like the off-limits order would be enforced for the foreseeable future, in reality, by the fourth week out from the incident there was access given back to the black troops. However, the Majestic Theater was still not to be entered—but an improvement in the screenings at the base allowed for more showings and alleviated the need to go to Seema to watch a film. By the middle of May things were fairly much back to the new normal.

The realigned status quo for the colored service constituency was being adhered to. They again could have access to the black community of Seema, but only within the town. Colored civilians still had no relations, business or personal, with the Negro troops at the Ft. Benning encampment. But there were considerations given, as well. Public buses ran for longer hours, now. And another line was added for persons of color. So, toeing the line reset for the Negro soldiers and Seema's colored, had not worked a calamity upon them, but a beneficial structuring of resources.

A small battle had been won by the disenfranchised citizens of the area because of what the forty black soldiers did at the Majestic. The small disquiet that the Seema incident brought about seemed to have initiated some goodwill, sensitivity, and an uplifting of the society, in general. But when Cleo Martin arrived in Seema on May 24, 1944 all the steps forward took four huge steps backwards.

Initially, she disembarked at a train station in nearby Phoenix City; she was somewhat disoriented and very thirsty. Her sleeveless light-yellow dress, with its fairly large white polka dots, pinched under her arms a little bit in the snug, humid air and for a moment she felt weak in the knees. A very dark woman, one who had been sitting near her in the Jim Crow car of the train, helped her off the coach.

"Are you all right, Missy?" the matronly woman asked the pasty looking Creole, half her age.

"Just thankful for some air, Ma'am," Cleo sighed, getting her bearings. She then smiled appreciatively at the woman she found out went by the name of Belle. A deaconess at the local African Methodist Episcopalian Church.

"Lawd knows you need some air," and Belle did a close-mouthed chuckle to keep her dentures in place. "With all that bad mess you had pushed up in your face back there. It's a wonder you ain't sayin' the holy ghost right now."

Cleo couldn't help but snicker at the pointed remark about her seatmate for the past hundred miles of the trip. A man she could only compare to a buffoon physically encroached upon her and verbally harangued her with unasked for conversation all the way to Phoenix City. His frame was a large one and he moved about like a bull in a small pen. He seemed to want to be perceived as being svelte and nimble, but he certainly wasn't. It seemed he thought himself a Fred Astaire but he was more a Fatty Arbuckle.

"He was just too country, wasn't he though?" Cleo teetered.

With some refinement from a well-placed palette blade and a sharp razor he could have shown some improvement in the looks department, but it would not have been enough to draw a second look from Cleo. Yet, he persisted in getting to know her, attaching himself to her like an overgrown leech once he'd set eyes on her. The overall effect he had upon her entered into the category of mild repulsion.

He had worn an out-of-date suit with a tie that had a dark grease spot on it. Cleo could see thick, yellowish build-up along his blackened gum line, above his even more yellowed teeth. His black skin was ashy and dry and he smelled like he hadn't washed for the trip.

Belle saw her squirming to get up from under the badgering oaf and she came to assist by giving the admirer a saintly reproach that bordered on a conviction of his spirit.

"Remember, Missy. We got prayer meeting Sat'dy mawning. And church start at nine, Sund'y. Hope y' can get by," Belle said in parting.

"Oh, I'll probably be gone before the end of the week," Cleo apologized, knowing outright that she had only gotten four days leave. But she would do with that time whatever she could manage. Prayer meetings, though, weren't on the list.

"Oh, that's a shame. Well—God be with you, sister."

"Thank you, Ma'am. God bless y'all too, now." Cleo waved her white-gloved hand goodbye as she watched the matronly acquaintance walk out of sight. Smiling at the kind deeds and words extended to her so far away from home.

She breathed in and out deeply, still smiling, with a satisfaction that came from her completing the first part of her excursion, and not being any worse for the wear. Cleo had never been south of the Mason-Dixon and had premonitions of what she could expect. Although, she was not oblivious that there was virulent social separation. She knew also knew that she had the ability to slant her image to her advantage, when needed. At this point, she believed most of her fears to be overactive ones. Ones that would be more dispelled, she was sure, as the days wore on.

With her little round white suitcase in one hand, and her patent leather white clutch purse in the other, topped off with a dainty white hat at the rear of her head, Cleo veritably glowed as she waited for her luggage, but it was the start of the sweltering part of the afternoon. Cleo just had her tan marble-textured *Samsonite* suitcase to pick up and she would be off to find a hotel. As the heat began to flush her cheeks she silently urged the porters and baggage handlers to expedite their work, but they worked slowly.

This train would be followed by thirteen others in the next four hours and the men knew not to overextend their energy. They especially became drained after having to crawl into the hot undercarriage luggage bins. One fellow would shimmy his way under until he disappeared and then could be seen, headfirst, tossing luggage forward to an awaiting handler outside the train. So, the bag handlers were not in a rush and paced themselves, conserving energy that got sweated out of them while they hoisted the poundage.

Cleo took off her gloves because of the heat and thoughtlessly slapped them a few times across the palm of her hand, as she began tapping her foot with growing impatience and began checking and re-checking her watch.

Then she heard a comforting sound; it was the sound of tinkling crystals, like chandeliers being gently shaken by a breeze. Cleo turned, ever so slightly, to look towards the noise and immediately saw why it sounded so refreshing, and familiar. Just inside the train station, to the right of the great wooden doors with their glass panes all tiffany- bordered, stood an umbrella-shielded lemonade stand in the tiled, open-air courtyard and it seemed to beckon her in.

She crossed into the station without hesitation, and all the while beamed a toothy, vividly white smile. Her teeth made all the more appealing by the red, fleshy, lipstick framed lips, upon on her attractive face. She looked all the part of a model and her posture as she walked into the building reflected such comportment, as well. She noticed some men staring as she passed, without any attempt to hide their lechery, she thought. But she kept her head straight, nonetheless, to make up for her darting eyes as she approached the stand.

At the crook of her left elbow she pinned her clutch against her side and the interior of her arm sweated uncomfortably from the contact with the non-porous, glossy plastic. With her right hand freed from the white cotton gloves which were now held in her left, she paused a moment and opened the purse to get her a nickel out of her change pocket. Acquiring it, once pushing aside her lipstick, compact, and fifty dollars cash she carried, Cleo closed her purse and stepped forward towards her intended stop.

The stand was made of dark wood, highly laminated, and the lemonade it store was filled in a twelve-gallon glass drawing well. Inside the dewy well three large pieces of ice floated around in it, like ice bergs in a milky-yellow sea. That unit, in turn, was surrounded by four square panes of glass with red and yellow letters advertising the product and what it cost to the consumer. A mockingbird was singing away in a potted tree just to the right and behind the proprietor.

As Cleo walked up to the stand her movement could not have been more elegant or graceful. Her skin smelled of lavender and her shoulders flared above her tiny waist and carriage. The small of her back ran down into a line of womanly flesh that could only be called statuesque in its design. When she stopped and lighted her hand upon the edge of the vending cart she placed her right leg slightly in back of the left, revealing a very nice calf. "I'll have one of those, if you please," Cleo said brightly.

She extended her hand with the solitary coin to a potato-sack waisted, large, blonde attendant who'd turned aside to Cleo when she came up to the station. Giving her the benefit of the doubt, Cleo tried to get her attention once again, this time in a little louder tone. "Excuse me—" The vendor was in no hurry sweeping up some spilt sugar from off the floor. "Ma'am—" Cleo went on, "I'd like to have lemonade please."

The woman turned to look at Cleo, and glowered at her when she pointed at the stack of paper cones behind the panes. The moon-shaped face of the woman reddened. She wore a white paper hat and her curly, blonde hair splayed out in frazzled mats from underneath it. "I can't help you," she said.

Cleo, still smiling, though trying not to furrow her eyebrows, kept her hand extended with the offered nickel in her fingertips.

"But I don't understand," Cleo said, "you do sell the lemonade here, don't you?"

The attendant had turned her backside to her as she scooped up the sugar pile into a dustpan and replied matter-of-factly, "Not to colored, we don't."

"I beg your pardon!" Cleo said indignantly, going into her assimilation mode. "I can't believe you would dare say that to me. How dare you. I am white as you are, and you will serve me what I want, now."

The attendant put away her cleaning supplies and faced off with Cleo, putting doughy looking fingers on her hips.

"I don't know who you think you are fooling. Up North, they don't know y'all like we'uns do. You can probably get by them all right, but I could see from the first minute that y'ain't nothin' more than a high yaller bitch. And

I'm speaking kindly by sayin' that. And believe me you don't want to raise no ruckus up in here. You understand me, gal?"

Cleo timidly withdrew the coin in her hand with the pain and humiliation she felt welling up inside of her. She quietly took a step back from the cart. "But, ma'am," she pleaded in a whispery voice, "please—you see, I haven't been feeling too well with all the heat from the train. And I was hoping—"

"I told you now, we don't serve niggers!"

That exclamation drew attention to Cleo, unwanted attention, and just as she had stood so tall and proud upon entering the train station, she was now imploded and shrinking in stature. "I'm sorry," Cleo apologized.

"GIT!" a septuagenarian man tried to bellow at Cleo, and though his order was not deeply-voiced, the disdain and objection he felt towards her was more than apparent. To make an emphasis that his voice couldn't, he swiped his wooden cane at her a few times. Causing Cleo to jump back and almost stumble. And then the laughter started.

Now far away from the lemonade station, Cleo could see a few younger men gently slapping the senior citizen on the back or shake his hand. They turned and guffawed more at her and pointed fingers. "Best do what he said, nigger. This'n here is just as sharp as any Johnny Reb, yet. And he get to his truck, it won't be his cane you got to worry about."

The atmosphere too raucous, too disquieting for even the mockingbird to remain, so Cleo too retreated. Looking hurt, and more than a little confused by her persona being totally ousted in such a vulgar fashion, she didn't even stop to get a drink from the clearly marked water fountain for "coloreds" by the door. Once outside, she quickly found her bag while the laughter still resonated from inside the cavern courtyard of the station, and that made her ear lobes burn in anger. "What kind of God forsaken part of America is this?" Cleo muttered to herself, and in addition thought, "And how did I honestly think I could separate myself from all this madness?"

She followed the path that her friend, Belle, had taken to get off of the depot area and would never try to pass herself off for white again for as long as she was in the South. And that couldn't be over with soon enough.

Therefore, instead of looking for a hotel room, and a bath, Cleo hoped that getting done what she'd come for—seeing Joseph and August, would quicken the way for her premature departure. Which she now wanted to happen immediately.

She wanted nothing more to do with getting to know the local culture, now. Or to finding out what type of environment her sons had been dropped into. She'd seen enough of that, all ready. And that was why she was on a bus heading to Fort Benning.

Cleo had given up on reflecting on what had occurred in any attempt to quantify or qualify the extreme environment of Georgia for blacks. When she boarded the bus and deposited her fare she had gone directly to the rear, with the other colored passengers. There were no pretenses made. Yes, in Detroit she could sit wherever she pleased, with the forethought that a white passenger could still displace her from her seat. But that had never happened to her in all her years. She had never had an incident as oppressive happen to her, either. But here was a different slice of life, indeed. The incident in the train station let her know in no uncertain terms, and made it abundantly clear that like Dorothy landing in Oz, she wasn't in Michigan anymore.

When she arrived at the base she re-situated the pin in her hair to steady her white hat and then walked to the visitors' reception area. That had been almost an hour ago. And now she somehow found herself in a base stockade holding cell. The stubborn hardness of the stone bench under her lean flanks reminded Cleo just how long she had been waiting, as well. Things were deteriorating at a rapid level of increase. When she couldn't come up with any specific reasons for the sergeant as to how she came to know about a "purported" special training endeavor on the base, she was escorted to the blockhouse.

She absentmindedly smacked her clutch purse against her leg a few times and then tossed it aside, towards the end of the bench. She was at this point so disheveled and tired from the day's activities that she now she knew how stupid she'd been in hurrying this chance meeting along.

All her responses to the sergeant who came to talk to her had been slurred so she was sure that he must have thought her to be a drunk. It had been a long, long day of travel and Cleo softly cursed herself for not being more patient and affording herself with some bit of rest and relaxation. This could have all waited for the next day, she now knew. Her constitution was just not up for such an emotional marathon.

Lighting a cigarette broke up the tedium of the thoughts coming to her mind in a creek of anger dammed next to a river of regret. With every cloud of smoke she exhaled she did it loudly, frustrated that the cigarettes weren't tranquilizing her, as advertised. The lipstick banners she once had were now ribbons, and showed no flash of a smile.

They had come at her, she believed, like she was being suspected of smuggling out plans for some bomb, or something. And they had also just as much as accused her of lying.

"Don't know my boys—humph! Yeah. Uh-huh, got no record of 'em, huh? They just disappeared into thin air, I guess."

That's exactly what the sergeant had told her, though. The sergeant had told her there couldn't be any colored privates from Detroit named Martin at the base, because there weren't any colored soldiers on the base.

She wasn't worried about being in the stockade, really, though. She wasn't worried because these people weren't the police and had no authority over her. She was a citizen, and whom they were supposed to be fighting to protect from fascists. She'd shown them the letter Gus had sent her, so that had to prove her story. But then why was she waiting in this human kennel for so long. The thought suddenly crossed her mind that though she hadn't done anything wrong, she may have brought calamity down upon Joe and Gus. And that caused her to light up another cigarette. After a few drags she felt more centered and less paranoid, until a wispy, brunette, white female officer came into the room.

She was from the Women's Army Corps and a captain, but who was paid what a male lieutenant made. And her nameplate read TREADWELL. Captain Treadwell was not happy being a WAC, in fact she had been tricked into the service by a bit of recruitment chicanery. While seeing her boyfriend off to his basic training, the previous year, an unscrupulous officer asked Treadwell if she wanted to do something to bring her man home sooner. She'd said yes and he had her sign a paper. She was mortified when a week later she'd gotten orders to report to an induction center. She thought she'd been signing a petition.

Since the recent advance trainings at Benning, Treadwell had found herself pulled from her usual clerical assignment to perform "other" duties. Today was her third such instance of performing the duty, and she had quickly learned to be impersonal with the formalities needed. For weeks, Treadwell had been called down regularly to provide the one skill that only she could provide in her service: the searching of colored suspects from the neighboring red light district. She hadn't particularly thought about the searches one way or the other.

In fact, she felt it somewhat odd that she should be searching for alleged prostitutes because before the WACs became part of the army, and they were the Women's Army Auxiliary Corps, the public-at-large believed many of them to be women of low moral fiber, themselves. She'd heard that the old motto: "Release a Man for Combat" had a duplicitous meaning when applied to women being in the army. She didn't get involved with creating empathy or concern while conducting the searches, which usually preceded the *visitor* being escorted off of the base; she simply did what was needed and how she'd been trained to do it. Upon concluding the examination, having the women gather their belongings quickly and getting dressed.

Somehow, Treadwell knew that she would be getting called by the sergeant with a request when she saw this one come through. Of all the visiting area sergeants, this one by far had the most requests in for summonsing a strip search. Treadwell could sense the sergeant got a vicarious thrill just from imagining that in the room next to him a woman was being made to disrobe, purely based on his personal whim.

Even though she knew he had no way of observing the search, she couldn't shake the feeling that it was with such an overactive ardor the noncom made his requests known to her; it left no doubt to her that he found the situation pleasurable to initiate. Notwithstanding that, however, what the captain found even more disturbing to her own sensibilities was that she actually enjoyed his apparent arousal; strained cloistering in his pants at times, as he got all worked up over her performing a search.

Once she even explained to him what the suspects had to do when she conducted the searches. The captain would touch herself—in a militarily demonstrative way, to explain the procedure. But though she said she meant it to be perceived as only an informative display, it was suggestive, nonetheless. So suggestive that she'd made it difficult for him to stand when she was leaving the room. And she didn't even find the man attractive, in the least. But she liked toying with him. Because it was just her way of letting him know that she had more power at her command than he thought.

"The sergeant tells me you've got some missing persons you're looking for. You—ah, are from Michigan and yet you come all the way down to Georgia looking for your—"

"My sons—yes, that's right."

Cleo's right foot was waggling in the air after that leg crossed her left. Her left arm was at a forty-five degree angle across her midriff, the elbow nestled. And she had her right arm crocked at a matching perpendicular angle, with her fresh cigarette held in place by her index and middle finger. She had done a quick once over of the WAC when she entered, and wasn't impressed. Giving her a hard stare through eyes that had grown smaller from irritation. Treadwell was nonplussed and sat in a chair at a small table across from Cleo, and folded her hands.

"You've lost track of your boys? James and George?"

"Joseph and August—I showed you people the letter and you tell me I'm mistaken. But I know my own son's handwriting."

"I'm not calling that into question, Ms. Martin."

"Then may I have my mail back, please."

"Not at the moment. How did you lose track of your sons?"

"Seems to me, you people are the ones who have lost track of them, not me."

"We contacted the Service Command in your area and they claim they are still in Wisconsin, ma'am."

"Not according to my son's letter, they're not."

Captain Treadwell rose from her table and crossed over to a sink and mirror to the left of Cleo. She preened herself in front of it for a moment and then sighed before saying, "I can see we're not breaking any new ground here, I'm afraid—and that is—well, that's unfortunate."

"Look," Cleo interrupted, finally disregarding propriety, "I'm really getting tired of this. I have done nothing wrong. Where are my sons and can I see them, please? If not, then you'll have to excuse me. You have no right to keep me locked up in here."

Treadwell cleaned some lipstick from off the corner of her mouth with her little finger. "Oh, I'm sorry—but that's where you're wrong."

"What?"

Treadwell turned to face Cleo, propping her butt against the sink she'd been standing in front of. "I need to inform you about a few little things. Whether you know it or not, your civil rights—such as they are, cease to take precedence over the authority that's vested in a military base during a time of war. On this property we can detain you, even arrest you. Do I make myself clear?"

That announcement made Cleo change her attitude because she had no desire to be placed in a southern jail on the whim of some disgruntled debutante in uniform. She knew that colored folk got lost—permanently, in the to-and-fro tipping of the southern scales of justice. And then never seen or heard from again.

"Captain—what is it that I've done so terribly wrong to have you all treating me like this? Please, I really don't understand and I'm tired. I'm so, tired."

Treadwell retrieved the chair from behind the table where she'd previously been sitting and placed it within an arm's reach of where Cleo sat, who was no longer smoking in a cavalier fashion, but now had her face buried in her hands. Treadwell sat in the chair and gently patted Cleo's left shoulder and when Cleo looked up at her the eyes looked misty and moist. The captain switched up her approach and began employing the demeanor of the friendly inquisitor.

"I know this seems absurd to you," she said. "Maybe even somewhat overzealous, if you understand what I mean, but you must know that we have men on this base who have been receiving company on a regular basis. Company—female company, which we found in some cases to be women of questionable character. These women conduct immoral business on government property. They introduce all sorts of contraband. They may even be moles for enemy forces, truth be told. So, it's because of this that we have to screen our visitors just a little more carefully than our usual policy would dictate."

"But what does that have to do with why I'm here? And why I came?"

"Well, ma'am. The reason why you were brought aside is because—ah, frankly, you don't look old enough to have boys in the Army."

"Wha—"

"And—" Treadwell emphasized, "we have no records of your sons that you're claiming being assigned to the base. Based on those facts, perhaps you can understand our position?"

"But I showed you all my birth certificate. That proves who I am, doesn't it?"

"Yes, Mrs. Martin. But again, you must realize that we have dealt with sophisticated individuals who could supply you with the documents you've produced."

Cleo began to gather her belongings and then stiffly rose. Sighing, accepting the fact that she'd come all the way down there for nothing. "Then I guess there's nothing more you can do for me, then. Is there? So, I'd like to go now."

Captain Treadwell positioned herself in the closed doorway and folded her arms lightly atop one another. "I'm sorry, ma'am. I'm afraid you can't do that just yet."

"But I have answered every question asked of me!"

"Yes, you have. But we still have some unfinished business."

"What more could there be?"

"You need to be searched, ma'am."

"You've looked in my purse."

"You don't understand. I'm talking about a more thorough search. We need to examine—your clothes."

"My clothing?"

"It will all be returned to you, and won't leave this room. But I have to search them, and then I have to search you."

"What?"

"So, if you please. I need you to remove your dress and shoes, ma'am."

"You can't be serious! I'll do no such thing!"

"You will," Treadwell shot back. "You will do it, and do it now, or I will have other soldiers in here to assist me in disrobing you. It's your choice."

Cleo was totally caught unawares by these new developments and the shock blanched her face and loosened the grit in her jaw. Drawing her arms behind her to unzip her dress, one she had so carefully chosen for the special trip she was making, Cleo held the dress fabric with one hand's fingertips and pulled the white zipper with the other. She did it slowly, hoping maybe the officer would relent, change her mind. But Treadwell's eyebrow just arched up higher on her forehead, an air of expectancy accompanying it. Cleo finished and took the dress off her shoulders as she slipped out of one shoe and then pushed off the other with her painted toes. In quick order she was standing in her bra and slip and handing her dress over to Captain Treadwell for inspection.

In the darkness, behind the cell's wall the desk sergeant inched his way along the plumbing channel, trying not to make any more noise than possible. His mannerisms were always the same when he couldn't resist this urge, this curse. For indeed this was a curse to Sgt. Vincents, and it had all begun one night when he was a teenager who unexpectedly witnessed a voyeuristic fornication on a loading passenger train. Transfixed on the distant, unsuspecting lovers, as he stood in the shadows and high brush near the railway station, he'd released himself along with them in their cabin, spilling his ejaculate on the gravel of the railroad tracks just at the moment it seemed that they'd climaxed. It was at that moment that he felt his soul's magnet drawing its moral compass askew, and he could not set it aright again, for the life of him. Several times, as the years passed and he grew more slovenly, he'd almost gotten caught in various instances. Almost, but not quite. It had quickly gotten to the point that the girls, or women, needn't be unclothed to get his mind imagining what they would look like if they could see him doing what he did. And then it would begin, one step leading to the next. The change came over him. Like *Lon Chaney*, once the spell hit him, he was powerless to suppress it. Even joining the Army couldn't stomp it out.

As a young man, the dates he did end up going on usually were embarrassingly awkward for him. Most times ending early and leaving Vincents only to prowl the boulevards looking into hotel and apartment windows, or if not successful in that, unfolding a pornographic magazine on his bed as a last resort. But he refused to "pay for some pussy". He was adamantly against prostitution.

And then by a fluke he'd been reassigned to visitor detention. He found out about the way the cells were engineered when he had to cut off water to an overflowing toilet in one. His deviant mind instantly wrapped itself around the opportunity created when the new orders came out. This was a dream come true, for Vincents.

Secluded from the rest of the visiting area, the plumbing chase tunnel was conveniently situated near the staff restrooms. When the right situation arose, he would take a short excursion into the bathroom and grab a handful of tissue, stuffing it into his right pocket, and then head to the iron grill door. Inserting the large brass Folgers-Adams key into the grill's lock quietly, he turned his moist and pudgy fingers on its flat oval base to the left, and then pivoting sideways, crossed the entry; he was all but invisible to the world once he closed the bars behind him. And he had no one to answer to for his comings-and-goings because this was his unit. Perfect.

Rubbing the flint wheel of his *Zippo* lighter quickly produced the glowing, whitish flame he found so pleasing. The smell of the naphtha. The dankness of the area. It all made him feel like he was an explorer, inside some ancient tomb.

Still keeping his body sideways as he inched his way between the sweaty walls, his protruding girth made it difficult to move, his lighter's flame only disturbed as he moved along with clumsy attempt at stealth.

The catacombs of the inner stockade had electrical conduit behind him and near the ground, and the larger piping for the plumbing was in front of him. Which he painfully sometimes rammed a knee into. Wincing and cursing, more than once, Vincents still kept moving towards the objective, though. Hoping not to tear a hole in his service pants. As he crab walked his way down the enclosed corridor, he was counting softly to himself each set of pipes. There really wasn't much of a need to do that because the light from the observation hole he'd made, just a few feet away from where he stood—a third of the way in, clearly cut a horizontal beam of light across the span of the tunnel. It easily identified the cell he had put the suspect in.

The block there, especially, was somewhat calcified and soft, or softer than what it should have been. Vincents found it gave way easily to the jabbing of a pocket knife or a large Phillips head screwdriver. A well placed strike with a ball-peen hammer made getting past the outer block easy enough, punching a two and-a-half inch hole in the cement, but it took a good deal of time to peck out the inside cinder layer. The one that made up the actual wall of the cell. But with persistent scraping and chiseling—when he could get away with it, Vincents eventually gouged his way through to the back of the mirror. From there it was just a matter of etching away the lead paint and the thin aluminum plate of its backing, to allow a direct view in. A two-way mirror. Worth all the work.

Vincents didn't approach the half-dollar sized peep hole immediately because he needed to get his respiration rate under control. Instead, he placed his hands against the cool, perspiring wall behind him, leaning his back against it, he stood waiting while his gasping eased. But he could hear the clopping sounds that her shoes made as they hit the cement floor. And even though his breathing was still coming in paced gulps and bellows, he felt compelled to make the approach before he missed everything. He extinguished the lighter and slid down the wall a few inches.

Mopping his face with his handkerchief and then eyeballing the women through his surveillance aperture in the cell caused the sergeant to quickly unzip the fly of his pants with a short grunt, and expose his already fully erect phallus. He was a large man but his manhood was not hidden beneath folds of flesh. He was of above-average length and girth where men are often times, though arguably—measured. The sight of Cleo in there gave Vincents cause to suck in his breath loudly, making a low whistle in the clandestine corridor. "This certainly ain't no field nigra," he barely whispered as he slowly began squeezing his fascinum and swaying his hips forward, and then back. Stroking himself.

Shadows caused by the harsh, unshaded light, were illuminating the fine depths of fleshy body Vincents ogled. Her back was to the sergeant but there was just enough light to make out everything he needed to. She stretched her arms out to either side of her body, the top of them appearing to be a light ochre coloring and the back a darker sienna cast. The mustard colored moons of her butt, as well as the sides of her breasts still seemed firm and shapely from what Vincents could tell from the highlighting the overhead bulbs revealed. Captain Treadwell was in the foreground, nothing more than a head peeking over Cleo's left shoulder. He looked her in the eye and began jerking harder and then slowed down.

"Okay," Treadwell began her instructions after placing the last of the clothes on the table. "First open your mouth slowly and show me all your teeth. And pull out the sides of your mouth with your index fingers, too. I need to see the back of your teeth."

Cleo did as she was told, but not before having to press her lips together and looking up at the ceiling, trying to get the tears in her eyes to roll back behind her eyeballs.

"Now—roll back your upper lip with your fingers, so I can see all of your gums, now. The lower, too. All right, now tilt your head back and I want you to touch your tongue to the roof of your mouth, and hold it."

The order perturbed Cleo but she complied, just wanting to get this done with as quickly as she could. She'd gone too far to have any more feelings of decency left—or so she thought.

"All right," Treadwell continued, "you can lower your head. Now, I want you to fold your ears over and let me look behind them."

"Both sides?" Cleo asked.

"Did I say ear, or did I say ears?"

Cleo pinned her ears down and turned her head side-to-side. She then crossed her arms across her chest and glared back defiantly at Treadwell. She wanted to scratch her eyes out.

"Lift your breasts."

"What?"

"Lift your breasts, I said!"

Cleo timidly hefted her chest upwards, but Treadwell shook her head. "No, that's not what I meant. All the way up." Cleo didn't care if the WAC recognized how angry she was making her. She brought her dark brown nipples upward, pointing them at the ceiling.

"Is that more like it?" Cleo asked flatly.

Treadwell finished lighting a cigarette and waved a hand at Cleo, "Okay, you can put 'em down, now."

"Are we through?"

"One more thing," Treadwell paused as she picked a loose scrap of tobacco from off her tongue. "I need you to turn around, your back towards me, and spread open your buttocks."

In the tunnel, Vincents did all he could to prolong his debauchery. As Cleo was turning to face his way he scanned her over quickly from head-to-toe, quickening the nihilistic manhandling of his sex tool...She bent over from the waist, swaying pendulous breasts that looked like erotic plum lines to Vincents. And then she cast a glance to the captain, over her right shoulder, and kept staring all the while she reached back and brought her hands to pull on the sides of her flanks, exposing herself fully. Vincents could not hold himself in check any longer. He pumped his veined stub of lust with increased fervor.

Treadwell told the woman to do something and evidently had to repeat it. Vincents looked at the captain's face and then the visitor, feeling some wetness on his right knuckle. The look on the colored woman's face. The reluctant cooperation mixed with disgust began sending the sergeant to the point of no return. But he stopped pleasuring himself, to only make intermittent pawing at his groin in an attempt to delay the inevitable.

"Don't turn around yet," Treadwell still commanded. "I want you to squat down and cough for me, three times. And you have to do this nice and slow. Squat and cough, then stand up. Squat—cough, squat——cough. Got me?"

Each request this crazy bitch made seemed more insane than the last, Cleo thought. This was the epitome of outrage, but she could not risk not complying. That she knew, too. Cleo dropped down, resting her weight on the pads of her feet and placing her hands on her knees and coughed. She couldn't help but smile a little as she broke wind slightly on the second squat. Cleo hoped the officer got a good whiff of it.

Between the second and third cough Captain Treadwell thought she'd heard a moan come from the detainee, but she couldn't be sure. The acoustics of concrete rooms are notoriously indelicate, and whether she had, or not, as far as Treadwell was concerned the matter required no further investigation. The gal didn't keel over in a faint, and she had nothing secreted on her, or in her. End of story.

"Thank you, ma'am," Treadwell said, "You're free to go, now." But before leaving she ground out her cigarette next to Cleo's clothes. "You can get your letter from the sergeant on your way out."

Cleo slowly reached for her panties, lying on top of her crumpled yellow and white polka dot dress. Now it seemed not even to matter if she put her clothes back on. Her lower lip was quivering with each intake of her breath, through short sobs of indignity. Yes, she thought, she may as well walk out into that foyer without a stitch on her—everyone knew she had been stripped down. Down to the very core of her humanity. And no amount of clothing could erase that from the eyes and minds of those people from the War Department.

She gathered her things and while dressing, remembered how her mother used to tell her about her great grandmother. She had been a full-blooded Indian. Sometimes she'd have to watch Cleo, when she was little. When "the Indian" watched her, she was unmoving. Dressed in a small patterned dress, with her shawl, always sitting in Momma's lawn chair.

When Cleo would get too far away for the old woman's liking, she would take this big, black bullwhip she carried and deftly—lovingly, wrap its end three times, exactly, around little Cleo's ankle and pull her back within reach. "Outward scars can never blemish the spirit," she would assure Cleo's mother. "But I never harmed you. I would never hurt your babies," she said.

Cleo wiggled into her dress and smoothed its front. Her mother had said that her grandmother was the daughter of a Blackfoot witch doctor, who had been stolen by some fur traders. They'd sold her to a circus, from where she escaped, and that's supposedly where she learned to use the whip so well. She always reproached Cleo's mother with not being more watchful of her baby. But momma had understood why, Cleo thought. And she also thought, before leaving the cell, how she wished she could have had such kind of protection before she came all the way down to Georgia. Somebody who would have pulled her back from the danger she presented to herself, apparently. Someone who wouldn't have let her get on that train in the first place. She swore she would never let anyone know about this happening to her, as she snatched the letter extended to her by the smirking sergeant at the desk.

CHAPTER TWENTY-EIGHT
A Father's Remorse

The aluminum storm door had barely closed from little Bradley Martin running inside when Sackett, just now approaching the concrete path, heard Jim Martin's raised voice and the loud smack of hand striking the youngster's backside. Frank quickened his pace and didn't bother knocking before going inside.

Lorraine rose from out of her chair where she'd been reading her new *Ebony* issue, shocked at the intensity and suddenness of her husband's assault on their son. Brad was howling, running in place and flailing his little arms in his own quandary as to what he'd done. "Jimmy—what you doing that to him for?"

He still had Brad by the arm and his own arm raised, ready to deliver more of the spanking, but Lorraine's entreaty made him let go. "You stay right there," he ordered Brad not to move. The quivering boy stood fast. "I've told him before about coming home late—after the sun's down. This the third time and I'm through talking."

"This is my fault, Mr. Martin," Sackett said loudly. And James and Lorraine whipped their heads to their house's threshold. "Please, don't hit the boy, anymore—I was the one to make him late. I'm so sorry, Bradley."

"Go to your room," Jim told Brad. And Lorraine walked over and put her arm around her son's shoulders, leading him away and bending over to kiss the top of his head.

"I know it's not my place to tell a man how to handle his family," Sackett apologized. "Far from it—but your littlest one is so beaten down in his mind, it seems. If you put hand to him right now it will only push him over an edge, Jim. He's really that fragile. If you need somebody to take your anger out on—someone who can't fight back—you can swing on me."

Jim took a half minute staring at Sackett and then back to Brad's bedroom. "Have a seat, Frank. And—excuse me a minute." And without another word the old man was left alone in the living room.

When Jim entered Brad's room he saw Lorraine holding the nine year-old on her lap and rocking him, sitting on the edge of his bed, like he was a child half his age. Brad's head was buried into her shoulder and his little chest heaved between taking breaths and the conclusion of his silent weeping.

"He eat yet?" Jim asked softly.

"Mr. Sackett took him out to a *White Castle*, once they missed their bus."

Jim shook his head in acknowledgement. "Brad?"

"I don't want to talk," the boy said, barely more than a whisper. "I don't like you, anymore."

Jim came to the side of the bed and knelt down and cautiously alighted his hand, the same one that he had struck the boy with earlier, and patted him tenderly between the shoulder blades.

"Brad, I'm sorry. I'm sorry because I didn't give you a chance to explain. I forgot about Mr. Sackett coming, and I didn't even think of the possibility that you two might be together."

Lorraine caressed the top of her husband's hand and then wrapped her arms more tightly around her son. Who it seemed, still needed comforting. The sighs were still convulsing out of him, though now without the tears in accompaniment. It was times like these when Brad started thinking, "Daddy hates me."

"You know, Brad—sometimes, we parents don't always know what is the right thing to do," said Jim, "But I do know when it's right to say, I'm sorry. And I hope you'll forgive me."

"No, I won't."

Jim kept his hand on his back and Lorraine grinned at him and closed her eyes momentarily and then tugged at Brad with a few quick squeezes. "Hey, young man," she said. "Your daddy is trying to be kind, and make nice. Don't you think you can be nice, too?"

"No."

Jim sat down next to them on the bed, Brad turning his head away from his father, but still resting it on his mother's shoulder. "Did he tell you about where they went besides the burger stand?"

"Yeah, he said he met Mr. Sackett after he'd gotten done at the Boys Club and they were over at Mt. Olivet—"

"Mt. Olivet?"

"That's what he said."

"What the hell he want to take the boy there for?"

"Said that he showed him our family plots—your mom's, ours, and your Grandma Cleo's."

Brad sat up then. "Your Uncle Joe's and your daddy's, too."

"Did he say why?"

"I think he knew your grandma."

That gave Jim more things to pause over and consider, but they weren't as important as Brad talking to him again. "Brad, I been pretty hard to get along with—I know. When people come after you for money you don't have, well, it wears down what few good words you can have left in you, sometimes."

Brad didn't say anything. Just looked into his father's eyes, which were more like larger versions of his own.

"And I can't say there won't be other times when I'll get too quick to give you my hand, or a strap, but I will tell you this. The next time that you do something that deserves a whuppin', you got a pass coming. Okay?"

Brad didn't respond.

"You don't believe me? Look, your momma's a witness."

Brad simply folded himself back into his mother's shoulder, and soaked in all the comfort she exuded. Jim stood over them for a moment, feeling his heart softening, and perfunctorily kissed them both on top of their heads and quietly left the room. To himself, Brad thought he'd rather have his dad feel guiltier about the hole in the ceiling, than his hurt feelings. Lorraine knew there were things to do in the kitchen, but this little light of hers, which she held in her arms, needed to have some shielding from the imposition his father could be. Jimmy wasn't a bad father, just stern.

Mr. Sackett had waited patiently in the living room, without taking a seat or even removing his coat. He didn't know if he'd be thrown out, or not. So, he didn't want there to be any misunderstandings. He hoped he hadn't overstepped his boundaries with the Martin boy, and he would understand if he was asked to go. But, he fervently hoped he would still be allowed to continue on his discovery.

When Jim came out of the bedroom he couldn't remember if he'd asked Sackett to take a seat, or not, he'd been so upset with his son. But now much of that disappointment was turned back on him. Walking across the room to a hutch, Jim brought out two snifters and a bottle of single-malt whiskey.

"Can you handle three fingers, Frank?"

"Two would be fine, thank you."

When Jim turned around with the glasses he nodded Sackett an assent to take a seat. "Can I take your coat?" Jim asked, handing Frank the drink.

"No—no, thank you. I'm amight chill at the moment, yet. But this should help, shouldn't it?"

Jim sat in his easy chair and slowly stretched his long legs forward, crossing them at the ankles and then taking a good swallow of the fine distillation. He swished it around in his mouth like it was mouthwash, for a moment and then swallowed hard. "I—I, ah, want to thank you for getting the boy his dinner today, Frank. I appreciate that."

"My pleasure, Jim. I'm really sorry about the late hour. By the time we got done walking through the cemetery—"

"Yeah, excuse me for interrupting—but what was that all about?"

"Your boy is pretty astute, Jim. He let me know that he was somewhat aware of my interests in your family, and because of that he suggested that he show me where members of the immediate family were laid to rest."

"But why the—"

"Cemetery? In his mind, I guess, he took all our talk to be about ancestors that were ancient. And to his credit he associated that with his understanding of place. Place in time, and where he fit in that span."

"I guess I should be proud."

"And it was that sense of personal history that had him take me to Mt. Olivet. It was quite the serendipity experience for me."

"Seren—what?"

"Serendipity—a profound coincidence. Usually unexpected. Your momma's last name was Troubles, wasn't it?"

"Yeah. But some troubles you can't hide, Frank."

"You have a point there, son. You have a point."

CHAPTER TWENTY-NINE
Trouble, Don't Come No More

Concussions of air, Thor-like charges, blasts so awful that they threatened to loosen the very sphincters from fright, caused pressure on Sackett's ears. Shrugging his shoulders and ducking his head was the instant, futile reaction, as far as protection goes, it wasn't on par with the blasts from the cannons he heard. Outside the artillery division headquarters 70 mm howitzers festooned over and over. Save for one incident, maybe two, the captain had never felt anything to set him in such a panic. The very hardwood floors of his office vibrated and thumped underneath his well-polished shoes. At first, he grabbed hold of the corner of his desk on the way to take cover. He'd raise himself halfway when another volley was loosed.

There had been seven bombastic detonations in a matter of minutes and then Sackett heard whoops of excitement, and men shouting. Indistinctly, the cheers rose over escalating small arms fire. When Captain Sackett finally, cautiously stood erect he peeked through his window blinds and saw Sergeant Davies running up the walk, arms flailing. And by the time he'd gotten into the hall, Sackett was sure the man had lost at least half of his senses. "We done it!" Davies railed.

Now he was in the doorway, and bracing his arms against the portal's jambs like an earthquake was preparing to dash him to the ground. "Cap'n, we just done did it!"

"What the hell are you talking about, man? Done what?"

Davies joined his superior over by the parted window blinds. "We're over there, Sir! We're over there, and we done did it, awright."

"We have been in the theaters several years, Sergeant."

"Not this way, Sir. Naw—I'm talkin' invasion! The European Invasion's underway."

Sackett looked over at Sergeant Davies with a puzzled glance when someone loudly cleared his throat behind them. It was Colonel Krech.

The non-com and junior officer quickly righted themselves and saluted. Krech casually returned the salute and walked over to the men by the window, their skin highlighted by blue and orange flashes of light from the celebration. "Sergeant," Krech said quietly, "would you be so kind as to give me and the captain some privacy?"

Davies swung his arm down to his side instantly at the command being spoken, "YES, SIR!"

"And close the door on your way out, please."

"Yes, Suh," Davies clipped.

For a matter of ten seconds after the door was shut, maybe more, all the sound from outside was silenced, as the two men looked at one another. Both looked a little more than uncomfortable at how to start the conversation, but Sackett took it upon himself to breach the subject. "I gather you didn't come to personally advise me of what everyone's so hopped up about?"

"I'm afraid not, Captain. Even though D-Day has begun, the mood is troubling for me, at least. It's something that has made quite a damper on what should be a celebratory evening, I'm afraid."

"Sounds serious."

"I assure you, it is."

"Shall we retire to my office, then?" Sackett opened his door. "In case some troops decide they need to get in here."

"That might not be a bad idea, but first I must let you know something."

"And what would that be, Sir?"

"I've got a couple of M.P.'s outside in a jeep. Do you have any idea why I would do such a thing?"

"Colonel, I would not presume to answer what you already know so well. But again, could we adjourn to my office?"

Krech looked hard at Sackett. "After you, Captain."

The colonel could not detect any chink in Sackett's armor as he ushered him into the reading chair, which already had its lamp on. The captain then swept himself behind his desk and fanned his hands across his blotter before leaning back into his comfortable chair. When he looked up he saw that the once-friendly colonel had opened his jacket and was finishing the straightening of his pants crease.

"I guess to answer your question, Colonel, I would hope that you had brought those men because of my extreme sense of duty in trying to get those logistic spreadsheets completed. Seems about the only way to pull me away from out of here."

"I wish I could banter with you in kind, Franklin—but I can't. The Inspector General's Office has been in touch with the Service Command, recently." There was still no waiver in the captain's demeanor. He was playing a good poker hand, the colonel thought.

"This has something to do with one of my men?"

"I'm afraid not."

"Something about the riot?"

"No, Captain." Krech paused for affect. "An investigation has revealed that Franklin Sackett died as an infant. Some twenty-seven years ago in Dearborn, Michigan."

"A case of mistaken identity. I'm sure there's more than one Franklin Sackett around."

"Not according to the 1920 census, Captain. Your aunt did not place you in her household that year, nor did she list you ten years later. The 1930 census gave us some neighbors who we got information from, though. In 1919 your aunt had a baby who died of dysentery just before his first birthday, we were told. It was a male—"

Colonel Krech picked up the leather bound book sitting on the night table next to his chair and rubbed his palm slowly over the cover a few times before setting it back down. Sackett sat motionless, frozen in anticipation of the next word. "Who are you, Captain?" And what would drive a man to assume such falsehood?"

"Colonel—you probably can't imagine what it would be like to feel the need to be reborn again. Where you plainly see that there's no sense moving forward, that you have to completely erase whatever came before the one moment that changed your life, forever. A moment of bad decision, or happenstance. Who can say? Regardless, it was a time that I could never take back who I was. God knows I wanted to."

"A Superior Court in the State of Alabama is seeking your extradition from the Army, Sackett."

"I guess they want a fourth trial."

"Beg pardon?"

Sackett rose from his chair and turned his back to Krech, first blowing a heavy sigh into his closed fist and then peeping out between the thin metal shutters of his window. He saw the service men outside policing up the grass areas from the celebration they'd had. He also saw the two M.P.'s that the colonel told him about, smoking cigarettes and laughing occasionally. "I'm waiting, Captain."

When he turned back around, Sackett was not pleased when he saw Krech holding his pipe that he'd left in the ash tray. The colonel smelled the bowl and placed it back exactly as he'd found it, unaware of his faux pas.

"I wasn't from Alabama, directly," Sackett began. "I was born in Kansas, but I don't recall actually where because when I was about seven or eight my mother took me to an aunt's home, in Alabama. Her name was Clavelle, and I only knew I was from Kansas because that what's she had told me. The last time I saw my mother I remember she had this hat on—with a feather in it. You know, one of those long feathers, like from a pheasant. I was told she'd come back for me. Told to keep my stuff packed and ready to go in one of the two suitcases I had. But after a month, Aunt Clavelle came and told me to un-pack the other one. And—I don't think I was really all that shook up about it, really. Because I had siblings with her family, my cousins. When you're an only child, it's nice to have someone to talk to that isn't a parent—and looks like you. Talks like you. Me and my cousins got along fine, and Aunt Clavelle didn't show me any ill will—until the Depression kicked in.

I was eighteen, then. And she expected me and my cousin, Haywood, to be out making a way for ourselves and not just be two grown-ass men under foot in her house while she still had little ones to care for. So, we took out to find some work.

We'd hop trains and move from town to town, pooling our money to-gether. Scrapping together enough to get us a case of beans, or some rice, something to last us a week. And my cousin comes up to me one day and says that there were some jobs working coal, up in Tennessee. He said a group of boys he talked to were going to catch the *Southern Railway* and ride up to Memphis. So, I threw in with them, but some was pretty young. One, no more than twelve. We caught the train in Scottsboro that evening. There were ten of us."

"Good Lord, man—Do you mean to say? You were one of..."

"The Scottsboro Boys, yes."

"I find that rather hard to—"

"Believe? Can't say as I can blame you, seeing as you caught me in my lie. But let me speak now, about the truth— so I can finally get a full breath and let it out for the first time in over a decade." And Sackett did just that, and it was a forceful, heaving, relief of a sigh. Followed by still a few seconds of cel-ebration—distant firecrackers, or small gunfire off in the distance. "My real name," Sackett continued, "is Marcus Patterson. My cousin, Haywood Pat-terson, who I'm sure you may have heard about, brought along a gun with him that I didn't even know he had. The ten of us had gotten into a cattle car, and it was pretty bad smelling, so after awhile we decide to go up top and move into one of the forward gondola cars as we was getting up by Lookout Moun-tain. There were a few white guys and a couple of white girls with 'em, and I think they were drinking some moonshine. We were moving close to the front of our car, by the ladder, when Haywood falls and his gun fires. I recovered it before it went over the sides, but the men start causing a fuss—cussing at us, and Haywood cussed right back. When they heard that, they said they were going to throw our uppity black asses off the train—that is, they were going to until they saw how many of us there were climbing down that ladder. Me, I didn't want any trouble, so I decided to stay where I was, on top of the cattle car. Saw everything. There were a few punches thrown but the whites were overpowered and ended up jumping, leaving the girls behind. I mean—one of 'em, the younger one, tried to jump, but she was grabbed before she could make it a go for it. If they hadn't snatched her—she'd have gotten thrown under that rail car, for sure."

"Captain, if you saw everything, why didn't you go back to testify for the others. You had ample opportunity—"

"Are you crazy? For every one of the Scottsboro Boys who were released, two faced hanging. Me going down to Alabama wouldn't hold any weight with the court system, believe me. I ran as soon as I heard that posse approaching because I knew my cousin and the rest of them might not even be given the benefit of a trial. I wasn't about to be put into a bowl of strange fruit picked from a hanging tree. No, Sir."

"But they did have trials, Frank—I mean, Marcus. It's a little befuddling to know how to address you, Captain."

"I've told the lie for so long that someone calling me my real name probably wouldn't get any response, Colonel. Frank Sackett is fine."

"Not to be morose, Captain, but your words are more than specific because Frank Sackett, the real Frank Sackett, *is fine*, in a manner of speaking. That is when you consider he has no more earthly worries to contend with. Marcus Patterson, however, cannot make such a claim."

"That's true, Colonel. I've taken whatever sin burdens he might have had coming to him and added them to mine, so it seems. In a macabre way, I guess I still am resurrected through blood. As blasphemous as that may sound, it's still true. Oh, and forgive the dogma, Colonel, I know you aren't Christian. But it helps me to think about it that way."

"Getting back to my assertion—Frank. You can't say for sure that you mightn't have been able to help. They had three trials. Didn't you feel any tug on your conscience when one after the other led to such miscarriages of justice?"

"Again, Colonel—what good would it have done me? All of them had a strong legal defense team from the Communist Party, and *they* couldn't get them off. Even after the girls recanted their stories, they still couldn't get acquittals. Once you plant that seed of race mongering, you see, it has to run its course in the South. The juries all had their minds made up just from looking in the papers and seeing pictures. That's all they needed to know. Antebellum culture is the truth."

"Captain?"

"Sir?"

"Speaking of the truth—"

"You want to know about what happened with them, don't you? Don't be ashamed to admit it."

"Well, it is a rather indelicate topic. But you were—"

"An eyewitness?"

"Yes. An eyewitness who can debunk facts for me, if not for anyone else."

Sackett smirked slightly, wondering how much the inquiry was one of curiosity, and how much of it was a by-product of licentiousness. He crossed his legs and leaned back in his chair while he thoughtfully cleaned his glasses with his white handkerchief.

"Yeah, I 'spec most people would want to hear those details," Sackett smiled. "The two girls settled back in the gondola and started conversation. And they were bragging about how they had turned some favors, down in a hobo camp the night before. They sounded like they'd been drinking, though. And it seemed to me both of them had it in their minds they were going to make some more money on that train. One of 'em got up next to one of the boys and starts kissing on him and everything. Before long he yells out that she's trying to take money out of his pants pocket. She said she'd do him if he gave her fifty cents. The boy told her, 'You a crazy woman. I can get a whore for a nickel.' And she says, 'Not a white one, though.' So she and the other one are performing oral sex on the guys. Well, except for the one fella who was almost lame from syphillis. So, I do not believe what I'm seeing happen, you know, when all of a sudden I see these trucks hightailing it our way, on a frontage road. So, I set out from there. Because I knew nothing good was going to come from me being on that train once those men caught up with it."

"You ditched the gun?"

"Yes, Sir. And it was never found."

"And you proceeded north?"

"Sweating like a pig on a spit, all the way, too. When I called my auntie, she said she heard about it on the radio about a day later."

"And she told you not to turn yourself in, either?"

"Colonel—you really don't get it, do you?"

"I understand that you chose self-preservation over accountability in the matter, Captain. But if anything that only illustrates the flaw in your character."

Sackett's jaw tightened in anger and he pursed his lips momentarily, speaking after gaining his comportment, "Up until this point, Sir, I'd always thought that I'd become something more than a nigger being hunted down from the bottoms of Alabama. The only thing I've ever lied about, in my entire life is what my true identity was. And I swore it would be the last one, from the day I took on this name. You may say I have rationalized things a bit, but I see it kinda like the story of *Les Miserable*. Stealing bread to feed your family shouldn't be a crime, and neither should be telling a lie to save your life. Not when you haven't done anything to deserve what's coming. No, Sir. I will not apologize for that, no. Under the circumstances of my life, I believed I could prove to be maybe a little better than what anyone else would have expected of me." Sackett's voice was beginning to tighten, cracking with emotion. "Everything I had ever pinned my hopes on, for a better life—one better than what was handed to me are now about to be taken away." His eyes now began to shimmer with the wetness of impending tears. "I'm proud—Sir. I'm proud of my service," and Sackett nodded his head, grinding his teeth slightly to hold back a sob. "Proud."

Three quick raps on the door.

Colonel Krech pitched forward in the chair and rose to his feet, pulling at this jacket's hem and opened the door to the office. Sergeant Davies stood on the other side, and immediately snapped to. "Begging the colonel's pardon," Davies said, "But the men waiting for you have asked me to inquire as to when you may be leaving?"

Krech looked over at Sackett, who sat staring directly at the vacated chair that Sergeant Davies had presented him. His eyes didn't blink. As if awaiting word on a trial's sentence.

"Sergeant," the colonel said finally, "have those military escorts outside to stand down, please. Tell them—tell them that there's been a mistake."

CHAPTER THIRTY
Castaways

Cleo Martin got her first letter from Gus three months after her traumatizing visit to Georgia. Seeing the envelope brought a mask of guilt and concern over his mother and it deeply manifested itself in her face. Turning it over to its backside quickly, so she wouldn't have to look at the post mark; she had to close her eyes to compose herself, the rocking and rolling of the bus swaying her like the rapture of a spiritual exchange between the Holy Ghost and her soul. So, too was the connection she now felt being tapped into between she and her son. Simply because he had touched the envelope.

It is arguably a universal constant, something that tendrils itself into the very nature of all living things that bear their young. It is a germ of vitality that expands with time and follows a vibrant course. Something that lends itself to a profound nexus, a link between biological mothers and their children. And that is the germ, the mental umbilical cord that all of nature maintains; a cord that constantly seeks to reattach progeny to provider, and vice versa.

The letter was shocking because it brought back memories that had not yet been composted in Cleo's subconscious. True, she believed anybody who'd undergone what she had would have flinched at anything revivifying that kind of an experience, but it also bothered her because she sometimes believed she had been run off too easily. She felt maybe she hadn't shown the determination that a "real" mother would have had, even in those dire circumstances. Though Cleo knew she couldn't imagine bringing herself to think about making another such trip, the letter in her hand blunted some of the humiliation she retained from the last one, and it urged some temptation. Those were all the intangibles she was dealing with, at that moment. The sealed paper in her hands, however, was real, she thought to herself. And having it in her hands, her dry trembling hands upon her lap, truly brought back what she thought had been successfully put out of her mind, and once again placed it into its own conflict of unwilling considerations, between nurture and duty. She turned it over, saw with some alarm a postmark from New York, and opened it.

Meanwhile, on board a transport ship crossing the Atlantic, Gus tried to get comfortable in the bilge hold of the vessel so he could begin writing another letter to Cleo. The light there was dim and the space confining—no air circulation, to speak of—but Gus would not be deterred. He sat upon a few twenty-five pound bags of coffee that he had propped up near a kerosene lantern that hung precariously by a seated bolt, one that jutted out from an angle iron beam. With his cushioned back against another channel strut, he tried writing when the lamplight was most steady.

A colored soldier passed by, steadying himself against the bulwark as the ship pitched to the side dramatically and then yawed upwards. Both of them braced themselves for the stomach-flipping moment that occurs just as the bulkhead begins it plummet back down. "I wouldn't be writing under that lamp," the man cautioned. "The whole thing could spill on top of your head any minute. The sea is acting a fool."

"I'll be careful—thanks," Gus replied, assured that the aged appearance of the lamp, and the mutually rusted metal of the channel and its ringed handle, left little reason for him to believe he was in imminent danger.

Back in Detroit, Cleo fanned her fingers over the pages that she unfolded in her lamp, straining a little to read the cramped handwriting as she traced over the paragraphs. *Dear Momma*, it began. *So much has happened since the last time I wrote you, when we were in Georgia. I don't know where this letter will be sent from, as Joe and I are presently out to sea! Heading to Europe. Ships heading back to the States take our mail and drop it off from whatever port they're about to make. So, I know I've caught you by surprise with that bit of news, I'm sure.*

It's still all about keeping secrets, too. Just like it was about our little stint in Georgia. I can't tell you the name of the ship we're on or where we're at, exactly. Even if I knew to tell you, I couldn't. All I do know is all there is to see is water.

Have you ever seen an ocean, Momma? It really makes you stand and take notice, just how small you really are in this big old world. If you had seen one, something with all of this big blueness that I've been seeing for about a week or more, I'm sure you would have told me about it. Anyway, by the time this reaches you, I'm sure you'll have already heard about the D-Day Invasion...

In the tomb of the ship's stomach, illuminated by the halo of clean, yellow light around his shoulders, Gus stretched his legs out and yawned loudly. No one was around to have even noticed him, because save for the warning soldier who passed through, no one else was near him. Gus liked the feeling of solitude he was feeling down there, while he wrote. He liked the smells of the steel, the bagged cargo, the coffee and crates. Back in Detroit, though, Cleo felt more than a little uneasiness as she read on from her son's former letter. True feelings seemed to be coming out, betraying him.

People are quieter now, the letter said, *especially now that the fighting has gotten harder in the months since the first landing. Used to be, on board ship, it wouldn't take too much to get the chests puffing up and the old fighting juices ignited. But now—now it seems like everyone one of us just walks around kind of numb. With big ol' puffy eyes and bad gums because we have trouble keeping down most of the food. We don't seem to look right or left anymore, because really what's the use. Our faces don't see nothing—our eyes don't light up anymore, unless it could be something mistaken for land...Even Joe's a little homesick.*

Cleo looked again at the postmark and by the date stamped on it she figured that her boys had been out to sea for two weeks, maybe more. Didn't the Army have a duty to tell people where their family was being shipped off to? Didn't she have some rights to know, as their mother? She returned her gaze back to the pages, knowing that answer from her experience with the military, all-too-well. They were a heartless bunch. And the letter concluded with some attempt to putting on a brave face during adversity. Gus signed off, writing: *If there is one thing that you should take from all these words I've written, it should be that even though now an entire ocean stands between us, the tie that binds me to you is not diluted. That link stays strong and will remain so, forever. Don't worry about me and Joe, Momma. Both of your nappy headed weasels know the way home is always opened wide for us. We'll see you, soon. I promise.*

Cleo reverently folded the letter and put it back into the envelope. Before she put it into the handbag she carried she took out a crumpled tissue to dab at her eyes and lightly blow her nose. "Damn head cold," she said softly. As if she'd been caught in her weeping and needed to make an excuse. The bus driver called out her stop, and she went home feeling like she'd worked a double-shift.

Gus continued writing in his third letter to his mother, not realizing that she had only gotten his first. He wanted his letters to sound like he was sitting right across from her, and talking. But if he were, she'd not have been pleased by the demeanor. The usually hard to provoke Gus Martin was in a rare spoiler mood on this night. He was not happy. The "i's" were dotted with hard taps on the pad upon his knees, the "t's" crossed off almost dismissively. *The promises keep getting broken, Momma, or so it seems. They easily are set aside,* Gus wrote sitting at his oceanic perch, and his stomach growling like a hollow metal dog in the bowels of the ship that was hankering for a bone. *Before we left for Europe,* he continued writing, *the general, the one in Georgia—he told us we had trained in the largest colored training unit ever fielded, historically. He talked to all of us, black and white, about how we had performed with distinction and set aside differences that didn't matter. A real cheerleader for patriotism, that one...*and here Gus paused, stopping his writing with a moment of introspection. Looking over the last thing he'd written, he couldn't help but think how much it sounded like Joe, instead of him. A faint grin and a scratch behind an ear, and he was back into his letter. *If I sound frustrated,* he wrote, *it's because it seems we will never get there—wherever over there is. And once we do, what will happen? Like I told you in my last letter, which I shouldn't have, we have matched the white soldiers in everything that's required—everything. But when push comes to shove, we'll be the ones having to do both. Probably be over there unloading ships, or stuff of that nature. Most of the others on board that I've met have told me I shouldn't get my hopes up for seeing any kind of action. Two weeks now, and I'm starting to see how crazy I must have seemed to them. I should feel like some of them: just sit back and go on a government paid tour of England. Ain't no chance of getting hurt, really, because we'll be way behind the front line, Joe tells me. I guess, some of the older ones at least, are just tired. Been fighting too many battles for too long, and nothing to show for it but big ol' knots upside of their heads. They are tired of fighting in wars where you don't get medals. There, inside of them, sometimes you can see it in their eyes out here. Just keeping on this side of being sane.*

Gus nodded to himself as these last thoughts came out the tip of his pen to his tablet. He looked up and thought he saw Joe approaching at the other end of the cargo bay, near a bulwark whose shadow cut through a dim, half-light, but not creating such a mask that Gus couldn't pick up the glint of the two mess kits his sibling brought. Or seem so far away that he didn't hear the clatter made as Joe maneuvered around crates and tried to keep balance.

We eat here late, Gus continued, picking up the pace of his recording because he would have to end soon. *Usually,* he wrote, *it's after all the whites have had their fill. They don't get more than us, or different than us. They just get it all first.* Gus looked up again, and could see Joe's eyebrows knitted together in an apprehensive bead, casting shadows over his eyes, but eventually he came past a huge stack of burlap casings and then the irises were illuminated by the lanterns of his white orbits. Gus could see him stop, bumming a cigarette from a soldier.

I see Joe coming over to get me for chow now, Mom. He's been kind of worked up since he saw some rats on board the other day that probably weighed eight pounds.

Don't worry though. They haven't chewed on anybody at night, or anything. Joe's different out here at sea than he is on land. He looks like he did when he was little and Daddy would get on him about his stuttering. He used to always be looking around like some big hand was getting ready to swoop down on his head every time he opened his mouth. He's like that on the ship, now. Gus looked towards his brother and saw him putting out the cigarette. A bemused, but loving grin lilted a moment on Gus's face. And then he continued, *I miss you so very much, Mother. That goes without saying. And don't bear Joe a grudge for not writing you any. Guess it's just the way he's going to be and we both just have to accept that. And that's so ironic, because when I need to see you, when it's such an overwhelming need for me to just be able to hold you in my arms again, have you stroke the back of my head like you do. When I feel that I'm likely to go crazy if I don't have that connection, I just have to look at Joe. And when I do, Momma, I swear sometimes I see you, fresh to my eyes.* Gus signed off quickly and hurriedly putting his writing materials into the locker by his bunk, so Joe wouldn't be asking him questions about who he was writing to.

Joe didn't slow any as he passed by either, just turned his head to the side at Gus and said, "Le's go. See if they got us some deck bird to eat." Gus stared and then rose.

They moved together purposefully on their way to the stairs that led to the upper level. Joe didn't bother asking why Gus's eyes brimmed with emotion when he first saw him just then. Because if he had he'd also have to let him know he was concerned about him. And if he cared about Gus, he would then be asked why he could not give their mother that same kind of consideration. And he didn't want to go there, so, Joe just let the observation stand as a mental note.

When they got to the crammed colored dining area of the mess hall, near the scullery, the line for eating was on the opposite side of the normal steam line. They stood in the now empty white soldiers mess area. Smelled the recently applied disinfectant. The colored troops could pass by, but they had better not attempt to sit down at any one of those tables.

Gus hadn't been exactly truthful in his letter when he talked about the way they were fed, and what it was, either. It was edible—barely, but it wasn't always what had been given the white troops on board. Being that it was the last meal of the day, it seemed fitting that it was the culmination of the day's entire faire. Many of the men in line who were off-duty kitchen servers noticed what remnants came from breakfast and lunch. Complaining would have no purpose.

The main course for the men was a succotash conglomeration ladled over a large ball of rice. Ingredients inside the mélange included: corn, beans, carrots, peas, pork, beef, chicken, and even raisins. All suspended in a viscous brownish-gray sauce that couldn't be qualified as gravy. In other words, it was the proverbial kitchen sink. To balance the meal nutritionally there was a little bit of salad that had been served at lunch, and two slices of bread that partially covered a hardball-sized orange. Urns of water, milk, or coffee against the bulwark completed the culinary display. Essentially, the men knew they were being fed the garbage of the day—albeit garbage that hadn't been delegated to a dumpster yet, or pulled from one. But for many of the imbibers it may as well have been.

The galley area of the ship's prep area had a dozen park benches set up for the men to eat, with white non-commissioned policing in between the rows. And while there were metal trays being ran through a huge washer, at that very moment, none of the clean trays pulled from the other end were for the use of the Negro troops. They had to bring field mess kits with them to the dining room, and were responsible for cleaning them before leaving. An aluminum basin for that purpose was right to the side of the washer. The noise of the kitchen, shutting down for the day, created the ambience for the quick repast given for the meal. There was not time for much conversation. All talking pretty much had to be done in line, and that was moving very slowly for some reason.

"How come it takes 'em so damn long to serve this crap?" a disgruntled soldier, with blanket lint in his hair, complained to no one in particular. "What they run outta now?"

He was six people ahead of Gus and Joe in the steam line and Joe pulled on Gus's sleeve. "Oh, that's just what we need, now. Somebody to start acting all riled up and ignorant before we get to eat."

"They bringing up some more, Joe. Hope he sees 'em."

"That's what I said—no good," the complainant went on, "and no good means no good. Make me wanna holler what they puttin' us through fighting for this no good country."

Two mess soldiers carried over a steaming, partially filled gray kettle, and restocked the emptied pans on the steam line with more succotash. "Well, it's about damn time," the complainer jeered. "Y'all are bringing it out like ya the maitre de at the Chateau Mimosa, or something. Sorry ass. Strictly sorry ass."

But no sooner had the line started moving forward again, and things appeared to have settled, another commotion—louder than the back-stabbing soldier complaining at the steam line. There was a roar of anguish and a thin-faced but broad featured Negro soldier threw his mess tray at the feet of the white soldier monitoring the mess hall. "You feeding me pork!" screamed the offender.

"And you got that crap on my pant's leg!"

The black troop jumped to his feet and pointed an accusing finger, "You devils! Devils!" And then the five white soldiers pounced on top of him, but the crazed soldier broke free and picked up other empty trays and began running around and sailing them through the air like projectiles. Then some of the Negroes nearby lent a hand to get the guy under control, who kept screaming, "Aaaugh, you damn devils! Shoot me! Shoot me, why don't you? Why don't you shoot me instead of poisoning me with that rat meat?" They dragged him out on his heels as he went limp and became a sobbing rag of a man. It had been quite a show.

"What's his problem, Joe?"

"He's a nationalist."

"What's that?"

"Goes around spouting off about Africa, all the time. Talk about going back there, to Liberia or somewheres. Some like him consider themselves political prisoners back home."

As the black troops saw their misguided peer carried off, grabbing his shirt collar, sleeves, or pant leg, they all knew that as soon as there was some cover and concealment for the monitors, a rain of blows and kicks would come down upon the unbalanced transgressor.

A pot-bellied, dingy-smocked white mess sergeant stood at the opposite end of the serving line. Rolling a stump of a cigar around in the corner of his mouth. Seeing the situation under control, he turned his attention back to the other men.

"Come on, boys," he said, "a little pork ain't gonna kill ya. It's good for you. Le's get that line moving, now."

The serving resumed and Gus and Joe became separated during the realignment of the line after the skirmish. Now Joe was in front of the guy who'd first been complaining. He and Joe received their rice scoop, the suspect salad, and their orange and left Gus back on the line.

"Sackett! Don't be so stingy with that stew ladle," the sergeant roared. Mainly for the benefit of the trying to placate the tensions in the room. "Make sure they get plenty."

Gus's neck ratcheted quickly to the side to try and see if the sergeant had actually spoken, or if he'd heard correctly. At first he thought he might be talking to somebody who was a relative of his former commanding officer, but a stare and a reciprocating glance back his way let Gus know there was no doubt as to who it was.

Private First-Class Sackett, looking subdued, humiliated, abstracted from his assignment, and had come aboard the ship two days ago when the carrier made an at-sea refueling. He placed one spooning of the gravy mix over Gus's rice as Gus tried to open his mouth to speak but couldn't produce a sound.

Sackett held up a flash of a precautionary finger over his closed lips, and gave a curt swivel of his head. He grabbed the edge of Gus's mess tray and approached it with another half-filled ladle of food. "I'll talk to you up on deck, at nine." He then turned aside and dipped his utensil into the service pan for the next enlistee.

Within the span of the three hours of time it had taken Gus to write his letter, eat, and change to meet Sackett, the entire sea the ship had been travelling upon changed. Where that afternoon the skies had been sullied cotton balls of gray and slate, striped by white lasers of rain, now the moon appeared. Unveiling itself as a dusky, bone-colored circle on the inky velvet stage of night beginning an ever-arcing heavenward ascent until reaching the extremity of the celestial dome; but for the moment, newly risen, it was only bisecting the little silver thread of the water's glistening horizon. A cosmic lantern now turning into bluish-white brilliance.

Gus stood by himself in the area known as the afterdeck, behind the ship's bridge, or sometimes referred to as the poop deck area. This was where the Black soldiers were assigned to when on deck, and none of them were romantically inclined to perceive what the moon was doing. "How sad," he thought. "If they could only just look around. Yes, this is a transport carrier, but look at this night!" The moon was now the size of a white, half-dollar sized circle. "If this had been a cruise ship, everyone would have come up for this", he surmised, and couldn't help staring at some of the disinterested soldiers. But— he also knew that the business end of oblivion would probably be their final port. It was only the fact that Sackett had come aboard that had gotten Gus so upbeat. So, he dreamed of being on the imaginary cruise.

On that kind of ship there probably would be the nouveau-rich, as well as some of the common folk who'd probably gone through all sorts of sacrifice to get passage. On this late autumn night, unusually warm, the civilians would have been having muted conversations punctuated by cocktail glasses ringing from toasts—chattering with ice. On this ship, however, the harshness of a verbose crap game from across the way was what kept interrupting Gus in his fanciful vision.

Gus had been stationary for so long waiting that soldiers passing by were designating him a landmark as they repeatedly walked passed him during the shipboard laps. They all seemed to follow one another in a counter-clockwise fashion.

On the cruise ship, Gus thought, there would not be men cursing and having vulgar conversations. There would be discussions, or maybe some inside jokes about mercantile dividends in pork bellies, and professional and personal whispered propositions. Live music from a swing band would probably be setting a light mood, too.

Over where three soldiers were arguing over 5 cigarettes lost in an errant toss of die, Gus turned to see some GI pick up a banjo and begin to softly play. It wasn't quite as good as he imagined what would be heard playing on the cruise ship, but the melody held its own under the soldier's offer to the night. No, these men couldn't see the big picture or let their minds roam free. In this reality's proscenium, there was only talk of disappointment and poignant longing for the sighting of terra firma. And of course, he too had felt the urgings of that same expectation, but all of that had been set aside. After the day's surprising events, the night, and all its romantic relays sent confusing and conflicting messages to his mind.

Gus was, in so many words, actually waiting for a date. How lonely could a man get? He had no other feelings towards the former officer but a deep, abiding respect because Sackett's comportment and his sensibility were admirable traits, Gus believed. But he couldn't explain the exhilaration or titillation he was experiencing, at the moment. There had never been a time when he'd behaved in such a fashion concerning another man. At the moment their eyes saw one another in the galley Gus knew they had connected on an uncommon level between men, and non-commissioned officer and commissioned; a brotherhood of extroverted loyalty had grown, of that he was sure. At least, Gus hoped that it wasn't all about Sackett just wishing to acknowledge his past service, since they so happened to have run into one another. Now, while waiting, he listened to the churning progress of the ship slipping through the ocean and saw the vectors of sea froth the waves left behind on either side of the stern. And then the corporal began to have doubts about the situation.

"And why did he want to see me?" Gus questioned himself. "There certainly is no obligation for him to. Maybe he'd been sent in disguise," Gus thought. "But why—for what?" Then Gus saw him from across the deck opening a bulwark door. Shoulders hunched, and head lowered, Sackett fell in line with the others and followed the counter-clockwise trekking, but at a quicker pace. Soon he separated two soldiers who were near to approaching Gus' position and extended his hand to his former subordinate. A closer look revealed that the former officer was not focused, in fact, he seemed an untouched casualty.

Gus hesitated to touch the hand, for a moment, it was offered so carefully. "You got a smoke, Martin?"

"No, Sir. I don't participate in—"

Sackett stepped quickly to his side a few steps and turned to intercept fellow enlistees going by. He was able to mooch a cigarette not only for him, but one for Gus too. Such chicanery was expected among the lower ranks, but for an officer—even a former one, well. He'd replaced honor with pragmatics.

Returning to the railing he then lit the hand-rolled tobacco and gazed quietly over the side of the ship before saying anything else. Then a yelp of excitement, and Sackett pointing with child-like glee, made Gus jump. Who was this man? "Look," Sackett blurted, "flying fish! You see 'em?" Gus suddenly became aware of the sound, and could see metallic-looking projectiles of trout-size fish as they leaped out of the spray. Though the locomotion of the ship itself was quite boisterous, and there were the sounds of the waves, but there was an unmistakable subterfuge of united flapping of thousands of fins. Miniature umbrellas, opening and closing fervently.

"That means good luck," declared Sackett.

"How they do that?"

"I dunno—some story I heard. About a fisherman becoming lost at sea, or something. And just when they're about to start eyeballing one another, a school of flying fish comes leaping into their boat. They fill the goddam thing up and made it back with a helluva story."

"I was wondering what they was going to do with 'em."

"Do?"

"Well, they out at sea. Can't make a fire."

"So, you think they'd have eaten 'em raw?"

"Don't suppose they taste like sardines?"

"I think not, Martin."

"Sir?"

"You need to stow that, soldier." Turning from the rails Sackett took two quick inhalations and cupped the tobacco nub towards his palm. "In fact, If I'm not mistaken," he said with a smoky exhalation, "you outrank me."

"Sorry," Gus apologized. "It's just my habit. That's all you've ever been to me." Fanning his hands with an exasperated motion, he finally asked, "So, what should I call you then?"

"Many to choose from, son. Sir—just isn't one of them."

Several crude disparagements went through Gus' head but they did so, involuntarily. Of course he'd only be able to address Sackett honorably, regardless of his status.

"What's your first name?"

"The War Department has it as Frank."

"All right then, how about I call you, Mr. Frank? Is that all right with you?"

Sackett flicked the butt of his cigarette, barely missing a fish. "Sure, whatever toots your horn, kid—just don't keep treating me like I got something special coming. Cuz' I don't. Not anymore, okay?" The fierceness of the statement almost silenced Gus from speaking any further.

"No, no problem."

"Good—How, ah, how did your training go for y'all, down in Georgia?"

"Can't say it wasn't hell—just like you said, but not all the crackers gave us too hard a time. We got through it all, all right. I even think we're ready, to be honest. Leastways, Mr. Frank, we're going, ain't we? Ready or not."

"What's that supposed to mean?"

"Ready to fight for freedom's cause, all that."

"You are, are you?"

Gus shook his head once.

"Tell me something, are we fighting two wars, or one?"

"One war, Suh,—Mr. Frank. With three enemies."

"Not us, home skillet—not for us. You can't mean to tell me you standing here after all the crap they done put you through, and you still ain't taken out that hook, yet? You believe it's really about us saving the world?"

"Sure—And I thought you believed that, too?"

"Let me give you the inside on this—The bottom line of it is, kid, is that war is not about fighting for the salvation of human rights, okay? It's about fighting over national interests. Not human interests. Notice I said 'human', not humane. There is no humanity to it, and I've seen seventy percent of the big picture. Seen it from both sides. War's not about people, it's about politics settled through aggression. Do you know what we are here—you, me, and all the rest of these sorry sonuvabitches walking around? We are political expedients."

"What do you mean, Mr. Frank?"

"I mean we're 20,000 tons of beef being tossed through a high-speed grinder to make into lean cuts to feed the hungry national interests in our country. You see, they got to maintain control and all that work that it has us doing keeps making it hungrier and hungrier. The rich and the powerful of the world, all they want is to make sure they get fed on time and that no one steals their food while they're trying to eat it. Whether you know it, or not, that's the way it really is. Take it for what it's worth—or not." Sackett now lit the last cigarette he'd bummed and stared out at the waves below.

"You always feel that way, Mr. Frank?"

No answer.

"If I might ask, how long since you lost your bars?"

"There's nothing more either one of us can say about that, Martin. Now, I know you must be thinking that may be the reason behind my sounding so particularly bitter, some would even say unpatriotic, but that's not the case. There was a time when I couldn't talk to you, like this. When I was your commanding officer, I could not let you know my personal feelings. That's not the way the military operates in order to keep the chain-of-command enforced, but even that is to train you for objectifying everyone—everything. It makes killing someone a less conscionable thing once you sterilize the act with a purpose of curing a moral outrage. All those contacts you've made since you've been in the military—the camaraderie of daily life in the Army. That can't get in the way of what this is about. One personal stabbing of consciousness, you see. That's all that's needed is one soldier hesitating, and it can lead to the demise of the whole operation. Cold-blooded business it is—this war thing. You can't have people getting all sulky-eyed when they need to worry about slitting a guy's throat."

"If I'm reading you correctly, you're saying you didn't see what was going to happen when it was coming at you, is that right?"

"I got sucker punched into making an either/or decision, Martin. Yeah, I was bamboozled. They told me what was on one side of the hoop and what was on the other, and then they knew I'd jump it."

"But to lose all your commission. I could understand if they made you a 2nd lieutenant, heck, even a sergeant major, but a PFC?"

"That's the consequences, Martin."

"Was it bad? What you did?"

"I, ah—ah. Got caught having forged some documents in order to get into the Army."

"But why?"

"I didn't have much choice. Who I was, you could call a victim of circumstance. The army is the only type of structure where a man could lose himself, if that's what was needed. I had to go from where I came, change who I'd been because I never had a feeling of being from anyplace, really. I felt like I belonged to the biggest goddam family a person could have. Even an orphan can feel like he's got family in the army, boy. And it was a glorious time for me, when I found that with hard work I could better myself and make a difference for me and those around me. Do you know what I'm trying to say?"

And Gus did—nodding his head, almost to a point that it was continually rocking, acknowledging ascent to more and more of the genuflected feelings Sackett exposed about his predicament.

"But, you know Martin," Sackett interceded after a tirade of audacities he remembered came out, "the thing of it is, is that I really didn't think it through, carefully enough. I got so caught up in the entire hullabaloo about wearing a nice uniform and saving the world—and that in turn from that someone would forgive me for my transgressions, that I forgot the truth."

"Truth?"

"You got two kinds of men on the front line, Martin. Those running to glory or those running from infamy. The truth is neither one matters. We might for a minute when there's a few quick words said over our remains, but when a man falls—there's another; and another, and another. Each fool thinking that he can be the one person out of the whole bunch that can be the straw breaking the enemy camel's back. All for the sake of having someone say things about you that you'll never hear, or really care about once you're gone. Lot more dead heroes than there are ones alive, Martin."

"But at least it meant your life had a purpose."

"What?" Sackett grabbed Martin by the shoulders and looked squarely into the younger man's eyes with a squinting concern. Then after several moments, Sackett released him and turned away. "I'm through talking. Why don't you go on and get outta here?"

"What's the matter? What did I do?"

"You got yourself convinced of it. That somehow the noblest thing you could ever do would be to lay down your life for your country. Martin, let me tell you something. You should never wish to die, it ain't healthy. It's disturbing."

"You got me wrong, Mr. Frank. I don't plan on dying, but with us being deployed now, the chances are greater than they were back home. If my time comes, I just don't want to be alone."

"Don't worry, Martin. You'll have plenty of company." Sackett's lips curled up in a grin at the corners as he finished taking a last drag from his smoke, nervously pushed up the collar on his coat, tipped the bill of his cap and went down the hatch at the far end. Gus kept his eyes trained on the hatch, and started to take a few steps forward when he ran into Joe.

"How the mighty have fallen, huh, little brother?"

"You saw him?" Gus felt like swinging an arcing right hand at his brother's jaw line.

"Joe, what are you doing up here? You never like to come out topside when I'm out here. Are you spying on me, now?""

"If you really didn't want me to know—shoulda kept your mouth shut."

"Joe, you ain't planning on giving him any trouble, are you?"

"Sackett? I wouldn't bother wasting my time with him. No good would come of it. But I will say one thing, though. Chickens coming home to roost around, the farmers tell you that's a good sign."

"I wouldn't push him on it, Joe."

"Why?"

"His bed is hard enough to lay on, and we don't need to add to any more burdens than he already has."

"Well, what he do?"

"Got busted for falsifying some documents."

"Why you so surprised," Joe asked.

"Whatever it was, when he did it, it was bad enough to make him lose all level of rank."

"Will you give up on all this hero worship you have for him, Gus? The man has done a 180 degree turn, and he don't piss ginger ale or make thunder when he farts. He puts his pants on just like me and you."

"You really don't understand anyone, Joe. You know, for a long time, when I thought of somebody I wanted to be like, I thought about Captain Sackett. I'll admit that—and I know it's not the proper way to show respect for your older brother. I know that could make you angry with me. But you shouldn't. When he was an officer, I saw the way he handled himself. All the responsibilities—the power. He was happy to do it, though. But you're right he has changed. And you'll never believe how much the two of you sound just alike."

CHAPTER THIRTY-ONE
Dawn's Too Early Light

His eyes opened very slowly, but his head did not make a move. Though without his glasses, Sackett's unassisted eyes could still make out that he was not waking up in his hotel room. And he was thirsty from all the conversation the night before, tinged scotch. A splash of the apple juice colored liquor still waiting to be finished off in the glass he'd sat down hours ago. He felt the pillow under his head, resting against the couch arm, and ran his right hand along its width. What time was it? Was there anyone still in the house? The slate blue blanket covering him gave Sackett a very comforting feeling and he wanted to enjoy the warmth longer, but knew he shouldn't. He must get up. With a grunt, he carefully pulled himself to an upright sitting position and did the wide-mouthed silent scream that accompanies riveting stretches.

Subsequently, he noticed that his shoes had been removed and were set neatly in front of the couch. Sackett was thankful he didn't have holes in his socks, or sweaty feet. That would have discouraged anyone from doing any such kindness for him, but apparently someone had. Whomever it was, probably was the same person now tapping intermittently on the other side of the closed drawing room doors.

"I'm decent," Sackett spoke up.

He couldn't get up enough momentum to get off of the enveloping seat and to meet Mrs. Martin as she partially slid open the opaque, wooden doors of the room. And Lorraine did so as quietly as she could because they usually made a good deal of protest at ingresses. Sackett's head appreciated that. Bringing in a flower-covered TV tray with some scrambled eggs, a few bacon strips, grapefruit juice, and black coffee; she set the hospitality by the living room table. "I came down last night about two. Both y'all was just a-snoring and asleep in your chairs. Didn't have the heart to send you on your way. So, there's why you're here."

"I'm much obliged," Sackett said, his mouth and stomach acknowledging the still-hot, tasty faire put out for him.

"Everybody gone?"

Lorraine brought the tray towards the couch, "Uh-huh. It's about 10 in the morning."

"My lands, I feel so—"

"Ashamed? Needn't be. Sorry, I don't have toast—but I can make you some English muffins."

"No—no, that's fine. Had my fill of those." Sackett scooped up some cooked eggs with his bacon, clinking utensils. Lorraine sighed and put her hand on her hips, grinning slightly. "Tell me, Mrs. Martin—is there anything in that gay-rage outback of the house?"

"I imagine so, but not from me seeing Jimmy pulling anything out of there."

"I'd like to take a look around it, if you won't mind."

"What do you have in mind, Mr. Sackett?"

"Repaying hospitality, ma'am." Frank stood, having hurriedly demolished the small portions given him and stacked his dishes. "Now, if you'll allow me to put these to the kitchen, I'd like to take a stop by little Brad's room and check something out."

Lorraine watched from the front room as Sackett moved past her and lighted his dirty ware on the kitchen table, stopping directly in front of the open door jamb of her son's room. The hanging lip of the opened ceiling still pointed down towards the head of the boy's bed. Sackett looked to his right, his left, and then stepped back into the kitchen and turned, slapping his hands together. "Now. I know what I need, let's see what we got."

Watching from the kitchen window, as she cleaned up after breakfast, Lorraine saw him bring out a rust-claimed toolbox. Then after several minutes he followed up by bringing out some gray, old lumber. Then what looked like a half-full jar of nails—a saw—then a large portion of half-inch sheet rock and a couple gallons of paint that had faded, once water-soaked labels. What the old man was putting into motion was worth far more than the breakfast he'd imbibed, she thought.

Sackett stuck his head in past the back screen door. "You got a stack of newspapers around, Mrs. Martin?"

They spread whatever could be used to protect the worn furniture, ripped linoleum, and bedding where Sackett would be working. Some drycleaner plastic and garbage can liners were in the mix of tarps, as well. When Lorraine could only produce a kitchen step stool for a ladder, Sackett declined its use and balanced himself atop Brad's bed to cut away the wasted ceiling. He took the sheet rock cutter in his right hand and cut an uneven square about eight inches around the hole's edges, then he began to gouge out the deeper indentations. Within minutes, the ceiling joists were seen. Sackett took the whole eyesore down, turning his head aside to not breathe in any more of the dust he'd kicked up. Sackett then laid the discarded sheet rock on top of the replacement and made a similar sized cut.

"Mr. Sackett?"

"Ma'am?"

"How'd you come to know about this? It was like you knew where to go to get everything."

"Well, ma'am—can you hand me some more of them sheet rock nails, please." Sackett began tacking down the unblemished drywall patch and concluded by saying, "Your son has some strong values, Mrs. Martin. And it don't seem he likes to press much to get things done his way. Thought I'd take that burden off of him—having to ask his daddy, and all."

"What a nice gesture."

"He's a fine boy, ma'am."

Sackett didn't have any joint compound to properly set the tape he prepared to use on the board, but he did have a partially used can of *Spackle* he found between two wall studs in the garage. And that would be good enough. He tore the drywall tape to approximate the perimeter of the fix and put them in his shirt pocket. Then Sackett scooped the gray fixative onto an old broad knife with a used paint stick and made a thick layer of paste over the exposed cracks from the repair. "How did your husband get along with his dad, Mrs. Martin?"

"Jimmy never got to know his daddy, so—you can imagine that some of what Brad gets from him is..."

"Parsed with some frustration on his part?"

"Yes."

"What about Jim's mother, did he have—oh that's right."

"Yes—his mother didn't make it past the day he was born. And Jimmy always got such scrutiny from everyone. He used to stutter and they'd go and blame that on his position in life."

"How's that?" Sackett finished pressing the last strip of joint tape into the compound he'd put on the ceiling.

"Well, you know it wasn't a natural act."

"What do you mean, Ms. Martin? Giving birth to babies is the most natural of acts."

"A baby by your first cousin?"

Sackett wiped at his nose with the back of his hand like it itched him.

"The way it all happened was such an unexpected thing and it seems that the one who got the brunt of it—until Brad, was Jimmy."

Sackett pulled the broad knife along the patch at a low angle and with a light touch, "That will have to dry overnight before I can put a finish coat on it." And he quietly cleaned up his work debris without saying another word. Brad didn't notice the ceiling until he'd gone to bed for the night because he's just gotten used to ignoring the damage over him. And he made it a point to ask his mother in the morning how all the wondrous things occurred while he was at school that day. The only thing that the boy knew for sure was that someone had taken account of his feelings and done him kindly.

But the patch was still rough, and he hoped that it wouldn't be left with being half-done. His dad would start to do some things, but he never seemed to finish. For a long time, Brad just looked at the patch, as if staring at it would ensure that it would not disappear. Soon, he slept. A sound sleep. One that came with being satisfied.

CHAPTER THIRTY-TWO
A Change in Plans

"One thing is painfully evident," the Negro general said, the glint from his epaulets single silver stars almost non-existent, so far was he away from the fireplace in the Supreme Headquarters State Room, "if Washington had any plans to send us more men—needed men, they would have done so by now."

General Eisenhower and General Bedell Smith, his Chief-of-Staff, stood near the cinder-glowing fire and continued gazing at it. Their backs turned to General Lee, the European Theater Logistics Command, who didn't feel any of the hoarded warmth of the fire's heat as he still stood in the doorway. Eisenhower had been leaning with an extended arm upon the mantle but put his right arm into his pants pocket when he turned his blue, cow eyes, to Smith. The staffer mouthed a silent message back to the Supreme Commander with a deliberate, oscillating shake of disapproval. Eisenhower still did not speak. Finally, it was Smith who broke the lack of communication. "John," he said to Lee, "I think we'll have to forego what you proposed for the Third Army. They won't even consider it as an option."

"I didn't know General Patton had any problem with employing Negro troops, Bedell?" Lee's voice barely hid restraint on his part, but he was used to off-handedness.

"There's no offense intended, General Lee," Eisenhower apologized for his aide, "but the incident with that group of his in that tank battalion left him with a bad taste in his mouth."

"I've never known George Patton to shrink from a challenge. What exactly did he say?"

"Well, John," Eisenhower said turning now, "he—ah, made some comments to—"

"To the effect that, 'They can't think fast enough on their feet to fight in the armor division," Smith interrupted. "I know that sounds blunt, but I can't sugarcoat this issue with you."

"Mind you," Ike came back, "that's not the Supreme Command's feeling on the matter, whatsoever."

General Lee looked with pensive distaste at the two men, and they stared back at him in unblinking disconcerted caution. Lee thought to himself, what would the outcome have been had he been a white general making the kind of initiative he had? For one, that man probably wouldn't even consider making the meeting an opportunity, or to see it as an opportunity. It was because of Lee's special circumstances—the status of his human, ethnic, hierarchical placement, that the plan and the meeting about it were highly-prized. It was a thing that would leave a mark on history, but clearly a part of history that Major General Smith wanted no part of. Lee could see that by the scowl that darkened his face as he quoted Patton.

"General Eisenhower, will there be any censure on this?"

"We happen to be fighting this massive war over the very freedom to hold an opposing view on things, trivial and important," Eisenhower said with patriotic sincerity. "No, this does not require that kind of action."

"Sir," Lee resolutely pressed, "I've kept you in steady supply going on for six months now. Whenever you needed anything I got it for you. All you had to do was to say, 'John, I need this here,' and it was there, wasn't it?"

"I can't argue with you about that. From the day the First Army landed on Omaha—you have done an outstanding job, but the thing is—"

General Lee sighed heavily and then charged his response.

"Begging pardon, General. I don't waste. Nothing. If I'm telling you this is a way to handle a serious shortfall of troops, you can bet a star on it. Period."

Eisenhower passed by the conference table between them and picked up the classified documents General Lee had set on its highly-waxed surface. He seemed to study the order for a half-minute of earnest review, but the paper soon rested against his right leg. "Maybe—as a way to not dilute the advantages presented, maybe we can just put the men who you're talking about and put them in a colored division that can be placed behind the Maginot."

"Sir," Lee pleaded, "what possible good would that do? It's the infantry that is decimated. If you wait for white infantry and cavalry, you're facing three months of down time for training them. Three months before you could use one. And you and I both know a week is an eternity on the field when you can't hold position."

"Yes," General Smith said, "but it also might take as long to smooth over all the ruffled feathers from civilians and soldiers who were not canvassed about this move."

"Since when did we start making military strategy based on public opinion, Bedell?"

"The locals in the United Kingdom would be taken by surprise, and our allies deserve better than that."

"General Eisenhower," Lee pushed, "it's almost to the point of it being sacrilegious not to allow ten percent of your fighting force not be able to fire off one round."

Eisenhower folded his hands at the small of his back, right over the left, and walked slowly away from both debaters. His bald head pitched forward momentarily and then he stopped to look out the large cathedral window. He held ground there for a moment, looking forward and then quickly to each side. His back still to the junior officers, he turned his head to look at them both before speaking. "The presence of Negro troops in this Theater of Operations will present a variety of problems, to be sure. And General Lee, I'm sure you know all too well what those details can be. If you would, I'd like to ask you to help yourself to some coffee in the foyer, if you don't mind. I need to have a moment with my chief, here."

General Lee began to speak again but thought the better of it and just saluted his superiors as he retreated. He imagined Bedell Smith as being comparable to Caiaphas, in the Bible. Or like a Brutus—lurking around the Supreme Commander to thwart any plans that could derail hidden agendas. Always offered in the terms of advice. Eisenhower turned to face Smith once Lee had closed the doors, and he folded his arms casually across his chest.

"Permission to speak freely?" Smith asked.

"Let's hear it, Bedell. What's really eating you? I think it's a damn good idea."

"I flew it past the rest of the lieutenants of the command, Ike. And let me tell you. If you have any plans for life after the war, any political ambitions—for God's sake, I'm begging you. Don't do this. It would not go over well at home. You know that."

"There's nowhere else to draw from. Do you think I make this decision lightly?"

"What will the enemy think? Have you thought of that? What kind of message are we going to send our enemies by them seeing colored or, even worse, integrated battalions? Or did you forget Hitler and Jesse Owens meeting at the Olympics?"

"Hitler be damned, General. If General Bull can't get congress to authorize fresh enlistment, I'm going to let Lee's Christmas surprises go through."

"You're betting it all on him?"

"General Lee doesn't need an answer today and this order is only a draft. Bull just got into Washington yesterday and he is meeting with the Joint Chiefs."

"He better come back with something in writing, Ike."

"Have some faith, Bedell. It's that time of year."

Henry Stimson looked directly at General Bull as he slammed a thin metallic pointer against a tactical map set on an easel in Roosevelt's Oval Office. Though the president and Bull tried to employ all their rhetorical skills, Stimson created an inertia of rebuke concerning the solicitation for troops. He did so with a fervent and heavy-handed deliberateness. "Here! Here, and here," Stimson slammed the cylinder like a metal whip against the land graph of France. "The Germans are encroaching around every point we've locked down in the last four months, General Bull. This was all meticulously planned, this invasion—we told you how many troops you had to work with. And now because of mismanagement of those resources, you are coming back here to get more? Why have Hitler's men been allowed to get so close to our positions, General?"

"General Eisenhower is requesting more men and ammunitions, Sir, because without them we can't keep the Nazis at bay. It's not for lack of trying, Mr. Secretary."

"Sounds reasonable to me, Henry," FDR chipped in, repositioning himself in his wheelchair. "Why should we begrudge the European Theater that?"

"Because Anzio and North Africa's fronts depleted those reserves. Mr. President, there are no more divisions left in the States to give him. It's just math, simple as that."

General Bull would not be repressed, however. "There has to be time for the front line to catch their breath, Mr. Secretary. They've been humping it all day and night for what seems like forever. An invading force has to be reinforced and we have held our own, until recently, through the summer and fall. And if you're worried about those jerries now, wait till another month goes by without some backup."

"The fact of the matter remains, General Bull, and it is what upsets me so much about your request, is that we gave major appropriations, after the fact. But our positions are tenable, at best."

Roosevelt considered what each man's assessments were of the situation and came up with his own summation as commander-and-chief. He put out his hand, palm down, and looking at Stimson, quietly brought it down on top of his desk. "Henry," he said, "there are Nazis past the Maginot, of that we are sure, but are they a force to reckon with or merely an irritant? And look at our forces. If they had enough people to really make a counter-strike they'd have been right behind the front—but there are no advancing divisions. We're in good shape in comparison to them. That's my concern, to ensure we hold that advantage. While our forces can't contribute at this bulge, Britain is freeing up some troops. And General Bull? Has your Headquarters looked at optimal utilization of all the forces we have in the European Theater of Operation?"

"The Supreme Headquarters has been in touch with the general in charge of logistics, Mr. President."

"And I presume the jury is still out on that?"

"I've no word on what they discussed, Sir."

"Well—General. That doesn't give me much. I can't go to Congress and simply order up more enlistees, more ammunition, based on what you've just confirmed. Eisenhower must show me a way that things can be reordered to cut men loose—and where they are to be garnered from."

"Yes, Mr. President," Bull said flatly.

"Have you thought about amnesty for non-serious offenders that are incarcerated?" Stimson suggested.

"I'll tell Ike." But General Bull was more than aware of the Article 15 violators who could safely be called upon. It still wouldn't fill the demand. Even if he let loose attempted murderers, it wouldn't. Bull rose and nodded. "Thank you, Mr. President."

Now it was up to the hidden agenda of General Lee, who would be directed to post the classified orders for Negro soldiers to commit to the front. Bull didn't mention it, for he really didn't think it would have come down to that. But the whole world was doing the unexpected, so why not the Army?

Not all the things set into motion that day, or that hour, came about from the decision made in Washington. But within seventy-two hours, it was evident that a chain-of-events began involving the military transport the Martins and Sackett were on. Events signifying that General Lee had won out became apparent to the men on that ship, on the morning of November 14th, though they could make no connection to it due to their shared ignorance of command decisions.

Breakfast on the transport was abandoned midway through its serving when shouts of 'land' and cheering were distinguished in the lower decks of the ship. Hunger was supplanted with earnest preparation for making landfall. Food had grown tasteless and nothing more than filler, long ago. It wouldn't be missed, especially since they could purchase food on shore after landing. But the sight of what was to be the first docking dampened the soldiers' appetites even more.

The quays of London were an eerie vantage point to the arriving troops as they surveyed the shore from aboard the ship. The Luftwaffe ruined flats and stores revealed blackened decimation on the streets. The men on the decks, both white and black, thought they'd been experiencing hell aboard the ship. But now knew they'd had it easy in comparison. From what they could see, a real inferno had to have been unleashed. It was sobering to them. An order given caused large hemp nets to be tossed over the side of the docking ship, scramble nets. Two hundred of four hundred and fifty soldiers, mostly from the Detroit unit, scaled their way down to the pier and lined up for embarking on awaiting deuce-and-a-half trucks.

Their destination was Paddington Station, where a British Rail train would convey them to a forward base camp in the midlands. Neither one of the Martin brothers, or Sackett, had been chosen for that group. They were still on board the transport, and as the ship eased away from this docking they didn't know whether to consider themselves lucky, or not.

"They a bunch of sitting ducks for some Messerschmitt," Joe said loudly. "All the strafe runs they been doing on trains—I wouldn't want to be one of them."

"From the air, a transport ship is a bigger target than a train," Sackett said. Joe cut his eyes towards his nemesis and didn't take the opportunity to start another quarrel.

"Well—I still say we're better off."

"The Lieutenant just got through saying we're going to Bristol," Sackett disputed. "Train runs there, just as well. There are two other stations we could have used, Temple Mead, or Parkway. It's just pragmatics. You only put half the eggs in the basket. Just in case—better a few broken eggs than no omelet. We're all sitting ducks. Each and every one of us."

Bristol was one-hundred twenty miles to the west, and to the south of London. It was the largest city in what was referred to as West Country, second only in size to Bath. A channel separated the city from Wales, although Welsh food had a mainstay in the diet of the Bristol citizenry. The ship navigated south with no concern, and after travelling several miles along the coast entered the mouth of the Avon River, that led to Bristol. All hands were on deck as they made the turn in from the sea, not at all raucous. Their ship progressed slowly in the fresh waterway, embellished by autumn crimson in the late afternoon.

The natural splendor made it seem sacrilege to be loud and boisterous and the men were shushed in their assembly, talking to one another in low voices. But when they approached the town of Clifton their sotto uttering turned into whispers.

The river narrowed here and was being squeezed by tall, steep, rock walls formed by sheer ancient stone, which towered two-hundred and fifty feet above the river bank. The rock face resembled humongous slabs of butter toffee. There was no danger of running aground; the river was deep enough and navigable, but the banks were very close to the sides of the ship. In fact, an average swimmer could have made good time getting across from either side. Once the soldiers on board passed an upcoming bend, however, everyone began diverting their eyes from below, to fixating on what stood before and above them. High over their heads, expanded over the gorge's floor and its river was a suspension bridge like none any of them had seen before. Necks strained upwards as the ship passed underneath the viaduct.

"Good mother of god," Gus said, marveling at the century-plus old span.

"Bet that's what every one of them suckers said while they were building it, too," Joe kidded.

"Yeah," Gus acknowledged, "that's a mighty long way up."

"Or down," Joe quickly added.

And that was as far as Gus wanted to take the conversation. He was deathly afraid of heights, though he preferred calling it having more of the proper respect for the odds of calamity. One of his worst experiences during the training in Georgia had to do with rappelling from a seventy-foot tower at Fort Benning. He never felt complete confidence in the situation, even with controlling the descent. Joe couldn't figure him out, either, because his younger brother had no such compunction about jumping out of a plane with a parachute. Didn't bother him one bit. To Gus, it probably seemed safer relying on a mechanism, than it was to depend on an unsteady hand the only thing keeping you from sure death.

As the soldiers were further transported by vehicle through the English countryside they eventually arrived at a town where an American-like antebellum fabric inexplicably seemed to have woven its way through every setting. The houses, many of them along tree-lined streets, had pillars at their front entrances. Arches and pediments over the tall windows on slate and thatch roofed abodes. They were told they were supposed to be based there, in Bristol, but to their regret found out that their accommodations were not nearly as romantic. The Georgian architecture didn't apply to the camp where the Blackbird troops were going to be.

Although ensconced in the grounds of the prestigious and stately Bristol University, the bivouacs the men were assigned to, and the encampment, were strictly government issue fabrications. But seeing that they would be having access to a nearby town, and a nice pub on the campus, many of the soldiers believed this visit could turn into a pleasant stay. And for at least twelve hours after disembarking the men were left to their own devices and were able to explore. And that may have been a mistake because the men soon found out they had found a land filled with lotus, and they could not help but to feel a rush of malaise.

The command rolled out a welcoming mat, so to speak. Though they hadn't given out off-base passes, they did allow the PX to supply beer and gave each man a consignment of scrip for purchases. The officers knew the men wouldn't be so annoyed with being off-limits from the pub if they could get their beer for free. Be they Negro or white, everyone got some ducats and though segregation, per se was adhered to on base, they were all having a rollicking party together and kept on good terms.

The following morning was like something out of dream. They'd been allowed to sleep in until 7:30, two hours later than their usual reverie. But one couldn't call they way the men were awakened even a call to arms. A well-coiffed corporal with broad shoulders and a square chin came into the barracks area quietly and calmly and pleasantly announced that breakfast would be served from 8:30 to 11:00. The men could come in at their leisure during the hours given. And with having said that, the noncom was gone.

Joe picked up his toiletries and snatched his towel at the head of his bunk. "Next thing you know," he whispered to Gus, "they gonna start serving us breakfast in bed." Gus had to chuckle. Their agenda, one that they already had been briefed on, was a sundry one for the day, dealing with mostly how the lay of land was going to be.

The afternoon began with a history lesson where the soldiers learned that Bristol exported to many of the colonies in the 18th century. In fact, legend had it that the name for America got its derivation from the surname of a certain Bristol clerk during that time, a Richard Ameryke. It was interesting enough, the seminar, but soon a few troops started nodding off. They had an hour to themselves and were to meet at the chow hall for "tea", another acculturation the command wanted to imbue the men with. They learned the country stopped daily at that time to enjoy a hot brew. But coffee was available for the more reticent yanks.

The white troops thought cucumber sandwiches a curiosity but many of the black soldiers had made similar edibles when meat was scarce in their homes. Gus got Joe to laugh about how he and his brother would have all the fixings for a cheeseburger put together between two buns—except for the burger. But, surprisingly, it was enough of the reminiscent flavor to fool their hunger. That, however, was not going to be a concern on this particular night.

The new troops had been given an invitation to a dinner reception for the Humanities department of the university and the course was world-class: Beef

Wellington, asparagus, brussel sprouts, mashed potatoes with chives, melt-in-your-mouth rolls, and lovely brown gravy. For dessert, there was cheesecake with blueberry compote, and a three-layered chocolate cake if a diner preferred something more deliciously decadent. Not many of the men had ever had such a fine repast served to them, certainly not Gus, or Joe. They politely listened to some poetry before leaving and they all decided they wanted to bed early—sleepy from distended stomachs and spoiled into lethargy. But at four o'clock the next morning all the whetnursing came to an abrupt halt. The new soldiers had expected as much, though. They knew that it was too good to last much longer, but that didn't make the realization any less for them when it occurred.

The whining din of distant voices barking in the night started from outside, increasing as it got nearer the Negro barracks. Someone was banging non-stop on a garbage can lid. But the slumbering men in the colored barracks didn't budge and if these soldiers didn't hear the racket, one could be sure the white troops on the other side of camp were completely unawares.

Then the door to Gus and Joe's barracks entry crashed open with a slam against the wall, pushed open forcefully enough to cause a framed picture to fall loudly—and then that was quickly followed by the high-pitch trilling of several white soldiers fully deploying pea-whistles. There were sergeants and corporals, no one lower-ranked than a PFC, and they were all white. Stomping up and down the aisles, high-stepping and clanging pot lids. Then they began plodding in between the bunks, where alarmed bronze troops catapulted forward in surprise and disbelief. They were under attack by military demons, incarnate. Any thoughts that these soldiers ever held any kind notions towards them were quickly set aside when they gave an entreaty to the men that in no shape, or form, be called flattery.

The men were ordered to fall out and prepare for PT—physical training. Starting with a full repertoire of calisthenics, the cadre then ran the perspiring men out into the cold, early morning, Clifton Valley. Far away from Bristol, yet splendid in its tree-lined hills, the run didn't slow down for the recruits until well after the sun came up. Still headed in an easterly direction, the cadre staff had the troops finally slow the pace down to a single-file formation, and in that design they kept walking for twenty more minutes. Most of the men too tired to talk.

Sometime during this cooling down period water could be heard lapping along holding banks, and Gus, who was near the end of the line, suddenly realized where they were going and his intestines tightened. They were going to cross the suspension bridge at Avon.

Midway out upon the bridge, a number of white cadres awaited the arrival of the fifty black soldiers, and uncoiled carefully wrapped piles of eleven and thirteen millimeter rope. Rope thick enough to hold a man.

A corporal walked over to the approaching group with a swagger in his gait, carrying a duffel bag full of leather gloves. "All right, boys," he said, as he began passing out the wraps, "looks like we're all going to be one big happy group of Swinging Richards, today." Gus's heart fell out from the bottom of his feet. Just as he surely would be doing the same, momentarily. Of that, he was all too sure. They weren't crossing over the bridge. They were going to rappel it. Instinctively, in a manner of self-preservation, Gus withdrew himself from the direct eye line of the trainers after he'd gotten his gear: the gloves and a d-ring carabineer.

While their Swiss Seat rappelling trusses were being fashioned around their waists and between their legs, it bothered Joe when he noticed with some disconcerted awareness that his brother was having Sackett adjust and check over his particular knot work.

Once everyone was haltered up in their gear the company walked out onto the surprisingly stable bridge. But all the same, Gus kept to the center of the group and to the rear.

Looking over, no one could see any outcropping of land, a slope, downward grade, or anything. It was sheer rock. A wall two-hundred fifty feet high of ochre-colored stratification, going straight down. The snookered recruits had been waylaid by their unfamiliarity with the area, and combined with the fact that they hadn't been able to see what the terrain was like at the top. Now, that vantage point was immaterial because whether they had wanted to, or not, every man was going over. And it didn't matter if they rappelled from nearer the end of the span or from the middle. It was over two hundred feet to the bottom from anywhere along the length.

Gus began feeling his breath start to become hard to catch for all the wild thumping in his chest, and his middle ear began to ache a little, as well. His fear, he knew, was making him physically sick. Much to his chagrin. Sackett looked back and saw the trepidation on Gus's face and he lagged behind a little bit to bolster him.

"You gonna be okay?"

"I'll probably have a heart attack before they can get a chance to throw me off this bridge."

"It's safe, Gus. Those belays are tied off by Rope Masters. There's no possible way you could fall."

"All right, people," the corporal yelled. "Let's have everybody make sure you got your rappel package squared away, correctly. Check each other. You check his package, I check my package, and then go ahead and check your own package again."

Many of the men laughed at the light humor, but it simply ratcheted up Gus's dread. "I don't think my seat's tight enough, Mr. Frank."

"You don't want it too tight, or you'll start cutting off your circulation in your legs."

"I don't want to fall."

Sackett could see the young man was clearly beside himself with his worst nightmares. Sackett blinked once and looked at Gus with a commanding look. "Nobody's going to be doing any falling, Martin. You just hang back and watch the others do it for a spell and you'll get the hang of it."

"Come on, bring it in here," said the Master Sergeant. "The sooner we're done here, the sooner we march back to camp and get some chow."

"What about tea time, Sarge?"

More laughter.

"Well, if you're quick enough with it, we should be able to make it back there in time for that. Although, real men don't drink tea. I don't care what the limeys say."

Again teeters of giggling assuaged the tension, but the moment of truth had arrived. "Who's to be first?" A sergeant who adjusted the wrap system, that looked liked some massive spaghetti of snakes, all clover-hitched into a pile asked. No one spoke a word. Fifteen seconds of quiet and then—

"Hell, I'll do it."

Joe, much to the astonishment of his brother—and to his shame that he could not match such bravery, was confounded by the bravado of his older sibling because Joe didn't like heights, either. But he also would never let another man know he was insecure, at any time. Gus would have taken a step back to delay his participation, but Joe had looked directly at Sackett and Gus when he spoke up. He wanted to prove a point.

"Here's the set-up," the sergeant began to explain as Joe took the doubled line and looped it inside of his carabineer and locked that down onto his seat's front loop. "There's a man on belay, way down there. At the end of your rappel, you then become the next belay man. Got that? Now, from here you should come down right at the river's edge."

"Okay."

"Now," the sergeant cautioned, "there's an overhang off the side of the bridge. Because of that, I don't think it wise starting your rappel from a standing position."

He motioned Joe down to a prone position with the doubled master line after he wrapped it around the carabineer and locked it. First grabbing the master line, high above its doubled sets of carabineers, and then bringing the braking line behind his waist to the small of his back, Joe made sure he felt his gloved fist constantly in touch with buttocks. Gus stepped forward to watch more carefully as his brother inched his way over to the edge in a lateral crawl. Scooting over by twisting his belly and hips.

"Okay," the sergeant said supportively, "just a little bit more. Make sure you keep your guide hand up and just roll to your right...all right, watch that anchor hand so you don't get it pinned. It will ruin your day."

"Roger, that," Joe said.

He was at the point of precipice and the sergeant placed his hand on top of Joe's brake hand. "As soon as you roll over the side let up on this hand a little, your brake. That will give you the slack you need so you don't go knocking yourself out by swinging back into the bridge. You tell me when to help you over."

Joe gave a thumbs-up with his anchor hand. "All right," said the sergeant. "See you at the bottom."

Joe's departure from the suspended extension was true to character; he flew off the span by whipping his right foot over and having that momentum to help him roll. But then he was gone from sight. Gus rushed over to the railing with a stifled gasp but he quickly peeked over and saw his brother swinging back and forth about six feet underneath the suspension channel. A collective whoop arose and he made his way down to the tree line cautiously. Some of the trees below him stood one hundred feet above the Avon River's banks, and Joe was one hundred-fifty feet higher than them. His suspended, spider-like appearance gave a humbling perspective to the men watching the defiance of the rappel. Joe was fully in control of his descent and felt even more self-assured because it seemed to him that this must be what it feels like to be a bird. At least, he had a bird's perspective on things, at the moment. And he remembered that he had a point he wanted to make.

For the sake of dramatics, highlighted by his one-upmanship of his brother's idol, Joe decided to put on a little show and loosened his grasp of both of his hands. The gravity of his weight immediately dropped him fifty feet, or more, in a matter of seconds. Joe didn't know whether it was smoke or dust coming from between the gloves' fingers but then the friction made it all too clear that the leather gloves only offered so much protection. Suffering some second-degree burns and stinging discomfort in the palm of his hands, Joe winced as he slowed his rappel descent. Eventually, he became lost from view again when he got past the treetops, but several seconds later it was seen that he had made it down to the carpet of wet grass by the river bank.

The jumpmaster on the bridge stepped back from looking over the railing and seemed to look directly at Gus, as the hesitant troop tried to encapsulate himself amid the others. "Who here is afraid of rappelling?" the sergeant shouted.

Gus was motionless, and cast his eyes from the left to the right nervously, contemplating whether it was errant to be honest. "Come on, now," The jumpmaster encouraged. "It's not a disgrace for you to admit it. Hell, as a matter of fact, it probably shows you got a lotta sense." Gus's eyes met a few other timid souls near him, but he believed the jumpmaster was a sincere man. He wanted to believe he would be a merciful one as well. He even wanted to believe that if enough of the soldiers stated their true feelings as to the propriety of the training, the cadres might even let them all sit this one out—or maybe even stop the whole operation, altogether. "By a show of hands," the jumpmaster declared, "who's afraid of going over?" Gus and four other men, soldiers who believed in democracy, raised their hands. Ignoring the stares and accompanying ridicule and snickers.

The jumpmaster, of course, knew which man he was going to pick all along. He'd been watching for some of them who looked like nervous kittens that just realized they were going to be drowned. Of course, he wanted to ante up the stress level for them by seeming to give a rat's ass about their mental well-being. "You!" he shouted, as he added a pointed finger and aimed it at Gus, for emphasis. "Get your scary ass over here."

"Sarge," Frank Sackett interceded, "I'll go."

The jumpmaster turned his head quickly from where he heard the disruption, and let Sackett know with a glare that he would suffer no interference kindly. Assured his message was received, the sergeant returned his attention to Gus. "Let's go," he said to Gus, "let's get locked up!"

Gus slipped the anchor line past the carabineer gate, and with shaky knees, laid down on the cold, unforgiving, hard ground. Then he did something that took everyone by surprise. He didn't wait for jump instructions, but followed only what he intermittently observed when Joe did his rappel. His sudden action didn't take into account the safety issues of rope fraying, etc. Things had occurred so quickly that Gus saw in a split second his left hand was about to be caught under the anchor line. He instinctively released his grip and because of that Gus didn't clear the bridge. He was hanging upside down. It had happened. His worst fear of the day coming to fruition. Now that he had put himself in this precarious position of being inverted, looking down at what seemed to him would result in a topsy-turvy, untimely and certain death—all he could do was scream—his brake hand firmly locked against his butt and the anchor line and his left glove gouging into privates. Above him he could see the black silhouettes of his concerned company, and he didn't want to think about looking down. He just concentrated on the bridge, and where safety lay.

Joe recognized the scream bouncing off the gorge's walls to be his little brother's, but he had no idea what situation Gus was actually in. There was too much distance between them. And the screams kept coming, too. Like a hundred forty-five pound newborn held up by the ankles. The sergeant tried to get Gus to calm down but each time he only responded with an even more piteous wail.

In between one of his laments, Gus heard a familiar voice, talking to him soothingly. "Martin, Martin—Gus, listen to me, now."

"Mr. Frank! I'm gonna die. I'm gonna die! I know it!"

"No—Gus, listen to me. You're not. You're all right. Look, you haven't gone down at all, have you? You've broken your fall by your brake hand. You just tipped over, is all."

It was true that nothing could pry Gus's fingers off from the rope system in which he was entangled. "Help me, Mr. Frank!"

Sackett got onto the ground, taking off his gloves, and stuck his shoulders out over the edge of the bridge. He could see Joe in a clearing down below, straining to see what was going on. "Gus—you're in a position that is called an Australian rappel, okay? There are guys that do this all the time, okay?"

"Yeah?"

"That's right. If you wanted to, you could go all the way down to the river just like this. But I guess, you might find that a little too unnerving."

"I don't want to do this anymore."

Sackett looked back over his left shoulder and nodded his head for assistance. Two big foot soldiers grabbed either of his legs, and still two more held them in place. Sackett pushed the upper portion of his body out over the edge, and by reaching down he could just touch the heels of Gus' boots. "Gus. I'm going to bring your feet down so they are pointing in the right direction, okay?"

"All right, but hurry. I don't know how long I can hold on like this."

"You'll be all right," Sackett assured him, knowing that Gus's muscles were frozen in place and that he wouldn't be loosening his grip. It was literally a death grip. "Okay. I'm going to slowly swing your feet down. When you start feeling the gravity take over, let your anchor arm—"

"The one by my package?"

"Yes, Gus—that one. In order for you to get in the correct position, you'll need to slightly release your brake hand a little bit—"

"No! No!"

"Gus. Once I have your feet turned, alternate the grip between the two hands to control the rappel. Here we go, now." Sackett gingerly pushed down and away from himself, against the soles of Gus's shoes and the imperiled soldier's body did a majestically slow one hundred-eighty degree pivot—ending with Gus bleating whoops of relief as he clutched the rappel line tight. Sackett was lifted back onto the bridge with a chorus of cheers.

"That was good work, soldier," the Master Sergeant commended Frank. "You got some sergeant material in you, son." Sackett didn't even look at the cadres when he got up.

Gus regained a modicum of dignity with now being right side-up and began his descent, hesitantly at first, but after inching down 30 feet or so, he allowed himself to look around and to enjoy—really enjoy the beautiful setting he was witness to. The myriad of late fall colors stretching along the river banks below him as far as he could see, visible from his left or his right, filled him with a peace. Then, almost in a drunken passion, he began shouting up directives to the next rappeller as to how to best maneuver off the bridge's expanse. Yes, he was drunk all right—drunk with relief. When he finally reached bottom, it was the only time Gus could ever remember when he'd actually been hugged by his older brother. It was an embrace like a vice.

"ON BELAY!" Gus yelled up, wrapping the master line around his waist. The two brothers grinned at each other. Then Joe hardened, "And don't you ever let yourself do something so stupid again."

CHAPTER THIRTY-THREE
Taking Requests

Jim Martin folded his pants trousers and placed them on a hanger. Standing in his white t-shirt and a pair of boxer shorts, with his black nylon stretch socks, he gave Lorraine another puzzled lock before crossing by the foot of their bed to the bedroom closet. "Don't you think it's weird for an old guy like that just showing up and making himself so at home?"

"I thought you liked Franklin?"

"Sure—he's not a bad guy." Jim closed the closet door and crawled into bed with his wife, sitting with her back propped up by pillows against the headboard and erasing an entry on her newspaper crossword puzzle. "It's just—I don't know what drives him to do all this. He comes here and has all these stories about my dad and uncle. He knew grandma—and he acts like I don't know how to handle my own kid."

"Did he mention something to you about that?"

"No, but—he's always stepping in, interceding for Brad when the boy clearly crosses the line. And they spend so much time together."

"Ah-hmm. Does that bother you?"

"What? Are you asking me if I think he's kinda—you know, lonely?"

"For what, Jimmy?"

"It's just not natural for a guy that old to always hang around a kid like that—one that's not his own."

"He spends a lot of time with you talking, Jimmy. Is that unnatural? And if he worried you so much, you shouldn't have gotten the both of you all liquored up, the other night. He fell asleep on the couch and I think it embarrassed him so much that he just wanted to make it up to us."

"I didn't even know we had that stuff in the back."

"You ain't looked, either."

"All right."

Lorraine smiled. "Do you want me to tell him to leave it alone and let you finish?"

"Naw—but I'm not responsible if he gets hurt climbing and stuff."

"He seemed to know what he was doing."

"But why?"

"Why what?"

"People don't do things for people and not expect nothing in return, Lorraine."

"It's not natural?"

Jim looked at his wife without blinking. His thoughts wanting to come out in the open. His shame over what things he could be counted on for, and what he couldn't. "Did the boy say anything to you?"

"Not about his room."

"About what then?"

Lorraine removed her glasses and set aside the newspaper on the nightstand. "He wants to meet your father, Jim."

Her husband grunted and cleared his throat, while turning on his side away from Lorraine. "Could you turn out your light if you're done with that, please?"

The room went dark as Jim requested and without any response to his wife. With ambient light from the streets still filtering through their closed bedroom blinds, Lorraine was staring at the ceiling with the same intensity that her son had in his room, before he'd fallen asleep. It was satisfying to her that Sackett made Jimmy think about Brad. Maybe it would spur thinking about other relationships, as well. She liked that. It made her feel satisfied, indeed.

But the next day for Brad came with a devastating revelation while he was in school. Everett "Bumpo" Wilkins sat in the row to the left of Brad and three seats up, at the front of the row because of his eye problems. So, when a week passed and Everett wasn't in class and it was the day before Brad usually went to stay with him after school, he became worried about being stranded.

As the class went outside for their morning recess, Brad held back and inquired to his teacher, Miss Katchmeyer, if she knew what had happened to his friend. He told her why it was vital for him to know, but all Miss Katchmeyer knew was that the family had moved. Brad felt a dual aching in his chest and stomach just then, but walked out into the open yard, wondering why he hadn't been told about anything.

It didn't take too many referrals before Brad found someone who knew what happened.

"They went to Indiana."

"Indiana? That's far, huh?"

"Yeah, but he's right near Illinois, though. My dad told me his dad got transferred to the General Motors factory there."

"Did he do something?"

"Naw—something about being able to see some special doctor there for his eyes. Next time we see him, I betcha we won't be able to even call him, Bumpo."

"They coming back?"

The boy in the school yard shrugged his shoulders and then turned to take his turn at tether ball. Brad let the news soak in for a minute, as he looked at all the places he and Everett used to occupy when they were together at breaks. His head felt like it was a helium-filled balloon, one that had gotten away from its owner. His mind floating above the situation, higher and higher, while his feet refused to move. Trying to imagine, just where his buddy could be.

He got excused from recess to make a phone call to his father, who surprisingly seemed to have some knowledge about what was going on. "I'll come by to pick you up, son. Wait for me out in front of the school."

Jim could see how dejected his son was feeling as soon as he set eyes upon him, standing at the curb. Climbing into the back seat of the car, as he usually did, Brad could see his father glancing back at him occasionally through the rear view mirror as he drove.

"We probably going to have to have you staying with the Foucault's again until we can find something else...somewhere else that you can stay until the bus comes. I think I know."

"Daddy? Do you know what happened to Bumpo?"

"Ain't nothing happened to him, son. He's fine."

"I mean, his family."

"They moved."

"I know, Dad, but do you know why?"

"No one told you, huh?"

"No, Sir."

"Everett's daddy got sent to jail, son."

"But I liked Mr. Wilkins, Daddy. He wasn't a bad man."

"He isn't."

"Then why'd he have to go to jail? Why'd his family have to move if only he was put in jail?"

"Because he's going to be there awhile, I guess. Got caught up sending some car parts from the factory to some people who rebuild stolen cars."

"Is that stealing?"

"Yes, Son. It is."

"Worse than stealing fruit pies?"

"The parts went from Michigan to Indiana, and when you send something across state boundaries that you stole, that's very serious. It's a federal crime."

"Did some bad men make him do that, Daddy?"

"Naw—he knew right from wrong. He just took his chances on not getting caught. And usually when you're doing something wrong for too long, eventually you're chances of not getting caught doing it are getting smaller and smaller."

"But what about his family? Mr. Wilkins seemed to like his family. Why would he do something—"

"Because he needed money. Quick money."

"What's that?"

"Money that you need—a lot of it...so much money that it can make you do crazy things to get it. You know Everett wasn't a very good student because of his eyes, right?"

"Yeah."

"His daddy heard he needed an operation on his eyes. Said if he didn't get it done that his boy was going to go blind. That was all he needed to know. The doctor gave him so much time to come up with the money. And he went out to get it for him."

"Is Bumpo still going to get the operation?"

Silence.

"Would you do that if I needed an operation like him?"

"Your eyes are fine, Brad."

"I know. But what if they weren't, or if I had something else broke that needed fixing bad. Would you break the law then?"

"Wrong is wrong, Brad."

"But, Dad—I just..."

"Son—to tell you the truth, I really don't even want to think about that happening. I can only imagine what he was going through."

"But why did the family move, Dad?"

"Well, they just wanted to be closer to their Dad, I guess. You'd want to come and see me if I was in jail, or in a hospital, wouldn't you?"

"Yeah," Brad cautiously replied.

"Of course, you would."

"But, Dad?"

"Yes."

"Why don't you like to go see grandpa, then?"

"Let's give it rest for now, Brad—okay?"

Brad started seeing familiar landmarks from areas near his home and began training his attention on whatever they were passing by. He wished his dad could drive him home everyday, just like this. Even if they would just simply drive without speaking to each other. It wouldn't matter.

He just gazed at the thinning plate of the back of his father's head. The unfurled ears on either side of his head, just like he had. The back of the neck, at the base of the skull. That was like his dad, too. Brad wondered if his grandfather had given him these, as well. His mother said, "You can't get what you don't ask for." He wasn't surprised his dad had shut him down.

"Sometimes you don't get it," the boy surmised to himself, "even if you do. Guess sometimes, you just get what you get."

CHAPTER THIRTY-FOUR
Keeping Things in Their Place

For the next four days that followed the rappelling incident at the bridge the cadres kept pressure on the newly acquired Black soldiers. When it wasn't some arduous routine, it was some other energy sapping ordeal; field tracer firing drills, obstacle courses, practicing building clearances and assaulting various structures and encampments. The men were kept up late into the night and then allowed only so much sleep before it all started all over again the next day. The reinforcements got the message...they should have lapped up all the niceties they had had upon first arriving. Because from here on out, no day was going to be spent picnicking. And then as quickly as they had begun, the torture put upon the men stopped.

After their seventh day in camp, the real surprise for the Blackbirds came with mail call, late in the afternoon. The men were given off-base passes for the first time and many deemed it the reciprocation for the trauma they'd been experiencing. All the conditioning the soldiers found themselves being subjected to now started to make them feel mostly that if they showed they would be willing to walk through hell's gate—there would be some reward waiting for them if they made it back. Then there was those men, like Joe, and even Sackett surprisingly, who knew intuitively that the time was fast approaching when that faith would be tested. A time when they'd all be expected to make that fiery march through a gauntlet of fountains of spewing lava and sulfuric, brimstone pillars, without asking promise or question. Notwithstanding the fact that they surely would one day almost certainly face such annihilation, the

333

men were quickly grabbing up the passes. As in the time of the Romans on the night before a gladiator spectacle—tomorrow, who knows—maybe then we all die? Therefore, they were yearning for the night to be filled with levity. Not the anticipation of any harm.

The charming facades of Bristol remained in the minds of many of the soldiers who were planning the evening. For the pious, there was St. Mary Redcliffe Parish. Its gothic spires some of the tallest in England. During the war, German Luftwaffe bombed a street near it and threw a train rail over several nearby houses and plunged it into the churchyard, standing practically straight up. And off of Queen Square, in the town of Bath, for the soldiers who came from more cultured families, ones that had been vacationing on the Continent for decades, there was the Theatre Royal. It is one of Britain's oldest theatres, one in a chain of prosceniums all over the country. This one, notoriously, was financed through Englishmen who made their money through African slave trading, slaves used mainly to harvest sugar in the Caribbean. Its 20th century competitor, the Hippodrome, had no such affiliation, but the men from Fort Custer were made aware of the dubious history of their whereabouts; they decided as a unit, to stay up the hill in Clifton and away from the smell of the quays and the stench of ancestral exploitation. Besides that, most of the tourist areas had been bombed out fairly much in Bristol, as it was.

They opted for a forage into the sleety, damp, blue-black night of Clifton, to investigate its local color, and made haste to the first place that looked warm and cheery inside. And that place happened to be called the Seven Bobbins Pub.

The coiled doorbell above the entry continued its dinning with each arrival of more of the immigrant troops into the ribald establishment. It was moderately filled, and there were already some colored soldiers that the Michigan group did not know, or recognize. None of them were being bothered, or ostracized. In fact, four of the men bellied up to the bar just as matter-of-factly as any white patron. Another two were playing a game of darts, siding up against a couple of miners. Sackett looked around and admired the setting. The pub had big, mutton windows that faced the street, where the exterior panes were underlined by vacant flower boxes. The walls were brick, covered with plaster and off the side of the bar was a marble fireplace with a roaring conflagration inside. The lighting was dim, and the ceiling was partitioned by dark wooden beams. There was a snug quaintness there.

On the other side of the bar were stair railings that descended into a lower level. In days gone by, the rooms down there had been wine cellars, but now made up a restaurant. Before any of them could make a decision as to what they were going to do, a busty, slightly overweight waitress came over to address the men. "Well, if you birds ain't a bit of the kettle calling the pot black, eh? In with you now—and might you gentlemen be caring to dine with us, this evening?"

Sackett looked around his companions and saw that everyone seemed to lose the ability to speak. It was so uncommon a thing to have happening to them, someone white offering them hospitality. "Yes," he said. "Hope you can handle us?"

"May take a bit—but we'll fix you fine. Come along, now." And they all followed her down the stairs. "You must be new, here?"

"What gave it away?" Sackett joked.

"You're all sticking together," she replied, pointing the men to a large banquet table in the dark, paneled wood, of the catacomb. Lamps on a wall nearby had cup-shaped coverings of beveled crystal. "You see, here," she continued, "we're not like across the pond, y'know. A dress perhaps, maybe lipstick—we chose those kinds of things by color. But not our friends. We are glad to have your business, indeed."

"Thank you, for a kind welcome, miss."

Gus, encouraged by the matter-of-fact sincerity of what the waitress had said, freed himself up to speak. "What do you have to eat, ma'am?"

She waited for all the men to be seated and then did a quick headcount. "Twenty-four of you—my, my. I expect you'll be wanting a bit of our ale, wouldn't you?"

"It looks like six pitchers should start things, fine."

"Would that be the *Bass*, or do you prefer *Newcastle*?"

"Newcastle, please."

Sackett motioned for her to listen more attentively, "If it's not too much of a bother—could we have our pitchers and schooners chilled, too."

"The American way—eh? You lads don't like warm ale?"

"No, ma'am," said Sackett.

"Very well, General," she replied. "Six pitchers of Newcastle with chilled pints and quarts. And now, let me tell you one thing, lads. Unfortunately, due to the lateness of your arrival we have to make do. We're all shut down for fish and chips, tonight. Not a cod left, Sir. And it's a shame too, for they rave about the Seven Bobbins all over West End, they do. But—we have other trays we can bring out for you."

"Well," Joe broke in, "whatever it is you got—just make it good, hot, and plentiful."

"Oh," the waitress eyed him with a raised eyebrow and a coy grin, "we'll be on that right away, Sir. You know your mind. I'll say that. Most insistent, aren't you?"

There was some nervous laughter at the table but the waitress broke the tension. "I don't mind, luv. I'll have you all squared away, presently. Just got to get me some help, is all."

Gus began to rise, "We can assist with carrying—"

She shook her head, "No. That's not the place for our gentlemen, at the Bobbins."

"You Brits could sure show a thing or two about how to treat a man over in the States."

"Be back presently with your drinks."

Once the waitress turned and her foot touched the landing of the bottom of the stairs, some of the southern colored men began complaining to Joe. "Man, is you crazy?"

"You saying I am?"

"What you doing talking fresh to a white woman, for?"

"I ain't hurt nothing," Joe retorted. "You all just need to relax. Besides, you heard what she said. This ain't the United States. Here, we're gentlemen."

"You sure about that, Martin?" Sackett questioned.

"Niggah, you was sitting here with the rest of us. I know what I heard."

"What did she say to us when we came in? Called us birds. Is a man a bird? No, if you really are respected you aren't made out to be something you're not. Don't you think?"

"Maybe she was trying to tell us something."

"Sackett, you crazy. All the British call people that."

"Called twenty-four of us that," a soldier who seemed to be agreeing with Sackett, "along with being as black as iron."

"What of it, then?" Joe responded defiantly. "Four and twenty blackbirds—all of us lined up to be put in a pie if we fuck up. So, here's what I suggest."

"What?" Sackett asked.

"Don't fuck up."

The table broke out with guffaws and teasing, and before Sackett could get back at him, Joe was taking the first of the sarsaparilla-colored ale pitchers from one of the three waitresses carrying them, one in each hand. Another three girls also came down the stairs with trays of chilled tankards. The waitress who had taken their order placed two of the urns down on the long table, relieving one girl who was having trouble with the heft of her order. "It's a shame you all want to waste a good stout with getting it all cold," she said. But," and she wiped her hands on her apron, "the customers always right, and here you are."

What struck the colored men then, something that was so disarmingly strange, was that the last two women on the serving team went around pouring their drinks. Black men, being served by white women. And the men were silent, admiring them; all the while this was done. Some had never been so close, before.

The men were presented with menus and didn't know what to make of the names on the bill-of-faire. The entire menu reflected the region, more Welsh than British. Regional food. But it would have to do. The men were ravenous. In the end, the waitress just begged the men to let her put together what could be gotten and she'd return with help. In twenty minutes a procession started heading towards them. At the front of the servers were two women with large, transfixing eyes. They were sisters, and very beautiful. Each carried a huge silver platter that was almost three feet long, and on them was steaming heaps of a dish known as Welsh rarebit. Usually beef was the source of the meat, which was placed upon buttered toast and slathered with a thick, cheesy mustard and beer sauce. But times being what they were, the pub had gotten down to transcending the meal and making it rabbit-rarebit.

Following the sisters, the original server brought in two large soup containers with potato soup in one and French Onion soup in the other. Other waitresses brought armloads of bowls and other place settings for the soldiers, as well. When from somewhere behind them, a white frocked chef pushed out a coaster tray laden with sliced up mutton and pork remains.

The fervor at which the men attacked their meals was astonishing to behold, yet some had become a little crude with manners by the time they'd had a third ale. Some bayoneted the rarebit off the trays and onto their plate, using field knives. But no one from their group reproached them. "What a memory to drink in," Gus thought. The whole world was topsy-turvy here.

"Will you be staying long?" a female's voice cooed.

Gus was startled. He quickly put his napkin up to his mouth to hide the large portion of food he was expeditiously downing. "Hmm?"

"I said, will you all be coming around?"

"I don't know how long we'll be here. What's your name?"

"Katherine—but you can call me, Kate. And yes, that's my sister, over there." They both hard large, pumpkin seed sized eyes, with irises that were kissed with St. Elmo's Fire. Their long eyelashes needed no modification with a make-up brush, and in fact they both appeared to be not be wearing much in the way of amplification. But they were captivating and they smelled of warm, baked bread.

"And that's my brother, other *there*."

"He seems to fancy my sister, I think."

Kate laughed and went around picking up dishes as they became emptied. Her hair was reddish brown, worn in a bun but with tendrils of wavy wisps gracing the back of her neck. Her cheeks were high and her nose Romanesque, with lips full and enticing. Gus couldn't keep his eyes off her. Even though he was inexperienced in the matters of the heart, he should have known better than to fall in love at first sight with a white woman. What could he possibly be thinking to make him do such a thing? The older sister had hair that was more toast brown, actually, and though her cheeks were as high, not as pronounced as her younger, auburn-haired sibling. Her mouth was more of a rosebud shape than the lily-like curvature of Kate's. He had to agree that if Joe had seen how he was fawning over the way Kate's sister turned her wrist inward towards him as she poured into schooner she held. Joe had some knowledge of what could be a black man's downfall. Gus didn't.

Well, he remembered, there was that one long-ago initiation that he had had into what the wiles of miscegenation could release, back in Michigan. Gus had just turned seventeen when he had his first innocent foray into what fleshly desire actually was. Joe had already moved out of the house, and Gus was waiting to see where he'd end up in the lottery when he met Gillian. She was part of a family of four kids and a mother and father from Tennessee, and they all could have been put in a box with the label 'white trash' on it and it wouldn't have mattered none to them. Being poor whites, they couldn't afford but to live amongst the blacks in the shanty. Gillian's family became the Martin's neighbors for a spell. Gus looked at Kate out of the corner of his eye as he remembered.

The girl was just budding, as young females do, and around the age of fourteen, or so, she had been caught doing some sort of sexual exploration with her brothers. Gus found that out after about three nights of staying out late in the summer—talking to Gillian. They talked about many things, but mostly what it was like to be lonely, and being out of touch with family. The yearning to be appreciated. And then they talked about what it was to touch— what it meant to the person being touched and the one doing the touching. They also talked about when touching was not good, and how to make touching feel good, so she would keep on liking Gus touching her. They kissed. Kate was much more of a woman than that. Then the next thing Gus heard was the clinking of the silverware as the place settings were being finished.

"And how long might you be staying, I asked."

"Hmm? Oh, I'm—excuse me," Gus stammered.

"Probably not for long, eh? What with it being the war." As she set Gus' drink down for him she pulled her face close to his. "You're all most certainly welcome here. Ever since the allies have come through here—you know, after the buzz bombs. It's been a lot, well…" She squeezed Gus' bicep, "The war's been good for business again."

But before Gus could think up any off-the-cuff banter to come back to the saucy bar maid with, she'd already moved on to the next soldier and giving him compliments, too. Gus let his hopes dismount the stairs to Olympus. She was just being pleasant to me, he thought. He made sure to remember, her name was Kate.

And she returned with many other wait staff once the biggest part of the tide of eating had subsided and there were several dishes that could be cleared. Everyone sitting was so full they offered no protest as the remaining portions were cleared. The matron of the waitresses gave a loud whistle by placing her forefinger and pinky in her mouth. "Listen, well—we're filling up, top of the stairs so we'll be having to open the cellar now for more of our guests. You're welcome to stay."

Most of Gus' crew took that as a clue to get their things together and the younger Martin was doing the same when he felt someone tug at his coat draped over his forearm. Startled, Gus turned and was pleasantly surprised by the strawberry-haired Katy.

"Hang back a bit, would you love?"

"Ah—eh, excuse me?"

"I'll be off the clock, now that dinner's all served. Nothing but work for the dishwashers, bar maids, and such."

"You all did a real fine job, too."

"Might you not be so generous so as to offer a hard-working girl a cold drink for the end of her day?"

"It would be—"

"My pleasure," she said, "I'm sure."

Gus was enamored. Never in his life had a woman ever presented herself to him in such a haughty, forward way. It intrigued him and beguiled him at the same time. This mystery would not play out of his subconscious until he could find out if he was simply a romantic, or actually an object of affection.

Sackett noticed from the opposite end of the room that both Gus and Joe were being propositioned by the two Welsh sisters. Gus and Kate were fully staring into each other's eyes, smiling warmly as they small-talked their way past introductions. He'd even noticed earlier that there was some energy between the two, that they were attracted to one another. And that made Sackett nervous. He couldn't help but consciously fight back a cringe each and every time her breasts drew close to the soldier's cheek when she was serving. How she practically heaved her bosom under his nose and, maybe not so innocently, took in a long and slow breath, to make her carriage all the more apparent, as she sighed slightly and poured more ale. "That was trouble," Sackett thought. The little time he'd had in jail had taught him that. Or, more to the point, it had taught him to assimilate in a response to unvirtuous white women in a socially acceptable fashion. Look, but don't touch.

That was not a concern with Joe Martin, however. In a semi-lit corner, Joe was glimpsed putting his right hand in between the pleats of the tartan wool skirt Kate's sister, Blair, was wearing as she sat on a bar stool. The impetuosity of the act seemed to thrill the older one, and she just as brazenly nuzzled against Joe's cheek and blew into his ear. And whispered something that ended in a teetering giggle.

Deciding that no good could come of the situation, Sackett retired upstairs and got involved in a few game of darts. And the two couples walked past him on their way out. And he followed, within minutes, turning towards the base where they continued walking on. Sackett would not go back.

It so happened that that first night turned into a week and more of evening trysts for the two foreign couples. But it wasn't long before Joe started bad-mouthing the Seven Bobbins, too. Though, he was the reason for his own unhappiness. Of the two Shaugnessy sisters, Blair was the least likely to take any guff from a "bloke", and she quickly tired of Joe's chronic abrasiveness. She soon found affection in the arms of another Fort Custer's Blackbirds, though. That was the term the native Brits gave the colored troops. Just like Sackett said they probably would. He stopped going out on the foraging for intimacy because of his own experiences.

Gus, however, had found his reason to come back to the Bobbin, again and again, and again. Where they had a drink together on the first night and he'd coyly escorted her to her apartment door, by the third night they'd escalated the amount they drank. Soon, standing outside, both tried to become semi-lucid by getting fresh air. But that seemed to only make their blood more embroiled with the alcohol. They just walked the lane tipsily, human lean-to's, arm in arm. But this time, Kate opened the door to her flat and held it open. Gus stood hesitantly at the raised cobble porch, not looking at her.

"Are you a vampire, or something?" she asked. "Do I have to invite you in, in order for you to cross the threshold?"

Kate's flat was a studio, two-room affair with a mauve colored, embossed wall covering, and a dark wainscot. The room smelled of heather and there were little knick-knacks of feminine accoutrements lined on top of a window ledge that made a breakfast nook because of a small two-person table and chairs, near a closed bedroom door. The only light that imbued the flat came from a grated fireplace and cast burnt orange and umber shadows, and accentuated the polish on the hardwood floor.

"Well, come on," she invited him once more. "I'll put another log on the fire and turn up the lamps, a bit. Make it a little less..."

"It's fine—" Gus said, crossing in front of Kate. "Really nice, real nice."

"Thank you, shall I take your wrap?"

Gus went over to the fireplace and removed the grill so he could put two more logs on the bank of glowing embers not far from a smart Victorian divan, careful not to tread across a white pelt spread in front of it. "Maybe I'll wait until I get the chill off for you. What kind of—what animal did that rug come from?"

Kate kneeled down beside her guest and whispered to him.

"Actually, that would be my landlord's rug and I couldn't tell you exactly where the sheep came from." And she mixed in just a trace of a mischievous smile when next saying, "I have the damndest problem with fleas, though. For some reason. Do you think that could be the source?"

Now it was Gus smiling at her as he finished with the stirring the flames of the fireplace and his heart. He was bewitched by Kate. Totally enthralled.

She brewed some tea, laced with a dash of rum in each cup, and they talked until more wood had to be thrown on the fire. Gus found out that Kate's family had moved to England, instead of America, during the potato famine. She and Blair were the fourth generation of Shaugnessy to live across the English Channel. Their forebears had joined in with others in the late 18th century, Quakers mostly, who questioned what the slave and sugar trade would bring upon the land if it continued.

And though they were against the trade of skin, her family did not have a particularly familiar relationship with any Negro, until she and Blair broke out of the mould. She and her sister had found some of the men they'd met to be quite attractive. But they had never acted on their curiosity. For one, they had heard the rumors about the men of the race having overactive libidos, and it certainly caused an undercurrent of electricity and infatuation when they would overhear conversations. Black men had a way of interweaving sexual entendre in talking, at least when with a woman, that she never saw employed by Europeans. The talk, combined with the way they carried themselves— cock sure, would be an appropriate phrase, was enticing to Kate. But she made sure to let Gus know that she could empathize with second-class citizenry feeling. "You see," she said, "My family and me, we're just as much a part of being one of the colonist trophies as your people were."

Gus wanted to press the issue but did not, for in many respects he could see where her analogy of what happened to Irish immigrants in America did compare with his ancestry. But it really wasn't even close to being the same. And he wondered if he could ever make her understand how he felt. To feel so, inalterable. So consigned to beliefs that were false. But for this short period of time he didn't want to think about the terms of color. For once, he didn't feel the need to, thankfully. And that meant not to bring up an argument for the sake of arguing.

Kate knew the moment she'd laid eyes on him at the Bobbin's cellar table that she wanted to make plans to cross paths. Had cautiously decided to begin dating him, if he'd have her, even before he'd accepted his pint. Blair was excited, as well, but she'd been trying to get Kate to do more than that. They had giggled in the pantry about how they could make comparative notes about the lovemaking. But Kate made them both promise to only fool around—not to allow any kind of mounting. Kate did not want to be a notch—she desired pursuit.

"You must slow down," she sighed. A husky titillation still in her voice as they disengaged from still another impassioned kiss. The auburn hair seemed to glow around her head as she lay on top of Gus. He rolled her over onto her back on the combed, sheep rug, and looked down upon her as she lay seemingly open to culminating desire. His bare chest as tangerine as an ember in the night's firelight. The bosom of Kate's dress horizoned at the level of her hardened nipples and after catching her breath, she reached up again.

Drawing his mouth to hers, Gus softly traced his tongue over Kate's as his upper thigh parted back the sweep of her dress, revealing sheer black hose that highlighted the flash of her inner thigh and its white exposure. Her breath came in short, little pants, blown into his mouth and then she unexpectedly ground her pelvis upwards, and then just as suddenly jerked herself out from underneath him. Overcome by her excitement and losing battle over her waning self-control.

"I'm not ready for that, just yet," she blurted as she sat up and brushed her hair back with her hand.

"I'm sorry, Kate."

"It's me who should be saying that."

"It's just that, I want to experience more with you than being—this is driving me crazy." Gus sat up.

"I know. And it's not your fault, love."

"I thought this would be going to new heights."

"It's just me," Kate apologized. "I haven't been able to understand all the ways I feel about you, yet. Sorry."

"Let's give it time. Some day, you will."

She playfully nipped Gus' lower lip and leaned him onto his back. Placing her hand on his stiff phallus, she delighted as it lunged in her palm through his pants, and without explanation unzipped the fly of Gus' military trousers and released its straining manhood. "This will have to do, for now," she whispered, lowering her head.

He felt a warm, wet, fleshy envelopment at the bulbous head of his fascinum, accompanied by gentle hefting and kneading of his testes. He felt the feathery hair along his thighs as his penis tracked into her mouth with deliberate passion. Gus tried to manipulate her mound but Kate stayed his hand from reaching. He knew now that for the moment she wanted him to just be receiving party. He happily laid back.

As Kate fellated him Gus took some solace in the manner in which the bar maid found pleasure. She rubbed her vulva against his lower thigh and knee which caused her moans to send vibrations of pleasure along the underside of his cock. And as the intensity of that moaning grew, along with it came the cessation of the pressure on Gus' leg. He looked up to see what was happening and saw Kate hips were now above his legs, one leg angled so as to allow a free hand to be placed deep within the folds of her dress. Kate kept sucking as she manipulated, with vigor, her own fleshy nub. Wet clicking.

He remembered, just before reaching a point to where he could not turn off the fount of fornication, that he'd told the hillbilly girl to work her mouth just like the way Kate was doing. She did him just as well, slathering him with her spit, but with Kate, she did not have to be told.

They retired to her room afterwards and spent the rest of the night in each other's arms. Asking for no purchase from one another, when none would be taken, as far as further intimacy, than their mutual explorations. But it was enough. In the morning, Kate was not to be found and that shocked Gus until he heard her padding back into the bedroom in her bare feet, carrying a breakfast tray with marmalade blintzes and scrambled eggs. In America, some would call what had happened a lie. Impetus for a lynching. But for Gus, Kate was bliss.

CHAPTER THIRTY-FIVE
Anger Not, the Child

Brad heard the tedious report of *Breakout*, which was the latest Atari game his sister was playing. But he didn't stop and occupy the place next to her in front of the television, even though he looked to be quite surprised by the largesse. He seemed too distracted, and it was because of the smell of paint in the air that grew stronger the closer he got to his bedroom. Something had happened, or was happening in his room that he hadn't expected.

Coming to the archway without its door, Brad saw Mr. Sackett in a garbage can liner outfit that protected his shirt and pants from paint splatter, bending over a five gallon bucket with a paint screen in it. His dress shoes were wrapped in layers of clear *Saran Wrap* that were stuck together by some duct tape, in places. Sackett ran the edge of a putty knife around and down the circumference of the nap roller on the extension pole, and its frame, not even knowing he was being watched until he stood up to stretch his aching back.

"Well, young Mr. Martin. How long you been there?"

"Wow, it's a big difference."

"Certainly should be, according to my back."

The entire ceiling of the room was a paper-white white, unblemished and eggshell opaque in color, but flat in its finished appearance. No trace of the former calamity was evident. Sackett completely eradicated it, and hopefully, now some of the boy's concepts about his self-worth. They both looked around at the sullied walls, however, and the disparity between them and the ceiling was apparent.

"Thank you, Mr. Sackett."

"You're most welcome, Brad. What's the matter?"

"The ceiling's great—"

"But you don't care too much for the rest of the room, now. Huh?"

Brad was ashamed to not seem grateful, and wanting more, "Maybe, my dad will—" And before Brad could finish his father was leaning against the door jamb.

"Will what?" Jimmy inquired.

"Your son seems to feel we need to move on to the walls. But I run out of all the paint you had in the gay-rage."

Jimmy frowned a little, hoping his son wasn't being too pesky. "Brad—you didn't..."

"It's all right, Mr. Martin. Can't say as I blame him."

"How much will you need to paint the walls?"

"I'd say four gallons would do it."

"What's the cheapest I can get?"

"White's always cheapest—in any brand. Probably run around thirty dollars to get what you'll need. Would you like that youngster? A nice, clean, white room?"

Brad didn't respond with an immediate answer and it seemed he was considering his options. "Daddy? Mr. Sackett? Would it be possible I could have some color on the walls and not just plain white?"

"It costs more to get tint put in 'em," Sackett said.

"I can't be spending that much, buddy. I wasn't expecting to have to get that, as it is."

"Getting it from a paint store?" Sackett asked.

"Yeah, they have one about five blocks from here."

"Well, what color you thinking about, Brad?"

"I want—I want a gold color."

A grin came to Sackett's face, and he offered an idea.

"Mr. Martin, if you'll allow—the paint shop should have some burnt umber and yellow tint in tubes. I can mix up any shade of gold your boy wants, if you'll get it to me."

"Will you be able to do it, tonight?" the boy asked.

"No, not directly. Take a whole another day."

"Okay," Jim agreed looking around with more interest. "I'll run down there and pick it up before they close."

"That way I can start in the morning," Sackett nodded.

Lorraine could be heard locating cooking utensils in the cabinets and Jim turned back, "You are welcome for dinner, Franklin. Lorraine's frying up a mess of chicken gizzards."

"Thank you," he nodded, and turned his attention back to the paint roller. He picked up enough *Saran Wrap* to keep his hands from getting an excess of paint on them as he disengaged the nap from the frame and placed the cylinder in a bucket of clear water. After that he sat down on the boy's bed with a loud sigh. "Whew—I am beat, today. Yessir."

"Did you used to paint, Mr. Sackett."

"More than used to. Still do."

"I mean, to have a job, did you paint?"

"Yes."

"You're awful nice, Mr. Sackett."

"Why, thank you, youngster. Thank you. Did you see the new A-tari game I brought?"

"I saw it."

"Well, go on out there and play it, then."

"I don't feel like it."

"What? Ain't that the latest thing?"

"You came back here to see my grandpa, right?"

"That was the main reason."

"And you knew him before?"

"I knew him from the Armed Services, I did."

"What was he like?"

Sackett contemplated his response for minute or two, and then surmised, "Your grandfather was one of the most unassuming men I ever met. He didn't stand up and point a finger at anyone and say they belonged in a certain group, or category. He took everyone at face value and changed his opinion based on how he was treated, individually. August Martin never said scat, about anyone. He always seemed to go by the motto that if you don't have nothing nice to say about someone..."

"Then, don't even say it," Brad finished.

"That's right."

"Does he look like my dad?"

"Not really. Favors his mother more, I think.

"You met her?"

"I thought I told you in the cemetery?"

"No, you didn't."

"We had—we made contact with one another both before and after the war. Couldn't say I really knew her, though."

"Oh."

"Have you ever seen your grandfather, Brad?"

"No, Sir."

"But you want to?"

"Yes."

"Question is, why?

"Well, you're nice," the boy said. "And if you liked him, then he must be nice, too. You just said so, so I know that must be true and he'd want to see people. Anybody—not just me."

"You know he's ill, don't you?"

"Yeah, but that doesn't mean he wouldn't want a visitor, sometime. Don't you think, Mr. Sackett?"

"From what I understand, he doesn't have any way to communicate with anybody. You could be in the same room and he wouldn't notice you—or know who you were."

"Oh."

"Brad, do you know how lucky you are?"

"Lucky? My best friend is gone forever and might be blind, soon. You bought my sister a game—"

"And I'm doing for you, too. So, don't be bitter. You thought your dad didn't care for you much, did you? But who's out there right now getting you paint for your room? I never had what you do, son."

"Momma says you go 'round looking up people you were in the war with. Like grandpa. You do this kind of thing for all the people you visit?"

"No...Takes special people to get me to do more than tip my hat at 'em and leave a package. You see, out of all the people I knew then, your grandfather and great uncle were part of a special group. And we saw things, and did things, well—if a man's lucky he only has to go through once, maybe twice. They did for me. So, this is my way of giving back to them. By showing gratitude in this way. But, no...Regular people don't get this kind of treatment."

"So, we're special?"

"That's what I said, didn't I?"

"I wish you were my grandpa."

Sackett turned his head away for several seconds. "What you want to go and say something like that, for? Your granddaddy is still your granddaddy, y'-know. Ain't a thing I can do to make me any bigger in life than what he is to you, son. But, I'll take it as a compliment. I never had the raising you did. People who cared. Family. Be thankful."

The young boy looked expectantly for Mr. Sackett to go on and say more, but the distinguished gentleman didn't even turn his head Brad's way as he kept on softly repeating that, touched by the boy's sentiment.

"Thankful...thankful."

CHAPTER THIRTY-SIX
A Letter Home

It so happened that Cleo Martin received her first letter from Gus that had a Clifton postmark on it, on a day that was seasonally inclement with wet, heavy snow cutting off most of the outlying city from easy access to Detroit's main thoroughfares. She had all she could do to walk three feet without a string of clear snot driveling down from her nostrils. She was suffering from her fourth day of having an attack of influenza that had been especially virulent, in Paradise Valley.

Iola Bumphus had told her big-headed, but good-hearted son to do a neighborly thing and pick up Cleo's mail for her when he went into town. "Hope you get to feeling better, Mrs. Martin," he said, pitying her as she wiped at her raw nose while standing at the doorway.

"Thank you, Amos," she hoarsely responded. And quickly shut her front door. He understood that Cleo was really sick and didn't feel offended by her lack of courtesy. Besides, no one really gave him much respect anyway. So, Amos didn't have a thin skin regarding his feelings. Unlike Cleopatra Martin. She turned the letter over in her hands, flipping it from front to back a few times, and brushing off the melting snowflakes against her robe. The paper started to warm by the time she got the letter open and she smiled. Smiled for the first time since she could remember, it had been so long.

When she'd gotten his first letter, while he and Joe were on the ship, Cleo had been concerned with the morose feeling the words seemed to be expressing. And there had been no return address, either. No way to convey to him what she desperately wished he could hold on to, during these times. But with the new writing—all that anxiety no longer cast a shadow over her moods. She had wanted to write him, and now she could, and that made her smile even more. Notwithstanding a low-grade fever. She began to read:

> *Dear Momma,*
> *Two weeks in Britain have been real eye-openers for me. I can't tell you all the particulars, about what I saw on the way here, but I think it's safe to say that the Army's got one hell of a surprise for that Hitler fella.*

Gus did tell her what he could about non-sensitive information about the sights and sounds of the London docking, the arrival at the base. Then it became more personal, again, rather than a laundry list of goings-on. At least, for Cleo it seemed more interesting—in a cautionary perspective, regarding military society her sons faced in Europe:

> *Mom, you wouldn't believe it till you see it with your own eyes, but there's no color line here—No Jim Crow, period! Some of the Southern colored boys just can't seem to get over it, but we saddle right up next to the whites, just as we please. The "Brits," as they liked to be called, say that we're "a bit all right". They call us from Ft. Custer, the blackbirds-—instead of "yanks". The guys like it, so I guess we're letting it stick. Joe's talking about moving over here, after the war. But, then again, it's probably just Joe talking like he do, sometimes. But I can't say that I blame him for feeling like he do. For the first time in my life I think of myself as just being me first, and not even worry that people may react to my skin. In a word, I don't feel colored, anymore. And while that's important, it's not the most important thing. I like this feeling I'm getting over here, a feeling of being treated with manly respect. Anyway, that's all I have to say about that. Oh, yeah. Momma, did you know that they got some new fangled candy that Joe and me tried out, called—get this, "white chocolate". And it's exactly what it claims to be, too. If you close your eyes you'd swear you were biting into a brown bar, but that isn't the case. Wonder how they did that?*

At this point, it was necessary for Cleo to set aside the letter in order to blow her sensitive, achy nose. She sighed again before beginning her reading. "How they getting on?" she wondered. Gus' letter continued:

Unfortunately, most of the white boys in our company say that chocolate looks like chocolate, and that people shouldn't make choco-late that looks like it really, should taste like, vanilla. They do make me laugh. They just can't stand how the British will go out of their way to make us feel welcome. And what really tears 'em up is all the mixed dating going around. Not really too much they can do about it, though.

And Cleo placed the letter in the folds of her bathrobe and rubbed her eyes. She sniffled because she didn't want to cause anymore irritation to her raw nostrils, and then dabbed underneath them. What Gus had written her took her back, back again to her humiliation in Georgia—the unseemliness of ex-posing her posterior for the white female officer. And she remembered too that all-too-knowing gaze the sergeant at the visiting desk gave her on the way out of the base. His eyes were trained on her unabashedly as she walked—eyes that she could feel ogling her from her heels to the back of her neck.

She read Gus' assumption once more and hoped he wouldn't be caught as unaware as she was. "Ain't nothing they can do about it," he said in his letter.

"Don't be so, sure, baby," she said to herself. "There is a whole lot they can do to you. A whole lot. If they did what they did to me, and I ain't in the Army—just what you think they'd do to you, and you is?"

The time was around two o'clock Central Standard Time, but in England, evening hours were being well-settled, and for the men at the Clifton base that meant another foray into the streets and trying to revive or drown out mem-ories of civilian life. "I can't tell you what to do about matters of turpitude, Captain. Nor, in all actuality, do I care to," the voice of Major Stryker railed against the office walls. "One thing I can tell you though," he continued. "I expect you to recognize that the morale of our men is first and foremost. Up-holding that is of major importance, do you understand?" The staff in the outer layer of the Bristol Camp Office did their best to busy themselves with anything that would get their minds off of the dressing down being visited upon their company chief.

"Yes, Sir," the captain apologized. "I understand that, full and well. But how would I go—"

"How in the blazes am I supposed to know? You find a wedge—some-where, and then drive that sonuvabitch home, you hear?"

"But again, Major. How do I do anything that restricts without making it seem like—?"

"Like what, Captain? I don't care what they think it seems like. They're not the point. The point is that, Good Lord, man! One of them was seen fornicating in the street one night with one of the local women." The imagery the statement made evoked unsettling sentiments that started to course through the captain's emotions. He imagined dozen of Bristol residents passing by while a colored soldier rutted on top of some girl in the town square. Not a thing that would go down lightly at home, at all. And even though this was only rumored to have happened, it began the impetus of a campaign. What had been actually witnessed was only just a very passionate kiss and some amorous groping in an out-of-the-way store front that was closed. But for the major, the foreplay connotated inevitable violation in his mind.

"I understand, Sir," the captain assured. He gave a slow and thoughtful nod before saluting, apparently having come to some sort of opinion as to how to put a fresh face on the piggish issue. "I'll get right on it."

"See that you do, Captain Bowers. See that you do."

It was some forty-five minutes later that the CO of the Blackbird Company, Second Lieutenant Ryerson, awaited the arrival of his clerk, Private Sackett, with a slight amount of intrepidation. He had sent the noncom over to the infirmary for reports, as per the captain's instructions after he passed on the dirty work for Ryerson to do. Ryerson was told in no uncertain terms that he had better have more of an awareness about the nocturnal activities of his soldiers, henceforth. And Ryerson hoped the plan would work, but he had some doubts.

The one thing about the story he'd concocted was that it needed a gullible person to buy it, and he worried because the new-found clerk, Pvt. Sackett, was skillful and adept. He needed no shadowing or second-guessing, appeared literate, but the officer just didn't know by what route he took to gain knowledge. It hadn't taken him long to know that there was something amiss in the medical reports he'd been given to deliver. And as foolhardy as it was, Sackett decided he was going to call the lieutenant on what he planned to do. He hadn't moved from in front of Ryerson's desk, all the while after he'd delivered them and they'd been inspected.

Ryerson lazily rose his eyelids to ascertain that Sackett hadn't left, "That will be all, private," he said with calm matter-of-factness.

"Begging your pardon, Sir."

"That is all, Sackett."

"Sir," Sackett insisted, "There's something amiss."

"How's that?"

"According to these reports, all the colored personnel should be on base restriction for the next three weeks."

"That's right, Sackett. And with the rates I see here, Private, *you*, meaning you colored boys, *should* be confined to base. Y'all a walking epidemic."

"Beg pardon, Sir?"

"Sackett, you're trying my patience."

"But, Sir. This is inaccurate. I took over different numbers of soldier venerals to the infirmary. Nowhere near as high as what I see here."

"Soldier," Ryerson tensed, "are you implying someone would change a government document in this camp? And if they did happen to, for what possible reason? It's just a bad run of clap, is all."

"Sir, you're our prophylaxis officer. Two white platoons just came back from a bivouac and that count is high. More like these numbers, than what we show."

Ryerson put a dense, poker face close to Sackett's, waving the reports under the subordinate's nose. "Now, you listen, and you listen well...Close that door, first." After Frank made sure to act deliberate, not in any hurry, he did as instructed and stood at attention. He knew what was coming. "Sackett? Boy, are you trying to tell me that you think—and you had better have considered this well; if you're gonna do what I think you're saying—You're telling me that these figures are a lie? Because if you are saying that, boy—and I believe you are entirely mistaken, if you are saying that you are going to raise a fuss about this. It will not be a good day, for you. Do I make myself clear?"

His shift at the Watch concluded, Sackett did not look forward to facing his companions. He slipped into the barracks, unobtrusively, for he was the person who usually carried the passes back to the soldiers. It was a Friday, early in the evening, and as per usual many of the Blackbirds were dashing about grooming themselves for what promises awaited them. Joe Martin gave him about just as disapproving a look to Sackett as the lieutenant had given, as he waited in line to shave, towards the rear of the line to access the communal basins.

By that latrine area the smell of cologne and pomade were sandwiched together in such a way so as to throw a passers-by sense of smell off-kilter. The aroma irritated Sackett, as well as did the exuberant whistling and cajoling shared between the soldiers. The uplifted spirits only dampened igniting his own and yet he was still trying to put the best light possible to the situation. In his mind.

Everyone hadn't noticed he'd arrived yet because he remained withdrawn from the enlivened enlistees, still wearing his lined trench coat and wool gloves. He snatched off the surplus hand apparel and flung them down on his bunk with great gesticulation and agitated excess. And when that didn't seem enough to garner more than a casual look, Sackett practically tore his buttons off getting out of his overcoat. They still hadn't noticed his disquietude.

"If you're all getting ready to go out to the Seven Bobbins tonight, you got another thing coming," he announced.

Some chairs could be heard scrapping on the linoleum floor, and Joe cursed softly standing at the shower area's mirror—almost cutting his ear lobe. His face was half-lathered and scowling, "What did you say?"

"We're shit-outta-luck, guys. On quarantine," Sackett matter-of-factly stated as he hung up his coat in his dark gray locker.

"QUARANTNED!" reverberated around the room's nooks and crannies, with an air of finality that made people start whispering and taking in thin breaths. But that was for about five seconds, and then a din of disappointment and curses began filling the air. Sackett had expected as much, and tried to assure everyone that he was only the messenger behind the dastardly deed, not the purveyor. Reaching for some book matches from his locker and sitting down on his bunk, Sackett rolled him a *Bugler*. He happened to be facing the main aisleway of the dorm, and he was getting a crowd gathering. Lighting the cigarette, he waited, and took three slow drags from the smoke. Hearing all sorts of scenarios, and hypothetical's as to why and what had happened. Gus, with his palm brush still in his hand, was the first to approach him.

"What they quarantining us for, Mr. Frank?" As soon as Gus said the pet name for Sackett there were obscene gesticulations and verbiage thrown at the younger Martin's way. By now, everyone knew that Sackett had been an officer and they didn't hold too well with the acknowledgement of authority that Gus freely and continually gave him. Sackett, who since the bridge incident had taken Gus under his tutelage, didn't forbear him from using the particular idiom, anymore. He understood. He even appreciated it, somewhat.

"Our venereal count is too high," Sackett answered.

"What are they talking about," another grunt broke in, "because I know for a fact that we ain't had nobody sick in here for at least ten days." And the hubbub arose again, only this time rejuvenated with a cause that allowed for curses. Many angry confirmations, of shared misfortune bolstered the defiant incredulity within the barracks. And through it all, Sackett continued sitting and inhaling. He was bent forward, contemplatively with his elbows resting upon his lower thigh areas. Thick blue smoke billowed out from each of his nostrils as he smoked what remained of his cigarette, which he clasped between two fingers in one of the two hands supporting his chin. As the smoke wafted upwards, through the haze, Sackett took in the group of half-dressed and bewildered soldiers about him. In a strange way he actually was enjoying his control on the opinions, and that it mattered what he thought could or should be done. But he wasn't about to act. Not on their behalf.

"Well, whether you like it or not, we're locked down," he said. But he knew it wasn't valid, and he might tell them what he saw in the reports, but at the moment didn't feel as inclined.

"Did you let Lt. Ryerson know that we ain't been sick?"

"He's the one who signed the Article 67, Gus."

A pair of highly polished boots flew over the heads of the troops as an agitated soldier let loose his frustration, "Dammit—why can't they just leave us be? Why they got to always keep messing with us?"

"I don't like to be the one to say it," Sackett added, "but I told you all what would happen if you went out there and tried to get a taste of the local color."

Sackett reviving his social position had the affect of admonishment and humiliation he intended, for everyone but Joe Martin, who stepped out from behind the privy area and made his way through the crowd to Sackett, holding the still opened straight razor in his hand.

"Oh—so, it's their fault?" Joe asked.

"No one's fault, in particular, Joe. It's just the lay of the land."

"Like the 'lay of the land' was back in Michigan, Sackett? Seems like you always about keeping your thumbs on everybody's plans. Just like you did at Ft. Custer, *ain't it, suh?*"

Frank stood and turned aside while Joe glared at him, and casually flicked his finished cigarette into the butt can nailed to the end of his bunk's frame. This seemed to get Joe even more riled.

"Ain't this just like in Custer, suh? Ain't this like Custer all over again, when you could have done something for your men—but you didn't?" And Sackett didn't move a muscle as he could see Joe approaching menacingly from out of the corner of his eye.

"If you know what's good for you, you'd better get out of my face with that razor, hear?"

"Oh—don't worry 'Mr. Frank'. There was a time when it would have been worth the effort, but not now. Uh-ugh, ah, no. I wouldn't bother spilling the blood of a man who don't have enough backbone to call 'stink,' shit. Even when he can smell it. Thought nobody could get shit by you, Sackett?"

It was awkward, even backhanded, but it was Joe's own way of finally giving Sackett his due, and the former officer knew he would never hear it said any plainer or more sincerely. How incongruous, Sackett thought fleetingly, that the older Martin brother actually had given him a compliment, while yet and still waving and pointing a threatening razorblade at him.

"All right," Sackett muttered and snatched his overcoat from his locker. "Can't say it will amount to much, but I'll go over to the watch commander and see what I can do." And that had been at least an hour from when he sat down at the well worn bench area of the command office. From his viewpoint Sackett had witnessed the sun's setting, with pink and cobalt stratifications of color that deepened into starlight.

He had been sent there directly after first meeting with Lt. Ryerson, who felt ill-prepared to handle the predicament the enlistee insisted upon triggering.

"My clerk says you want a blue letter inquiry form."

"That's correct," Sackett replied, knowing that the euphemism for the Inspector General's Office complaint submission would get the lieutenant's attention. Would let him know that he meant business.

"Sackett? Where'd you learn anything about that?"

"Learned enough to know that I need one of them, Sir."

Ryerson ordered Sackett out of his office and closed the door. Frank was close enough to hear the lieutenant's voice grow emphatic a few times and then, almost as quickly as he'd been told to vacate the office, the door came open again.

"The battalion commander would have a word with you about your request, private. Walk with me."

Ryerson took the lead in the crossing to get to the far end of the camp. He saluted lower-ranked individuals with the most abbreviated of salutes. Smiled at no one. In fact, the lieutenant's complexion had grown a rosy color, spiked by emotion. When they got to the waiting area, Ryerson pointed at Sackett to sit and the company commander went inside Bowers' office. Three minutes later he walked out and looked like he could have spit nails at Sackett. "Stay there, until he calls for you, soldier." And Ryerson didn't look back as he headed out of the door, closing it forcefully. That's when he got the first of the inquisitive stares from the office staff, and he met one of their gazes.

"I'm allowed to have a smoke, while I wait?"

The clerk waited almost a half-minute before responding, as he ran his finger down a spreadsheet table before him and then stopped his trek. "You can smoke. Make sure you use the can." Sackett rolled his tobacco and had his first cigarette.

Three cigarettes later, now, after crossing and uncrossing his legs. Standing up to stretch and look at various memorandum posted on the corkboard behind him, Frank picked a small string of tobacco from off the tip of his tongue and flicked it off his finger with his thumb. And the longer he waited, the more of a mess he was sure he'd gotten himself caught up in.

And as the time dragged on, there seemed to be more and more curious looks directed his way, by way of peripheral observances. Frank's eyes oscillated from one clerk to another, trying not to be caught watching them as much as they were trying not to be caught by him. One thing Frank noticed was that he saw they were growing almost as uncomfortable as he was. No one thought to offer him a cup of coffee, or a soda pop, nothing to make his wait a little more comfortable. They just poured looks of contempt at him and Frank only had the counting of papers being shuffled to listen to as one soldier collated.

Frank now began to see that there must have been some hubris on his part that allowed him to get into such a tight spot with the command structure. "All because of that damn, Joe Martin," he thought. When he alleged Sackett of being a hypocrite, and basically an *Uncle Tom*, well, Frank then had to make the sacrifice. Though he knew he would be asking for an inquiry from the very bureau that was investigating him, he knew that of all the men in the barracks—he was the most well-equipped to address the aggrievements—the disparity of treatment. He hoped he wouldn't have to go there, and that they would not take it as a bluff.

And at this point, Frank didn't care if he somehow would be sent to a jail in Alabama because of this. The lies against his men were all the variations of lies said about black men for centuries. But now, they had tried to cover it up with phony numbers. And if he didn't say anything, regardless of what became of him, it would make it just that much easier for the next group of colored soldiers to be hoodwinked. And that certainly could not stand, not if this grand experiment the Army was doing was nothing more than a sham. How could they go back to a Jim Crow Army after this? The face of the United States Army had changed, irrevocably, into a contrast of dark and light. "With this one act," he thought, "I might be able to have accomplished more than if I'd even stayed an officer." That's what he kept repeating.

The door to the captain's office opened slowly, "Sackett, would you come in here, please?" Captain Bowers was not a happy man, at that moment. He had no taste for crow.

Frank Sackett rose to face Captain Bowers. A man who at one time was his equal in rank. But now, clearly his superior. Yet and still, by the time Frank left that building after saying what he had to say, he actually felt as if he was one step above Bowers' equal. There was no light in the sky now at the time of his departure because a new moon held reign over the heavens after the sun yielded the celestial sphere to its less glaring beam. As Sackett walked back to his barrack the gravel crunched underneath his boots like surplus packing being mashed, and it made his stride sound like he was a giant. His fellows weren't appreciating the wait, however.

Not one man lay on a bunk, or lounged around playing friendly games of cards. The air in the quarters was thick with tension from the men having expectantly readied themselves for a positive outcome from Sackett's mission. They were dressed immaculately with their coats and hats at the ready. Just waiting for the return of their reluctant advocate.

When the door swung open all eyes were on Frank as he crossed over to his bunk area. Again, he didn't say anything or look at anyone when he entered, not even Gus. There was a slight deflating affect on the hopes of the group. "Did you talk to him, Mr. Frank?" Gus cautiously inquired.

"Yeah. Yeah, I did, Gus." But it was a mixed message Sackett sent because he was pulling off his overcoat when he replied. His gloves, as well.

"Well—tell us what they said, man," Joe insisted.

Turning his back to everyone, Frank pulled out his Class A uniform and shoes. "If you all would be so kind as to let me get properly dressed. I'll buy the first round."

Outside, a pair of white G.I.s passed by when a jubilant cacophony of whoops and shouts barely could be contained within the wood framed building they crossed in front of. The loud and sudden commotion had startled them, at first, but then one knowingly tapped his friend's elbow and nodded his head in the direction of the barracks while he pursed his lips and bulged his eyes. "Niggers," his pal said, smirking, "go figure, huh?"

PART III

CHAPTER THIRTY-SEVEN
The Insurgence

The passage of the fall season brought increasing pressure to bear upon the Axis forces in Europe. The United States and its allies had been tightening a ligature around the neck of fascism in the United Kingdom, and then in France. Backed up to military walls that allowed for no escape, by December 15th the Nazis decided to quit relenting, and to turn and make a stand in order to recapture what had been lost since that summer. Their buildup of forces had been gradual over time and Hitler's high command believed that their enemy would become complacent with their accomplishments thus far. It was during that time that tactical miscalculations could happen, and with the allies underestimating the resilience of the Nazis, Hitler felt he could divide the front at its thinnest point—split it into two, and then perform a simultaneous flanking maneuver on the bifurcated forces. And yes, though the allies had gotten air control over the Luftwaffe, the Nazis still had formidable artillery. And it was these batteries of mortality that crept closer and closer to the 28th Division's front line, in a classified area in the mountains near Luxembourg.

Two, perhaps as many as four days from their position, a Panzer regiment and its accompanying tanks and heavy vehicles crawled along through the range's snowy valley. That armored division's responsibility to the Fuhrer was to be the first of three massings to create the tear that would fold in upon itself to eventually, inevitably, turn into a "bulge". German planes monitored their movement and encapsulated the strikers from harm. Resistance information still, however, made its way around to the villages enroute. And the news it spread to the countryside caused many to flee earlier, in front of the oncoming horde. One such person, a terrified French woman of approximately thirty years of age, who'd stayed in place until it was too late, held onto her only hope. To reach the 28th Division before Hitler's men.

Though she was not dressed warmly enough for the stark mountain forest terrain she encountered, she still pressed on. Her coat material was made of thin, brown cord and was much more suited for an autumn outing rather than the teeth of winter in a chilling, clandestine trek. The torn and wet hem of her dress caused her to lose speed while she high-stepped through the snowy banks. She was having difficulty in feeling her calves, let alone her feet. Her arms, equally as cold, also flailed while she hastily made her way, trying to maintain balance, and at the same time, secure the wool shawl wrapped around her diminutive shoulders.

And just when it seemed that it would almost be a comfort to just stop and allow herself to succumb to the harsh elements, she saw the mountain pass she'd been told would be there. That gave her renewed purpose because American patrols were said to pass by on the quarter hour. But her legs and body were so tired that all she could do was scream out in frustration. She pleaded intermittently for strength, then for warmth, then for food—knowing all of that could be within reach, but also that she was the only one in her family to have made it so far. It wasn't long before a jeep espied the emigrant and brought her to their fortress.

"Okay," the hatchet-faced army interrogator said to his translator, "let's have her run her story once more."

"But, sir—look. She hasn't changed her story up in three separate tellings."

"We give her breaks, don't we? And we haven't denied her any food, or rest. Have we?"

"Well, no—but..."

"But, smut—I wanna hear it again."

The detainee looked at her inquisitors with such an innocence and naivety, borne out of ignorance in communicating in their native language. She might not have known what was said, exactly, but she knew what the inflection of the voices meant, the underpinning of disagreement. The smaller man, the first lieutenant, made her nervous when he spoke. But the other officer, the one with the single gold bar, tried to look at her reassuringly. It had been four hours since a perimeter team had found her and she did look much better than when she'd first been brought in.

She was given access to a hot shower, a warm meal that she could only eat a third of because her stomach had shrunk from hunger, and a change into some dry clothes. It had made for a startling transformation in the outward carriage of the visitor but inside, her fears stripped her mind of any solace. "I'm just saying that it might go a little better for us if you show her a little more heart," the junior lieutenant advised.

"We don't have time to empathize or sympathize with the locals."

"Her husband was killed three days ago. She's got kids holed up in some farm, near Clerf. And they've been there ever since then. What more can you ask of her? She left them to come warn us."

"I know. I know. That's tough—real tough. But we have to be sure that we're acting on completely accurate information."

"Maybe we should check the story out with Major Ludlow, then," the second lieutenant suggested, "see if reconnaissance can find any cracks in the story."

"Maybe you're right. But while I'm talking things over with him you be sure and keep on running her story. And try to trip her up on it, this time. Quit lobbing the ball in."

Major Ludlow, however, already had the initial report and was relying on its information when he notified Eisenhower of the predicament. Yet, the Supreme Commander still acted as if he had the luxury of being selective as to whom he would turn to as far as resources. Approximately at the same hour, General Eisenhower paced in front of a seated General Lee, who was reading over a draft of general orders. "Well, John," Ike interrupted, "is it a go?" But General Lee would not be rushed through the reading of this particular order, no matter how many scowls were cast upon him.

"Sir," Lee began with deliberate emphasis, folding his glasses, "this is almost completely changed from what's been posted at the bases, to this point."

"We had to change a few things, John, since last month when your order first was flown."

"Why?"

Eisenhower didn't acknowledge Lee's question. "I need you to sign this as it's been revised."

"But this isn't what I'd written—or agreed upon, either. Sir, it loses all the purpose and intent that I—"

"Yes—but will you sign it, or not?" Eisenhower snapped.

"If you are putting it that way, Sir-—I'd rather not."

Eisenhower's lips curled inward over the top of his upper teeth, momentarily. Scarcely concealing his being perturbed. He then turned the order around on the desk upon which Lee had been seated, and with a demonstrative flourish, signed his own name to the paper. "John—you're making a big fuss, over nothing." But Eisenhower could not look his subordinate in the face as the man stood and straightened his uniform before reaching for his hat.

"If that's all there is, Sir. Then I'll take my leave." And Eisenhower could tell that Lee had been stung by his last harangue, for he'd turned his back to him. That made Ike feel a good measure of regret because it had been a most undiplomatic way to handle the situation, and he was chosen to lead the expeditionary forces because he had such skills. But this had been handled poorly, all around, he thought.

"John—I want—I want you to know..." And General Lee remained in his impassive stance. His visage a stone-faced countenance that would be reticent to any form of patronization. "Never mind," Eisenhower recanted.

General Lee spun around on his heels and squared his shoulders to the door exiting the state room, just as Bedell Smith happened to enter when Lee left. "General Lee?" Eisenhower called, but the wound had been so inflamed by the abrasive tone of his former declaration that it seemed no entreaty given to him would cause him to do an about face; Eisenhower didn't press.

As Lee passed Bedell Smith he exhaled and turned to face his superiors, "Sir?" he responded.

"They'll make their mark before the war is over. Your people will. Just be patient, John. You'll see."

General Smith felt that when General Lee turned, it seemed he had a bit of a smirk on his face as he looked at the other generals in the room, but it was in reality just a minimalist grin. No trace of anger.

"Of that, I'm all too sure, gentlemen," Lee assured them. "Perhaps your mother feels that way at this very moment, Dwight?" And with that, Lee placed his hat on his head, saluted, and exited.

"How did he take it, Ike?' Bedell asked, noticing how ashen the commander was.

"He'll get over it, Bedell."

"My question is what we're going to do about all the men in the field?"

"At present, I don't think there can be enough to really be of any consequence to anyone, is there?"

"I hope not."

"Can't we recall most of those we already sent? Get them mustered into a colored division?"

"I think it would be hindsighted to do that now, Ike."

"What do you mean?"

"We've had them out there for over a month, and not just some insignificant few, either. The First and Second Armies have several hundred colored troops scattered all along the front."

"Oh—I see."

"What are we going to do?"

"Looks like we got to clean it up, don't we?"

"But how?"

"First of all, make damn sure that there aren't any more of them embedded with white infantry."

"That goes without saying, but again—what do we do about the men out there, now?"

"You can clean it up, can't you, Bedell?"

"I'll take care of it, Sir. No one will even know they were here."

Back at the 28th Division Headquarters an eagerly awaited for coded message made its way to the Operations Center's communication room and it confirmed what the French refugee had stated during her interrogation.

General Cota, who had played such a large part in getting infantry to this part of the front since the invasion, could only suck in his breath. The captain at the radio headset looked up and saw the exasperation on the general's face. His lower lip formed an anticline above his chin's divot.

"What should I reply, Sir?"

Cota placed a patient and assuring hand on the captain's shoulder. "Tell Third Army we appreciate the information and that we understand about their inability to perform strikes at this time."

Then Major Ludlow came into the room. "General, I need a word with you—alone."

"Take care of that in the other room for me, Captain. Would you?"

"Yes, Sir." The captain closed the door to the staff room on his way out as Ludlow motioned Cota over to tactical maps. There Ludlow used his index finger to show where the Nazi columns were.

"That goddam Quesada," General Cota muttered. "Who the hell does he think he is telling Patton that he has an entire Air Corps to look out for his artillery units?"

"One thing we got going for us, Sir," Ludlow mentioned, "is that the Krauts ain't moving all that fast."

"But that doesn't mean that they're going to stop short of us, Major."

"Can't say you're not right about that."

"But I wish I wasn't."

Ludlow turned away from the strategy board. "What do you think about that woman, Sir? One brave little package of nerves, isn't she?"

General Cota stopped penciling in some notes on a set of documents and looked at Ludlow and then back to his task before saying, "Yes, but to tell you the truth. I don't know if I totally buy what she's saying, Major. It just seems all a little too convenient. All a little too easy—finding her where we did, and when. Just showed up—from out of nowhere. Right behind our line."

"Thank God, she did."

"Yes, Major Ludlow. I know it's confirmed, and Quesada may be a hot dog commander but he's not a liar. And you know he would have stayed to take a whack at jerries—even with their ground-to-air, unless..."

"Unless what, Sir?"

"Unless the whole front's being moved."

"You don't believe..."

"As a matter of fact, I do believe that."

"What do you want to do?"

"We need some more recon, on the ground. Charlie Company was at what position?"

"Sixty-five clicks out, to the east."

"And they were drawing fire?"

"Last we heard."

"See if they've given ground any and at the same time post an alert. We'll have to hold these ridges our damn selves until we can get some help."

"We don't have men enough to hold the ridges."

"Notify communications we have to have troops or we will evacuate."

"They'll probably have to come from England." Ludlow picked up a clipboard of rosters and said, "We have a couple of field troops combat ready, Sir. The 66th Infantry."

"Out of Bristol?"

"Yes."

"Very good, Major. Tell them we needed them here about this time, yesterday."

"Right away, Sir."

At Camp Bristol a beefsteak white sergeant peeked his head into the Blackbird barracks entry way. Only the shaft of light from him opening the door cut through the blackness of the midnight hour. "All right, you monkey shining maggots!" began his ear splitting tirade, "Assholes and elbows, on the double! The 66th's moving."

"Sarge," one sleepy soldier croaked, "you gonna drill us to death." They had just come back to camp from a two day training exercise earlier, and had been thankful for an early retirement that evening. The men certainly weren't expecting this, however.

"This is no drill, soldier! This is 'Praise the Lord and Pass the Fuckin' Ammunition'. Now, let's go! You got seven minutes to fall out or I'll have all you 'Swinging Richards' nuts in my backpack! Ya pieces of shit. Do you hear me?"

The Blackbirds hated getting up to such a greeting but they weren't offended because this sergeant spoke offensively to all troops, colored and white. And he meant seven minutes to perform the three s's; shit, shower, and shave before needing to fall out in combat ready gear. Woe to the troop who missed being on point when time was up, but the fear of tardiness or punishment was not the great motivator in these early morning hours. The men quickly rubbed the sleep refuse from their eyes and realized that they were actually going to war, and there began a scurrying blaze of activity that exploded in all quarters of the barracks. Except for the Martin brothers and a few others.

"Sackett?" the sergeant yelled for his platoon leader. The command thought he would be a good ambassador between the Negro soldiers and those in charge after the quarantine incident. And so he was delegated the role.

"Yeah, Sarge."

"Where is everybody?"

"It ain't but one o'clock, Sarge. Some of us might be at the Seven Bobbins, yet."

"You're almost ready, ain't ya? Get down there and tell our boys we will be expecting them in the square, directly."

Between Sackett, and a few others, word got down to the restaurants and bars that the soldiers had been activated. But one person he didn't see was Gus, though Sackett had a good idea where to find him. While transport trucks were being assembled in the square, Sackett went down the lane for several blocks and knocked on the front door of Katy Shaugnessy's apartment.

Gus and she both came to the front door to answer the hard knocks which awakened them. Gus was buttoning his pants and had no shirt on, while Katy wore a night gown that was sheer enough to let one know she wore no underclothing.

"Sorry to interrupt—to bother, but we got to leave now."

"Where?"

"We got marching orders."

Katy took a step backwards, in shock. "This is oh, so sudden," she said.

"Get my things out from the bedroom, Kathy, please."

"They got trucks arriving," Sackett advised, "and they expect everyone there by 0300." Gus nodded, grabbed his utility shirt and closed the door when Sackett departed. Katy dressed too, while Gus hurriedly finished, but she would take considerably more time than he had to give her. Gus told her this as he trotted over to her room to check on her progress.

"Go on, and I'll meet you there," she insisted.

When Gus arrived at the departure area there was a deal of activity going on with the loading of equipment and baggage. He found out that his gear had been unceremoniously dumped into his duffel bag and thrown on to one of the deuces. The next thing he wanted to reassure himself about was the whereabouts of Joe, and he showed up in the company of a Seven Bobbins escort, not related to either Shaughnessy sister.

The mustering out of the troops was typically lessons of expeditious preparedness combined with prudent caution, or in other words "hurrying up, and waiting". When Katy finally got to the Bobbin and reunited with Gus, he secreted her away to a darkened recess of a door, nearby. Though much activity transpired about them and they seemed to go unnoticed, both Gus and Katy knew it wasn't acceptable for them to be public in their displays of affection. Katy wrapped her arms around Gus' waist and rested her right ear against his chest, hearing a strangely calm heart.

"Put your arms around me, Gus. Put them around me and don't let me go. Oh, Gus. Oh, my brave little soldier boy."

"What you crying for, Katy? You knew it would have to happen."

"I just thought we'd have more time. My mind's all awhirl about you. Dear, sweet August. I don't know when I'll ever be able to think clearly again. And when reason does finally bring me to my senses where will you be? I'll have lost you. I should have let you had your way."

"No. That wouldn't have been right. You can't risk having a kid by me. Or the possibility of having to raise it by yourself. You were right to hold off. I shouldn't have pressured you so much."

"Did I give you what you needed, though?"

"Katy," Gus whispered, choking back his own emotion, "as long as you draw breath and you think good thoughts of me, I'll never be far from you. And as long as I live, I'll never forget being with you. All the good times and tender things you'd do...I think you're the first woman—besides my mother, of course, that I've ever wanted to say 'I love you' to. And I do, Katherine. I do love you. The way we did it, made it a pure love. Not just about our bodies. I guess we're what you might call..."

"Soul mates?"

"Yeah—soul mates."

Katy sobbed audibly, now. A stifled wail.

"Oh, Gus."

Their combined passions for one another then welled up and over the dam of forbearance they'd had. Their tongues and lips did the things that mouths do to cause couples to grope at one another. And the muffled sigh from Katy caused Gus to grind himself against her dress folds. Grinding that soon led to thrusting of pelvises. It was growing so impassioned that the two were almost in danger of actually consummating their affinity right then, and there.

But, an indelicately loud and strong gastrointestinal protest from Gus' stomach distracted the lovemaking and caused both to laugh at the other's reaction. "Aren't you the romantic one, love?" Katy joked, drying her eyes.

"Guess my gut and my heart aren't on the same schedule."

"Oh!"

"What's the matter?"

"I just remembered. I brought you something."

"What is it?"

"Oh, a momento. That's what I'd call it."

She had Gus close his eyes. "You're not gonna hit me, are you?"

"Don't be a silly," Katy chided as she reached into her coat pocket. She placed three objects in his outstretched hands. He felt that they were wrapped in paper, and thick, but it was the smell that gave away what everything was.

"Mmmm...Now I think I know." Gus opened his eyes and hefted the bars of white chocolate like they were precious metal. "I'll be sure and save these for later." He put the candy in a supply pocket of his fatigue uniform and gave Katy a quick hug and a peck on her lips. "Thank you," Gus said.

"Don't eat them all at once, either. You'll get a tummy ache if you do."

The trucks' engines blasted out diesel fumes as they fired up and drew both of their attention to the square.

"And you'll write me, too?" she asked.

Gus saluted her and smiled, "Noted, and will obey, Ma'am." From the corner of his eye Gus could pick out Joe looking into the rear of each truck. "I'll be right there, Joe," he yelled.

"Come on with it, already."

Gus hurried through one final embrace and then ran towards the trucks that were actually beginning to move. The last thing Katherine Shaughnessy saw of him would be played over in her mind many times. And that was the sight of two of Gus' mates dragging him up by the seat of his pants into the back of rolling deuce-and-a-half, and then Gus unabashedly turning back to wave farewell to her. He was going to war in a vessel that was heroic—a body not sullied by the satisfaction of human desire, but one satisfied to make the most of whatever journey it would undergo.

The close quarters of the trucks and their canvassed cargo space provided an effective buffer from the cold. Cadre informed the groups on the vehicles that they were rendezvousing with planes at an air strip a few hours away. Everyone on the trucks then knew how exactly they were going to be deployed. They weren't going to be making a beach landing, and they weren't going to be driven to the front.

"Parachuting ain't so bad," Gus said.

"I don't know," a nervous soldier replied. "I hear that if your chute gets caught up in the trees when you land, the Nazis will put a plug into you, right where you're hanging from."

"Oh, I don't think we'll have to worry about that, none."

"Says who?" Joe asked Gus.

"They'll probably have some *Mustangs* laying down cover fire for us. Won't they, Mr. Frank?"

"They'd better."

The raising of an issue of reasonable doubt was all that was needed to place a pall of quiet contemplations throughout the assembled crew. Even Sackett's thoughts momentarily resigned to a morose imagining of what such demise would be, and the agony of it. What the odds were of such a thing, but that was before they'd boarded the plane that would take them over their destination.

There were no Mustang escorts for their mission, in fact, there wasn't an American plane involved at all. The Blackbirds were placed upon a Royal Air Force (RAF) Lancaster and it would be preceded in the air by three British *Spitfires*. The men boarded, strapped on their parachutes and clipped their carabineers to the guy wire over their heads and then sat down on the jump benches. Approximately fifteen minutes after they'd departed a lieutenant came back to the payload area and addressed the occupants.

"Now that we're near the drop," he began, "I can inform you of our mission. That being, we're going to be the second Luxembourg. There are Nazis encroaching on a mountain ridge approximately thirty clicks from a Division Headquarters." The plane's guts resounded with roars of adrenaline and testosterone. The lieutenant appreciated the valor, but he was wary of his soldiers' following through on their intent. He let the noise abate and then continued, "We are going to drop back of the line, there. We've got a hill we need to support. If we don't hold that ridge, gentlemen, it'll only take a day, at most, for the jerries to reach that HQ. That is unacceptable, do I make myself clear?

"SIR, YES SIR!!!" they said in unison.

"Alright, smoke 'em if you got 'em. We'll be there, soon." Unspoken to the men was the officer's plea for God to help them reach the ground safely.

Meanwhile, back at the division headquarters, General Cota received the first message that troops were coming his way. He could feel his chest relaxing and being able to take in full breaths again. For awhile his anxiety levels were almost enough to put him down with a mild tranquilizer. But Major Ludlow notifying him that they would have reinforcements changed Cota's general disposition. That is, until General Cota had a coda of information added to Ludlow's first one.

"They are what, Major?"

"Colored men, Sir. I don't know how it happened but they're sending us Negro troops. Communications must have misinterpreted our request."

"That they mistook infantry reinforcement for logistical support, Major? Not hardly. It smells of something Quesada would put together."

"I got a confirmation."

"You mean to tell me that was all we had there?"

"Apparently, Sir."

"Have they been...?"

"Dropping them in now, as we speak."

"Good Holy Moses—Ludlow. I'm telling you right now. They better be able to pass muster out there and fight their asses off. If not, we'll stack 'em up in front of us to use as concealment while we sneak out the back door."

"General?"

"You know I don't mean that. But I truly believe our chances of survival just depreciated, considerably." And General Cota's sentiments were widely felt among the members of the 66th Regiment, who were now stowing away their used parachutes.

They and the Blackbirds saw the tracer rounds coming at them from the ground as they flung themselves out of the plane's bay. Intermittent, red, strafing bursts of oscillating lights coming up towards them heightened their fears much more than what Cota had been experiencing. They all landed in a meadow on the hill, behind a grove of trees, midway from the base of the mound, which adjoined to higher foothills and then eventually mountain passes. Allies were at the base of the rising, and now the 66th awaited word from who was coming down from the topside.

As the men were setting up some intermediary shelters and getting radio communications erected, a captain, stained with dirt and sweat, approached the newcomers along with a retinue of what was left of his soldiers. They'd obviously been involved in the battle to maintain security of the ridge, but they were not conventional. The soldiers, like the integrated 66th, were made up of white and black men.

They trudged along into the new camp, carrying some men on stretchers, and others needing help from two other soldiers in order to walk. They were in two columns and they did not talk to any of the 66th's members as they entered the area. No looks to their right or left—just grimy and dazed looks.

The captain inquired as to where he could find the commanding officer and a grunt pointed out Lt. Ryerson who was running from one platoon to another. The captain cut across and field and confronted Ryerson. "Hellzapoppin', Lieu. We need you to get a platoon, or two, up on that hill, there. And I mean ASAP."

Lt. Ryerson looked at what was behind the captain, and then turned to either side, looking at his men setting camp. "I can appreciate your desire,

Sir. But with all due respect, we're not really ready to be going anywhere, at the moment.

A few of the wounded soldiers, passing by Joe, Gus, and some of the others in the Blackbirds group, for a moment looked them straight in the eyes as they headed towards medics. What the Blackbirds saw in that instant were the eyes of men who had seen the inside of a lion's maw and somehow lived to tell about the appetite of the beast. They looked to be just this side of maintaining sanity.

Joe turned to speak to the men around him. "It must be a suicide job," he said. "I heard one of them say that the ridge is just covered with the bodies of our guys." About thirty yards from Joe and Gus, the captain pulled Ryerson out of earshot of any of his men.

"What the hell do you mean, you're not ready?"

"Sir, if we make a move at night with these men, we can't be sure they'll stay in position. Without such assurance, holding a perimeter will in all likelihood probably fail."

"I had 'em up there in my company. Probably as many as you got, and didn't run into that problem."

"Sir, I've been training these men for 3 months. Believe me, I don't like to have to say it, but I truly dread how many men would just slip away from their positions. And furthermore, although you have rank, my orders say that we are to stay put until the 28th HQ gives me my instructions."

"And I say you're underestimating your men, Lieutenant."

"Before this...Captain, had you ever commanded Negro troops?"

"I'm not about to put up with your crap, son. I've been holding that ridge for the last day-and-a-half. And when I saw the first backup coming up there I didn't worry whether the fingers laying down cover fire were white or black. Just as long as they were shooting the goddam gun!"

Ryerson could see he wasn't going to get the captain to change his mind, so he relented. "Sir—if you can get those boys to go up with you on that hill, you're a better officer than I am. You're welcome to have them."

"You can damn bet I'll take 'em up there. Let me show you how it's done, son." Intent on accomplishing his prerogative, the grizzled captain turned his heels on the lieutenant's position and made his way for the nearest black troops. And that happened to be Joe Martin and Frank Sackett being locked up in another one of their squabbles.

"And I say you're out of your mind, Sackett," Joe argued. "Tell me what sense does it make to scale a hill and try to hold it, when another company has just been run off of it?"

"That's the hand we've been dealt, Martin."

Joe gave Sackett another of his infamous looks of contempt. A look that did nothing to hide the animosity he held. "Well, *Mr. Frank*, I guess if we keep throwing enough men at them that they'll run out of ammunition. Is that called a plan? You make me sick."

"Okay...you boys. You boys over there," the captain yelled. "Get your buddies together because we're heading up to the ridge, understand?"

Joe, Gus, and Sackett all three looked at one another and then at the fast approaching captain. "Yeah, that's right. I'm talking to you three. Let's go."

"Sir, with all due respect, we'd like to know a little bit more about what it is you're proposing that we get into."

"I ain't got time to brief you, son. All you need to know is that I want your ass in line and ready to move out."

"But, Sir...we've barely had time to get our bearings or the lay of the land, yet you want us to engage with an enemy we know nothing about."

"I'm not gonna beg you guys. There are no Germans on that hill because we fought 'em off of it. But there damn well will be some if we don't get more men back up there to finish securing it."

The Blackbirds didn't move, confounding and angering the captain at the same time. "What's the matter with you men? And I use the term loosely if you have such reservations. It's just a matter of digging in up there. Shucks, I'll go back up there with ya."

"Shii-it," Joe hissed.

With that, the captain's patience had run its course, and been pushed to limits he'd never considered before. He drew his .45 and cocked the hammer, pointing it at Joe's face. But Joe didn't flinch, blink, or show any sign that he was afraid. "Let me tell you something, boy," the captain fumed. "If I ever hear anything close to that come out your mouth, again— directed to me or any other officer—I'll put a slug in your damn eye. You got me? I guarantee that, son."

Joe's eyes were becoming small slits of flesh with onyx pupils, and he balled up his fists. Lt. Ryerson, astounded by what he saw transpiring, ran over and placed a restraining hand lightly on the captain's extended arm, still at a ninety degree angle that pointed at Joe. "Sir!" Ryerson yelled. "What the hell do you think you're doing?"

Everyone was in a frozen stasis. Joe and the captain's stared one another down, refusing to blink, but eventually the captain pulled back the hammer just a little further and then let it slowly ride forward. "Lieutenant," the captain said, "I suggest you remove your hand." Ryerson dropped his arm away from the captain's but he stayed grounded to his spot. "Now, to make myself perfectly clear. I will shoot him, Lieutenant, and then you, if you ever touch me again. Do you understand me, Lieutenant?"

"Yes—Sir."

The captain turned his attention back to Joe. "Now, do you plan to follow orders, or not?"

"Let it go, Sir." Lt. Ryerson pleaded.

"Lieutenant? Lieutenant?" A runner started to run up on the situation but then saw the gravity of the predicament, and held his distance to make a report. "Lt. Ryerson—28th Division requests our men to pull back to their position."

"We are not to engage?"

"No, Sir."

Ryerson now insisted, "Let it go, Captain. Headquarters is expecting us." With some twitching of his upper lip, the judging officer lowered his automatic, which allowed Joe's lungs to fill, and Gus and Sackett could finally do the same.

Back at the front's division headquarters, where Joe's life-saving directive had been issued from, General Cota came to the doorway of the cafeteria and caught the eye line of Major Ludlow, who was dunking a cake donut in a black cup of coffee. Cota jerked his head indicating he desired a private audience. Ludlow finished the last bite of his donut and joined the general out in the hallway. "I'm afraid it's bad," Cota said. Just got confirmation that strong reinforcements won't be able to get here for another thirty hours. Be careful to not let on to the others about the direness of the situation, Major."

"The front's folding."

"We have to start making contingencies."

"Well, I can sure put that together, but if we pull out completely from here, say falling back to Wiltz, we're not allowing any place for our side to regroup."

"On the contrary, Ludlow. We'll have the troops provide our flank as they retreat. If we leave a skeleton force here, say about two companies, we then should be able to maintain this base. At least, until help arrives."

"And what of the Wiltz camp?"

"We can send out fingers of platoons from there and they can relieve men as needed."

Ludlow drank the rest of his cup of coffee. "Just give me the word, Sir."

"The word is given, Major." The general felt some reflux attack his esophagus, just then. And Ludlow could see Cota was in some sort of discomfort before leaving. "We're gonna set the line, right now."

CHAPTER THIRTY-EIGHT
On Point

In the crystal crisp dawn of the French countryside, the early morning's filter of diffused sunlight placed soft colors over the snow-draped farm structures the troops approached. Its ever-evolving detail created a semblance to pictures found on calendars, or postcards. Be it abandoned carts, or a retired tractor—they all were ensconced in shadows of soft, royal-blue. Covered hay stacks looked like scores of large, white goose-feathered pillows. It truly could have made one forget there was a war in process.

For some reason, Joe could not stop imagining himself being back home, out for a day of sledding. But even though the reality of his frozen feet and hands were just as painful as they would have been back in Michigan—his memory of his winters stateside seemed much milder to him. It had taken the platoon the whole night to make it to the valley floor, from the mountain, and cold weather plays with one's head if left open to exposure for too long.

The platoon consisted of him, a white infantry soldier who said his name was 'McPhee', his brother, Sackett, and a fourth colored soldier who liked to call himself, Brillo. This was the rag-tag reconnaissance unit which trudged their way through the linear trough of the valley. Drummed up because of the insubordination incident.

Joe led the way, followed by McPhee, who had his forearms wrapped over the crossbar his rifle made upon his knotted shoulders. Gus and Sackett were paired up and walking together, and Brillo, just a few steps behind them. Spotting something that could actually be called a road; Joe pointed at it and then couldn't stop giggling. "Hey, Martin," McPhee asked, "got a wild hair up your ass?" When Joe didn't answer, but instead began to shriek with laughter—louder and louder, Gus picked up his pace and ran up to where his brother's position was. He walked quietly alongside of him for awhile, trying not to directly turn and look at his seemingly crazed older brother. Just a wary glance from the corner of his eye.

"Joe? What's got into you, man?" And Gus wondered if Joe had even heard the concern raised, for his behalf. But he had at least stopped his mirthful shriek, now. Gus was wary. Intermittent chuckles could still be heard coming from him as he continued to lunge through the knee-deep snow that lay between the platoon and the road. A fear arose from Gus that his brother may indeed have gone mad, to some degree. Gus extended out his left hand towards him, and gently touched his brother's right sleeve. That stopped them both.

"Joe?"

With one glance at his bewildered younger brother, the Joe's seemingly private joke affected him again. But in an even more profound way. Howls of hilarity now bent him from the waist, and eventually caused him to have to wrap his arms around his lower ribs. He laughed so hard that his stomach muscles ached, as well. Then, still in throes of laughter, he just dropped to the ground and began to roll back and forth in the snow. Eventually, this irreverent folly left him deposited by the edge of the road's bank. And everyone circled around to watch Joe's lunacy run its course; or, if it didn't, figure out how to be inconspicuous with such a crazed man.

Joe's index finger pointed up at Gus, "Do you know what you looked like?" he asked haltingly between gasps for air that occluded the area of his mouth with miniature white clouds of exhalations. "Just like you did when that crazy ass captain put that automatic in my face." Then quite unexpectedly, Joe popped to his feet like a wrestler coming off the floor of a mat. In a crouch, he leaned closer to Gus and turned his expression into a caricature. Eyes that bulged, lips distended and relaxed, the silly look was amusing to everyone, including Sackett.

Gus didn't laugh, though—at first. Not until Joe added a comical grunt and an exaggerated, double-take glance. And then they all really cracked up, as Joe got under Gus' nose to do it again. And as suddenly as the whole thing had begun, Joe straightened himself and hugged Gus, warmly. "Of all the times for you to grow a pair, Gus. 'Can't we get the lay-o-de-land, furst, Cap'n?'."

"Aw, hush," Gus quietly said through a chastened grin.

"Yeah. Damn sure the last time I'm gonna jump in on any of your shit, youngster. Almost got myself killed. And you just standing there..." Joe put Gus at arm's length and made the face again. More laughter.

"After climbing down that mountain, all night," Brillo said, "I'd have rather gone up the hill to have a look at how many Nazis there was."

Sackett joined in on the roast, even. "Gus? Was it your idea to run this recon mission?"

"I didn't say—"

"You didn't have to say, anything," McPhee said. "We were toast as soon as he had a look at us."

"What do you mean, 'us'?" Joe asked, seriously. And McPhee turned his head to the left, and then to the right, his left eyebrow arching as his eyes scanned his dark compatriots. The silence held for a few seconds, and then Joe began roaring laughs and pointing at McPhee. The joke did the trick, and they all laughed together. "You're alright, McPhee!" Joe consoled him. "We'll make you an honorary brother."

"Don't tell my family, though. Ma wouldn't understand."

"Neither would mine," Brillo joined in.

Sackett, who had been looking through his binoculars, waved them all to silence. "There's a farm house a couple of clicks down," he said.

"Think there are Nazis?"

"I don't think so," Sackett advised. "Because we couldn't go over the ridge, and ended up having to move south along the front. Nazi forces shouldn't be this far."

"Yeah," McPhee agreed. "I think we're close to Clerf."

"Is that a good thing?"

"Eyes and ears open," Sackett recommended. I didn't see any trucks, but that doesn't mean there won't be."

"Roger, that," McPhee agreed. And began to lead the way.

Before long, though, their naked eyes could see obscured farm structures and equipment as they drew closer. This discovery meant that the equipment had to be approached strategically, as if all were enemy cover points, and the farm buildings had to be considered barriers of concealment. That meant each hut, each pen, had to be thoroughly examined, gone over carefully, prior to the soldiers checking out the main house.

"Hey, you think we'd get lucky and find some chow?" McPhee asked. No one seemed to have heard him. So, he rooted his rifle muzzle around the unfrozen portion of a hay stack and continued with his solitary conversation. "Maybe some coffee. Man, a cup of joe would be so great, about right now."

"Hey, fellas," Brillo called, "ain't nobody been up the road to that barn. No tire tracks."

"So, we're clear on the left?" Sackett asked. Gus and Joe gave a thumbs-up. "Clear on the right?"

Brillo raised his rifle and waved it forward.

"Okay, people. Let's move on to the barn."

When Joe crossed paths with Sackett on their way to the barn he made it a point to smirk as he passed, and said, "Yassuh, Cap'n, sir. Boss said the barn, y'all." Frank Sackett made it a point not to react to the slight, but McPhee was close enough to hear the pissing contest being declared.

"Knock it off, Joe."

"What? He thinks he's still the man, Gus. The way he talkin' to everybody. Sh-i-it."

Brillo, along with Gus and Joe, just entered past the threshold of the barn and then slowly fanned out, along the walls. Outside, McPhee nodded once at Sackett and asked, "They always like that?"

"Sometimes, McPhee—I think if it wasn't for Gus...Joe Martin would probably lack any values, whatsoever."

"Certainly turns on a dime with his emotions."

"Oh, yeah. Definitely needs a safety lever on him."

Crates filled with metal scraps, and old plows pushed into empty stables took up a good portion of the barn floor. On its rough walls, stored plow horse harnesses emitted tannery sweetness into the cold air. Despite the fact they hadn't been used in decades. "It's all clear, Mr. Frank," Gus reported.

"Did he check up in the loft?" McPhee asked.

"Yes!" Joe said exasperated, tired from the meticulous search they'd done, so far.

Brillo began to ransack one crate, and McPhee shoved aside another, when unexpectedly Joe began to wave his arms several time to silence them all, and pointed at the ground in front of him. Weary calf muscles tightened, and the weight of their bulk shifted in each man, to prepare for action, as they quietly raised their rifles in the direction Joe pointed out. The quiet made it possible to hear a small squealing noise and then, directly following that, an abrupt hissing sound.

There was the possibility that it may have been cats in the vicinity, but the minor commotion did not continue in the way it would have had it been cats. Not risking anything to chance, they all approached Joe, who knelt by the crate and alerted everyone to an eighth-inch crack in the barn's planking, at the front of the box. Heads nodded, all around. Sackett, who stood at the back of the box, saw clearly that at least two-thirds of the wooden crate was raised about a sixteenth of an inch above the floor. He motioned with a raised hand to tell the men they should prepare for attack. When they pushed it, the false covering slid back easily, mechanized by a loudly complaining pulley system. But the new opening presented no Nazis within its recesses. Only the frightened gasps and sounds of young children. Softly sobbing at the men looking. McPhee shone a flashlight into the dugout hideaway to reveal three shivering, and grimy French children who aged in ranges between four and eleven years old.

He spoke to them in their language, and pleaded to them to come out of the cellar, but the oldest child's reply soon had all the soldiers vying with the children for space of their own in the cellar. Monique, who spoke with McPhee, explained Nazis had been in the area the last 3 days and that the children had been in the cellar for a week

"It sure smells like they have," Joe said.

"Smells more like two," Brillo said as he found a full kerosene lamp, and asked McPhee to make an inquiry about the whereabout of any matches. Turned out they had never used it because no matches were to be found in their stay. But that was quickly remedied by Sackett's butane lighter. The paleness of the flesh of the children, and McPhee's became more illuminated by the lamp's sepia light. The other men, Sackett, Brillo, and the Martin brothers became more enveloped by the shadows, however,-—light externally covering darkness.

"They said their mother left them here and went to warn HQ, and I guess she said she'd come back to rescue them."

"Did the mother know where she was going?"

McPhee's translation was responded to with a despondent shaking of Monique's head. "She only had a little bit of an idea from their father, who had helped a Resistance fighter. With this weather the way it is, plus her Mom's ignorance—about the war, and all. Don't look too good."

"Hey—". Something was being rustled around by Brillo. The lamp moved, playing a cinematic wash upon the skins, further increasing the pallid look in the visages of McPhee and the children, and illuminating the variations of brown in the skin of the Martin brothers, Sackett, and himself. Brillo didn't have any hue of brown to him. Black as pitch and one mean sonuvabitch, he said of himself. "Look, fellas. Food."

"What do you got there?"

The lamp fell upon a corner that revealed a small stash of fifty pound burlap bags, which were alongside some vegetable bins. "There's onions in one the boxes, too."

"They must have been living off of them, the poor things."

Monique spoke again and once she stopped, and McPhee could begin translation, she had looked for acknowledgement that she'd been heard. Her wide green eyes hardly blinked as she passed from one to the other. "She says there's food in the house, but they've been afraid to see if anything was left after the Nazis sacked the place."

"Did she say how many there were?"

"They only had one jeep, but as many as three had been here."

"Probably a company passing through."

"Dime will get you a dollar that a brigade can't be too far behind," McPhee said.

"Oh, come on. You saw the road. Ain't no traffic been through here."

"He's right, Brillo," Sackett agreed. "If they've been back more than once..."

"They'll bring others," Joe warned.

"But what if it's a squad, like us? Who say's we'll run into them? What are the odds?"

"We would probably not have the best chance of success in leaving here," Sackett said, absent-mindedly opening and snapping shut his lighter. He looked at the children. "Thirty miles to the Division HQ. That would take twelve hours, at least."

"We can move faster than that—heck."

"Yeah, Sackett," said Joe. "We covered almost that in one night."

"But we didn't have children with us, Joe," Gus added.

Brillo came from out of the corner he was rooting around in, for a moment. "And as far as I can see, we don't need to have them with us when we go." He tried to make it an aside, but his deep voice carried in the chamber.

"Are you serious?" Gus asked.

"Well, what's our mission? Do our orders say that we have to nurse maid every kid we find?"

"We can't do that, Brillo." Gus was especially shocked to hear Joe say that. "I understand why you feel like that. And in many ways, it makes a good deal of sense. But, if we left them here, and Germans did find them. Right after we hightail it out of here. That wouldn't make us any different than who we're fighting. Nazis don't value human life."

"Leave them be—right here. We can send somebody back for them when we get to the base."

"Didn't you hear what Joe just said, Brillo?" Gus interjected passionately. "Americans don't act like that."

"Well, why don't you stay here with 'em, then?"

"Ain't nobody splitting up," Joe countered.

"Alright, alright—guys!" It was McPhee. "You got the kids scared. They might not understand us, but they can sure feel the sentiments being said. Hey, Sackett. Shouldn't the company be catching up to our position, soon? Can't they take them up?"

"We don't know if they're coming or not, McPhee." Everyone contemplated the magnitude of the moment, when they realized between them that their chances of staying alive were not good. Far less, in fact. "Truth of the matter is, Mack," Sackett continued, "they very well may have taken it pretty hard. Trying to give us a chance to get to headquarters."

"So, we hold?"

"Let's see what the day brings, gentleman. Make the best of our bad situation."

They went about in silence getting the hovel into some semblance of bohemian utilitarianism. Yet, they also knew, all of the time, to be wary of any sounds heard from above.

Gus emptied the chamber pots outside, behind the barn, near the tree line, using snow and a branch to wash out the slop jars. In the hideaway, Brillo peeled potato after potato. Placing them in a clean burlap sack, between his feet. The peelings that he left on the ground helped to absorb some of the fetid stench from the air, remarkably well.

McPhee fashioned a lumpy couch pile from the empty burlap bags, stacked away. He was opposite of Brillo's position, where the voluntary KP duty continued. Positioned ideally for the privacy, he sought in order to rest. Just outside the umbra of the lamp's glow. The nodding of McPhee's head on the swivel of his neck soon ceased its pitching and yawing, and the tired infantryman commandeered an increment of the sleep he needed, a vow made to make each minute seem an hour. He slept soundly, too tired to even snore. Too tired to even have Sackett's tinkering with a miniature stove, awaken him.

Tap, tap, tap...tap, tap, tap, tap—the sound of wood being knocked on the faux crate, overhead. Joe went part way up the stairs and nudged the covering back on its track. Gus handed him an armful of wood. "It's just like you said, Mr. Frank. You can go ahead and light that paper up the flue. The pipe comes up in the woods. I don't think anyone would see it from the road."

Joe put the wood underneath the stairs, "I'll take a look and see if I notice anything. Be nice to have some heat, down here."

"Stay clear of the house, Martin."

"You just get that fire going, Sackett."

Frank rolled a sheet of faded newspaper into a solid tube and lit one end, and then placed its flame inside the stove's enclosure, towards the rear. The smoke from the paper didn't billow out into the shelter, and the flame enlarged. "Keep the paper coming," Sackett nodded at Gus. "Have the kids help." Within five minutes a criss-cross of kindling was lit and glowing. Tap, tap, tap...tap, tap, tap, tap, tap. It was Joe, returning with more wood.

"How's it going?"

"Did you see, anything?"

"Barely."

"Hey, Brillo?"

"Yeah, Sack."

"Why don't you slice up some of those onions, along with the potatoes?"

"What you got?"

"Can of cooking lard, had some leftovers in it. If anyone wants to, figure we can cut up some of our *Spam* K-rations, and mix that in with the other stuff. Might have something there. What do you think?"

"Sounds better than a sharp stick in the eye," Brillo said, slicing potatoes like apples.

"Not by much," Joe commented.

But the hot food, prepared in Sackett's helmet, and scooped into the metal coffee service mugs of his comrades, was not met with distaste by any of the children. Gus thought they actually looked like they were happy. Warm food in empty stomachs had that effect, it seemed. And that was when he remembered. Kate's gift.

Gus drew closer to the siblings and sat cross-legged, putting his pack in between them and reached into a pocket as he raised and index finger in front of the inquisitive faces of his charges. They stood up on their knees and leaned forward to see, and Gus revealed an empty hand. Then, almost simultaneously, he reached behind Monique's head with the other hand. When he sat back the hand possessed the thick, bar of colorfully wrapped white chocolate. Now, of course, the children didn't know exactly what it was the soldier had, but they had some idea that whatever it was, was special. Special, for them. Their mouths worked like small beaks, chipping away at the bone-colored blocks of confection, as they pinched them in between their grimy little fingers.

Gus scanned around the room for components to make something, some toy-of-sorts, a thing that they could play with. There was a broken straw hand-broom, with its short handle splintered near its base, and a doll's dress attached to a shattered porcelain shell. Other refuse collected were the tin can lids from the army rations, as well. All could be utilized in the project, and Gus displayed the items on a blanket, before his curious, satiated audience, and began going about his work.

An unlikely duo were posted guard at their vault's entrance, on either side of the stairs. Sackett and Joe looked down from their observation point at Gus and the children. It was only a momentary distraction to them, however, for they were as anxious about being so close in proximity to each other, as they were about the sounds in the night around the barn. It was Sackett who finally broke the silence between them. "You know," he whispered, "I always used to hate being closed in. You know—cut off. Way back from when I was a kid."

Now, Joe didn't quite know how to take the initimate sharing that his former commander offered. His feelings about Sackett always would lean towards distaste, but maybe a little conversation would better help them to pass the time. "Maybe," Joe eventually got out, "what we imagine being out there—ain't half as scary as what we are, in here."

"Why would you say that?"

"We really don't know much about each other than we do about those kids, down there. We are all mysteries, here."

"How's that?"

"Oh—you know. A wolf in sheep's clothing. That kind of thing."

Sackett looked into Joe's eyes and waited for him to blink, but he just stared right back at him. Punctuating his insinuation. Sackett wasn't about to be involved in such childish antics. "Martin, watch the way you hold that rifle. You could blow a whole through the bottom of your chin."

"Do you really think I'm that stupid?"

"It's not your intelligence I'm doubtful about. Your carelessness could be a problem, though."

"Well—" and Joe shifted his weight with a little grunt of discomfort, "You just quit worrying about me, okay. It's not your job anymore, or have you forgotten?"

Effusive giggles chimed up to the rafters of the cellar; coming from the direction of the niche that Gus and the children occupied. Their merriment, accompanied by Gus's high-pitched nursery song, underpinned the hissing hot argument embroiled in the hearts and minds of Joe and Sackett. From the bits and pieces he'd acquired on his forage, Gus had produced two dolls made out of large potatoes.

The queen was fashioned from a large, oblong potato being spiked upon the broom's handle. The broom's straw made up for the lack of a dress. And what were left of the original porcelain doll's garment became a shawl, as well as the porcelain doll's eyes, now stuck into the potato Queen's flesh. They were close in proximity, and punched into a little potato bud head. Over that, some sparse pieces of yarn, took the place of a blonde coiffure; and they were held iin place under a makeshift crown fashioned out of pieces of tin can, that Gus had carefully used by crimping the edges back, so as not to cut fingers. It tamped down the yarn hair into the potato, well.

The king was another crude attempt. His torso was a potato that was long and cucumber-shaped. Spent rifle casings were used for his arms and legs. And risking yet further personal injury, again. For the sake of the children. Gus made another crudely regal crown out of the remaining metal scrap. The children "oooh'ed" their approval and then Gus began to actually perform for them.

The figures chased one another, under the direction of his puppeteer wizardy, speaking gibberish that would translate into a reason for laughter in any language. Then the chasing became the inevitable Punch-n-Judy routine.

Sackett smiled at the antics Private Martin went through for the sake of the children's distraction. And marveled even more that it had also taken his mind off from the anxiety abounding in the hovel. He gave a glance across from him,and Joe seemed to be troubled. "Hey," he called out. "Don't you think you should be holding that kinda stuff down, over there? But the squeals of contentment continued; Joe either hadn't been heard, or made no impression on them.

Gus bobbled the queen-figure as he warbled, "*No, no, you must go away. I want, I want to be alone. I want to be alone, now. I don't love you anymore!*"

"*Alone be damned, varlet.*" Gus's king fumed. "*I shan't remove myself. Not until thou favorest me with song.*" And the laughter of the children increased for Gus's enthusiasm.

"*No, no, no,*" the queen protested, "*You shan't have a song. You, are a cur—sir!*"

"*You had better sing, my dove. Or I will make you whistle.*" And then Gus had the smaller king potato harass his queen. The children were enchanted and could not keep the level of their laughter quiet. Gus was like a pied-piper to the children, Sackett thought. That's a gift, to make children laugh when the world is falling in on itself.

"*Oh, alright—please, stop.*"

"*I'm waiting,*" said the potato king.

"*Let me catch my breath.*"

"*Shall you, whistle?*"

"Your brother's talented," Sackett said to Joe.

"Yeah—used to make-up voices for imaginary friends when he was...a kid. Getting a little noisy, Gus."

"*Sing a song of sixpence, a pocketful of rye. Four and twenty blackbirds, baked in a pie. When the pie was opened, the birds began to sing—*"

"I mean it, Gus.

"*The king was in the counting room, counting all his money. The queen was in the courtyard, eating bread and honey—*" More fighting between the royal potatoes.

"Stop it—Gus."

"*The maid was in the garden, hanging up some clothes. Along came some blackbirds and snipped off her nose.*" A machined sound of metal sliding against metal told every soldier that a round had been chambered. "I told you to knock it off, Gus!" Joe said with a voice trembled by anger.

McPhee stood. "Hey—Joe, it's just a song. Just a little song for the kids."

"Yeah," Brillo agreed. You'd think your mother never used to sing to you."

Sackett just had the trace of a smirk on his face that Joe perceived was directed toward him, and that is what caused his better judgment to lapse. He turned in the direction of Frank, and no one could hear anything after that.

As for Sackett, for him, nothing was occurring in the cellar since the shot reported so thunderously. All he could see was white light. Blinding white light, enveloping him and causing the intense pain to subside. He didn't hear the shrieking of the children, nor the scuffling made when Joe was disarmed. What he did seem to remember was the look of Joe's face as he turned to point. And that's when he knew. When he knew what Joe had festering in his agitated spirit.

Seeing him had vividly recalled where he had seen that face before. In a time, long ago, where youthful indiscretion often led to embarrassing predicaments. The lifting of the rifle muzzle towards Sackett had become a catalyst to forgotten realizations, and failings. Now, in his unconscious state, Sackett recaptured the face—its tears brimmed Joe's eyelids like clear oil, and he was all of fifteen again. A shocked and dismayed boy who had pointed a double-barrel shotgun at him. When Sackett was only nine years older than the boy, and had no idea he even existed.

It had been in Detroit, when he met Joe and Gus's mother. Not too long a time, actually, from when he had made his derring run to the North to escape criminal justice in Alabama.

He hadn't quite gotten into a place, yet. And was feeling anxious to get out of his aunt's cramped quarters, where he felt he'd overstayed his welcome. She was always asked him so many questions about Scottsboro, which didn't make Frank any more at ease. They wanted to know if he'd actually done what had been reported by so many newspapers. Did he have sex with the white girls? But what Frank had encountered on the Scottsboro train was outside of his personal experience. Because for his part, he had been a virgin up until that time. He'd innocently been taught how to kiss a girl on the lips from a benevolent second cousin. But what he had seen transpire on the train, as the moonlight partially illuminated the rail car's interior, had been things only lent to his imagination about the female body. Let alone, the intimate anatomy of a white woman. In fact, it was that experience that seemed to have formed a lot of Sackett's thinking towards women. The one that he met that summer long ago in downtown Detroit had fooled him, at first. Her flirtatious nature caused his guard to rise up instinctively, that coupled with a complexion that could be mistaken for that of a white woman. And even though she was surely older than he was, Frank wanted to take her up on an invitation for dinner.

And since he'd had no luck finding employment that day, he was more easily compelled to make something worthwhile occur. He doffed his light-gray fedora, and smiled his acceptance, but not before first getting a name. Her name was Cleo—short for Cleophus? No, Cleopatra. That was what he remembered, now. It was her shortening of the name, Cleopatra. Why? It was like shooting the nose off the Sphinx.

Frank had a sense of how well-planned Cleo's trek had been and could already smell food cooking when he came inside; so much so, that when she returned, it seemed like she was a much practiced woman. She'd put a low flame under the big pot of cooking oil before she'd left. Oil that may have been used once before, recently, and still gave off the aroma of the deep fried past. This way, it would not be as long take to be ready would to eat. A few minutes to coat the fish, flash them into the hot grease. And before they'd know it, they'd be ready. Them, and the fish, was what Cleopatra had figured on. And that's what she went about doing.

She opened up her ice box, and situated by two salads she had already made, pulled out an aluminum baking tin with several catfish fillets. She set that down next to a blue china plate that had a cornmeal and flour mixture piled up in pyramid at the center of it. She poured some buttermilk over the catfish and then pressed them into the coating mix, while all the while continuing her flirtatious ways. Sometimes a quick smile, or at others, sometimes a gaze meant to be long. She put four filets into the pot, with a crackle of heat escaping while the fish became subsumed in the oil.

"You tell time?"

"Oh, yes. I can tell time, or read it silently."

Cleo's red lips curled up in a beckoning smile. "When ten minutes are up, we need to turn the fish." She turned to Frank and brought a cigarette to her lips from the pack she had in her apron pocket. She held the cigarette expectantly towards him. Her palm pointed upwards to the ceiling, and the rolled tobacco stick was gently pinched between her index and forefinger. "Light me," she said, almost in a whisper.

Frank nodded and lit her cigarette for her.

"Get you a beer?" she further asked.

"Please, and thank you."

Cleo stood, and turned, glancing back over her right shoulder at Frank. "Would you unzip my dress?"

"Uh—you, ahem, really want to do that. I mean..."

"It will be hot in the kitchen while I'm cooking. And I also don't want to splatter grease on my dress."

Sackett started to put his hand to Cleo's upper back, "I thought that's what your apron was for?"

"Too hot for an apron, too." And Cleo smiled and lightly bit her lower lip. "You still want that beer, or what?"

Sackett brought the metal tab down to the small of Cleo's back, where there was a soft down of strawberry-blonde hair. And then, she surreptitiously, let the dress fall around her ankles, and let Sackett eyes follow her into the kitchen space. Sensuous curves draped over by her chamois.

She dangled the cigarette from the corner of her mouth, and squinted her eyes to keep the smoke out of them as she pulled a can opener out of a sink drawer. Two cold cans of *Schlitz* were punctured with the opener, and Frank took the cigarette from between Cleo's lips when she came back to the couch. He took a drag off of it as she handed him the beer. Her hand, a soft caress as she retrieved her smoke.

"You got a man?"

"Let's just say, I had one."

"Don't care for surprises—y'know."

"Time to turn that fish, sugar."

Frank didn't press her, any more. He figured she had to be about 10 years older than he was, and should know better. He would take her at her word, or lack of it. After all, sometimes it was better not to know, how strange the stranger across from you actually is. "Is it alright, in there?"

"They done. I'll fix plates." Two clean china plates were placed on a wooden serving tray, on the counter. And with swift movements of well-placed hands, hips, and toes, Cleo had the salads and all the fixings prepared and sit-uated for them. Frank liked the shifting bounce of her still pert breasts, just in the eyeline above the tray in her hands.

"You make it look easy," Frank said.

"You talking about how I cook?"

Frank burnt his tongue a little on the large portion of his catfish that he'd taken off his plate, and could not get out any response. He went from fanning his opened mouth, to aggressively breaking the meat down; chewing, while covering his mouth, but not quite being able to close his mouth to swallow. Finally, he took a swig of beer to dowse and cool his tongue and palate. Cleo laughed—a laugh that sounded like wind chimes. Pleasing and delicate. "Sorry—", Frank apologized. "Hot."

"Well, you made darn sure you didn't lose any of it."

"Oh, yes, ma'am."

And that's how they passed through their meal. Occasionally asking a question between bites, or answering another query while the other's mouth was half-full. Informal dining, to say, the least. But that suited them, just fine. After awhile, once another round of fish had been consumed and a couple of more beers, Cleo burped.

Her beautiful brown eyes grew so wide, and her hand quickly went up to her mouth; before she could even get it closed. Frank smiled, and raised his eyebrows as Cleo's peals of laughter seemed larger than the room they were in. "Oh, excuse me...that sure was good, wasn't it?" Cleo giggled. "Do you know how women get after a good meal?"

"Sleepy?"

"No—silly. When I get full. I feel like a natural woman. You ever had a natural woman, Frank?"

"What? Am I about to?"

She then took literal control of the situation and proposed to initiate the young man into understanding exactly what she meant, and what she wanted. It wasn't long before he had come to figure it out. And though, not experienced in the pedantic of lovemaking, carnality bridged his understanding. They began their first union on the couch, and before Frank reached a point-of-no-return they halted—and proceeded to Cleo's nearby bedroom. A trail of Frank's clothing denoting the path they went. She sat on the edge of her bed after she'd pulled her slip up over her hips, and then tossed it like they were feathers over head. Letting it drop to the floor, Cleo, now fully nude, leaned backwards and held her hand out to Frank.

When he did come to her, his knees touched her widened inner thighs, and her arms encircled him in an embrace. But before she could take him any further Cleo felt his warm passion spill across her lower stomach. She couldn't help but giggle at him, for he looked all the part of puppy who had missed his spot on the newspaper. "Oh, you sweet thing," she chuckled as she pulled on his softening organ. "If the wind blows down there, you don't know whether you supposed to come, or go." Frank began to get hard again, as he kissed her deeply. After the kiss, she said, "Come here, baby. Let me teach you some love." The second time was much more what had been expected. A third, beyond dreams. And Frank was finally spent—until another fifteen minutes passed.

He felt good to Cleo, but he hadn't yet gotten her to climax. And while that wasn't absolutely necessary to her, she believed it possible with a little more strategizing. "Slow down, baby," she cooed in his ears. He pushed the palms of his hands over her bent knees and swayed into her wet softness. "Now, not too fast. Listen. Do it this..." And Cleo began to sing the old nursery rhyme in tempo to Frank's thrusts. Then, without warning, she turned over and somehow didn't miss a stroke. She liked it this way. "Sing a song of sixpence—pocket—rye...oh, my God. And the jumbled verses followed, changed under her passionate license. When the time came for the fabled pie to be opened, though, Frank released his last bit of sustenance. And it had been enough for Cleo, too.

Frank stepped away from the foot of the bed, seeing his whiteness sandwiched between Cleo's swelled labia. She reached over to a nightstand and grabbed tissues for the both of them. A silent assent made during the time of cleaning up, let it be understood to the participants that the deed was done. Frank put on his boxers, and then his pants. But before he could find his shirt, Cleo had pulled him back on top of her still unclad body. She began kissing him deeply once more, and tilted her pelvis up to his hips. Yes, she had had an orgasm, but her libido hadn't been bedded quite to her liking.

The unmistakable snap of a double-barrel shotgun being closed behind him, though, froze young Sackett in his movement. He slowly began to raise his hands in the air and closed his eyes. All he could imagine was some bearish, ogre of a husband, glowering at him. The inevitable became arrested in his memory, however. Cleo pushed him aside with a strength borne from panic, and stood between her lover, and her son. All of fifteen.

The boy saw the wetness of his mother's and Frank's viscous juices—still glistening like a snail had left behind its trail upon Cleo's thighs. He could also smell the pungent muskiness of the latent sex committed in the room. "What you doing here, nigga?" he asked, angrily.

Frank couldn't believe it. There, in front of him, was the tear-brimmed, wide-eyed eyes of Joseph Martin.

Cleo snatched on a robe from a nearby chair, "Joe! Put that gun down, y'-hear me?"

But the barrels stayed pointed in Frank's direction. Cleo stepped in front of him, causing Joe to take a step backwards, while Sackett quickly gathered his belongings.

"I mean it, Joe. Dammit, do what I say!"

A blast of pellets knocked a whole out of the wall, over the bed's headboard, to the right of Frank and Cleo. Taking the moment, he took a step forward with a cocked right fist and punched Joe on his chin. He was out. Frank then dressed hurriedly, and left Cleo Martin's without another word being spoken...he left there, walking into a white light.

"Hey—hey. Look, I think he's coming too. Let's give him some air," McPhee suggested.

The white light faded, and it dissolved into an indistinct haze of filminess over Sackett's now opened eyes. Joe had been separated from all the others, into the corner of the cellar. There, he sat guarded by Brillo, and repeatedly pounded the palms of his fist against his temples. His right hand had sprained fingers. Some mumbling from the assailant could be made out by Frank as he tried to align voices and faces to one another. "*I didn't mean to. God, I didn't want to do that,*" Joe sobbed.

Frank knew the location of his wound before even attempting to move his left leg. It was high, at the top of his anterior quad. The pain also existed because his sciatic nerve was innervated by the bullet. "You're lucky you saw it coming," McPhee commented as he saw Sackett's eyes flutter. He continued bandaging him and pulled the rolled and bloodied pant's leg higher. "Because you turned when you did, you got lucky. The bullet made a clean exit."

"Ahh—ow, damn that hurts. How bad?"

"I'm no medic. We packed the hole with gauze and wrapped it. There wasn't much bleeding, surprised by that."

"I don't think I can put weight on it."

"You know, Sackett. Infection sets in...It'll cost you that leg. We need to get you to HQ."

"Fat chance of that, now," Brillo said, giving a disgusted look at Joe. Where it had once been feasible to attempt making a passage to the command—even with the children in tow, now, a march would be nearly impossible to maneuver. Not only at some point would the children probably need to be carried, Sackett would have to be littered, as well. And Joe Martin needed to be escorted. Unless, he came back to his senses.

"I could stay here, with the kids," Frank volunteered, somewhat resigned.

"What if you start up bleeding, again?" McPhee asked.

"I could do that just as easily, enroute to headquarters, couldn't I?"

"Why not send one of us out, at a time?" Gus suggested.

McPhee shook his head, "We all got to go, lad. All or none—that's the way."

"We'll need every hand we got—the worse comes our way."

"What about him?" Brillo asked, pointing at Joe.

"I didn't mean to do it! I didn't..." Joe's screaming frightened the children again.

"Hush up, Joe," Brillo ordered. "You gonna trust putting a gun back in his hands?"

"But—I didn't mean for it to go off," Joe whined.

"S'alright," Sackett said through a grimace, and then looking into Joe's eyes, said. "It was an accident."

Gus looked up from the freshly comforted children. "Mr. Frank. As much as I'd like for it to have been. That was no accident with you."

"I said it was an accident, Gus. And anybody who says differently is calling me a liar. If anyone knows, I know. The truth of the matter is somewhere between me—and Joe. If he'd have been trying to kill me, he could have. It's over. What is important, though, is to figure out a way to headquarters."

The circumstances presented to the group were not favorable, however. Joe, through his own skewed, warped reasoning, had unwarily aided the enemy.

It was always better to wound a soldier than to kill him. Because a wounded soldier had to occupy two other men, in order to take him to safety. There just wasn't enough of them, here, to go around.

The night had worn all of them out, emotionally. Because there was heat in the cellar, and they'd eaten. Sleep came over them after they left it until morning to come up with a plan. Through the insistence of Brillo and McPhee, the hands of Joe were bound with rope.

But, at some time into the night, a few hours past them all sleeping soundly, a scuffle, followed by a loud shift in the heavy false entry ceiling. In the dimmed light, Gus saw his brother working at something by the stairs. He tried to push the false bottom with an upwards push.

"Joe!" Gus hissed. "What in the hell are you doing?"

"Shut up, and help me untie my hands."

"Are you—? You aren't trying to escape, are you?"

Brillo then snorted himself awake and scowled at Joe, sleepily. "Martin—what's your problem, man?"

Joe just kept on pushing, but then Brillo and McPhee, together, brought him down to the ground.

"I'm not going anywhere—listen!" And Joe pointed over his head. What they heard caused all misgivings about Joe Martin to become abated. "SSH-HHHH," he warned.

Together, all the men very quietly nudged the opening that had been made, just a little wider. What Joe had heard had been nothing imagined. A jeep idled nearby, and muffled voices spoken in thick German could be heard.

"Now, will you untie me?" Joe choked out his angered request. McPhee reluctantly began to unknot the bindings.

"Need to turn out that light as soon as we can," Sackett grimaced, as he shifted his injured leg.

The children were not a problem. They knew how to stay quiet and to make themselves appear smaller, more innocuous, than they actually were. They showed that at the very first; how they became one with the earthen walls, and their shadows. "Hey, Sackett?" McPhee asked, "Remember when I said those things about worse coming to worser, or worst getting worster...well, I think this qualifies."

"Shut up, fool!" Brillo cautioned. "Do you want them to hear us? Try to pick up what they're saying!" Their ears in the hideout made manifest in their minds all sorts of pictures of imminent doom as they sat in the darkness, trying to control the thumping of their hearts.

CHAPTER THIRTY-NINE
Farmhouse Guests

The aggregate noise of that beating itself would surely alert someone that they were there, right behind them in the barn. Because it was all the inhabitants in the root cellar could do as they strained to hear over each of their own palpitations. Compounded palpitations that hopefully would not turn into an auditory beacon. But after awhile of listening intently, for just a few minutes longer, it became discernible to them that there were probably two jeeps. One had a slightly irregular hitch while it idled. The American soldiers were getting more apprehensive at that, when a curious thing happened. The unexpected laughter of a young woman could be heard, actually, several of them. The motors suddenly now stopped, and all the voices were heard distinctly. Echoed on the frigid air without any interference from wind or warmth, they were not discussing anything to do with the American front.

"You're the one who went out looking for Panzer men, not us," said one of the two heavily bundled young women sitting behind the Nazi driver as he lustily finished kissing their friend, who'd accompanied him in the front. "You will give a bad name to all us French girls, Babette."

It seemed the opened-air ride had stifled the thrill of having a party. And Babette's friends were also not particularly enthused about the looks of the three Nazis in the other jeep. Besides, that, even with an elk skin cover placed over and around them, it was an extremely cold night. Unintentional tears from the cold had to continually be wiped from the corners of their eyes as they drove. And just as one of them feared, as she looked at herself in her compact mirror, their mascara had run. They quickly tried to re-apply their make-up. It wouldn't do to remind the Nazis of the dead-eyed Jewish girls they had in the camps. Even if they were unattractive—they could give a girl nice things. Things like a bottle of liquor.

Barbette reached over the back of her seat to hand them the bottle. "I'm the randy one? Maybe this is not good enough for your liking?"

The other Nazis stopped apprising the situation and leapt from their jeep as soon as they saw the other two girls take a couple of good nips, apiece, and began to giggle. They knew it was safe to approach. "What are we going to do with the three of you? Four guys and three girls?" And the Nazis, between passing cognac amongst each other, began to state their case as to why *he* should not be the odd-man-out.

Barbette didn't have any trouble with her mascara, but there were other things about her that her friend's feared would make her be mistaken for Jewish, or that she looked more like *them* with her very short hair. It was because she had been so filial with each military group that passed through. Russians, Germans—she'd even show a good night to an American, if that's who was running the town. And it was precisely because of that kind of attitude, that a pack of women from her boarding home held her down one day several weeks ago, and sheared her hair off. "What's wrong with a full stomach and some new hose every now, and then?" She had screamed when they had begun, and each limb was immobilized.

Now, six weeks later, Barbette sported a cute little pixie cut, hairdo. And it harangued the older women in the village to no end that she still looked just as vivacious. "Come, let's have a look inside," she said.

"What they say?" Brillo hissed.

"Could anybody make that out?" Sackett asked.

Joe, with a diffident glance upwards to the stairs whose base they'd been gathered around, made a move and poked his head out above ground, and then quickly drew it back under cover. He placed his wool skull cap atop his head.

"What are you doing, Joe?" Gus asked.

"What ears can't conceive, eyes believe, little brother." He poked his head up again, and then looked down at the others. "We got to see what's going on, don't we?" Joe slinked his way quickly away from the hole as he low-crawled to the ajar door of the barn. There hadn't been any cautions, or entreaties not to go. It stood to reason somebody had to do what he was doing, and it might as well have been accomplished through volunteering.

The meaning of what the term "baited breath" actually meant crossed through Gus's mind as he sat there in the dark, imagining the worse. His chest was not expanding as far, breath coming out in short, little respirations. No gunshot rang out, at least. Or any shouts of an encounter, either. It was just still. But Joe didn't just crawl back to the cellar. Heavy footsteps were heard. His boots firmly hit the fake crate as he pushed it backwards on its tracks, with his strong legs. Fully exposing their position. Then he reached down into the hole and grabbed the lamp sitting at the top of the stairs. Without hesitation he brought up a flame in it.

"Man! Is you crazy?" Brillo said in a forceful sotto voice.

"Put that out!" McPhee demanded.

"It's alright," Joe said, placing a blocking palm forward of the lamp's wick. "You can believe they ain't worried about us. They're headed for the house."

They all vacated the stairway to allow Joe to get back in, then Gus and Brillo rolled the crate closed. Having the cellar lit again was an especially comforting sign for the children. McPhee seemed to be the most confused by what was transpiring, and he lightly touched Joe's arm to address him as he passed. "And just how in the hell do you know that's what's going on?"

"Had an uncle who taught me some German. He used to cut hair for them. Now, it might not be as good as your French, McPhee. But, I'll lay you odds they got plans to be wrapped up with a bottle or two of alcohol, and a little ménage action, y'know what I'm talking about?"

"If that don't beat it," McPhee said, letting Joe pass and then joining with the others. "Out there, making whoopee while on duty."

"There's more, too."

"We get sloppy seconds?"

Joe smiled at McPhee's attempt to douse his authoritative knowledge of the situation with the ribbing. In fact, he thought what McPhee had said to be very funny. But he held his laughter in check. Joe wondered if all the levity would be as pervasive after his next divulgement. "One of the jeeps," he said, with a raised voice, "has a set of keys in the ignition." Sackett sat up from his convalescence, and Brillo and Gus, along with McPhee began to congratulate each other. They had a way out, now. But it would be hours before they had chosen the best plan; the best out of three, that they would need to mull over more completely, before doing anything. And it would mean doing it all before the sun rose very high in the morning sky.

Joe was all for absconding with the jeeps while they were still warm, but McPhee put the kibosh on that idea because he was the only one who knew how to hotwire a car. He wanted some daylight to do that in.

"Besides that," McPhee added. "Wouldn't they be a little less likely to respond to a backfire after a night of drinking, than they would, say an hour from now?"

"Who's gonna be the one to drive, then?

"Yeah...I'll hotwire the damn thing, but you can't expect me to pop the clutch and give it the gas, too."

"I can drive it for you," Brillo volunteered.

"Hey, why don't I take that?" Sackett countered. I only need my right leg to drive—"

"What about the clutch, Sackett?"

"I can do it."

"No, Sackett," Brillo flatly rejected him. "It's gonna be risky enough without worrying about your leg locking up."

"I don't know how to drive a four-speed manual," Gus admitted. Sackett looked over at Gus with a look that said, 'You've got to be kidding me.' And Gus gave a sheepish smile.

"Well, too bad they're not staff cars, huh, Gus?"

"My hand's sprained," Joe added. "So, that takes me out."

"Mr. Frank should drive the one with the keys—and the kids should probably be in that one, too."

"Well, Mac...looks like it will be me and you riding the rocket. Put the Martin boys with the kids. Keep 'em from getting tousled out."

"Let's get some rest while we can, a few hours at least."

"O.K.," Sackett finalized, "we'll synchronize, now. Reverie at 0400, gentlemen." And with that, seeing everyone was in a rest position, he blew out the lamp. Only a pumpkin- colored glow from the wood burning stove provided any light.

In the farmhouse, angry looking embers in the living room fireplace kept the nip from the air. The repast of debauchery and intoxication had all of the fornicators sleeping soundly, and due to the inequities of gender, proper morals became suspended during the party. But notwithstanding that, one soldier had stayed in his full uniform, all night. None of the girls had wanted anything to do with him. But everyone else was semi-clothed.

The driver, Gunther, who had brought them all out to the farm, had gotten to bed both of the best looking girls. He was exhausted, lying on the floor in his long johns and the women crooked under his large arms. Their heads rose and fell gently from the movement of the pectoral muscles as Gunther slept. It was like a human sandwich, or something. One girl had her right arm draped across his corded stomach, and her right leg draped over his massive quad. And the other girl was in the same position on the opposite side, extending her left appendages. Their skirts still remained on them, but they were stripped down to their sheer bodices, otherwise. One pink nipple of a breast profiled itself as one of the consorts repositioned herself.

The dressed Nazi had fallen asleep in the corner of the living room, after walking back and forth from one unnatural coupling to another. He had re-treaded his steps so many times in his drunkenness that night that he began to feel if he hadn't been moving, at all. In the bedroom off the living room, his two comrades shared a girl between them. At first, it was a taking of turns—and listening to jeers thrown out about the other man's prowess as the other looked on. No one even looked at the silent Nazi who watched. But at some point, the trio became entangled carnally. The girl was stacked between the two soldiers, and as one filled the space between her vulva, the other prepared to take her through her rectum. When one soldier asked the other if he could feel the sensation of the other's penis working behind the woman's anal mus-cle's wall, the uniformed Nazi shook his head. He had seen enough.

He had retreated to the living room, but only saw similar goings-on hap-pening with that group. There, Gunther's face had been completely obliterated by a girl sitting astride it, rocking her crotch in tighter and tighter circles around his swirling, lapping tongue. Gunther made the sounds of a drowning man. A happily drowning man. And the other girl sat over his very stiff and thick penis. Slamming her mound to the base of Gunther's shaft, while at the same time holding onto Barbette and kissing her deeply in the mouth. "French women," the Nazi thought.

Left with only the choice of voyeurism, the clothed Nazi quickly took two more quick shots and decided, the hell with it. He unbuckled his pants and let his drawers hit the ground along with them. He didn't mind, if they didn't. He steadied himself with one raised arm on a wall and leaned forward, expos-ing himself, and stroked furiously. Hoping one of the girls would see him, or look at him, his eyes glued longingly at their enraptured faces. His grunts did not disturb them, however, and now a small bud of semen was being formed at the tip of his average penis. It made some licentious noise—but again, not enough for anyone but him to notice. He tried mightily to keep going, to co-incide his stroking with the plunges of the girl's hips. But, alas, it all ended way too soon for him. He noticed he had dribbled some on his left pant legs' knee as he gathered himself, but didn't bother with wiping any of it off. As stated earlier, he just retired to his corner that served double as a bed, and fell asleep.

At some unclear, unknown hour of the morning, their libation and orgy ended. It ended with all of the farmhouse squatters passed out. And whereas at the time of them falling asleep, the succor of their arranged closeness had clearly been pleasant. But, as the night evaporated, and the dawn prepared to beat back the night, so did the delusions of enchantment the fornicators had had with one another. With Gunther's situation, curdled breath from one of the women sleeping on his pillow chest wafted up to the level of his chin whiskers. And just alerted his nose. But he still dreamt, for now.

As for the other paramour, she was similarly bohemian, except her problem had been a stomach that could not handle a rough culinary combination of alcohol and summer sausage, and old biscuits. As she moved to regain her comfort as she slept, the fermented biscuits in her alcohol laden stomach caused intermittent flatulence. But the big German didn't seem to notice the foul odors. The malodorous company had put him to sleep sexually bedded; time passing after that escapade seemed to disperse all enmity he might have felt. Besides that, she wore a cheap, flowery perfume that could have been used to mask the smell of a corpse.

Gunther's eyeballs began to roll back and forth rapidly in their sockets, the fleshy envelopes of his closed eyelid folds began to tremble. One of the consorts moved a little next to him, started to snore softly in his ear. It didn't wake him up, though. His eyes subconsciously moved in the direction of the auditory stimulus. Gunther was, indeed, waking up.

The escaping group from the cellar had had all of their preparations made in quick order; due to coffee and shortbread cookies being served first thing, to get everyone moving, they went over their final plan. It seemed, proportionately, that the attempt to commandeer the enemy vehicles had the type of deliberations that were used to initiate the D-Day Invasion. For these individuals, it was something as dire. One miscalculation—one delay—one second of not concentrating—not listening, could cost them all their lives before they'd even know that they were dead. If there was any type of precognitive awareness, some sixth sense their doctors may have developed—anything that could have alerted the Nazis of their presence—there would go their element of surprise.

Because Sackett would be driving the keyed jeep, he needed to be the first one out of the hole. The rag in his thigh muscle irritated the traumatized nerves of his wound but Frank could control his reaction to the pain, for now. He had to. Next man up the stairs was Joe, who would be in the passenger seat, next to Sackett. Joe had the shotgun position, it would be up to him to have to lay down cover fire for them, should the need arise. Gus's assignment was to safeguard the lives of the children he'd befriended, and who followed him up the stairs, out of the cellar. Even though he didn't know their language, the children were quite fond of him. Then the others came out of the cellar to join the rest.

Standing around the exposed hiding place like it was a warming blaze, none of them could fully raise to their full heights' because their muscles were so stiff from their cramped night of repast, spent underground. Their combined rank breath fogged the air over the opening. As McPhee came up he said, "We'll need forty-five seconds, at least, so my question to all of you is:

do you want to stay in here while I hotwire the jeep? Or do you want to be outside?" They moved over by the barn doors, and Brillo and McPhee began their cautious low-crawl. Leaving trails in the snow like they were snakes crossing sand.

Once at the jeep, Brillo sat in the driver's seat, and cocked his .45 and put it in his lap. Underneath, McPhee pushed away snow from the bottom of the carriage to give him access to the wires he needed. McPhee gritted through his teeth as he released the wires from their ground, and blew out a forceful exhalation. "Whoooa—it's cold," McPhee complained. The stripped leads were rubbed against one another, over and over, but the flywheel wouldn't engage. "Come on, you cocksucking sonuvabitch. Turn over, dammit." When a few abbreviated sputters began coming from the other jeep, Gus helped anchor the hobbled Sackett so he could walk. And Joe, forgetting his sprained wrist, scooped up the two youngest refugees. Monique stuck close by as they scurried, and she moved with fear-motivated purpose while her jeep's inhabitants got in place.

Inside the farmhouse, Gunther sighed once. He was the picture of contentment, until he began to hear aberrant noises, things that sounded faintly like the putter of backfire. ..it must have been the snoring mistress beside him, he thought. The sausage really had her bloated stomach going, apparently. But then, the tempo of the combustions grew more rapid, less human, and Gunther snapped open his bloodshot eyes in a panic. He unceremoniously threw the women off of him and ran to the bedroom to collect his men. When Gunther did find the other Nazis he was embarrassed to see that one trooper's hand casually laid resting along the inner fold of the thigh of his friend. The girl still between them.

Picking up a boot, Gunther threw it at the footboard of the bed and caused a loud enough noise to wake everyone in the house.

"Did you hear that, Mac?" Brillo panicked. "Sounds like they's moving."

"Give it some gas, Brillo."

Carbuerated hiccoughs turned into a commotion of combustion, for an instant, and then began to sputter once more. Sackett was having some difficulty getting his jeep to turnover, as well. Brillo and Sackett gave one another several furtive glances as they tried to will the jeeps to keep running. "Come on, man," Joe began to urge more loudly. Come on, Sackett. Get this motherfucker moving—and now would be good."

McPhee screamed encouragement to Brillo, "All right, you fucking Swinging Richard—double clutch this sonbitch." And then, suddenly, with a grace that would have befitted a miracle from Lourdes, both jeeps kicked over, simultaneously. And just as it seemed fortune had turned their way, finally,

Sackett's injured leg went spastic. The muscles damaged or displaced by the bullet had nerves that were highly agitated, and raw, from the cotton strips brushing against them during the escape. Excruciating, near blinding pain, flared with cramping in the rear quadriceps of the clipped leg. And Sackett screamed out loud in agony.

"Shut up, fool," Joe yelled at him. "Screaming ain't getting the job done. Get it in gear!" Then their jeep began to convulse a little bit, like it might stop running. Joe saw that Sackett had his hands wrapped around his extended leg, and where blood oozed from in between his fingers.

"I can't pull the clutch," Sackett grunted.

Then the rear of the jeep became panicky as the children screamed, and each of them pointed a finger at the back porch. Exiting hurriedly out of the farmhouse were the four rumpled Nazis soldiers. Each had a look on their face that was halfway between disbelief and a terrible hangover.

They were half dressed in thermal undershirts and their gray service pants, shaking their fists at the Americans and their refugees. And then, as one, they turned back to the opened door, and sped inside. They quickly grabbed their boots, searched for their misplaced weapons and shouted curses at each other. Of course, they paid no attention to their guests. And when Barbette took offense to the slight, Gunther roughly threw her to the ground, and turned away from her without compunction, to lay his hands directly on the iron barrel of a mortar launcher.

McPhee's jeep was operational. "Thank you, Jesus," Brillo said under his breath to his personal savior. The Irishman quickly cleared himself of the jeep's undercarriage and leaped into the passenger's seat. Sackett, at the same time, had been able to get his vehicle to roll back in reverse, and he stomped on the gas.

Gus was able to see McPhee and Brillo just begin to pull out when the Nazis reappeared. The enemy were completely fixated on assembling their weapon, assured that the jeeps wouldn't outrun their shells. Gunther told the spotter to make one little adjustment and tapped him on the soldier. The fired shell struck the last jeep squarely, and a blast of orange, white, and black rose as the explosion pocked out the dirt where the mortar struck. Sackett gunned his way forward, ever forward; widely meandering a course up and over snow drifts, threatening to dislodge them all.

Another round was fired from the porch, and careened near the Americans but missed by a foot. Sackett kept up with his defensive maneuvering in light of the repeated attack. His bum leg, however, screamed for attention. Biting pain knotted his stomach in waves of nausea, but he continued on.

In the open-air rear of the jeep, all the tossing to-and-fro caused the potato doll to become disengaged from the littlest child. Fearing that she would lose the treasure, the toddler broke her way across the cargo compartment and grabbed. Gus yelled for her to stop, Gus's alarm strong enough to make his brother turn to assess what was happening. Then, Sackett would recall later, the shrieking started again. But this time it sounded like there had been ten rounds honed at them. "Jesus!" Joe scolded Gus, and the child. "Would you keep your asses down?"

Joe had to place himself halfway back into the rear of the jeep to grab Gus, who, in turn, had almost been thrown out trying to reach the girl. And the round that hit the ground was closer this time, Gus was sure, although he could not see because Joe was still atop of him. The jeep's course, all of sudden began to straighten out. "Joe, hey. Message received, big guy."

Gus didn't hear any response and his pushing against Joes' torso failed to make his brother climb off of him. "He might be unconscious," Gus thought. "Joe?" The younger Martin began to get a tightness in his chest and he pushed his arms up with the same kind of force Joe had used against the cellar door. He straightened his arms, relieving himself of his brother in order to pull away momentarily and prepare for the incoming rebound. Gus shoved his way up Joe's chest, in this fashion until his hands fell into a slick, dark abscess.

Raw mush that had previously been Joe's face, and a side of his neck, filmed Gus's hands with blood and pinkish, clear fluid. Pumped with shock and grief, and added to by the discomforting repulsion he felt as the corpse danced about him with its arms, Gus lost himself in the careening dance of the jeep. The mortar had peeled back several layers of Joe's face flesh. Some of it still slough-ing off the skull, and revealing the white bone beneath. It was like watching a ball's hide shrink back from its core during a fire. The few seconds of recogni-tion it took to know his brother was gone passed for Gus, and he was brought back further into the reality by the screams of the still shocked children.

The body flopped around the cargo compartment and draped itself mo-mentarily over all of them. Gus's shock and alarm, mixed with the splattered matter and fleshly carnage made the children cry out all the more hysterically, as well. Gus tried to protect them from Joe's body, fighting his own repulsion, but each time Sackett made a turn or found a rut, Joe catapulted lifelessly against them again. It seemed like the macabre madness would never come to an end, so Gus began to kick at the demon who had once been his brother. The first kick rolled the taunting specter over onto its back, and into the pas-senger seat. The body grazed Sackett's shoulder and he got his initial assess-ment of Joe's condition. Vomit spit up into the back of his throat and Sackett turned to the left and spat it out towards the ground.

"Get him out of here, Gus! I can't shift like this!" Sackett pushed Joe back towards Gus with his right elbow, and the children helped their protector accomplish what had to be done. They kicked it, and pushed it, together, until they had expelled it—unceremoniously, from the freewheeling jeep. His body hit the ground with a hollow sound. But it was too much for the children's young minds to tolerate, and they fainted.

No one, save Gus, had looked back as they drove forward. Sackett concentrated on his driving, and Gus could see Joe's body lying on the white snow. He remembered everything. And all he could think about—over and over again, was the last look he had had of the dead Cyclops that was once his brother. The noise his body made when it landed hadn't sounded like it had ever lived. And now, as the jeep began to turn, he captured another memory. One leg bent akimbo in the snow, an arm raised. The fingers from that one bloodied hand still refusing to stretch upwards to heaven.

CHAPTER FORTY
The Great Reveal

"Thank you," Franklin said after pointing to the level of scotch he wanted in his empty glass. "That will do, nicely." There was a long pause after Jim had his drink replenished, and he brought up his glass in a silent toast. The story had left him speechless, but it was the story's teller that he really wanted to show appreciation. The heaviness of the conclusion was an amalgamation of depression and guilt for him. "I've told this ballbreaker of a story, for what seems like a hundred times. Heck, talk about it more than I do Scottsboro."

Jim was still reflective. "Did you ever check on my father after he was brought home?"

"Not your father," Sackett said, shaking his head. "But I did get an opportunity to talk to your grandmother, though. She didn't seem to remember me. She said, 'I don't think I ever heard any colored man who sounds like you. You must be mistaken.' Ha! That was something. I told her that I'd served with her boys. She kinda, she kinda got real quiet, then. Said something about it being such a shame about Joe. The Army told her he'd been run over by a truck. I didn't have the heart to tell her no different, though. It was best she had peace with what they told her. Just seemed more decent, considering your father was shell-shocked permanently. But no—no. Never took the time to see how he was."

"I didn't bring that up to make you feel guilty, Franklin. I got my own stuff to deal with over that."

"I understand."

"You've turned the whole world upside down about everything I knew about my dad. And even though I know it should change the way I feel—I don't know if I'm ready to embrace him yet. Not on so short a notice. I need time."

Sackett put his drink down and pulled the turquoise case from out of his overcoat pocket, and placed it on the table in front of Jim; he ran his fingers over the slick feeling, silver engraving on top of the case—noting the detail on the Congressional Seal. "Earth has a hundred percent fatality rate, son. Don't fool yourself into thinking you have the luxury of time to take; the moment is spent before you have a chance to think of it. And there's no way to get any of that back. When you get an idea to make something right—don't turn down the heat on the kettle. You do, you'll probably end up not feeling too well about yourself."

"The first person in twenty-five years looking to have anything to do with my Daddy, and he's bringing him a medal? Man, if that don't beat all."

"Well—to tell the truth. This here, is your uncle's. Your dad, shoulda had a Purple Heart. But back then, if you weren't wounded physically..."

Jim opened the case, but didn't dare touch the light-blue neck ribbon and its thirteen white stars. "This if for my uncle? I thought it took legislation to get a Medal of Honor?"

It's given by the President on behalf of the Congress. No vote involved, or anything. Just need a commanding officer to write the commendation and—"

"So, who referred him if they weren't supposed to even be there?"

"Kinda went through the back door, to get this here."

"Alright, I'm intrigued. They don't just hock these out."

"Actually, you'd be surprised. Not the government, mind you, but there are individuals who could get you one that looks amazingly similar to the real deal. That's what we'd been doing with all the other Blackbirds since nobody was paying attention to us. But, no—this one here. The real deal."

"Conferred by the president?"

"Yes, Sir."

"How'd you get it. And why didn't we get told about it?"

"My friend, Colonel Krech. He made general. And after he retired he'd become a big supporter in the Democrat Party. His brother, after I made contact with him agreed to approach President Carter after McPhee's family started getting upset. You see, the corporal had friends who knew what had happened to him as far as the reconnaissance assignment."

"He didn't get a medal—but why? He was white."

"It was part of the systemic denial. Anyway, the family compared the two stories: what the army said, and what they'd learned. They demanded he be given proper recognition, or they were going to call a news conference."

"That would have been a helluva mess."

"Oh, my-—yes."

"But that still don't explain—"

"I had a chance to confirm their suspicions, and Krech, took the ball and ran with it. Got two medals out the deal. One for Brillo, and one for Joe. Posthumous recognition for them was a proviso for not going public with the cover-up."

A nerve in Jim's jaw started to cause a slight ticking spasm that flexed perceptibly several times. He frowned, and took down the rest of his double. "My moth—my mother, Mr. Sackett, didn't live long after birthing me. She wasn't—", here, Jim struggled to put things in the context he wanted. "She wasn't ready to have children."

"You don't have to go on, about it. Your wife told me a little, but I didn't get any particulars. Didn't need to."

"Oh, but I want my turn. I want my turn at spinning things around for you...maybe you'd have a better understanding why I am, the way I am."

"When was the last time you saw him, Jim?"

"Oh, it must be six, no—eight. Eight months."

"You know, when I came through those doors for the first time, I marveled at how you have nothing of father's features. But there is a resemblance to your Uncle Joe."

"Well, that suits me fine. He's the one getting decorated—not my dad." Jim made a contemplative, somewhat morose look away from the table for a moment. "Granny told me about how everything happened. The room where she had him in at the attic of her new house. Right by hers, at the end of the upstairs hall. You could pull a ladder down from the attic when you grabbed ahold of the door ring, though I wasn't big enough to ever do that, when I was little. For the most part of every day, my father was in his own little world. She had to spoon feed him—everything. The only thing he could do for himself was tend to his own toilet business. Guess she was thankful for that, at least. But resentment was there, too. And at times, she would tell him off, too. Said it felt like he was trying to climb back inside the womb. She put up newspaper clippings for him, model airplanes, posters. The kind of things that can help snap people out of certain doldrums. But they didn't help, none. VA couldn't tell if he ever would get better. And you know, my grandmother was a young woman—even for being a grandmother."

Sackett smiled and chuckled, "Yes, I do know that."

"She said she weren't going to be spending all of her time just sitting with my dad, and she began to entertain. You know, throwing barbecues with family and acquaintances stopping by. They used to have some good parties, then. Last sometimes up to three days. And it was during one of those clan sleepovers that my father and mother *met*, you could say. They tried to say that she was messing with him—she had his stuff on her hands. They had to sew closed the holes he made in her. Then, had a hearing and placed him out at Lakewood Nursing—for reasons of public saftety is what the order said. And that's that. That's where he is, to this day. Not speaking nary a word, to anyone."

The next day, Franklin came to grips with his own deep-seated aversions to hospitals, or anything medically needed, and made an excursion to the nursing/convalescent home. It was a good deal to do with him staying away from the VA hospital, like he did. He felt the air in most places like that had a sickly-sweet, disinfectant type of smell. Intermingled, without fail, by underlying weak strains of urine. He could never stomach eating in them, either, because he just found it so disgusting. It was just a little too overpowering, and definitely guaranteed to spoil his appetite. In his own recovery, for his leg injury, he had lost fifteen pounds.

"The medical history of Mr. Martin can't be divulged to non-family members without a release, Mr. Sackett." The chief-of-staff, Dr. Hardaway, stated this with a matter-of-fact monotone. And it didn't make it seem any more empathetic to have him repeat what the head nurse had told Frank. The man had a sparsely populated comb-over and smaller than normal looking eyes. "I'm sorry, but I think you can understand why."

"I just want to know if he'll come out of his condition."

"Look, I know you've come some distance...So, let me say this about people with catatonia, and apply the information as you will. Catatonia is a form of schizophrenia. The patients can become agitated, or in some phases aggressive. And then turn around and become docile. You see, there is still usually a pattern of behavior with it. But, that's simply not the case here."

"What are you driving at?"

"Patients who don't respond to stimulation with excitement or motor activity—chances are, they have what we call shock retardation."

"I understand."

"I hope so." But Dr. Hardaway was flummoxed as to why Sackett didn't turn to leave. It was like he continued taking in a breath that he couldn't let go until the visitor had left. But the insistent acquaintance of the patient doggedly wagged a questioning finger in the air.

"There is one other thing, though, doctor."

"What's that?" Hardaway said, and glanced quickly at this watch and then put his left hand in his pocket.

"My visit. I'd like to see Gus for myself, if you would?"

Hardaway sighed in exasperation, "I thought we had an understanding. You must be on a family-approved list of contacts for Mr. Martin."

"But I'm only coming for the one time."

"Then come back with a first-blood family member."

That evening, with some trepidation because of what he'd been directed to do, Sackett found himself on the Martin's porch, once again. What would make it even worse for gaining any favors from Jim was that it was meal time. Even with all he'd done and been through with the Martins, Sackett still felt like an intruder. And he was sure Jim would take it that way. Especially to ask what he had to ask of him. Jim, who answered the door, however, didn't seem bothered.

"Hey, Franklin!"

"Excuse me, Jim. Forgive me for interrupting—"

"Psssh, come on in here. Have some supper."

Lorraine smiled when she saw Frank, as well, and pulled up an extra chair for their guest. Looking at the partially eaten fare, Frank could see the meal was probably halfway over. The menu included meatloaf, broccoli, and scalloped potatoes. "Sure smells good, ma'am," Frank praised Lorraine as she put a full plate in front of him.

"That's not too much now, is it?"

Sackett was distracted for a moment because he noticed that there was an empty chair at the table, with a plate of food set for someone. Little Brad wasn't there. "This is just fine, Mrs. Martin...mmm, now how do you keep the meatloaf so, tasty?"

"Family secret, Franklin."

"My Bernice, God love her—but that woman couldn't make a meatloaf. Turned out so dry, you could toss slices in the air for skeet shooting. Hmmm, kinda miss it, though."

Lorraine was touched because she saw the faraway look, and melancholy in his grin. Which couldn't be called one, actually, but more like an attempt to make one. A grin mixed with a grimace. "He still misses her, Lorraine thought to herself. She saw a little tearing up in his eyes, and looked quickly away.

"What's a skeet, Mr. Sackett?" Bernadette asked.

"A clay pigeon."

"What?"

"Something they use for target practice," Lorraine answered.

"A bird? Made out of clay? How does it come alive if it's not hatched?" Mr. Sackett lowered his head as he swallowed and shook it slowly from side to side, chuckling.

"It's not a real bird, Bea," Sackett said. "They are little round discs. About yea-big." And here he held up both hands to form a five-inch circle. They're stacked on a machine that flings them up into the air, and you shoot 'em with a shotgun."

"Oh...Is that why you're so skinny?

Frank chuckled again, "A contributing factor. Let's say."

Lorraine noticed that her husband wasn't laughing, however. Jim just rolled his broccoli in his mouth, as he chewed. Absent-mindedly foregoing the enjoyment of eating because his gaze and concentration were on the door off the hallway from the dining room. And the missing family member.

Jim's temper had been put in check for awhile because of Frank being in the house, but it was precisely because there was a guest present that Jim felt all the more miffed by his son's behavior. Finally, he set his fork down. "Lorraine," Jim said softly, feeling his temper grow. "How much time are you going to give him? The boy's had twenty minutes to get it together and come out here for dinner. His food's good as cold. What's the matter with him? Bea? Do you know?"

The young teen shrugged her shoulders, and momentarily feigned she had no knowledge. "I don't know, Daddy."

"He's ran into a rough patch at school," Lorraine said.

"What? He been fighting?"

"No—it's a class he has. The teacher rubs him the wrong way, for some reason."

"White teacher?"

"I think so."

"Then, I can imagine why there might be a disconnect."

"Is it something wrong with what they're teaching him?"

"To be honest, Jim. I really haven't looked at his books."

Jim pushed his chair back from the table and stood, all powerful in his authority. "Well, obviously it's got to be something pretty upsetting. And I'm going to—"

"What is the subject, Mrs. Martin? English?"

The Martins looked like a group of deer that all heard a twig snap at the same time, but didn't trust their hearing. "It was history, I believe, Mr. Sackett." Frank believed he now might be a way for him to bring up the matter of going to see Gus.

"Maybe I can be a little—"

"No, thanks," Jim said curtly. "Bradley Allan Martin! Get to stepping in here, right now!" The only person not ill-at-ease was Jim. Everyone heard a door open and then close. And in a few quiet steps, Brad stood just beyond the table's membership. But he couldn't bring his eyes up to meet his father's hard stare. "What's your problem, son?"

"I don't know."

Bernadette made eye contact with her mother. Things were about to get bumpy. "You don't know? You been holed up in that room for a half hour. Didn't you hear your mother? Now, what's the matter?"

"Is it some problems with your history, son?" Sackett asked his little friend, Gus's grandson, whom, unlike his father, looked the spitting image of him. Sackett tried to de-escalate the tension by his soothing voice.

"I tell you what's causing his problem. It's that damn Ay-tarie game. It's got him all wigging out, and stuff. When he plays it he don't act human! Eyes all bulging out, blinking too much, or not at all. Like somebody on drugs."

"Jimmy," Lorraine interrupted, "don't be that way with him. Come on and sit down, baby." Fortunately Brad's seat was next to his protector. "What's the matter, baby?"

"Bussing him to that white school. That's —"

"I'm not having any problems," Bernadette said. Simultaneously, Bea's mother and father both told her to hush. "Dang!" the girl said under her breath. The clicking of metal upon china resumed. Brad picked at his cold food, and Frank was a little surprised his mother didn't offer to warm his plate in the oven. But, the house rule was if you let your food get cold. Cold food was what you were going to eat. Finally, after he'd been able to get a few bites down, Brad spoke.

"I get to feeling sick sometimes when I have to go into the history class, lately."

"Do you know why? You don't look sick," Lorraine said, stroking the back of the boy's head a few times.

"The feeling is different. I mean a different kind of sick feeling. But sometimes, I'm okay. Then other times..."

"Do you like your class?" Jim asked, taking a lighter tone with his son, now. And Brad shook his head. "Is there something about the class, or the classroom?"

"I don't like going to it."

"That's not—"

"Jim," Lorraine reminded her man. "Let's stay helpful."

"Son," he then said, "is it the work? Too hard for you?"

"It's not the work—it's just..."

"Come on, Brad—I'm waiting."

"We've been studying about Afro-Americans."

"Well," Jim relaxed, "you should get an 'A' on that, then."

"Every time they talk about our past. Lynching—or, they show pictures of slaves. *Little Black Sambo*, one of the kids called me."

"Sticks and stones, son. Sticks and stones."

"But they all look at me when we read that stuff. Especially when it's read out loud. They all look at me like they're waiting for me to run screaming from the room. Or, I get asked by the teacher to explain how it is to be me. To be black. Is being black for you the same as being black for me, Dad?"

Now, it was Brad who caused the table to become silent. "Out of the mouths of babes," Mr. Sackett finally commented.

"I'm not a baby," Brad insisted.

"Son, everyone's experience with being black, with who we are, is an individual thing. No two white people have the same experiences in life; so, why should you or I be painted with the same brush?"

"So, what should I do?"

CHAPTER FORTY-ONE
Getting Up Morning

Brad knew what he should not have done. And that was to have overslept for school the next morning. He batted his alarm clock around in his hands—stopping them from shaking long enough to see that it was nine o'-clock. He knew his father would be beside himself, angry. Wide-eyed, Brad was overcome with anxiety and then terror. He leaped from his bed and wanted to cry. Just stand there, knowing his moments were numbered. The door opened, and his father was there.

"You got fifteen minutes."

"But, Dad," and then the boy started to whimper, knowing the whipping he was going to catch would go hard on him. "Dad, I set this clock. I did."

"What you getting so tore up about?" Brad couldn't reason as to how his father would be in such a state of calm, knowing he was late for school. "Fifteen minutes to breakfast, son. I'm making our favorite. Blueberry pancakes and sausages. Let's get it together."

"But—school?

"You want to eat cold pancakes?"

"No, Sir."

"Then, get dressed. We got some family things to do."

His father left without even loosening his belt and wrapping it around his hand. Brad remembered a science- fiction movie he'd seen. Maybe some creature from another world had come to their house during the night and swallowed his father whole. And had now come for him, to have dessert.

Just as strange, possibly even stranger to him was that Mr. Sackett was back at the kitchen table, again. Almost like he'd never left. It was like he just got a new plate of food put in front of him, and never moved a muscle. "Good morning, Bradley."

"Good morning, Sir," Brad said, puzzled.

"Your father and me, been talking. And we think we'll need your help finding something."

Jim placed Brad's breakfast before the boy, "You want some more, Franklin?"

"I'll handle a couple more, I think."

Brad could not figure out what the adults had in mind. Bea and his mother were gone, just like any other school day. But he was treated to a Sunday morning breakfast, prepared by his father. Jim Martin, though a capable culinary artisan, didn't proffer his talents for any common occasion. This was indeed a special thing. But he was still just as perplexed when they all left the table with their slightly distended stomachs and went downstairs to the basement. Brad following his father and Sackett. After they'd turned on the light.

"It's here, Franklin. If it's anywhere."

"I hope so."

Jim displaced boxes and rustled through irregular looking packages. He pointed to some stowables nearby and told Brad to search those. "What am I looking for, though?"

"It will have an address on it; '517 Lundy Street', just look for that somewhere on the outside of them."

Brad guessed that he was responsible for the scavenger hunt because of the conversational abstract he remembered hearing the prior evening. While he looked for what he was told to search for, he let his father and Mr. Sackett carry on conversation; because he, being so young, had no idea what he could add to their discourse, or even what he was meant to say. For now, he would be a silent assistant, foraging, but without purpose. Which made him a better listener.

His father and Mr. Sackett spoke about cycles in relationships; the love a child needs to have for their father. Mr. Sackett explained that boys deprived of a central paternal male figure in their life, often grow into men with no perception of what it is to be a whole man. No filters on their thoughts, or words. No interest in hanging around for a child's eighteenth birthday. No desire to work, for the most part. That certainly wasn't his father, though. But yet, Brad still asked himself how finding a certain box was going to prove something about his situation. Or his dad's.

"Here it is," Mr. Martin said enthusiastically. Like this was comparable to unearthing a pharaoh. He flicked off some collateral debris, Christmas garland and such. When Brad saw what it was that was supposed to have had such prominence to the occasion, he was disappointed. It was not a big, distressed-looking wooden chest with the Lundy Street address burned into its side. It turned out the thing was only a small parcel, really. But they all gathered around. Jim brought out a pen light to help them fully inspect the contents.

"Wow."

"Yeah, pretty neat, ain't it?" Mr. Sackett chuckled.

"I know there's got to be more than this around here, somewhere." Jim Martin sounded disappointed, but Mr. Sackett knew that this small gleaning of Gus's entire memorabilia could be enough to stimulate the aggression in the convalescent survivor. If that's what the chief-of-staff said had to be done. They took things out and laid them atop a larger box's surface.

Brad was immediately transfixed with his grandfather's dog tags. Sackett admired the condition of the mess kit. "That's all right, there," he said. "Good enough for a bivouac, right now." There was a Mackintosh overcoat folded into an olive drab square; its belt, flecked with bluish-white mold, cinched it in place. There were thirty-five year old unopened *K-Rations* that Sackett set on top of the kit.

"I wouldn't try to open any of those, though,"Sackett warned. "They're supposed to have a shelf life of a few years. But they'd be a might suspect, now."

Three photo albums had made up the base for the package, it seemed. They had clippings from American and British newspapers in them. Each of them carefully flipped through a collection. Pressed in the middle of one of the forgotten heirlooms were three rectangular, wrinkled, but flattened, blue and silver foil wrappers. On a dark brown oval were the scripted words *Alpine Bricks* fine Bavarian White Chocolate. Jim was transfixed. The old man had indeed been telling him the truth. "Look at this," Jim said, carefully holding up the wrappers.

Brad had no idea what the significance about the old candy bar wrappers was all about. He was more inclined to be pre-occupied with the dog tags, he'd found. However, for the very first time that Jim Martin had known Frank Sackett, he actually found himself smiling at him, standing there in that basement. Hope can rise up from a basement, you know. All it has to do is go up the stairs with you.

The ride over to Lakewood was silent, pretty much. Except for the low, white-noise of Jim Martin's car radio. Brad felt mixed emotions, at the time, because his father had demanded that he dress up. Shirt and tie, slacks—his shiny *Buster Brown* shoes; the whole Sunday thing. Now, all three car occupants were dressed like gentlemen. Brad was not enthusiastic about it, but they got on their way. A box, where the transplanted memorabilia was placed, sat next to him.

"Dad?"

"What son?"

"You going in to work?"

"Not today, son. I was able to take some time off."

"Oh."

The local weather report said that there could be lake effect snow for the next two days that could end up being eighteen inches deep, in some places. They were at a stoplight now.

"Dad?"

"What Brad?"

"You gonna write me an excuse from school, aren't you?"

"Yes, Son."

"So, who's going to write one for you?"

Jim looked at Brad in his rear view mirror for a moment, when the light turned, just before putting his foot to the gas pedal. "I think I got it covered, little man." Sackett knew he certainly couldn't do any good in that regard, either. After all, he wasn't blood family. The process, and its hoops, had gotten to make even the patient Mr. Sackett, more of a cynic than he'd already been.

Jim drove the four door sedan into the crowded parking lot at Lakewood and found one of the last visitor parking spaces. Once his father had turned off the ignition, Brad flung open his passenger door and discovered there was a large muddy puddle underneath his car portion. But remembering what Mr. Sackett had said to do, he improvised and exited the car from the other door. "Is that box too heavy for you?"

"No, I can carry it," Brad said, shifting the bulk. He then joined his father and Mr. Sackett at the front of the car. Mr. Sackett had certainly turned everything topsy-turvy around his house the last couple of weeks.

"You know what this place is, Son"

Brad read the sign with the missing metal letters on its cinder block retaining wall: LAKEW OD ARE FACIL TY, and found he couldn't intuit what specifically was missing from its letters in order for it to make sense. He shrugged his shoulders and admitted that he was getting bored. All the questions he was being asked, but none of his getting answered. Brad thought that maybe this wasn't worth a day off from school, but they began to make their way to the facility entrance.

"You know, Brad," Jim said, "Last night, your mother and I had a talk. It was about how you've been acting, but more importantly, how I have been acting. She feels I smother out any way for you to speak your mind...I don't know, maybe it's because I have unfinished business in here that makes me so disagreeable at home. You follow me?"

Brad nodded, but didn't really understand. He just gave the slightest acknowledgement possible, as if his father expected that he did understand. Brad just kept hoping he wouldn't ask how, it proceeded to be, that he understood. The boy didn't obfuscate his confusion that well.

Still strolling to the convalescent home, Jim began to speak again. "You know, Brad," he began. "I can relate to the trouble you've been having. Trying to fit in, and I'm up here trying to compare what you do in school with your sister. Guess I expect more from you. Not saying it's right, but I guess I do."

"That's okay, Dad."

"No—it isn't. But can't change what's already done...Kids at school weren't no better when I was your age, neither. White kids would come up to me and not even ask, just start feeling on my hair. They said they couldn't help themselves, it was a fascination to them."

"Really?"

"Uh—huh. One time I had my sixth grade teacher tell the whole class that I didn't need to comb my hair because a comb wouldn't be able to work through my kinks."

"Wearing one of them Afros, then?" Sackett asked.

"Trying to—but I had it blown out. I oiled and picked it out. But as soon as he saw some print from a copy of *Huckleberry Finn*, well, he just saw fit to make me the object of identification to the reading. You understand, what I'm saying?"

Brad grinned, and looked up into his father's face.

"Hell, I remember—" And they stopped, at the sidewalk and let some visitors who were leaving pass. "I remember sitting in segregated seats in the movie house after the Civil Rights Bill was passed. And this was up here, not past the Mason-Dixon Line. Son, both of us men, me and Sackett. We know how it is when you stand out, for no reason other than because you're black. Like you talked about last night—about being asked to represent the mind of all of us. The reason why they expect you can answer that is because they know they haven't changed any to make things better for us, as individuals. Not as a group, but individuals within the group."

"That's the difference," Sackett agreed. Jim opened the double glass doors for his son and the old man. They didn't stop at any station, or have any need to. Jim matter-of-factly walked them into the wing, and right up to the door.

"Okay, Brad. Past this door here—my dad, your grandpa. Ready?"

Brad nodded from behind the awkward box and Jim let him go in, first. In a chrome-railed hospital bed that was positioned at an angle was a brown, human cocoon. An empty bed, just like it, was to the right. The appearance of Gus had the most shock value, of course, on the young boy and Frank. Brad couldn't believe that it was a younger man than Sackett asleep on the bed. But it was.

For Sackett, what startled him the most was the absurdity of his recollection; the always and forever young Gus, is what he remembered and locked into his memory. Notwithstanding that, Sackett wondered how over three decades had passed, and Gus was in worse shape.

"That's your grandfather, Brad."

Sackett shook off his own uneasiness and took the box from Brad, and walked up to Gus's bedside. He set it on top of the covers, at Gus's feet and neatly laid out everything in it. Then he opened a small, tan shaving kit, and produced a stiff, black-bristled hairbrush. The base of the brush fit in the entire palm of his aged, corded hand. "Hello, Gus," Sackett said softly, but trying to sound upbeat, even though the sight of him saddened Frank, so. "Can you hear me?"

"Probably," a female voice from the hallway said. "But you won't get any response." It was one of the home's nurses. She said a quick hello and then proceeded to plump up Gus's pillows for him.

Sackett returned his attention solely to Gus, even while the nurse flitted about him. "Gus? They ain't done nothing to your hair today, have they? You remember me, don't you? You remember, Mr. Frank? This is Sackett, Gus."

Silence answered the old vet, but Gus's brow furrowed slightly, meaning computations and configurations were now probably going on. But not in any place that could qualify or quantify what his mind was doing.

Brad was finding the whole thing to be a little creepier and creepier. Even Jim began to think that maybe it hadn't been such a good idea to expose his son to this strange part of their family. His grandfather had a funny smell, he felt. And not in a pleasant way. It was that mothball smell that their pain liniment left, and there was a lot of that being slathered around, it seemed.

"Gots some people for you to meet, Gus," Sackett persisted. And set the palm brush aside on the bedstand, only to open an orange flat can of *Dixie Peach* hair pomade, which made a new bouquet in the room. Frank rubbed the grease into his palms after scooping some out of the tin, and nodded for the Martins to draw nearer to their relative. "They have brought you some things. Show him the dog tags, Brad. Your grandson has the dog tags you used to wear. This your grandson, named Brad. And you know your boy, Jim, he here too." Gus did nothing. But Sackett knew he had to keep at him. "What, you don't think these are your tags?" He showed the dull gray chits of metal to the invalid. "Let's look and see here, Gus. Private August J. Martin, private first-class. That's you, all right." Sackett brought them closer, "Remember when you used to shine these up? Yeah, you sure would—and all the brass buttons on your Class A's."

"Oh—you got him to open his eyes, at least," said the nurse. She applied long-lasting moisturizing drops to his eyes. "How the hell, are we doing today, Gus?" No answer. Not that the nurse expected any differently. She ensured his catheter was in position, and that his disposable diaper was not in any need of changing. He'd had some second, borderline third-degree bed sores on his tailbone area. "Wish I had twenty four more like you,"

Sackett tried pulling Jim and Brad closer to the bed. And as he looked back at the two generations, Sackett realized the Jim had a face that looked like his uncle—in the forehead and eye areas, at least.

The stupored look of the patient's eyes held on Jim. Gus heard the word "son", but that meaning didn't come to mind while looking at the thing-person by his bed. All Gus could bring to mind was the word, "ghost". It was Joe's ghost, now returned, to absolve Gus of his cruel spurning that he committed during the escape—that so long ago escape, in that cold open-aired jeep. Sackett picked up one of the candy bar wrappers and gave it to Brad.

"Go show him what you have there, Brad. Tell him about it."

"Mr. Sackett told me how much you liked children, Grandpa. He told me about this." Here, Brad held up the candy bar wrapper. "He said it was your favorite candy. He said you were brave, and kind...uh, Daddy likes candy, too. I wish we could know you more, Grandpa. Bernadette, too."

With his prepared statement given, Brad stepped back to stand by his father, once more. And as for Gus, he tried to focus his eyes from the taller ghost to the smaller one. Some words the small one said made some sense.

"Now, show him what I brought him, Jim." And with no ceremony to the request, Jim pulled out the medal and displayed it briefly in front of his father. Gus remained transfixed, however, on nothing in particular. He saw beyond the ghost, beyond the walls.

"Come on, Brad," Jim said with curt displeasure, and tossed the Medal of Honor onto the bed. "This isn't going to happen. We tried." The irritation in his voice was apparent, but this time he wasn't angry with his father. Instead, he resented that Sackett had duped him into thinking that they could do a therapeutic presentation. And that it would somehow unravel the damage done to Gus's psyche. "He's just not there."

"I could have told you that," the nurse commented, in an aside. "He's totally passive, you know?"

Gus, however, was holding his own private conversation: *Words, swords, word, swords, numbers—come down the middle; words, swords, numbers—come round the outside, and end up for—me. No stopping. No stopping them. I see them. I count. Thirty-four times three hundred and sixty-five is twelve thousand, seven hundred and seventy-five. Stop—stop—no stopping. Can't stop. Said it would not last, but now it's three hundred, make it stop. Twenty-four. Twenty-four of us—just twenty-four. Baked. Twenty-four. Pies. Twenty-four. Baked in pies for—for—Kate...*

"You coming, Franklin?" Jim asked.

"May I have a few more minutes, Mr. Martin? I got this grease in my hands, and I don't want it to go to waste. If you don't mind?"

"We'll be in the car.

The nurse walked out with Jim, who was holding Brad's hand. "He's the perfect patient," she said to him. "Like I said, wish I had twenty more just like him. Quiet as a mouse peeing on cotton." Sackett was relieved to see her go. He began applying the pomade on his hands to Gus's temple's areas, and then, all over his head. He massaged it into the scalp. Lubricating each follicle, it seemed.

"Does that feel good? When's the last time they run a comb through your hair?" Sackett picked up the hard bristled brush and began grooming the fallen veteran. The waves began to stand out. "Why'd you go and act like you did, Gus? Hmmm?" Sackett put the grooming gear away, and wiped his hands on a facecloth by the sink in the room. He then picked up Gus's dog tags, and tossed them in the air before he caught them. "What happened to this fella? Huh?"

Sackett turned away from the convalescent veteran and saw a dresser bureau with Joe's framed service picture sitting on top of it. A doily serving as a carpet for it. This chastened Frank's irritation with Gus. Yet, he also believed that maybe if someone just shook him up a little, well...maybe he could come out of his fog of dementia. As he picked up the tags, the medal, the toiletry case, and the candy wrapper, and transferred them to the bureau, he was careful to have them have form some sort of a fashionable placement. Or if failing that, at least not to make them appear to have been just tossed up there. And he went back to Gus's side for just one more attempt.

"People, over the years, have put a lot out for you. And that's your family, mister. Don't care whether you know it, or you don't. Take my word for it, and you know I wouldn't lie to you. Hummph, who am I to be up here telling you how to act? Pretty self-righteous, you say? Alright, I can agree with that assessment. To tell the truth, there was probably a good deal that we never talked about. Now, I didn't lie to you, now. I mean, I was an officer, you know. But through omission, certain facts hadn't come to light. And if this is how you're going to stay for the rest of your days. Ain't no reason for me, or anyone else who loves you, to come back. But before I do go—those things that Joe used to say about me? About me and your mother? Well, turns out they were true. I didn't realize that until he shot me, but when I met her I was a kid. I didn't know any better. And Lord knows, if I'd foreseen that a youngster could come walking in on us. By jingo, I'da done differently. But—I didn't."

Two times four is eight, three times four is twelve, four times four is—

418

Sackett looked at Joe's picture once again. And the unsmiling Joe Martin still sneered at him. "Want to know what I call myself, these days? I'm Franklin Sackett, now. No more Frank—changed it when we came back. But, as you know, that wasn't why I'd lost my commission. I'd used the name Frank Sackett to hide who I really was, you see. Think the statute of limitations is up, but I'm not sure. That's why I changed my alias. Still trying to keep one step ahead, you see? My real name, Gus, is Marcus. Marcus Patterson. They say I raped a white girl, but I did no such thing."

Five times four is twenty—

"We're the last two, Gus. There are no more Blackbirds."

Six times four is twenty-four, twenty-four, twenty-four...baked in a pie.

Sackett had no idea what effect his words were having, if any, but he continued, nonetheless. "It's gone down in the annals of history that we did nothing more in the war than tote barges, and lift bales. And I wasn't about to let the United States of America get away with that. I wanted them to make a public declaration. Wanted them to have it read from the Halls of Congress...But in the end, we got just one. After all that...just the one. You just go ahead and rest now, Gus. You earned it." And Franklin Sackett, Marcus Patterson, whichever one, never turned back once he walked out of the room.

It was quiet in the hallways, and he looked for a public restroom, which he found not too far away. But even though Sackett left, Gus was not alone.

He saw a figure come into his room, maybe another nurse. He wasn't sure. For she was all in white. But the white of the clothing she was in had an incandescence—a purity that no bleach could endow it with. Her dress was that of a Native American woman, and it was made of white buckskin. She wore matching white moccasins, and at her waist she had a skin gourd on one hip, and off of the other, a rolled bullwhip. She spoke not a word, but looked Gus evenly in the eye, as unblinking as he was, and came to his bed. Removing the gourd, she parted Gus's lips with its tip and poured a small mouthful of the liquid inside of it past his gums. It warmed Gus like alcohol, but it didn't taste like it anything known to be fermented. His great-grandmother smiled down upon him...and he remembered.

Outside, in the parking lot, Jim still had the engine running to keep the car warm. "Brad," he said, "Go on in there and tell him to come on." Brad didn't say a word but was happy to get out of the boring car, even if it meant going back inside the old folks' place. He couldn't stand to listen to that *Paul Harvey* station.

The youngster walked towards the wing where his grandfather was housed in, but Brad made sure to take aborted breaths, so he wouldn't be forced to fully smell the warehoused codgers. He blocked out of his ears the screams of delusion and cries for water. He didn't return the stares that came at him.

When he came to Gus's room he stood in front of it as motionless as if he were playing a game of Red Light. He cracked the door open, and hoped Mr. Sackett could just be told to come along without him having to go inside. But instead of seeing Mr. Sackett bending over his bedridden relation, Brad saw something that made his eyes grow wide and his mouth to slacken. Gus was standing—up by his bureau. His smock gown was opened to the rear, but the revived patient didn't seem to care. He ran his fingers of one hand over the medal he had found. Now it rested over the corners of his brother's portrait.

Hearing a gasp, Gus turned, sensing he was not alone. Turned and found that he'd been discovered. His eyes blinked a few times, and he had to wipe them with his fingers momentarily, to be sure he was seeing something real. Gus wasn't sure what he saw was… but he knew it to be a person, and some-one…for whatever reason, he made smile. Could ghosts do that? But at least this one he made smile. And Gus smiled back at him, too. He even gave a fairly appropriate salute back to the little ghost standing at the door.

Many things became initiated from Gus having awakened, and all of them were positive. Jim and Franklin were notified from the general alarm Brad had raised. The facility staff just allowed them to stay long enough to confirm the change in his condition, though. "We'll give you a call as soon as the doctor completes an evaluation." Jim reluctantly accepted that.

Extra staff had been called into his room, and they carefully placed him back into his bed.

They then began running a series of diagnostics on him, physiological, as well as physical. Blood samples were drawn, etcetera. And then, he asked for a drink of water. The first words spoken in over thirty years. Then still, it seemed that maybe he didn't have the strength to keep his eyes open any longer, after all of their disuse. Whatever the reason, Gus just went back to sleep. Only this time with his eyes closed.

The numbers and words from before he'd awakened; the ones that had jumbled incessantly in his subconscious, for one time in a very long time, abated by a short reprieve of lucidity, returned again—like they were Disney's *Pink Elephants on Parade* from the movie, *Dumbo*. Gus wasn't mentally present in his body, anymore. He still lived and existed, but on a different plane of understanding. For himself, and others.

No stopping. No stopping them. I see them. I count. Thirty-four times three hundred and sixty-five is twelve thousand, seven hundred and seventy-five. Stop—stop— no stopping. Can't stop. Said it would not last, but now it's three hundred, make it stop. Twenty-four. Twenty-four of us—just twenty-four. Baked. Twenty-four. Pies. Twenty-four. Baked in pies for—for—

Needless to say, Gus' doctor was disappointed to have missed the moment, but believed it might be one of many. He therefore ordered a CT scan and EKG to have slides to compare to the baseline films already processed. The head nurse, Mrs. Skullcraft, had gotten his opinion about whether patient Martin could share his room. "Getting stacked up. People are in the hallways, and that's just not acceptable. Don't you think?"

"Well, I don't think there should be any problems with that. Everyone else has to share a room, don't they? But I would run it past Dr. Hardaway, first."

"Of course..." And they began a whole new conversation as they walked out of the room. Concerning things that had no bearing on the patient they left behind; the one who began to dream about spending sweet, lazy summers in his mother's attic. Before they put him away.

CHAPTER FORTY-TWO
Patient Collins, Bynum

The family of Bynum Collins consisted of maternal grandparents, and his widowed mother. Widowed because her son killed his father, in a fit of rage because he refused to take his medication for schizophrenia. While serving time in a state psychiatric institution, Collins went into cognitive dementia. That happened after he developed clinical depression once he became stabilized, and been informed of his actions. He and his father had been close—which was all the more the tragedy for Bynum. It short circuited him, and he shut down. Though not to the point of Gus's condition.

He could still communicate when spoken to, however, he just chose not to interact with people. He didn't like noises, and had to be on pretty heavy doses of Lorazepam every six hours. Bynum was forty-nine years old, six foot-two, and had considerable girth due to body fat. He weighed 280 pounds. And he breathed through his mouth because of a deviated septum. Gus weighed 135 pounds.

It was late in the afternoon when Bynum was wheeled into Gus's room—which was now, their room. Collinses' grandparents and mother didn't know Gus was their relative's fellow occupant, for his privacy curtain had been pulled close. They stayed only for five minutes or so, offering to do whatever he wanted to make him comfortable in his new room.

Bynum had a large head, which seemed bloated even more because of the meds he took, and magnified by his brow line having a distinctive, thick ridge. He didn't appear to be quite normal, but again, he could talk if he desired.

"Do you want some juice?"

"Maybe just some water, please.

"How about some soda?"

"No, father. That will spoil his dinner in a half-hour."

"I—just—want some water."

"Papa," Bynum's grandmother clipped, "get the boy some water in one of those dispenser cups, over there."

"That boy, dear—as you are so fond of calling him, will be fifty in a few weeks." There was a sound of a wax paper cup being pulled from the bottom of its container, and then the trickling water coming from a tap. "There—now, how's that?"

"I think—you should go, now." Bynum said it very softly, but the family was used to straining to pick out any bit of communication from the man.

"What did he say, Miriam?"

"He wants us to go, father."

"Oh—well, I s'pose, so. Bynum? You take care now."

And the trio of Collinses kept on with their chattering as they left, though still not out of earshot of their ward. "That is a great improvement, wouldn't you say?"

"Oh, yes, he asked so politely."

Silence.

They were finally gone. Bynum looked around his familiar, yet new room. There was a plastic pitcher on a night stand next to his bed. A plastic emesis basin alongside of it, and oral hygiene equipment. He could hear the person behind the curtain on the other side of the room. He was breathing deeply, but not in meter with Bynum's gasps. The color of the breathing was purple. Purple smoke coming over the top of the curtain...and it tasted funny in his mouth.

· · ·

Gus could smell the burnt-sweetness of the detached meat still attached to the barbecue grills, outside. It rose with the air currents, right up to his bedroom window. Or rather, his attic room. Because Cleo had found it necessary to go on with her life, she trained some relatives to be able to help her when she had to work, and Gus needed to be assisted. Or, maybe when she'd want to go out for the night. Just like a mother would do if she had a toddler to consider. Except her toddler was thirty-four, and didn't move a muscle.

He needed to be turned every three hours, and have his pillows adjusted. The pillows kept him supported; with one in between his knees; two wedged behind his back when he was turned to his side. It helped to prevent him from getting sore. And he even had a pillow to rest his unpinned arm on.

Because they had already gone to the carnival the prior night, the two cousins, Imogene Troubles and Yolanda Spears had the duty to stay and watch out for Gus. Imogene, though just fifteen, had taken on a good deal of responsibility helping out her older cousin with Gus's care and maintenance. There was no wind blowing outside and the heat index had it feeling like 100 degrees. It was brutal to have to watch over all those slabs of baby back, and beef ribs, but this had all been pre-arranged. Imogene, who had had her hair neatly pressed with a hot-iron, and adorned with pretty bright barrettes, partially opened the back screen door, and called out to Yolanda, "Did you know if Auntie bathed Gus, yet? I was going upstairs to turn him for you." Imogene had a long slender neck, and sloping large almond eyes. Very pretty, and untarnished.

"Naw, she didn't. But you never bathed him before. So, just wait—" And the ribs fire had a flare-up. Yolanda quickly grabbed the water, vinegar, and paprika mixture that she had nearby the grill. In a spray bottle. With a few well-placed blasts, she got the fire under control. But she also needed to reposition the meat; and be watchful that another flare-up didn't burn up everyone's dinner. With the immediate conflagration eliminated, Imogene, who was bored, asked her cousin again. "I know how he gets that done. You've shown me before."

Yolanda knew she had to watch her meat. "Okay—you go on ahead. Sponge him off good, and then be sure he gets the baby oil so his skin doesn't turn ashy."

Imogene filled up the wash pail with hot water and put a fresh washcloth down into it, and after that she then reached into the pantry, and placed a bar of *Ivory Soap* in it, as well. She could hear Yolanda's powerful transistor radio. They were playing a Four Tops tune, *Bernadette*. Imogene started going through the procedure it took for anyone to get into the attic. She had to first, put the bucket down, and then grab the capture pole in the corner. The end of it had a metal angle on it to fit into a ceiling loop. The song ended just as Imogene pulled down the attic hideaway ladder. There was no noise coming from there, at all. Just as usual. She climbed up the stairs, and could smell the hot dryness of the wood that made up the rafters.

Imogene was a nice girl, and budding into maturity, but lately, her mother had some concerns with her being a little too "fast" with the boys. She'd been caught coming in late from sundown curfew because she'd been teaching some of the younger kids in the neighborhood how to French kiss. Her mother didn't know that for a fact. But she had some suspicions. Developmentally, this was to be expected, after all. It was just a curious exploration of heretofore unknown taboos. But her mother wasn't about to be taking care of brats from her daughters.

Imogene overviewed the whole scene. Gus lay on his bed in a utility t-shirt and some boxers. The skin on his head and neck glistened with a light sweat, giving it the appearance of unwrapped caramel. But of course, he didn't make any complaints. Cleo had told Yolanda, and she relayed to Imogene, that it was important that people tried to have a conversation with him. "Do you want to get turned over, for your bath, Mr. Martin?" But first, she needed to open the windows wider. Over in the corner was a standing electric fan. She turned that on, to create cross-currents of air.

Gus was on his left side, facing her. Imogene took the pillow from under his head and fluffed it, like she was in a band and crashing cymbals. Readied it for him, to be laid on his back. "Make you all, good and comfortable." There were pillows placed for support under either of his arms, laid out to his sides. And a pillow moved from in between his legs, was changed to a position where his knees were now bent over the downy comfort. By the time she'd done all the preparation, Imogene was dripping with sweat, herself.

She vigorously lathered up the washcloth and gently wiped Gus's face, his neck and shoulders. Then she rinsed the cloth and squeezed out as much soap as she could. Imogene pulled up at the t-shirt close to the waistband of Gus's boxers, and got it to roll up and off of her subject.

His eyes, were closed, in a repose of sleep. Imogene washed his chest, the corded stomach, and his underarms. Then she lathered it up again and sponged off both of his legs, and his feet. Drying her hands off, Imogene then took a small bottle of *Johnson's Baby Oil* and drizzled a few drops of it on his arms, face and legs. Then, with a quiet tenderness, she began to rub the oil into all the crevasses of his dry skin.

She made sure to catch especially needy areas, like the elbows, and the knees. She poured more and massaged it on his hands, with their long, strong fingers. She was pretty much done with the sponge bath, but wondered if she should dare to make it a complete sponge bath. She noticed that Gus had some man-bulging in his drawers.

About six weeks prior Yolanda had called down to Imogene to come up to the attic. As she reached the top of the attic ladder's rungs she could not make out Gus, for Yolanda had her back to the entrance, and blocked Imogene's initial view. But as Imogene drew closer, her eyes widened. And her mouth, grew even wider, still. Yolanda had pulled Gus' shorts down to his knees—his penis, large enough to be bent slightly by gravity, had the breeze pulse over him, and it lunged in the air, struggling to stay erect. "Yolanda! What are you doing?"

She turned her head and laughed at her younger cousin, "Girl, you better get to know what a real cock looks like. Cousin Gus is 9 inches of circumcised, fine man. And it's a doggone shame he laying here, going to waste. Yep. He alright, there. Guess they grow 'em like that in our family." She laughed. But Imogene didn't know what to think.

Since Imogene wasn't repulsed by what she had seen that day, Yolanda then showed her something even more fascinating. She put her hand around his penis! And then she slowly pulled its skin up towards the fascinum crown of the phallus, and then back. Imogene could see Yolanda trying to control the snake she'd let loose, and it throbbed more intensely. Then with one last run up to the top of it. Clear fluid tear-dropped out of the head, and oozed its way down to Yolanda's index finger. But Yolanda didn't masturbate him to ejaculate.

"That there little bead on top there, that thing that looks like oil? That's got sperm in it, millions of 'em. They get to one of your eggs—down there in your coochie, and you'll be knocked up, for sure." But Imogene's school friends told her differently. They said that you could do it more than once, and that when you're too young it's harder to get pregnant, anyway.

Imogene could not understand why Yolanda would do that to Gus. After all, they were cousins. And she also knew that her eggs were in her ovaries, not her vagina. Yolanda lowered her head over the head of Gus's penis a few times, making big slurping sounds. And then, just as if she'd become totally disinterested, spit his penis out of her mouth. She waited. Gus's member became flaccid, once again. Yolanda stuffed it back into his boxers, like nothing untoward had happened. She could not believe she saw Yolo put a man's penis in her mouth, right in front of her. Like she had done that, probably, more than a few times. Was that what was considered the definition of lewd? Now, Imogene wasn't so sure of what was up or down.

"That niggah still got ammo," Yolanda crowed. "He shoot a bullet, honey. Yes, yes. Shoot a bullet in a minute."

•　　•　　•

So, with all the conflict of messages about sex, it was no wonder that Imogene felt that she wanted to feel the same kind of control that her older cousin had displayed. It had fascinated her. Yet, she didn't know why? She didn't just pull Gus's drawers down. She removed them from him completely. And then, as the cool breeze blew over them both, there was the first twitch of Gus's condition. One of uncontrolled vulnerability. Bynum got up from his hospital bed and quietly walked over to the curtain where, whoever it was behind there had started moaning—as if in pain. "You all right, in there?" A few seconds would pass and Gus was blabbering a little more, like a baby, this time. "Hey," Bynum said louder. "Do you think you can hold it down, over there." Gus grew quiet, but just when Bynum was about to lay back down, a curdling squeal came out.Bynum had a furrowed brow when he slid back the curtain of his neighbor's bed. He wasn't shocked that a black man was in the bunk next to him. But he didn't appreciate it, either.

• • •

Imogene could not help giggling when she saw how Gus's cock could not stay in one place, even though it was now fully erect. First, she used good old fashioned soap and water on him. Thinking about rumors. Some girlfriends she had, told her you didn't have to use anything on your hands when you jerked a guy off. Others said you just had to spit in your hand, a few times. But seeing as she had the baby oil handy, Imogene let some small rivulets of it drip downward. She carefully massaged the excess oil onto Gus's testicles, and in back of them. His penis was in her left hand, and she played with his scrotum with her right, like some of the boys liked for her to do. She wondered how this could even be possible. Gus's cheeks started trembling with excitement, and his respiration increased. Imogene was startled when he lifted his hips up towards her hand as she flailed away on his member. "Kate?"

He spoke! But who was Kate? Imogene tried screaming but Gus's hand was quickly over her mouth, and he flipped her underneath him on the bed... When they found her, after coming back from the carnival, they thought she had gone as crazy as Gus had. She was truly hysterical, because when they came up to the attic Gus was slurping at all of her virginal juices, his head in between young thighs. Thighs covered in blood after he'd ruptured whatever could be salvaged, into coming out. Blood was all over his face, and he just kept on grinning. But now, the scene suddenly changed. Gus could still see that he had blood on his face, but it was his own. He was in the front seat of a jeep. It was 1944, and he had to crawl over the seat back, to help his brother duck. BLAM! The mortar didn't hit Joe, in this dream. It was Gus who took the full brunt of the blast, ripping his face apart. Joe, and the children Joe had saved, kicked Gus's body out onto the snow...and then the whole thing rewound over to the beginning.Gus reached over the seat for Joe, BLAM! And Gus could feel what Joe experienced, he began to moan, but just as before, his dream had him deposited outside the jeep once again...and it happened again, BLAM! BLAM! BLAM!

Four point restraints were tightened by two orderlies on the bed that they'd gotten Bynum into, after a violent struggle. Before getting a shot of thorazine the berserk white patient wasn't going to let go of the fire extinguisher he'd been using to assault Gus with. It was surprising that he could even talk, but due to his great heft, not entirely impossible. Collins said that Gus wouldn't shut up when he told him to do it. The blood splatter had gone across the room, flung, with such kinetic energy that it strafed the Medal of Honor and Joe's portrait, among other things. The head nurse made a hasty assessment and called the Director; and Dr. Hardaway called the police, and then the Lakewood Facilities attorney. Once they had their stories all in synch, that's when Jim Martin got the call that his father had been taken to the intensive care unit of the closest hospital. Jim then called Franklin, and woke him up—told him he'd pick him up in an hour. Sackett couldn't believe what Jim had told him, happened. Gus had half of his head crushed! Smashed in by some lunatic, convalescent patient!

"Look—somebody had better goddam well tell me why I can't have any information about the man who took a fire extinguisher and started batting practice on my father's fucking head!"

"Please, Mr. Martin," Dr. Hardaway appealed. "That man is a patient, and he has rights to privacy."

"What!" One of two police officers who were taking statements from the head of nursing looked up from his pad, and glanced in the direction of Sackett and Jim. "Let's be cool, Jim."

"Damn that."

"I understand your feelings, Mr. Martin. But by law, I am prohibited to say anything about the other patient."

"One who committed a crime, Dr?"

"I can only suggest you seek counsel, and perhaps they can get you the answers that you seek. But I, unfortunately, cannot."

"Doctor—when I left here this afternoon there was no one else in my father's room. If you were planning on putting a man in my father's room, why wasn't it brought to my attention while I was here, on site?"

"I don't want to be rude, Mr. Martin. But, contrary to what you may think, that room is Lakewood Facility's room. We have a reserved right to assign patients in a co-habitation environment, if and when needed. Now, we only have so many beds...I am sorry about what happened, believe me. But there's nothing more I can say, now you will please have to excuse me."

"Let it go, Jim. They got the upper-hand. Places like this have the contract set up to protect them from just this sort of thing occurring."

"He don't think I can get a lawyer."

"Can you?"

"I can get an ambulance chaser if I have to."

"I wish you well, then."

Sackett pointed at an orderly coming from the crime scene, carrying a box. "Hey—ah, are you supposed to be taking anything out of there?"

"Police said we could clean it up."

"Is that my father's stuff?" Before the kid could answer, Jim had brusquely taken the container out of his hands. The orderly didn't take offense, though. "I'm sorry, but it...some things got blood on them." And that drew Franklin's attention. As feared, blood streaked and spotted, the fine royal blue material of the Congressional Medal had the permanent blemishes of the assault on it. Jim felt Franklin's pain, and gasped a little. Not expecting the rush of emotion to become manifest in him, so quickly, after years of denial about having any feelings for his father. Jim now had no emotional compass, but guilt, upon which to navigate.

"Let's go talk to these officers and find out where we can see your pa, Jim." On the way to the hospital, Franklin felt the case for the soiled medal in his overcoat, yet. With Jim minding the road, as it had started snowing, Sackett took the medal out of the box and put it in the pocket, with the case.

"This is so jacked up," Jim fumed. He pounded the top of the steering wheel a few times. "Shit! Just give me three minutes with that motherfucker, that's all. Three minutes is all I want, or need."

"You're lucky the police shared with you what they did."The light changed and Jim cautiously pressed the gas pedal, for an inch of snow had accumulated on the ground since they'd left Lakewood. "They put a psycho in the room with my dad, man. That shit ain't right, man. It's just not right."

And Jim had gone on stating his overall displeasure but, Franklin felt a sinking within his chest that prevented him from making further comment. He definitely remembered one of his worse experiences with driving to see someone at a hospital. The graphic detail of the injuries to Gus didn't help to dispel any of Franklin's déjà vu.

Collins had raked the cylinder of the fire extinguisher from the top of the left frontal lobe, downwards, several times. He wasn't stopped by responding staff until he had also used the bottom of the extinguisher to mash Gus's left eye orbital, his cheek, and his jaw. Neurosurgeons were working dexterously on him at that very moment, in fact, just as Jim's car rounded the last corner to the hospital.

The doctor who met the Martin party looked liked he'd been doing a long surgery; his reversed blue smock was still on. And the scrubs underneath, had a large sweat mark on the shirt. Jim and Franklin steeled themselves for the update coming their way. The doctor introduced himself to Jim. "Mr. Martin? How do you do? I'm Dr. Stevick, head of neurosurgery."

"Pleased to meet you," Jim said, and squeezed the physician's hand with a pressing, earnest grip. "Tell me what happened, Doc. And what kind of surgery did you have to end up performing to save my father?"

"The police told you nothing?"

"Just the facts of the assault. But what damage was done, we have no idea."

"I see, ah-huh." Stevnick ushered them over to some available chairs. "We had to remove a large portion of your father's skull, over in this area, the occipital area, to help prevent swelling of what's left of his brain. A majority of the left gray matter is...well, there's no other way to put it. It's gone. What structure had been there is destroyed from blunt trauma and massive amounts of bone fragments. His left eye is gone. And there's been some damage to vertebrae in his neck. Mr. Martin, you have a choice to make, and it doesn't have to be immediately. In fact, I'd say take a few days. Because your father can't function anymore, even in the limited existence he had before. He's on a respirator and there's just enough brain activity from the right lobe to keep his heart functioning. But for how long? I could not begin to guess...Would you like to see him?"

Neither Franklin, nor Jim could say anything. The facts presented dazed them. They just shook their heads yes, in assent. Dr. Stevick allowed the family to walk in the patient's room ahead of him. There wasn't much of a face that showed visibly because of all the heavy packs and gauzes wrapped around Gus's head. The room was a symphony of beeps, clicks, and tubes attached for feeding through his stomach. Even if he'd had a whole face, Gus would not have been able to eat. He had to have a trach, which got suctioned out PRN.

"Can he hear, Doc?" Sackett quietly asked.

"Not likely—autonomic functions are functioning, but auxiliary motor function, and stimuli are just dropped off in a void. It can't connect one hemisphere to another."

Gus was not working hard to breath, but that machine he was hooked up to sure was putting him through some paces. As for Jim, he considered what extra care he would have to have, and how expensive would it be, if they just kept him alive artificially.

"Is he suffering doctor?"

"We're using morphine, but I'm sure he is cognizant of pain, at some level."

"You mean, on a 1 to 10 scale, he might be having a 11, and would not be able to correspond that, to anyone?"

"At this time, we can't say. He can't speak. We can make him comfortable, though."

"If we took him off that machine right now, that one that makes him breathe, would the brain still keep his heart beating?

"No—it would not."

"If there are family members to consult, please feel free to take a couple of days. The hospital knows how to reach me."

In the car, Jim began figuring out what needed to be done, next. It was not a question of if, but of when, someone would give the order to pull the plug. Jim was starting to think of what relative's he should invite to the funeral.

"You going to tell your boy?"

"Ah-huh. But I'll leave all the gory details out."

"I don't' expect you'll be wanting to keep on with the medal, then."

"It's ruined, a fair amount of blood splattered on it from what I could see. Hell, I didn't know it existed before you brought it. Keep it."

"Thank you. And not just for this, but for everything you've done for me since I been here. I couldn't appreciate it much more. You all are a fine family, and I want to thank to making me feel like I'm related. This old man appreciates this."

"You're welcome to come back up to the house, Franklin. No sense in your spending good money on a bad motel."

"Thank you, no. I'm thinking about heading back to Iowa. Got a young man interested in writing a book around all this. You can drop me off at the motel, Jim."

The next morning, the area around Detroit, was in the middle of the winter storm's vortex. Snow, and snow showers were expected to increase until steady flurries would be falling by 3:00 p.m. Sackett's phone rang, and it was so early that he put his glasses on to look at the clock radio. It was 5:45 a.m. Jim was on the other end.

"Franklin, this is Jim Martin. So sorry to interrupt your sleep—dad passed this morning, a couple hours ago. Started having seizures, and he went."

"Oh, I'm so very sorry, Jim. Truly, I am."

"Thank you, and I hope you'll stay for his service."

"I'll have to change my train ticket."

"It'd be great if you could...for Brad, especially."

"What's the schedule gonna be?"

"They are starting the backhoe, today. We could wake him tomorrow, service should be Saturday."

"I think I can do that. Saturday?"

"Yes."

"Okay, then. I'll come by Friday and go to the wake with you all, I guess.

"That won't be a problem, Franklin. Just call when you're ready to come over."

Sackett set the phone receiver down on its cradle very slowly. So, slowly that he heard Jim hanging up his line.

EPILOGUE

In this story it would have been preferable to be able to tell the readers that everything from that point on went ahead as planned; but that would not be accurate to say. The resolution in the story is probably not going to be in its ending, but in the story's entire telling. Franklin Sackett bundled himself up—and took the yellow line bus to Mt. Olivet. And even though there was plenty of snow on the ground, he remembered Brad's directions for getting to the Martin burial plots. But before Franklin even came down the rows of tombstones, he saw the pitched tent and the grounds equipment, working.

Franklin took his left arm and pushed four inches of snow off of the nearby bench and sat down, silently contemplating things while the backhoe was digging deeper, and deeper. Gus's grave was right next to his mother's. Which was to the left from where Sackett put himself. What was in front of him were Jim's and Lorraine's final resting places. It was a nice place. Franklin admired the slope of the ground, so, when standing from the sidewalk, one would see the markers at eyelevel.

He reached into his overcoat and pulled out the bloodied Medal of Honor and its pristine carrying case. Brad didn't need to see that, and Franklin commended Jim for his decision to let him keep it. He waved at the grounds crew as they passed his bench, and his heart seized up just as the truck passed, causing him to moan out a shocked, "Oh, my!" It began snowing heavily again, and hours later, when the crew returned with the burial crypt, they discovered that the old man hadn't moved. Frozen stiff. And he was covered in snow.

•   •   •

The death of Sackett put the whole service for Gus on hold. The Martin's contact information was on the body, and Jim received a call from the police once they came to the scene. "He had a Congressional Medal of Honor, Mr. Martin. Do you know anything about the blood on that? Or how he obtained it?" Everyone in the Martin household was as upset about Sackett passing, as they were for Gus. The family decided that they could not face the idea of Sackett's body being placed in an unmarked pauper's grave. Not after all he'd done for them. It would be the ultimate disrespect to the military and societal warrior. Jim and Lorraine decided to have their tombstones removed from their positions, and replaced with Gus's. Along with, would stand an additional, simple white cross for Franklin. Now, these two would have resting places befitting them. And their friendship.

Because Jim could produce no Army separation papers for the man, Franklin could not be buried with honors. Whereas, Gus got the 21 gun salute, the folded and encased flag, and a bugler, to boot. But Franklin had none of these accoutrements—however, what he did have draped over his folded hands, was the medal. Jim felt it was a fine way to honor this mentor and friend. A man who showed them that one solitary person could be the deciding factor in making a difference in people's lives—if—he chose to do so.

•   •   •

The following day the history teacher quickly wrote down names on a chalkboard in Brad's class. He'd decided to come to his class everyday, even if the other students didn't understand him. Even if the teacher didn't like him. He would no longer be a shrinking violet when he was asked about his political views. Mr. Sackett, he'd thought, wouldn't have wanted him to. "Now," the teacher began. "You all should be quite familiar with what each of these names have in common with the upward mobility of Afro-Americans in the U.S. How is their life different from say, just before we entered World War II, and the time of the Korean Conflict. Anyone? All right...you guys have a quiz coming at the end of the week, so you need to get with the program, here. Here's another question. Why is it that the military is so important for Black America in their struggle for equality?"

"Because it was the first thing they could do voluntarily?"

"That's correct—to a point," the teacher said, "But there were many Americans, white and black, who went into the service out of patriotic duty, or for a chance to learn new skills that would serve them at home. But black soldiers didn't feel equality in the army. Why?"

"They couldn't ah—they had separate units. Separated by skin color. Integration wasn't used in the Army until Korea."

"Who separated them? Did they separate themselves, or did the government do it?" Just then, Brad shot his hand in the air as if a string from heaven had yanked it up there. He leaned forward passionately, tapping the top of his desk with his other, to garner the teacher's attention. In the past, he'd been non-existent in class discussions, so this intrigued the teacher as she called on him. Brad had a window seat. And his hand, with its stretched, wiggling fingers, looked like burnt gold surrounded by the brilliant white light of that new day. And when he spoke, it was without hesitation. His voice was strong, respectful, but adamant in making a point. Usually he was asked to explain it all to them, but today the words were easy to volunteer. And the boy drew pleasure from how his voice echoed off of the walls.